Koontown Killing Kaper

(Based on a True Story)

BILL CAMPBELL

rosariumpublishing.com

Koontown Killing Kaper

Published by Rosarium Publishing
P.O. Box 691, College Park, MD 20741 U.S.A.
www.rosariumpublishing.com

ISBN: 978-0-9891411-0-9
LCCN: 2012941128

Young and old live together
In the dust of the streets;
My young men and maidens
Have fallen by the sword.
You have slain them in the day of your anger;
You have slaughtered them without pity.

Lamentations 2:21

CHAPTAH WUN

Lookin' at my girlfriend's black skin
You wanna jump in, but she don't like white men

—*Ice Cube, "Horny Little Devil"*

I LOOK GOOD. I know I do. I'm not bragging, not boasting. I'm not even trying to be conceited—I fear that comes naturally. It's definitely not a case of wishful thinking or self-deception. I'm not bouncing around like a Sky Cap with extra baggage for five people talking about how *fine* I am in the hopes that you may one day believe me.

I don't need any of that. My ego is utterly and completely comfortable with the truth—sometimes they even go out and have a drink together. It can stand tall all on its own and has not needed a man to lift it up in a very long time. After all, when the clock strikes twelve and the last beer is drained, who won't a man talk up? And when that foolhardy negro swaggers up to me with his "winning," Hennessy smile, and Barry Whites, "Damn, baby, you'd look good in a burlap bag," I just say, "I know," and sashay away. Because it's a fact. I did look good in that burlap. I still have the stills from that shoot. Benetton '91. I have that sack, too. It still fits.

My beauty is well-documented. You know it. You know me. Genevieve Noire. "Jon Vee." International supermodel—back in the day when that meant something. Cindy Crawford, Christie Brinkley, Iman, and me, Jon Vee. But what does any of that mean? I just know it was important to a lot of people. I can't even tell you why. My vamping for Versace never brought peace to the Middle East. Maybe hands to some perverts' members. But that was about it.

I just know that no matter what I've done since—and I've done a lot—and no matter how important my work is now—and that can be a matter of life and death—I will never be as "important" nor as influential as I was when I was "one of the most beautiful girls in the world."

Those days are far behind me now. And though they were great for my bank account and definitely helped make me the woman I am today, I mostly look upon them as a silly blur. Paris, Milan, New York. Versace, Vuitton, Vanderbilt. A completely self-important world of absolutely no consequence.

And my place in it? My beautification of it? Utterly meaningless. After all, what is a pretty face worth? It can easily be replaced. Mine was. So yes, I look good. After all these years and all this added muscle, I am still a beautiful woman. It hasn't always been that way, and part of me wishes it had never been. Yet, another part of me, that part that can walk away from those Hennessy smiles and their mountain-sized promises in molehill packages, that part can still get a little thrill when I can look into its eyes, and still say, "Yes, I look good." After all, the eyes never lie.

IT WAS THESE emerald orbs sprinkled with gold dust that set me down this path in the first place. It happened innocently enough freshman year of college. The last thing I was ever thinking about being was a model. I was going to be an electrical engineer. My father had spent a lot of overtime, risking his life as a beat cop and eventually a homicide detective to get me into college, and I was determined to see he got a healthy return on his investment. I picked the safest career path I could think of: math, science, engineering. I was going to "make it."

It was an anonymous fall day. I was walking along with my backpack and favorite red sweater. Elizabeth poetry was heavy on my mind. *Death be not proud, though some have called thee mighty and dreadfull ...* I was never much into reading and writing, and I couldn't figure out how iambic pentameter was going to help me in life; but I had a freshman requirement to fulfill. I was not going to mess it up.

I was muttering, "Death be not proud ... Death be not proud ..." on my way to the student union when I ran into him. Gianni Aragon. A 6'5" Vesuvius of a man with a lithe, soccer build and Tommie Lee jet-black hair. We both gasped on impact, and I dropped my backpack.

"Oh, oh sorry," he said, with a deep, rich Italian accent, bending down to pick up my pack.

His voice made me melt. I was definitely blushing. Thank God, he couldn't see me. I managed to stammer. "N-no, no, that's—you know—that's OK."

He shot back up with my backpack, beaming a truly winning smile.

"No, mi—"

The smile instantly gasped. "*Sei bellissima.*" He started—I don't know—gawking? "Your eyes..."

"What?" My hand shot up defensively. Did he accidentally hit one in the collision? Was it starting to blacken? I went to cover up.

He gently touched my hand. "No," he cooed. He moved my hand away. My blush intensified. "Your eyes," he continued. "They are so—so—so green."

"Yeah. I think I have some Irish in me."

"Irish?! No!" he scoffed. "They are pigs! And drunkards!"

"Well, I wouldn—we're mostly Fren—"

"And your skin. So perfect. So—exot—are you ... near—I mean, a negro?"

"Not since the '60s," I quipped, nervously.

"The '60s?! How old are you?"

"No," I chuckled. "We just prefer to be called 'black.' Even though, the other night, they said on *The Cosby Show* that we're 'African-American.' I guess we're that now. I don't know. But I still like 'black.'"

"Black?!" Gianni scoffed. "No, *bellissima*. You are definitely not *black*."

"I've heard that a lot actually," I confessed. "I guess 'cause I grew up in the 'burbs, ya know."

"No. You are not black," he continued, adamantly. *All right, already*, I thought. Why was this foreigner trying to revoke my Black Card? "You are ... caramel. Caramel and French vanilla ice cream. *Deliciosa*."

"Oh ... well ..."

I smiled.

"And those eyes. They go straight to my heart."

With a tongue that smooth ... I started thinking.

"Have you ever modeled?" he asked.

"What?!"

The man started digging through his pockets. I suddenly realized he had on one of those vests photographers wear—the ones with all the pockets. Then I saw the strap and a really expensive camera dangling against his right side. It was a pretty elaborate ruse for hitting on college girls. What guys won't do to get laid. He pulled out a business card.

"My name is Gianni. Gianni Aragon," he smiled, grandly. "Perhaps you have heard of me."

Blank stare.

"Well, believe me, in certain circles, I am quite famous."

"I thought fame encompassed all circles," I said, taking his card. "It's not like you can be a 'little bit' famous. You know, like pregnancy?"

He huffed. "Anyway, I am on your campus shooting this year's *Girls of the Big Ten*. I would love to include you, bellissima."

"For *Playboy*?" I gasped. "No. I couldn't. I wouldn't even get naked for my father. Wait, that didn't come out right."

"No matter," Gianni waved dismissively. "You, you are so ex—so beautiful, so *striking*, you will never have to be nude. No. You could even wear that sweater. It does not matter. I must have you."

"Hunh?"

"To photograph," he added, hurriedly. There was an odd, steely look in his eyes. I didn't know what to do. "It will make all my sorrows worth it."

Wow. I was blushing so hard I thought my face was going to melt.

"Caramel, French vanilla, and maraschino cherries," Gianni amended.

"Wow," I croaked. Talk about your embarrassing *Brady Bunch* moments.

"You don't have to answer now," he continued. "Just call that number on my card. I will come running if I must—" He leaned in closer and arched a perfect, black brow. "—and I must."

NOW, THERE HAD never been an hour, minute, nor second before that moment when I'd thought I was beautiful. Gangly, awkward, "Spidergirl" had been my nickname in high school. You see, I'm 6'3". And it really did feel like I got that way overnight. I suddenly went from wondering if little Jimmy Scott liked me, like *liked* me, liked me, to wondering if I could take two, consecutive steps without falling on my face. I was constantly stumbling, bumbling, and tumbling over my brand-new, size-thirteen feet.

By the time I'd finally regained my balance, I towered over every boy in my class. I was basically untouchable. It was to be expected, though. My father had been an offensive lineman in his college days. My mother had been a power forward in hers. I was bred to be big. My father's being a big-city cop everybody feared made *me* feared. Boys wouldn't touch me with their friends' ten-foot poles. I might as well have had the plague.

Sure, those first few weeks freshman year in college brought a few boys with poles of their own who wanted to touch me. But they were chasing any fresh meat with a vagina. And, tall though I was, I definitely had one of those. That didn't make me special. And none of those fools made me feel special or beautiful or particularly wanted. That didn't happen until I bumped into Gianni.

But it had to be a scam, right? Me? A model? He was trying to take my money. Or this was going to end up like some kind of *Carrie* prank. He was going to take me to some place nice and fancy, I was going to be all dolled up, and out would come the pig's blood. I could definitely see it. Gianni, John. And he did look a little like Travolta. They were both Italian, anyway.

"Don't be ridiculous, Genevieve," my girl, Shondra, scoffed.

A Different World had just gone off, and we were sitting in her dorm room trying to ignore our studies. Besides, I had to talk to somebody.

"OK," I started, "maybe it's like this made-for-TV movie I saw where this guy convinces this girl to become a model and go to Japan with him. Next thing you know, she's a prostitute servicing Japanese businessmen, and she can't get back to America."

Shondra was unmoved.

"I'm telling you," I continued, "this is just how white slavery starts."

"You're black, Vee. That's just called 'slavery.' Besides," she countered, "those made-for-TV movies are all made-up ... for TV."

"It said it was based on a true story."

"So does the news, and you see how they treated Tawanna. Saying she lied, and shit."

It was too much to think about. I remained silent.

"You just need to stop bugging," Shondra commanded, "and call that man and become a model. School will get you a job, but you never know where this white boy will take you. It could be the chance of a lifetime."

Shondra was right. There was no slavery—white, or otherwise. It was, indeed, the chance of a lifetime. Gianni Aragon really was a photographer for *Playboy*, and I really did end up in the "Girls of the Big Ten" issue, fully-dressed in the middle of the Quad with my bulky red sweater on, and my arms crossed over my chest, my Calculus book, and my copy of *Othello*.

Even my father had been proud.

Soon afterwards, Gianni called again. *Sports Illustrated* wanted me for their swimsuit issue. I skipped a week of classes and suddenly found myself sandwiched in between Cathy Ireland and Cindy Crawford on the white-sand beaches of Negros Occidental, trying not to faint from all that fame and excitement and the Filipino heat.

I ultimately held my own, though, and life became a whirlwind after that, with Gianni guiding me through the storm. I soon dropped out of school and was doing photo shoots in Zanzibar, Rio, and Moscow. I was taught how to walk the runways and found myself in Paris and Milan. I met Prince in London and Crispin, Danny, and Cory Glover in New York. I was wining and dining with celebrities around the world. I was in magazine after magazine. On billboards and on television, I quickly became famous. And rich. Nobody was calling me Spidergirl anymore. Everybody wanted to be near me, with me. Some even wanted to be me.

There were drugs and sex, but Gianni kept me away from all that. And there was always Daddy Terror. No matter where I was, I always felt that the old man was watching me, admonishing me to "better behave in public." And private! Like I would be in some hotel room in Istanbul, bent over a line of cocaine, with a gangbang of naked folks on my bed, and Daddy would come busting in with Detective Washington and a SWAT team, and he'd bend me over his knee and spank me in front of all my naked friends. "Don't think I won't, girl."

God, I miss that man.

My father never did like Gianni. He didn't like Italians. Lord knows why. He just knew my mentor was a lecher and a pervert and would somehow take advantage of me. But Gianni wasn't like that. He was a perfect gentleman. And he protected me from all the things that ruined a lot of other girls in the Industry. I had quickly fallen in love with the man—I was only nineteen, remember—but he refused to touch me ... that first year.

IT WAS A cold November day when I'd thought my chance had come. Gianni and I were inseparable at the time. I could've sworn I was in love, and the look in his onyx eyes told me he felt the same. I was a virgin and didn't know how the whole "love" thing worked. But I was sure it was about to happen, and, though terrified, I couldn't wait.

An early blizzard was battering Paris. You could barely see the Eiffel Tower from Gianni's studio/flat. The entire town shivered while I stood proudly in my brand new bathing suit.

"Are you ready, *bellissima*?" Gianni asked.

I pulled myself away from the window with a smile and walked into the other room. I was cold, bitterly cold. But I glowed in my feelings for my mentor and protector and the amazing opportunity he had thrown my way. See, by that time, I'd gone from Flavor of the Month to full-fledged fame. *Time* had already had me on its cover, asking if I were the '90s version of "Black Beauty."

"With those green eyes of yours, thin lips, light skin, and good hair, who are they foolin'?" Daddy had scoffed. "It ain't just the '90s, baby. I mean, *damn*."

He—all the Noires, actually—were quite proud of their centuries-long genetics experiment that had produced the likes of me. No Wesley Snipes had ever muddied our gene pool since the first Frenchman dipped his quill in the family ink. "You have cousins passing, as we speak!" my grandfather had once triumphed. My Uncle Flavian once drunkenly shouted, "Fuck the paper bag test! We goin' for Ziploc, baby!!!"

Needless to say, there was a lot of controversy around that cover story. Folks were furious. Al Sharpton threatened a boycott. Jesse Jackson threatened an even bigger boycott. Dick Gregory tried to sell me dietary supplements.

While some old college friends refused to talk to me (one had even thrown her X cap at me in disgust), the furor only made me a bigger commodity. Anne Cole cancelled their contract with Paulina Porizkova and wanted me to be their exclusive model for their new swimsuit line for the upcoming season.

So, I walked into Gianni's studio shivering in their "Safari Swoon" zebra-print, two-piece suit, my frozen nipples leading the way. Gianni suddenly stopped fidgeting with his equipment to look at me. I'll never forget the look on his face, the desire. I could almost feel it. I blushed immediately. As Betty Wright sang, Tonight was the night.

"*Squisita*," he gasped.

"Hunh?"

"Oh … uh … nothing." Gianni cleared his throat. He pointed to the floor beyond me. There was black sand spread out everywhere. "There," he directed. "Just lie down. I want to test the lights."

I lay down, propped myself up on my elbows, closed my eyes, and let my hair melt into the sand. I pretended that I was sunbathing in those harsh, studio lights—a piña colada by my side. Soon, Gianni was standing over me, his camera snapping and whizzing frantically. He suddenly stopped.

"Hmmmmm…"

He sounded dissatisfied.

"What is it, Gianni?" I asked, nervously. You can't understand how much I wanted to please that man. As I said, I was nineteen. His approval meant the world to me.

"I—I don't know," he pondered. He just kept looking at me, thinking, tilting his head this way and that. I always hated when photographers did that. It made me feel naked—especially when I was. And, with Gianni, too vulnerable. He suddenly snapped his fingers. "I got it!"

"OK!"

"Quick! Quick! Turn over!"

I was wearing a two-piece. What was he going to photograph? The spaghetti straps? But he was the professional. I was only the '90s version of Black Beauty. What did I know? I quickly flipped over.

"*Sì! Sì!*"

Gianni suddenly leapt over me and landed in a crouch with his giant lens in my face.

"What are yo—?"

"Quick! Get on all fours!" he demanded.

"Hunh?"

"Get on all fours!"

"Uh … OK? … Like this?"

"*Sì! Sì!*"

He suddenly couldn't stop taking pictures. The shutter rapid-fired in the artificial light. He frantically twisted and contorted his body and lens. "Now! Now!" he continued.

"Now what, Gianni?"

"Now *growl*!"

"Growl?"

"Growl!!!" he roared.

"But it's a zebra print, Gianni. Zebras don't growl."

"This one does. Now, *growwwllll*!"

"ggrrrr?"

"No! No!" he protested. "Like a tiger. A fiery pantheress! GRRRR! GRRRR!!!"

"Grrrr."

"Louder!!!"

"GRR! GGGRRRRRR!!!"

"*Sì! Sì! Voi puttana! Sì!*"

He vaulted over me again. Before I knew it, he was above and behind me. His camera going made in his hands.

"Now! Now! Arch your back! No! The other way! Now, shake it! Shake it!!!"

Confused, I shook it for all it was worth.

"Urrgggghhhhh … Don't stop, Genevieve! Don't stop!"

I wouldn't have—even if they would have had to put me in traction afterwards. I was making Gianni happy. What could have been better than that?

"Now look at me! Look at me! *Sì, puttana!* Over your shoulder! *Ay*

... *si! Si!* Move your ass up! Up! Up!!! Now—now growl! GROWWW-WLLLLLLL!!!"

"GGRRRRRR!!! GGRRRRRRRR!!!"

"uhhhhh…"

Gianni suddenly shuddered and went limp. His eyes rolled into his head.

"Gianni?"

"*Ay, stu cazzo,*" he croaked.

The camera fell from his hand and clattered onto the floor. I had no clue what was going on. I was scared.

"*Puttana,*" Gianni whimpered, falling to his knees at my feet, shivering. Terrified, I took him in my arms. He was shaking and covered in sweat. He panted, somehow drained.

"Is everything OK, Gianni?"

"*Mama*!!!" he wailed, and started crying. "Genevieve, hold me."

I did. I was happy to. It was all I had ever wanted to do. Something was seriously wrong with this man. I would have done everything in this world to make him better. Gianni wearily started tugging at the crotch of his black leather pants.

"*Ay,* Genevieve," he sighed.

"Yes, Gianni?" I asked, expectantly.

He yawned and nuzzled against my shoulder. Perhaps the worst of whatever it was was over. "Genevieve," he yawned again, his eyes getting heavier. "*Cosí violenta…*"

"*Violenta,* Gianni?"

He smiled, bemused. He was definitely on his way to sleep.

"*Cosí selvaggia,*" he continued. "How was it for you?"

"For me?" I asked. "*Violenta? Selvaggia?* Gianni, what are you talking about?"

But it was too late. He was already asleep. I lay his head on top of the sand, not knowing what else to do. He immediately started snoring, with the most cherubic glow on his face. I went to the window—feeling sadder than I could ever remember feeling once having first laid these eyes on Gianni Aragon.

It suddenly felt colder. I found my bathrobe, put it on, and went to the window. It was now night in the City of Lights. The blizzard had calmed to a constant snow. An ivory blanket covered the grounds. The Eiffel Tower looked majestic, aglow in its own reverie. I started to weep.

I hadn't known much Italian at the time, but I had been secretly studying. I had wanted to surprise Gianni after the first time we had made love. I had wanted to show him that I was willing to be totally his—to share his bed, his culture, and his tongue. I was not sure what *violenta* meant, but that was not too hard to figure out. I had come across *selvaggia* once late one night just cruising through my English-Italian dictionary. I knew exactly what it meant. My tears grew hotter on my face as I thought of the definition—"savage."

I FELL OUT of love with Gianni and with modeling that night. I had then felt that no matter how high I climbed, no matter how hard I worked, no matter how professional or intelligent I became, somebody would always want me to growl like a zebra. Mostly, I was proven wrong, but sometimes I was proven right. It did not matter, though. Once suspicion takes root, it is almost impossible to root out. After all, just because they didn't ask didn't mean they didn't want to, that they weren't thinking it. There was just no fun in it anymore.

"It doesn't matter what others think of you," my father told me. "It's what you think of yourself."

"I don't know, Daddy."

"No matter what you do in this world, no matter what other folks think, you just got to maintain that dignity, child," he advised. "As long as you can hold your head high, don't shit-else matter, Vee."

Gianni and I quickly parted ways. We just couldn't look each other in the eyes. I still modeled. It wasn't fun. But I didn't know what else to do. I didn't want to go back to school. I didn't want to be an electrical engineer—I'd already "made it." I just didn't know what I wanted to do with the rest of my life, and I was making great money. I was stuck on this glamorous, mind-numbing path, getting richer by the minute. I was going to stay on it until something knocked me off.

A GANGBANGER'S BULLET did just that, killing my father as he was leaving a 7-Eleven. A damned drive-by. Three blocks away. Daddy had been nowhere near the scene of the crime. He hadn't even been on duty. In fact, not one of the actual targets had even suffered a scratch. But my father (three blocks away) and a 42-year-old neighborhood grandmother (one block away, in her bed, eating Cool Ranch Doritos, and watching a *227* rerun) were killed.

I was devastated. Daddy and I had always been close. When my mother died when I was seven, he really stepped up. He was hell-bent and determined to raise his little girl right. I'd never gotten the chance to really thank him. The chance to say good-bye. I hadn't even really spent that much time with him the last few years of his life. We talked constantly on the phone. But that's not the same. I was just too busy floating around the world being a super model.

How "super" had I been, really? I never had an *S* on my chest. I couldn't fly around the world, spin the Earth on its axis, turn back time, and stop that 9mm bullet from shattering my father's skull. I couldn't convince drug dealers to stop shooting innocent neighborhood grandmothers and children, or photographers that I didn't need to be on all fours and growl for every photo shoot—especially for a Tampax ad. I couldn't do anything.

I didn't want to do anything, anyway. Or be anything. Especially not the '90s definition of Black Beauty. What was beauty? Other than money, it hadn't gotten me anything but trouble. I was sick of it. I wanted to be ugly. As ugly as humanly possible. I mean, I didn't go crazy and throw battery acid on my own face, or anything like that. But I started shopping at K-Mart and wearing thick, gray sweatpants in public. I even had a fanny pack. As I said, ugly.

And the only way to top it all off was to take the ugliest, grittiest, nastiest job I could think of. I became a beat cop—just as my father had done. I hung up my halter top and replaced it with a holster. I breezed through the Academy and quickly landed in a squad car.

It was a disaster at first. The Department wanted to milk the story for all it was worth. "Super Model Turns Super Cop!" The paparazzi were all over the place. The worst was on a night when we'd caught some teens joy riding in a Testarosa. I called in for some back-up, and we heard the dispatcher say, "You hear that, boys! Jon Vee's on a call!" Suddenly, we were surrounded by twenty cars, five helicopters, and scores of Italian photographers.

A simple car chase turned into a high-speed caravan. Tires screeched. Horns blared. Camera flashes strobe-lit the night sky. People died. The teens in the Testarosa never made it out of the hospital. We ended up charging thirty photographers for vehicular manslaughter and one reporter for reckless endangerment of lives and having to bury a puppy, Sparky, who the man flattened on the highway.

The fanfare died down quickly after that. Sparky's death sobered everybody up. The paparazzi quickly moved on to the next pretty face. Adoring gazes soon gave way to vague recognition. My fame was something of the past. My life became petty crimes, yellow crime-scene tape, and "Didn't you used to be somebody?"

The guys and gals on the Force were great. My father had been a legend in the Department. If there had been any hostility for the Super-Model-Turned-Super-Cop, I never felt it. Noel Noire was loved there, and so was I.

I hated giving it all up to become a homicide detective. But my father's best friend, Detective Washington, was promoted to Chief of Police Washington, and he wanted to see that I got promoted, too.

I quickly fell in love with being murder police. Even though they had a dress code and I had to go back to looking good, I loved the mystery of it all, the challenge, the purpose. I loved walking right in the middle of a bloody jigsaw puzzle and just staring at it until all the pieces fit. I loved solving the crime, arresting the perpetrator, and giving the victim and her family the justice the world so often denied them. Finally, I felt like I was making a difference in the world.

I'd still be making that difference right now if a few, well-placed bullets hadn't ended my career a year ago. Nobody has given me that little bit of justice—though we all know who tried to kill me. I try not to let the bitterness eat away at my life. I try not to let the anger consume me. I've mostly let it go by giving up my detective's shield.

I thought there was absolutely no way I could go back to that place knowing what I know. And knowing they all know it, too. But here I am, on my way to another murder scene. Not as a homicide detective, but as a private dick—if a woman can be that. I didn't want to take the call, but I have a client and a job. I know I can do this, and, when I do, I know I can hold my head high—just as my father would have wanted. I have no shame in what I had done.

I look at myself in the rearview mirror yet again. I'm nervous. Perspiration has popped up on my forehead. But I look good. All those boys in homicide will be expecting me to. I can't disappoint. Not again.

Traffic is light tonight. I turn off of John Wayne Lane onto MLK Boulevard. A large billboard lights up the night. "Welcome to Koontown!"

A knot instantly forms in the pit of my stomach. I try to laugh it off. I haven't been here in a year. This is where I got shot.

"Welcome to Koontown," I chuckle to myself.

I drive past the sign.

The bullets immediately smack into my Prius's windshield.

Chaptah Tu

"Mad niggaz is sucking dick"

—DMX, "The Industry"

LIKE RATS TO cheese, folks in Koontown are drawn to yellow police tape. It's utterly irresistible. *ESPN, BET*, not even sex can break the hold that thin, plastic strip has on them. And they come. I don't understand it. I grew up in the suburbs. But I'd seen it all throughout my police career, and tonight is no different.

I don't know how they got past all the security below to amass here in Sugar Top Estates. This is where all the Koontown royalty lives. Lawyers, doctors, actors, rappers who've made it, and their producers all have their McMansions on this hill. And Sugar Top is protected by a large brick wall with broken glass embedded on top, a barbed wire fence on top of that, Rottweilers and guards on patrol, searchlights, security cameras, four manned guard towers, motion detectors, a guard post at the only entrance, a secondary electrified fence, and a six-foot-deep moat filled with piranhas. Yet, there must be close to one hundred people here now. Of course, nothing was going to stop them tonight. The tape is protecting Funky Dollah Bill's house, and word on the street is that his body lies cold within.

Security and the police are making people park outside Sugar Top and walk up the hill. They're only letting other police, the media, and me drive through. My Prius creeps along with the milling throng. It's like a pilgrimage to Mecca out here.

I park a little ways away from the crowd and get out. I inspect my poor, little car. Not a single scratch. Hundreds of 9mm rounds smacked into my Toyota as soon as I crossed the Koontown border and not one ding, nick, or scratch. As pristine as the day I bought it. I have to give the boys at Sam's Body their propers. It took some convincing, but they've done a fantastic job.

"Armor plating for a *Prius*?" Sam asked, blue eyes bulging.

"I'm trying to be environmentally conscientious," I answered.

"Doesn't armor plating defeat the purpose?"

"Look," I sighed, wearily. "I work in Koontown."

"Oh. Well! You should've said something." Sam perked up. "In that case, I've got just the thing for you, Ms. Vee. Top of the line. Stops bullets, grenades, RPGs, and IEDs. Everything! They don't even have this shit in Afghanistan!"

Well Sam, I have to hand it to you. My Prius is still in tip-top shape. Even the windows are unscathed. Smiling, I look up and study the crowd, inhaling deeply.

I even miss the smell. It has been a long year away. I try to figure out the scene before me. See, except for the slam dunks where the murderer stands bloody over her victim, murders are mostly puzzles, and any good detective will tell you that one or more of the pieces is gathered right here in this crowd.

Hardly anything goes unwitnessed these days. Someone has seen something, and that person or someone who knows that person is standing right here. But who? That's the challenge. Finding that person, making them talk, climbing that ever-growing "snitch" wall of silence.

But people do talk. They don't want anybody else to know, but they do. Of course, with a known murder on the loose, who can blame them? Those bloody hands can reach out and touch them at any moment.

I scan the crowd, looking for the owner of those hands, anything or anyone who looks out of place, a little too nervous, a little too calm, maybe even a little too happy. But nothing looks particularly off-kilter at the moment. Just the size—so many people, and the ... no, wait ... no, it couldn't be. I shake my head in disbelief and move through the crowd toward that infamous yellow tape.

"And she was like, 'You little bitch,'" I hear someone say. I turn. It's a young, scrawny brother talking to a friend. "'Always cryin', an' shit. Bein' a muhfuckin' pussy.'"

"She know yo' moms just died, right?" the friend asks.

"We was at the damned funeral, yo," the man continues. "Then she was all up in my ass. 'Bitch cain't love no bitch, Lamar. Shit ain't natural. Bitch like me, she need her some thug lovin'.'"

"So, what you do, nigga?"

"Beat that bitch down right there in the middle a the gotdamned funeral home, cuz. Disrespectin' a nigga in front a his family. Fuck that. Put that bitch in the hospital."

"LaTarfarneshia press charges?"

"Naw, bitch axed me to marry her right there on the spot. Right next to my moms's coffin, yo." He wipes a tear from his eye. "It was a gotdamned beautiful moment, nigga."

Koontown. Gotta love it.

I make my way toward two uniforms, a younger guy I think I know and an older, plump sergeant I most definitely do. The scar on my left hip starts throbbing. They turn. The boy gasps.

"Jon Vee."

I smile and nod. The other turns. His walrus chops droop.

"Sergeant Perkins," I say.

"I thought you were dead," he says. Is that a smile?

"I was." I flash my private detective's badge. It feels so much lighter than my former one.

"Were you hired by FDB's family?" Perkins asks. He looks like he's itching for a fight. I'm definitely itching to give him one.

"No," I state, breathing through my nose. "I'm working on Hustle Beamon's dime."

"The hip-hop mogul?" the younger brother marvels. "Dope Beat Records?"

I nod. "They might as well be family."

"Well, he definitely owned that boy's ass," Perkins concedes.

"Looks like somebody else was trying to jump his claim," the young one chuckles. Perkins joins him. I don't get it.

"My baby!!!" I hear someone scream. I turn. There's an elderly black woman in purple wig and tattered housecoat on her knees, screaming up to heaven. Several camera crews are filming her. She'll definitely make the eleven o'clock news. "They done got him, Lawd! Oh Jesus Lawd hab mercy!!! They done got my baaaaabyyyyyy!!!"

"You'd think FDB would've dressed his momma better," the kid says.

I turn back to the two police.

"Can I go through now?"

Perkins raises his chunky thumb and forefinger like a gun and shoots. I fight a cringe. "Your funeral," he smiles malevolently, and raises the tape.

I brush past him. Remind me to get that tub of lard later. I make my way toward the McMansion.

"What was that all about?" I hear the kid ask.

"Remember this, boy," Perkins growls. "Cops don't snitch."

A FRANTIC, YOUNG uniform sweeps past me into the crowd as I step onto Funky Dollah Bill's veranda. I love the sense of urgency a murder brings out in us all. The large door's wide open, and two more uniforms stand in the doorway staring straight up at something on the inside wall. They pay me no mind.

I clear my throat and flash my badge.

Nothing.

…

Still nothing.

I finally say, "Genevieve Noire."

"Naw, looks nothing like her," the one on the right says, still looking up.

"Wish she did, though," the other one chimes in.

"No," I correct. "*I'm* Genevieve Noire. Here to investigate the crime scene."

What in the world are they looking at? Whatever it is, they don't want to look away. The first officer points nonchalantly. "Gloves and booties are over there."

I squeeze between the two brothers and retrieve a pair of plastic gloves and booties to put on. If OJ has taught us anything, it's that you better not corrupt a murder scene. Who knows what a clever defense attorney will throw at you? You don't want to give them any additional ammunition.

I look around as I cover my shoes. There's a grand piano here in the foyer with a clef note rug on the marble floor. To my left is a grand dining room with Louis XIV-like furniture, a grand crystal chandelier that almost sags to the table, a grand jungle mural that looks like it was painted by a second grader, and a grand flat-screen TV that's … that's playing …

"Holy shit!"

I turn back to the officers. They're staring up at another grand flat-screen TV above the doorway. I turn and turn again. There are flat screens everywhere. In the study, behind the golden stripper pole. There are several lining the stairwell. A few more are going down the hallway to the kitchen, which has another TV plastered above the stove. They're all on, and they're all playing the same, disgusting thing.

"That's one helluva woman!" the second officer continues.

One … two … my goodness, five men are penetrating this large, dark-skinned woman dressed in a tattered loin cloth. It's … She's on her knees with two men rapidly thrusting behind her, another on the ground pumping beneath her, while two more men are jostling inside her mouth.

"Annabel Chong ain't got shit on Nzinga here," the other one laughs.

"What is this?" I venture to ask.

"*Analubian Queen 7: Ass of Africa*," one answers. He has a goofy smile on his face, which is covered in a sheen of sweat. I look him directly in the eye, afraid to look any lower. "One of Funky Dollah Bill's movies."

"He did porn?" I ask.

"No. He *produced* porn."

"Hm."

"You know, these rappers today aren't so much musicians as they are franchises," he continues. "I mean, FDB has albums, side groups, a clothing line, his and hers perfumes, these movies here, and a line of children's books."

"Children's books?" I echo.

"Shit," the other police chimes in, "my granddaughter refuses to go to bed until I've read *My Daddy, My Pimp* to her at least twice."

I look at the man. "How old are you?"

"Thirty-three. Why?"

"No reason." I look back up at the screen, but it's too painful to watch. I turn back. "So, why's this thing playing now?"

"Rumor has it FDB used to play his movies twenty-four-seven."

"So, no one felt the need to turn it off now?"

The grandfather smiles. "Can't corrupt a murder scene, now can we, Detective Noire?"

Men.

I suddenly hear a loud cheer coming from upstairs. From the echo, I'm guessing the third floor. I look at one of the screens. The money's been shot. That Nzinga woman seems ecstatic. The cheer becomes a chant as more change is let loose.

"Nzinga! Boom-bah-yay! Nzinga! Boom-bah-yay!"

"I guess the body's upstairs?" I ask.

"*Bodies*," the grandfather corrects.

I turn and start climbing the stairs.

"Now, that's one strong, African sista," I hear grandfather say.

I hope he's not talking about me.

I REACH THE top floor and am hit with the odd scent of ass, feet, and blood. Did FDB shoot his movies up here? I wonder what I'm about to walk into.

The hallway seems to stretch for miles. I walk past a guest room where there are a bunch of uniforms crowding around, their backs hunched to me. I can only assume they're watching more of *Queen*.

"Where the hell is that uniform?" I hear someone growl. I know that voice. I smile. I look toward the voice. Just outside the master bedroom there's a medical examiner taking pictures of the right-hand wall. The main event is in that bedroom, however. I head that way.

But I can't resist. I glance at the ME's wall. "REEL NIGGAZ AINT GAY," it reads in crimson. I don't know if that's true, but the graf artist felt strongly enough to write it in blood. But not strongly enough to run it through a Spell Checker first.

I'm suddenly seized with apprehension. I don't know what I'm doing here. I really don't want to be here. What was I thinking? Why did I finally let Hustle Beamon hire me? He's been chasing me for nearly twenty years, always wanting me to be in one of his booty-shaking videos. I'd always refused. But now? Now, I let him hire me to be his private detective. Why, Genevieve? Why? I definitely don't need the money, and I definitely don't need to be here. I could be anywhere. Cancun, Casablanca, Cleveland. Why am I here, choking in the stench of ass, feet, and blood with the most horrific pornography flashing before my eyes?

"Vee!"

Hunh? Oh yeah. Right. I look up and smile. Detective William O. O'Ree is making his way toward me, a grand smile spread across his dark, chocolate face. I immediately relax. Well, as much as is possible. My father was Willie's mentor when he first hit Homicide, and Willie was mine. I don't look upon the middle-aged man with well-manicured afro and salt-and-pepper van dyke as a father figure, though. He's more like an uncle. I've known Willie since I was a teenager. And, while we've partnered up on more murders than I care to count, and he was my secondary on the Standish investigation which retired me from the Force with seven bullet holes, I definitely look upon Willie as family. The only family I really care to claim, anyway.

"Now, how are you doing, girl?"

He hugs me. I'm warmed ... a little.

"I don't know," I whisper. "All these *police*."

He looks into my eyes. "Yeah, but we *know* these fools. Come on, Genevieve."

He releases me and leads me into the room. I don't know how to feel. A large part of me wants to jump right in, take command of the scene, and be police again. But that's what got me shot in the first place, and, while nothing's been proved, we all know the shooter/s had a shield, too.

"*Comment-allez vous?*" Sandino, a fine Nico-American detective in his early thirties, asks, in his buttery voice. We almost dated once. Who can resist gray eyes in brown skin?

"*Comme ci, comme ça,*" I lie.

"So, how was Paris?" he follows up.

"*Très magnifique,*" I lie again.

"What she say?" a uniform asks.

"Fuck if I know," Sandino chuckles. "It took me a year just to learn that '*Comment-allez vous*' bullshit."

The cops and MEs in the room laugh. So do I. A camera flash goes off. I immediately forget the room and zoom in on the bed.

I gulp. "Hustle is *not* going to like this," I say.

Two, powerfully-muscled black men like naked, one top of the other. Dead. Funky Dollah Bill's on the bottom, a cherubic smile frozen on his face. I don't know who the scarred man on top is. Their bodies glisten, reeking of stale sweat.

"Nzinga! Boom-bah-yay! Nzinga! Boom-bah-yay!"

"What are you talking about, Vee?" Sandino asks. "This is like Biggie and Pac. You know how much money he's going to make off this?"

"Who's that on top?" I point.

"My God, woman. Didn't they have *BET* in Paris?" Sandino smiles—oh, so perfectly.

"Or *CNN*," a uniform adds.

"That's Irie Man," Willie informs. "The Dancehall King. He sang, 'No Batty.'"

"Wait," I say. "Oh yeah. I read they had a beef between them."

"Apparently," Willie snickers. "At least, six inches."

The room explodes in laughter.

"Oh, Willie," Sandino sighs, "give your brother some credit. Make it nine."

I look at the two naked brothers sandwiched together on the bed.

"What are those strange scars all over this Irie Man here?" I ask, over the din.

"Man," an ME pipes up, "this man's been shot, like, *ten* times. That's how he got his record deal."

Hm. I grab a pen from Willie's breast pocket and move over to the Dancehall King's body. I gently nose the pen under a shoulder blade scab and flick up. The "scar" flips in the air, landing bottom-up on his spine, the adhesive glistening in the light. The skin underneath is perfectly smooth.

"Wack rappers," someone grumbles.

"How did you—?"

"I know bullet wounds," I interrupt Sandino.

The room falls silent.

"Nzinga! Boom-bah-yay! Nzinga! Boom-bah-yay!"

The harried uniform from the veranda rushes into the room. He sheepishly hands Willie a ticket and tries to rush back out. My old partner looks at the ticket.

"What the fuck?!" he erupts. "Boy, what the hell is this?"

The uniform freezes, scared.

"Four thousand fifty!" Willie continues. "We've got a celebrity double murder, and you're telling me I'm four thousand fifty?!"

"It's a busy night, sir," the uniform trembles.

"Get the gotdamned coroner on the phone," Willie orders. He looks at me. "Can you believe this shit?"

I shrug. "Koontown." I point back to the corpses. "There are no bullet wounds, no blood. How did these boys die?"

"My guess would be … forbidden love," Willie quips. The room explodes again. "No. Seriously. We have absolutely no clue, Vee. There are no entrance or exit wounds, no spent shell casings, nothing. All we can tell is that they were crying at the time."

I look at their beatific faces. Tears had been streaking down their cheeks. I can see the traces.

"It was a tender, fucking moment," Sandino snickers. Everyone else laughs. I groan.

"The stone coldest of stone-cold whodunits I've ever seen," Willie declares.

"Then whose blood's on the wall out there?"

He shakes his head. "That's for the MEs to say."

"Got 'em, sir!"

"Put them on speaker," Willie commands.

"Thank you for calling the Koontown Coroner's Office. Now serving number two thousand three hundred thirty-two. Thank you and have a nice day ... bitches!!!"

Willie looks down at his ticket again. Four thousand fifty.

"Shit."

WILLIE WALKS ME back outside. The night has turned muggy. It will be a long one for my former colleagues. I miss it, but I'm glad to be out of there. I take off my gloves and booties.

The crowd has grown. There must be at least a thousand fools out there now. Off in a corner, there's a field of glowing candles. There seems to be a liturgical chant spreading among the crowd. They almost sound like cloistered monks. Like Enigma without the beats.

> Suck dis dick, bitch
> 'Til a nigga sees God
> Open dat gap, ho
> And gobble dis nigga's rod

"What the hell?" Willie gasps.

"I have absolutely no clue," I confess.

"Look, Vee," he squirms, "with all that's—"

"I know, Willie," I interrupt.

"No, Genevieve, you don't," he says, forcefully. "I … I should've … two more seconds. Two more seconds and I would've been there. Two more, fucking seconds."

"And you would've gotten shot, too, O'Ree," I contest. "And your black behind is too old to take a bullet, Willie."

"You're damned right about that, girl," he chuckles. "Look," he continues, seriously again. "I know I can't convince you to come back to the Depart—"

"No."

"Right. And neither can the Chief … I'm just—I'm just glad to be working with you again, Ms. Noire. Even if it *is* on Hustle Beamon's dime."

"A girl's gotta work, right."

"Yeah. I know," he smiles. "Upstairs. I don't know. I mean, we got nothing here. Your help's going to be really appreciated. You know Sandino's a fuck-up of the highest order."

"But those eyes."

"Anyway."

"Hey look, Willie," I point. "Perkins is here."

He suddenly stiffens. He wants a piece of that sergeant's lard, too. We trailed his boy, Presidio, for the better part of a year. Everyone knew he was the one who strangled, sodomized, hanged, and incinerated that poor boy, August Standish, alive, *and* smacked the boy's mother. It all happened in the middle of the day in the middle of their precinct in the middle of Perkins's desk. But nobody talked. The entire weight of the Koontown PD, the Mayor's office, the DA, the Feds, Amnesty International, and NAMBLA, and not one person said a peep. We know Perkins had been behind that silence, perhaps behind, at least, the sodomy, and most likely behind the bullets that had tanned my light-skinned hide. And now here he is. I tried, Lord knows I tried, tried to let it all go. But a year's a long time. I can't wait another minute.

"Do you want me to say something?" Willie whispers.

"I don't want you to say a single word," I respond, walking away. "To anybody."

I make my way back to the police tape. There's a well-heeled, middle-aged sister in a Dior nightgown haranguing the sergeant.

"Are you going to do something about these—these—these *niggers*?!"

"Oh no she di'n't!"

"I've got to wake up early in the morning and go to work! Do you know what *that* is, *bitch*?!"

"Uhh ... I ain't gotta answer that, heifa!"

"And you're letting these fools loiter in my lawn! Drinking their forty ounces! Singing these *offensive* songs! Selling their—their *crack*! I've got children, officer! I pay your salary! Do these fools?! No! I don't think so!"

"But, ma'am," Perkins sighs.

"Do something, officer! Call in the riot police! The SWAT team! Something!"

"Nzinga! Boom-bah-yay! Nzinga! Boom-bah-yay!"

"Perkins," I shout.

He turns, looks temporarily relieved. I throw my gloves and booties at him. He reflexively moves to catch them. I move on him.

"RRRR!"

Thwack! My fist finds his jowls. He stumbles.

"You go, girl!"

I pursue, double my fists, swing!

Crack!

"Whoop! Whoop! Git it! Git it!"

Swing! Crack! Swing! Crack!

"Sarge!"

"Whoop! Whoop! Git it! Git it!"

Perkins groans, falls.

"Nzinga! Boom-bah-yay! Nzinga! Boom-bah-yay!"

I stomp. Stomp again. Again!

"E'rybody in the club getting' tipsy!"

"Now, that don't make no kinda sense."

"Sorry."

"Talk now!" I scream. "Talk, Perkins! Talk!!!"

He groans, eyes swelling. He spits out a tooth. A hand grabs my shoulder. I twirl, ready to drive my fist into something else. It's the kid.

"Jon Vee?" the uniform ventures, tentatively.

I exhale and look down at the groaning Perkins. Revenge could be sweeter, but this will have to do. For now. I look over at Willie. He smiles proudly and walks back into the McMansion.

"Jon Vee?" the kid repeats.

I look at him, my vision clearing. He doesn't know what to do. Arrest me? Help Perkins? I exhale deeply.

"Cops don't snitch," I say, give Perkins's ribs a kick that produces a snap, and walk back to my bullet-proof Prius.

"Nzinga! Boom-bah-yay! Nzinga! Boom-bah-yay!" comes one last time from the house before I drive away.

Chaptah Free

"You don't treat a ho like a queen
Who behaves like a dog"

—*Geto Boys, "Let a Ho Be a Ho"*

"**YEAH! YEAH, NIGGA!** Hit dat shit! Hit it, nigga! My pussy quiverin', muhfucka! QUIVERIN'!!!"

Every day? Does it really have to be every day? I mean, doesn't the woman ever menstruate?

"Oh yeah, nigga! Ram dat big dick in this bitch! My pu-pu-pussy THROBBIN'!!!"

Every day I come down to my office, and I have to hear the state of my cousin Grey's vagina. I didn't even want an office here in Koontown, to make that twenty-minute commute from Sherwood Forest every day, only to be shot at as soon as I hit the border (my Prius held its own again today). But this is where the action is. If you're going to open a detective agency, check-cashing place, or liquor store, Koontown is the place to be.

So, I bought this former childcare center for a song and converted it into my office. Before the workers even began removing the asbestos and lead paint, my cousin came knocking, talking about how "we's" family and I owed her and she needed a place to stay. I can't see how she always does this to me. I'm not the cause of her problems.

Those stem from her father. *His* problems stemmed from marrying a very *black* woman despite his family's wishes. As I said, the Noires have spent centuries getting to be the color we are. Uncle Connolly, however, actually *believed* that "Black Is Beautiful" stuff in the Sixties and married the darkest berry from the African bush he could find. That's right. An *African*. He actually married an actual African. My uncle was a very intelligent man. Yet, no one could understand how he couldn't understand that all that "Beautiful" talk was just a rhetorical device. Even the Panthers didn't take themselves *literally*.

The family tried to save him from his delusions, tried to persuade him to come back to the Noire ecru fold. But when Umfoofahloofahklik!klak!klik! got pregnant and Grey came out quite brown, it was over. The Noires disowned my Uncle Connolly, completely cut him off from the family fortune, and proceeded to ruin his life.

My uncle, at the time, had been a tax attorney for the prestigious African-American law firm, Knott, Seaux, Black & Brown for ten years. Suddenly, he got fired. No other firm would hire him. He'd wanted to sue for discrimination, but no one would take the case. He tried to start his own firm but couldn't find any clients. His house, which the Noire family had owned for seventy-two years, was suddenly foreclosed on. His car got repossessed. Desperate, he tried to leave town to start over, but Greyhound wouldn't sell him a ticket.

Umfoofahloofahklik!klak!klik! left him and refused to take Grey back to southern Sudan with her, afraid they'd mistake her daughter for an Arab. My uncle and cousin had to leave Sugar Top Estates and move into Porch Monkey Projects. Connolly took to hustling—women, drugs, short and long cons. My father saved him from several jail terms until he just got sick of caring for his brother. Uncle Connolly eventually took to heroin and then crack. He died a broken man in 1992. His epitaph read: "Hell Hath No Fury Like Some Uppity-

Ass Niggers."

My cousin Grey indeed had a hardscrabble existence growing up in the Porch Monkey: fighting the rats for food, the dealers for drugs, and the prostitutes for an education. But how was any of that my fault? I'd barely been alive when most of that mess happened.

Yet, I always feel guilty. Sherwood Forest is no Porch Monkey. My life's been just as charmed as hers has been cursed. I've been a super model. She's always been portly. She's my "Before." I'm her "After." While the world was my oyster, Grey was performing sexual favors for that rock. None of it's my fault, true, but I can't help feeling it somehow is.

Believe me, I do pay for that feeling, too. When my cousin claimed she needed rehab—all five times—I helped her out—all five times. When she wanted to get her GED, I sprang for the classes. I paid for her BA and didn't complain *once* when she got it in African-American Literature. She didn't even hear a discouraging peep out of me when she got the only job her degree qualified her for—barista at Starbucks.

But when is enough enough? Haven't I reached that point, yet? Grey didn't think so last month. She didn't even care—after the year I'd been through—that I'd wanted this building for myself. That I just needed a fresh start. She didn't even care that she was making her plea in front of a bunch of construction workers I'd hired. Men who were supposed to take me seriously as their client and boss.

She just came by, moping, like she used to look when she couldn't find her crack pipe. Apparently, her Starbucks was closing, and the bank was foreclosing on her new house (which I provided the down payment for) in Bourgie Circle. What would she do now? She needed her "li'l cuz." "We's family, Vee!" she screeched. I didn't want to help, but how could I even think about dedicating my life to my sisters and brothers without first helping my cousin?

Still, I hesitated.

"You owe me, Genevieve!" she screamed. "YOU OWE ME!!!"

I really wanted to remind her that *she* owed *me*. Eighty-two thousand ninety-seven dollars and seventeen cents for her Bachelor's degree. Twenty-five thousand dollars for that down payment. But who's counting.

And the fifteen thousand dollars I gave her to open that beauty shop after she saw that Queen Latifah movie. And I still think I've got those rehab bills laying around here somewhere. Betty Ford is not cheap.

"All right," I sighed, wearily. "There's an apartment upstairs. I was going to turn it into a gym, but I guess you can use it. There's still the basement ... I guess."

"That's what I'm talkin' 'bout, cuz!" Grey triumphed, snapping her acrylicked fingers. She started grunting and shaking her ample caboose in some weird victory/mating dance they must do down in the Porch Monkey. The construction workers all stopped constructing to watch her go. My stomach tightened. I knew right then and there that I'd never be rid of my cousin, Grey.

"You just have to answer my phones," I interrupted.

"Nigga, what?!" Grey squawked. "Answer phones?! Bitch, what I look like?!"

One worker tried hard not to laugh.

"This is going to be a place of business, Grey," I argued. "You just said you needed a job—"

"I said I ain't *got* a job. I ain't said *shit* 'bout *needin'* one."

"Well, now you have one," I declared. "You're my new receptionist."

We stared at each other long and hard. I knew Grey would never answer my phone.

"A'ight then," she finally conceded, and resumed her little dance. There was some snickering. My stomach lurched again. "Ooooh," she suddenly cooed, "Vee, you think one a these big, strong mens could put some mirrors on de ceiling. In my bedroom," she winked, "na'mean?"

"Grey!" I yelped.

"Jus' that my nigga, Night, he, like, he like to be lookin' at hisself when I be suckin' on that big, meaty, albino dick a his. I'm sick a always suckin' dat nigga off in de bafroom, an shit. A bitch's knees be *hurtin'*, gurl."

Every worker in the place roared with laughter. I just looked at her, speechless. Bachelor's degrees aren't what they used to be.

Grey rolled her neck at me.

"Bitch, what?"

I sighed then.

I sigh now.

I have no clue where Grey and Night are at the moment. The bathroom, kitchen, the bedroom. I do know it cost me $57,201.37 to remodel the upstairs for that woman. I don't know if Night's looking at himself in the mirror, but it's painfully obvious that my cousin's mouth is free.

"Yeah, nigga! Pound dat pussy! POUND IT!!!" she screams. I should've gotten the place sound-proofed. What if I had a client in here right now?

"My pussy be lovin' it, nigga! My pussy want it all! My pussy be *needin'* that shit, nigga!"

"Shut up, bitch," I hear a much deeper voice say. "I can speak for myself."

"Ooooh," Grey coos, "you hear that, baby? You makin' my pussy *talk*, nigga!"

I go downstairs to my basement gym to meet with Lucille Parsons. I just don't have the time nor the energy right now to be disgusted with my cousin Grey.

Chaptah Fo

"You a bitch, you a bitch, I'm a bitch
We all bitches
In this motherfucking game"

—*Da Brat, "All My Bitches"*

"GOVERNMENT CHEESE IN every pot!" my father used to rant. "That's all these Civil Rights negroes ever want!"

He used to rant those two sentences with cold-eyed rage every time he saw Lucille Inez Parsons on TV. He used to rant it a lot. For a lot of years.

Lucille has been on television longer than I've been on this planet. She first gained notoriety in 1961 when she was kicked off the Freedom Rides for slugging a Klansman in Birmingham. She became even more notorious some years later during her stint with SNCC. Stokely Carmichael had proudly claimed that the only position for women in the Civil Rights Movement was prone. Lucille Parsons strongly objected with such a powerful right cross to Carmichael's jaw that it changed his name to Kwame Turé, seething, "How's that for black rage, bitch?" That was when she became the "Black Rage Bitch of the Civil Rights Movement," or simply, "The Bitch."

It's a moniker she still wears proudly. She says it allows her to fight more fiercely than most women would even dare. When Lucille Parsons enters a room, people expect a no-holds-barred, knock-down/drag-out, and she refuses to disappoint.

The woman fights hard. Watching her now in my gym, practicing with her rattan bo staff, I know I'm in for a fight. She calls it "sparring," but I always end up with bruises. It's hard to believe she's charging headlong toward seventy. You would never know it by the way she handles that staff, and you'd never know it by looking at her.

Lucille is a statuesque woman just shy of my six feet, three inches. Her skin is a smooth chocolate that either defies age or obeys a really skillful surgeon. If it weren't for all the news footage from back in the day, you would think that she would never hurt a fly. She walks with a grace it took me years to learn on the catwalk. Her voice melts stone, it's so soothing. Her smile still lights up a room. But her eyes. Even when they're bewitching you with their ebony twinkle, you can see the fire beneath them.

It's that fire you need to stay away from. It has scorched entire planets. It's what has made her a fierce Civil Rights fighter and one of the most eminent defense attorneys in the country. It has allowed her to carry on this fight for our people for five decades now. She has spearheaded Civil Rights reforms, education reforms, health care reforms, and tenant protections. She almost got the governor to repeal the death penalty and commute everyone's sentences until people pointed out that it would only lead to overcrowding in Koontown and the man slyly backed away from the issue. But even in defeat, Lucille Parsons leaves her opponents burned—and fearful that she will one day return.

"Are you ready?" she asks, standing and twirling her staff playfully. I refuse to be fooled. The first time she uttered those words to me I ended up where I am today.

"One moment," I answer, securing my headgear.

I've known Lucille my entire life—adored her as a child, wrote a paper about her in high school, studied her in college—but I only met her a year ago. Why she chose me, I'll never know. I still have no clue what she sees in me. I'm really not that special. Yet, here we are. I still feel honored.

It's a feeling that has never left me and probably never will. It consumed me the very moment we met. I emerged from my morphine haze, lying in my hospital bed, still pained from all the tubes perforating my body, the bullets scraped out of my organs, and the one left lodged in my spine, floating in the dream between life and death. I thought she was an apparition at first, standing there above my bed in a Prada pantsuit.

"Are you ready?" she'd asked.

"Now?" she asks.

I stand. "Now."

I would follow Lucille Parsons to the grave.

LUCILLE GLIDES BAREFOOT across the exercise mat. She moves like a panther, you can barely hear her. I watch her twirl her bo staff.

"Are you ready?" repeats Lucille.

I nod. I refuse to take my eyes off that staff. Lucille's quick and deceptive. It's always hard to tell where her attack is coming from. You just have to know that it's coming.

The weapon twirls faster and faster in her hands as she moves in a stealthy circle. I can tell she's smiling, like a Cheshire cat, but I refuse to look up at her.

Just watch the staff, Vee. Just watch the staff.

It moves faster and faster. It quickly becomes a blur of light and motion. I watch ... and ... I watch ...

What the ...?

My eyes ... they're getting ... heavier?

I can ... hardly—hardly keep them ... open.

I ... no. I can't raise my, my arms. They're too heavy.

Thu-Thump! Thu-Thump!

My heart ... It's pounding in my ears. Lucille's talking—I think. I can't hear her, though. Only my heartbeat.

Thu-Thump! Thu-Thump!

My eyes! My arms!

Thu-Thump! Thu-Thump!

Oh no! Her staff!

Thu-Thump! Thu-Thump!

Raise your arms, Genevieve! Raise ... your ... arms!

Thu-Thump! Thu-Thump!

"Are you ready?"

Noooo!!!

Thwack!

THU–THUMP! THU–THUMP!

"uuuggghhhh"

Where am I?

It's hot, excruciatingly hot. Sweat and my wife beater are plastered to my skin. I move the headgear from my eyes and open my lids.

The sun's pale and intense overhead. I'm surrounded by grass. I move to stand.

"Ouch!"

Saw grass. Blood trickles down my palm.

Thu-Thump! Thu-Thump!

I gingerly come to stand. My head. It's throbbing. What did that woman hit me with? I heard of knocking the black off you. There's Ralph Cramden's "To the moon, Alice!" But where in the world am I?

Wait. The saw grass climbing to my chest. That baobab tree looming in the distance. I've been here before. Not that long ago.

THOOM! THOOM! THOOM! THOOM! THOOM!

The ground beneath me erupts, pounding and shaking like a frantic drum. I fall to the ground.

THOOM! THOOM! THOOM! THOOM! THOOM!

An earthquake?

No. Wait. The pounding grows. Almost on top of me. I clutch the ground, the saw grass slicing into my palms. The pounding promises to swallow me whole. I yelp. Close my eyes.

THOOM! THOOM! THOOM! THOOM! THOOM!

Just as suddenly, it recedes. I venture a look. A stampeding elephant rushes toward the sunset.

"Ayyy! Ayyy! Ayyy! Ayyy! Ayyy!"

What?

I turn.

It's ... me?

Thu-Thump! Thu-Thump!

I'm running furiously at the elephant. My face and clothes are caked with mud. My matted hair bounces in pursuit. A long spear jounces in my hand. I have a look of intense rage, determination, madness contorting my face. My eyes are emerald fire. I spring past me, taking no notice.

Wait a second. That's impossible.

"Ayyy!"

I throw the spear at the elephant. It strikes the beast at the base of its skull. It teeters and begins to fall.

"Are you ready?"

"What?"

Thwack!

"TWO SECONDS," CROAKS Willie, over the monitor's beeps. "Two, fucking seconds."

Thu-Thump! Thu-Thump!

My old partner's standing over my body in my old hospital room. I'm unconscious with all those tubes jutting out of my body. The Chief of Police, Derek Washington, my father's old partner, stands beside him, a meaty hand on Willie's shoulder. I love both these men. They're like my uncles. They love me, too. They're crying.

I'm standing on the other side of the bed. I want to say something, reassuring them. Everything will be OK. There will be a bullet in my spine, but it will be all right. I will survive this. But I already know they can't hear me. Whatever's going on, I know I'm invisible.

I look down at me. I look so pale, so gray, cadaverous. No wonder they're crying.

"There was nothing you could do, Willie," Derek consoles.

"Bullshit, sir. You can always do something."

Thu-Thump! Thu-Thump!

"Then pray," says the Chief.

"Are you ready?"

"No," I groan, tears streaming down my face.

"Too bad."

Thwack!

I BLINK THE rain from my eyes. What is it now?

It's way too dark here. It smells like wet garbage and feces. Where is this?

I look around. It's an alleyway. Off in the distance, I can see a street sign. Armstrong Lane?

No, no, no, no, no, no, no! I do not want to see this! What are you playing at, Lucille?!

Thu-Thump! Thu-Thump!

I see me run into the alley, my service weapon drawn.

"Nooo!!!"

But no one can hear me.

The call came in while Willie and I were at the scene of LaCaranequa Johnson's murder. It looked personal. She'd been beaten severely. Her head had been caved in by a brick. Her brains had oozed out all over her bed. Her clothes lay in tatters on the floor. It had to have been her baby daddy.

The call said someone saw that baby's daddy, Dontanario Mickens, running through this very alley. Willie and I immediately took off. It was only a few blocks away.

Running down the street, I was certain the place would be crawling with other police. This was supposed to be a manhunt. When I sprinted into the alley ahead of Willie and saw it was empty, I knew it was a set-up.

Thu-Thump! Thu-Thump!

Yes. There I am now, realizing what's about to happen.

"Oh, Perkins," I moan.

The night explodes into day with all the gunfire. Bullets rip into the walls, into the trash, into me. I dance as they rack my body.

"Nooo!!!"

I fall to the ground and watch my blood melt into the rain.

"Are you ready?"

"Please," I whimper.

Thwack!

THU—THUMP! THU—THUMP!

"Elephant hunters?" I croak. My throat is raw. The tubes have just been removed, and my vocal chords feel as though they've been scraped down to blood.

Lucille sits next to my hospital bed. She looks almost regal in her Prada. Her eyes burn with an intensity I haven't seen outside the interrogation room. She leans in closer, grabs my hand, and squeezes firmly.

Her eyes grab onto mine as she asks, "Are you ready?"

I swallow hard.

"Yes."

Thwack!

THE SUN HANGS bright and warm in the sky. Honeysuckle wafts sweetly in the air. It's a glorious day, but I look haggard. This must be a month after I was released from the hospital. I'm still walking with a cane and wincing with every tentative step.

Lucille looks glorious in her summer dress. The country air really suits her. I look like a wraith—crippled and all in black. The children hardly notice. They dance and laugh, encircling Lucille and me in their joyous song. I smile despite my pain.

One boy pounces on my leg. I yelp.

Thu-Thump! Thu-Thump!

"Samuel," Lucille gently reprimands. "Now, you leave Ms. Noire be. She just got out of the hospital."

The boy looks up with large, black eyes. "Sorry," he says, and runs along.

"Do you know what that boy's mother actually named him?" asks Lucille. I shrug. "Carnivorous."

"No," I gasp. "Do you think she knew what it means?"

"Who knows?" Lucille shrugs. "The number three reason behind our people's being held back is these *horrific* names we give our children."

"Really?"

"We have the data," Lucille confirms, gravely. "So, the first thing we do when we get one of these children is change their names."

I look around the grounds. This "orphanage" is more of a compound of several buildings nestled here in the mountains. The murder and mayhem of Koontown seem eons away. This is a completely different world. A world where all these black children frolicking around us seem to have a chance to succeed, to thrive. Even Sherwood Forest has nothing on this place. It fills me with pride—and hope—just to be considered to be a part of something so positive.

Thu-Thump! Thu-Thump!

"Let me show you something."

Lucille has already shown me several of the classrooms where there's one teacher per every *three* children. Their education is highly-individualized with a strong emphasis on math, science, and African Diaspora history. Each child, Lucille tells me, is at least three grades above their age level. When they were in KPS, they were all considered "unteachable," doped up on Ritalin.

She's shown me their pristine sleeping quarters, the computer lab, five-story library, and science lab. There were ten-year-olds already learning chemistry. I couldn't wait to see what Lucille had to show me.

We slowly approach the building with the "Strong Sisters" mural, where Rosa Parks, Nefertiti, Coretta Scott King, Harriet Tubman, and others are gloriously depicted in bold colors. I can hear an angelic children's choir singing.

"The music building?" I venture.

Lucille smiles proudly. "Let's go."

The children's voices caress us as soon as we enter.

You will not be able to stay home, brother
You will not be able to plug in, turn on, and cop out

"'The Revolution Will Not Be Televised?'" I ask, astonished.

"Yes," beams Lucille. "Grace, née LaQueefneshia, Mays arranged it into a chorale piece."

"It's beautiful," I gasp.

"She's eleven."

Something catches in my throat. "Wow."

"Come on." Lucille takes my arm and leads me down the hallway.

Thu-Thump! Thu-Thump!

There are all these sound-proofed rehearsal spaces. Each one is occupied by a child playing something. Guitar, saxophone, cello, trumpet, kora. Each child's at a different stage in their musical development. It's not necessarily pleasant to listen to, but it's definitely a sight to behold.

Lucille stops before large double doors.

"Here we are."

She swings the doors open. The music immediately smacks me in the face. I smile and start tapping my toes—despite the pain it causes. A twenty-seven-piece children's orchestra is swinging to "Take the 'A' Train."

Lucille beams proudly. "Do you remember when black folks used to play *instruments*?"

A single tear trickles down my cheek, and I sob. "Yes ... I do."

"Are you ready?"

Thwack!

"THE FRENCH CALLED us the 'Dahomey Amazons.' Our people

called us 'Mino,' for 'Our mothers.' We prefer 'gbeto,' the elephant hunters.

"In the 1650s, the great Fon king, Houegbadja, formed our mothers into an elite royal guard. Houegbadja's son, Agadja, turned us into a fierce militia, and, in 1727, we defeated the Savi Kingdom.

"We were originally recruited from the ahosi, or the King's wives. But as time marched on and our strength grew, men who could not control their wives or daughters sent their women, their '*bitches*,' to the gbeto. We refused the yoke of marriage. We were fearless women, fearsome warriors.

"We trained vigorously in hand-to-hand combat, knives, clubs, and Winchester rifles. All of Africa trembled before us. Any enemy who fell into our hands—including the French—were decapitated. We gave no quarter. We asked for none."

Thwack!

"BUT, AS GLORIOUS, as mighty as we were, we were also part of the problem. Dahomey was the largest slave-trading empire in west Africa. We gbeto were an integral part of that despicable trade. We Mino, we 'Mothers,' enslaved our own children. We sent our children to die in the Middle Passage, to live in chains across the Atlantic."

Thwack!

"AND THAT'S WHY you're here, Genevieve Noire."

I look up. I'm on my knees, dressed in a leather jerkin, headband, and several long skirts with a spear and Winchester rifle on either side of me. I'm covered in ash and fight the urge to sneeze.

On the ground before me there's an intricate diagram drawn in chalk. I'm surrounded by a large circle of lit candles. Beyond the candles is a large group of black women of every hue and color dressed exactly as I am, shouldering their own rifles. They look fierce, majestic. The gbeto. I am honored to be among them.

"See, those brothers back in the '60s constantly *talked* revolution," Lucille exhorts, a bottle of rum in her left hand. She starts whining, "'Revolution! Revolution! Revolution!'"

Someone titters.

"When their true goals were no more revolutionary than getting a government job and eating some white woman's pussy."

A throat is cleared.

"I know, Naima," Lucille hisses.

"It's just the hair. It's so fi—"

"Anyway," Lucille dismisses. "The revolution, *black liberation*, is much more than that. It's more than government jobs, more than—I know, I know, Naima. It's even more than having a brother in the White House!"

The sisters start chanting.

RRRRIIIIIIINNNNNGGGGGG!RRRRIIIIIIINNNNNGGGGGG! RRRRIIIIIIINNNNNGGGGGG!

What—?

Lucille takes a large mouthful of the dark rum. She points herself to the north and sends out a huge spray of the liquid. She swigs again and sprays to the south. She repeats the process eastward and then westward.

Someone slides a bowl of blood in front of me. Lucille points out a large knife and crouches down before me. The candlelight flickers in her eyes. I place the blade firmly against my palm.

RRRRIIIIIIINNNNNGGGGGG!RRRRIIIIIIINNNNNGGGGGG! RRRRIIIIIIINNNNNGGGGGG!

"Genevieve Noire," she whispers, "are you ready?"

A surge of power rushes through me. I brace for the impending cut. "Yes."

Thwack!

RRRRIIIIIIINNNNGGGGGG!RRRRIIIIIIINNNNNGGGGGG!

RRRRIIIIIIINNNNNGGGGGG!

"uuggghhh"

I open my eyes and wait for the world to clear. My basement ceiling stares back at me. I feel a little dizzy. I grab at my headgear and rip it off. I gulp air as though I'd just spent a lifetime underwater.

RRRRIIIIIIINNNNNGGGGGG!RRRRIIIIIIINNNNNGGGGGG! RRRRIIIIIIINNNNNGGGGGG!

Suddenly, Lucille Parsons is standing over me. She's fully dressed with a briefcase in her hand. She looks as though she's never broken a sweat.

"What was that?" I groan. "We can time-travel?"

"There is no limit to the power of the gbeto," Lucille declares with her trademark smile.

I chuckle and move to sit up. I wince. My hand. There's a cut across the palm. From the saw grass? The knife? I look up at Lucille, questioning.

"No limit at all."

"Bu—"

RRRRIIIIIIINNNNNGGGGGG!RRRRIIIIIIINNNNNGGGGGG! RRRRIIIIIIINNNNNGGGGGG!

"I think you need to answer your phone, Genevieve."

"Grey," I hiss.

"Maybe it's that race traitor you're working for."

"What?"

"I'll be seeing you, sister," Lucille says, and leaves through the basement's steel-reinforced door.

I huff and go to answer the phone my cousin's supposed to be manning.

"HELLO," I ANSWER. The phone has been ringing on and off for the past five minutes. It has taken me that long to collect my thoughts and climb up the stairs to my office. What did she mean by "race traitor"? Hustle Beamon?

"Vee, where have you been?"

"I'm still trying to figure that out myself, Willie."

"Well, it's already ten o'clock," he continues. "Can I come and pick you up? We've got work to do."

I look at my hand. The cut's not deep, but it is most definitely real. I'll have to go wrap it up.

"Do you really think I should be so intimately involved in this investigation, Willie?" I ask.

My former partner huffs. "I really don't have much of a choice here," he admits. "Besides, with Hustle Beamon's money, you've got to be making more than KPD ever paid you for a murder investigation. Even *with* OT."

"It's never been about the money, Willie."

"Exactly," he chirps, victorious. "I'll be by in twenty."

"All right."

I hang up.

"Ahem."

I turn. Night's standing in the doorway. He's wearing nothing but a towel, his red body hair dripping in sweat. He is sinewy but strong. Every muscle cut and rippling. He thinks he's being sexy, but there has always been something with his milky albino body that has turned me off since I met him.

"Hey, Vee," he croons. Night is one of those Barry White brothers I've talked about, but, with the way he looks, he might as well be Rick Astley.

"Hello, Night," I respond, stiffly.

"Now, why you gonna be like that, Vee?" he smiles, slyly. "You know a nigga like me can make that pussy *sang*, gurl."

"With Grey's already talking," I say, "could you really handle all that noise?"

I brush past him and go downstairs to wrap up my hand before Willie gets here. I hear Night mutter under his breath.

"Bitch."

Chaptah Feyve

*"Anything goes when it comes to hos, they go:
Pimpin' ain't easy"*

—*Big Daddy Kane, "Pimpin' Ain't Easy"*

WILLIE LOOKS EXHAUSTED. The skin bags beneath his red-rimmed eyes.

The first forty-eight hours are the most crucial in any murder investigation. Trails grow cold pretty quickly in this business. If you don't solve a murder within that timeframe, you may never solve it. If I know Willie, he's spent the last twelve hours canvassing Sugar Top, questioning everyone he could get his hands on, questioning the uniforms who questioned the people he couldn't, chasing down every lead, harassing the coroner, downing gallons of coffee, and nodding off at his desk or in his cruiser. By the looks of him, I still know Willie pretty well. He yawns grandly as I sit down in the passenger's seat.

I start to ask a question.

"No," he interrupts.

"What about—?"

"'We ain't seen shit,'" he mimics.

"And—"

"Three thousand eight hundred ninety-seven."

"And you're—"

"Four thousand fifty," he answers. "And that?"

"Oh, nothing," I answer, rubbing my bandaged hand. "Four thousand—"

"Fifty." He exhales deeply. "Their damned eyes are gone."

"Whose?"

"Irie Man's," he answers. "And Funky Dollah Bill's."

"Their eyes?" I ask.

"Gone," Willie reaffirms. "I got curious about those tear streaks down their cheeks. They looked—I don't know—milky somehow. So, I had an ME open Funky Dollah Bill's eyelid. There was nothing there."

"Nothing?" I parrot, perplexed.

"Nothing but socket," he sighed. "All four of them. Gone."

"Wow." I exhale deeply. "And you're four thousand—"

"And fifty."

"Right."

Willie suddenly reaches into the back seat. He produces two plastic ponchos.

"Pimpnakang?" I ask.

"Pimpnakang," he confirms, throws the Crown Victoria into gear, and we're off to King of Sheba's.

PIMPNAKANG, NÉ NUNYA Damned Bizness, is the plaque-incrusted heart of Koontown. If something dirty has happened here, it has either run through him or has touched him in some way. He's what every rapper claims to be— "The Ruler of This Pimp Game."

He was just a Pimpnasquire when my father first ran into him some twenty-odd years ago. He'd been arrested by Vice for running girls out of the Porch Monkey. He told the detectives that he could finger the perpetrator of a triple homicide my father had been working. His information was good, the beast got electrocuted, my father got promoted, and Pimpnasquire got a Get out of Jail Free card.

As Dad always said, "A police is only as good as his best informant," and Pimp was the best. Whenever my old man had a trail grow cold, he'd go to Pimpnakanightserrant (at the time) to heat it back up. Oftentimes, the case would turn red hot. Though they were on opposite sides of the law, I think the two men actually respected each other, may have even liked one another. Pimp even showed up for my father's funeral.

Dad left his best informant to Willie in his will, and I exercised the legacy clause several times to help me solve a sticky murder or two. I know I should hate the man—I definitely abhor what the man does—but I kind of actually like Pimpnakang, too. I hate to say it, but it'll be good to see him again.

His "wife," on the other hand …

SCREAMS SMACK US in the face as soon as we enter King of Sheba's Hair Care and Beauty Salon with our rain slickers on. It's Welfare Queen in her custom-made chair farthest from the door. I swear she never leaves it. She has her feet hiked up on stirrups with her muumuu folded up over her knees. Her sweat-covered face is furiously contorted with pain. Her seven-inch acrylic nails dig deeply into the armrests, the foam padding crumbling to the floor. She thrusts her head forward in a mighty grunt. Her tiara nearly falls from her weave.

"LordJesusFUCKAlmighty!"

Willie enters first, holding out a bottle of Chivas Regal. "Pimpnakang! The Ol' School Bruvvaaa*Shit*!"

He slips and falls. The bottle flies out of his hand. There's a collective gasp in the room. I catch it with my good hand just inches from the floor. There's now a collective "Phew."

Kang laughs, spraying a mighty dose of activator into his hair. Like most pimps, the man *is* Old School. Except where most of his cohorts are trying to be "Superfly," Kang is "Funky Fresh out the Box." This pimp is strictly '80s. Rimmed gold teeth, diamond-encrusted Gazelle glasses, laceless British Knights, nylon Adidas track suits, and a juicy Jehri curl he keeps nice and moist.

"Watch your step, homeboy," he laughs, big belly bouncing, as Willie groans to get up. "You too old fo' dis shit."

"Who you telling?" grumbles Willie. He looks around for a place to wipe the grease off his hands, then decides to swipe them on his poncho.

"Told de fellas you be comin' round today," Pimpnakang boasts.

There are three graying brothers sitting around Kang's barber shop throne. They're all middle-aged and overweight and look like they just stepped out of a Fat Boys video. They nod their Kangols in agreement. Kang nods my way. "Glad you brought you some comp'ny, dough. How you doin', Vee gurl?"

"We—"

"CocksuckinsonofabitchWHORE!!!" Welfare Queen screams.

A newborn's head suddenly pops out from underneath her muumuu. Before any of us can react, a young uniform emerges from the back room with scissors and a cloth. He immediately catches the baby before it can hit the ground. He snips the umbilical cord, wraps the baby up, and announces, "It's a boy."

"Good," Queen exhales.

The police moves to the back room, shouting, "Another one for Angola. Someone come in here and grab the placenta. Come on, people! We ain't got all day!"

I hand the bottle of Chivas to Kang. He smiles contentedly. "Dis 'bout dem Irie Man/Funky Dollah Bill murders?"

"Yeah," Willie confirms. "What do you know about them, Pimpnakang?"

The big pimp shrugs. "Just 'bout as much as anybody else here in the KT."

"Which is more than the police will ever know," I add.

They all laugh. Welfare Queen grunts. Her placenta plops to the floor. I'll never get used to that.

"Why do you think those two were together last night?" asks Willie.

"Guess dey was feelin' lonely," Pimpnakang answers, to more laughter.

"BitchassniggaFAGGOTS!!!" Welfare Queen screeches. Another baby head pops out. Another police pops in. He snips, swaddles, says, "It's a girl," and sweeps out of the room.

"Damn," huffs Queen.

"Naw, seriously," Willie continues. "Word has it there was a beef between them."

"'Bout twelve inches," Prince Markie Dee chuckles.

"Niggas is always 'zaggeratin', an' shit," Queen huffs.

I chuckle. No one else does, though.

"Naw, look," Kang continues, spraying his hair, "dese young niggas *today*, dey *always* beefin'—"

"I-i-i-it sells re-re-records," the Human Beat Box interrupts.

"Damn skippy," the pimp concurs. "So, one day Irie Man beefin' wif FDB, den FDB beefin' wif him. Den Yo!Nutz an' C-Word beefin' wif de bof of 'em—"

"Dem bitches crazy," adds Kool Rock-Ski. "'Member what dey done did to MC Spit and DJ Swallow?"

"Dey never shoulda come out wif dat 'Goin' Down' diss record," Kang says, gravely.

"CumlappinWHORES!!!"

"It's a boy!"

The uniform leaves with another new baby.

"Den HNIC come out beefin' wif all dem uva niggas."

"HNIC?" Willie asks Kang.

"That doesn't mean what I think it does, does it?" I mutter.

"'Course it do, gurl," Kang grins, and sprays. "Yall ain't heard a *HNIC*?! He got de hottest new j'int out in the KT … 'Bitch! Ho! Bitch! Ho!'"

The Fat Boys start waving their hands in the air, chanting, "Bitch! … Ho! … Bitch! … Ho!" Welfare Queen squawks, "Partay ova here! Partay ova dere!" Kang starts popping and locking, jerking his ample torso, thrusting his right arm, right hand, left arm, left hand, jerking his—Oh no!

Ugh. He popped his neck. Now, Willie and I are covered in activator. Thank God for the rain slickers.

"Yeah. HNIC an' FDB," Kang wheezes. "It's de biggest beef goin'."

"D-d-did you s-s-see *Rollin' Stone*?" stammers Beat Box.

"Yeah," Kang chuckles. "HNIC called out FDB's sista, momma, *an'* third-cousin twice-removed *by name*. Said he did some real Nzinga-type shit to dey asses."

I shudder.

"I'd start there if I was you," Kang advises.

"CockteasinCUNT!!!" Queen screams.

Another baby, another police.

"Excuse me, Queen," I venture. "What do the police actually do with all your babies?"

"De gurls all go into foster care," she informs, wiping the sweat from her upper lip. "Boys go down to Angola."

"The penitentiary?" I ask.

"Three hots an' a muhfuckin' cot," she beams, "an' dey got dem dat cotton plantation down there."

I try to hide the shock from my face. I don't think it works, though.

"What?" Queen screams. "Dey pay twenny-five cent a hour."

No. It definitely didn't work. She's angry now.

"I don't know how it be fo' yo' ass, *Miss* Innermuhfuckinnational Model, an' shit," she fumes, "but round *here*, niggas gots to *earns* dey keep."

"Word up!" someone shouts.

Queen grunts. The placenta plops onto the floor.

"Look," Markie Dee interrupts, "yall might think I'm straight buggin', but I heard it was dem gotdamned *crack* babies."

"Oh yeah," agrees Beat Box. "I h-h-heard dat shit, too."

"Crack babies?" Willie asks, incredulous.

"Oh yeah!" Markie Dee confirms. "Not dem li'l shits you seent shiverin' an' shit on de TV all dem years back. *Naw*, dem li'l niggas done growed up now."

"An' dey crazy *as hell*!" roars Kool Rock-Ski.

"You got dat right," continues Markie. "Ain't got no respect, neiver. Never look a nigga in de eye. An' dey kill yo' ass fo' no reason whatso*ever*. Not like a nigga step on yo' sneakers, lookin' at yo' bitch, talkin' shit 'bout yo mama. Naw, I mean, over absolutely *nuthin'*."

"Yeah. A-a-a-a-ain't like we was back in de d-d-d-day."

"Yeah. *We* killed a nigga ova territory."

"R-r-r-r-respect!"

"Ova a nigga's kicks," Markie Dee continues. "Fly-ass Eight-Ball jackets. *You* try shootin' a nigga ova his jacket. You gots to be a *real* good shot—fo' *real*."

"Word! Strickly headshots," Kool Rock adds. "Cain't be sportin' no new duds wif bullet holes in yo' shit."

Willie clears his throat. Everyone looks his way.

"Not like *we* ever did some shit like dat," Pimpnakang chuckles, uncomfortably.

"TrickassbitchassNIGGAS!!!"

"It's a girl."

"Shit."

"I hears dey gots *powers*, an' shit," Kool Rock adds.

"Powers?" Willie looks over at Pimpnakang, who shrugs.

"Yeah," Kool Rock affirms. "Like my gurl, LaShareesa, heard dey found one bitch wif bite marks on her neck, an' dey wasn't a drop a blood lef' in de bitch's body, neiver."

"An' dey ain't never found her killer," adds Markie Dee.

"Do they ever?" Queen grunts.

"Dat's 'cause dat li'l crack baby nigga jus' flew de fuck *off*."

"Flew off?" asks Willie.

"Yeah, Detective. His black ass done melted into de night, an' shit."

"Jus' like *yo'* black ass, nigga," Queen pants. "Dat's why we always makin' you smile when we's out at night, Markie. Dat's de only way we can see yo' ass."

Folks start laughing.

"Aw, Queenie," Markie Dee groans.

How quickly it all turns to nonsense. I look over at Willie. He looks like he feels the same way. He clears his throat.

"Thanks, Pimpnakang." The detective reaches over and shakes the pimp's hand.

"Ain't nuffin', O'Ree," Kang says, and sprays his hair with activator.

We gingerly make our way to the door, careful not to slip on the floor grease.

"SuckacockyouWHORE!!!"

"It's a boy!"

"Cha-Ching!"

OUTSIDE, WILLIE WIPES his hand on the poncho and starts to take it off. He shakes his head in disbelief.

"Vee, what was that famous line from *Scarface*?" he asks.

"Uh, 'Say hello to my little friend'?"

"No. Not that one."

"'Say good-bye to the bad guy?'"

"Not that one, either."

"I don't know, Willie. I'm running out of rap lyrics here."

He sighs and nods his head back to King of Sheba. "'Don't get high off your own supply.'"

Chaptah Siks

"God bless the dead and buried nigga
Don't worry if you see God first
Tell Him shit got worse"

—2Pac, "God Bless the Dead"

WE LEAVE THE bulletproof glass, pork grease, and the fact they hate touching our money behind and take our Chinese food out to the parking lot. This is one part of the job I do not miss. Ghetto Chinese food always wreaks havoc on my complexion. All that grease. There had actually been times when I'd get a pimple on my nose after eating this stuff. But what can you do? I'm rolling with Willie now, and you will never be able to pry those BBQ spare ribs from his cold, dead hands. It's amazing he's stayed so trim over the years.

The old man sets his food onto the Crown Vic's hood and immediately grabs a sticky bone.

"They make our toys, our dog food, and now our ribs," he marvels. "Is there nothing the Chinese can't do?"

I pluck at my spring roll. I'll be Rudolph in no time. "I hear they're making African masks now."

He shakes his head. "Damn."

"Willie?"

"Yeah, Vee?"

"Pimpnakang and the Fat Boys," I open, "do you think they know that crack babies are a myth? That some reporter just made it all up to make us look bad—yet again?"

Willie licks the red grease from his fingertips.

"Crack babies a myth, eh?"

I nod.

"Like vampires, right?" he smirks.

I laugh.

"And the female orgasm, of course," Willie continues.

"Funny," I huff.

"And I just *loves* me some Welfare Queen, now," he jokes. "Fuckin' Angola. Can you believe that shit?"

"Koontown," I shrug. I grew up in the suburbs. "So, what do you think, Willie? Should we be out looking for crack babies? Or at least go home and watch *Blacula*?"

"No, but—" Willie waves a bone in the air "—I think they may have something with that, that beef shit they were talking about. With those rappers, uh, HNIC, and what was that? Yo!Nutz and C-Word?"

"Those names," I groan. "Whatever happened to Kid 'N' Play?"

"Damn, Vee. You work for Hustle Beamon now. Catch up."

> *Open dat ass*
> *Bitch, you know dis dick pleases*
> *Open dat ass*
> *A second cummin' like Jesus*

"What was that?" Willie asks. "Singing?"

"Yeah. Like last night," I confirm. "A choir, or something."

Suddenly, a large crowd of teenagers emerges from the corner of Vesey and Prosser and head straight toward us. Mostly boys, they're all wearing the same, oversized white T-shirt with a picture of Irie Man on the front. They walk slowly, uniformly, with lit candles in their hands.

"A vigil?" asks Willie.

"For Irie Man?" I add.

They sing with all their hearts.

Suck dis dick, bitch
'Til a nigga sees God
Open dat gap, ho
And gobble dis nigga's rod

"Trouble?" I ask.

From the opposite corner, Prosser and Turner, comes a group of black T-shirted youths. Mostly boys again, with their own lit candles and Funky Dollah Bill's face on their shirts. They're all singing just as heartily and are headed straight toward the Irie Man "choir."

As the crowds converge, the singing grows louder, angrier. They are shouting over each other. "Bitch!" "Ass!" God!" "Dick!" fill the air.

Willie throws his rib down.

"This *is* Koontown," he groans, and moves toward the teens.

The two groups are on top of each other. Candles are thrown down. Kids are in each other's faces, cursing, spit and middle fingers flying. I can see L-shaped lumps in the smalls of some of the boys' backs. This *could* get fatal.

The two leaders are spitting and jabbing fingers into each other's faces. Willie steps between them, flashing his badge. "Police!"

"Fuck de po-lice, nigga!"

Thwack!

Willie drops the Irie Man leader with a right cross.

"Sorry. Allergies," says Willie, shaking his right hand. "Now, what the hell's going on here?"

"Dese bitch-ass Irie Man niggas talkin' shit 'bout Funky Dollah Bill, Officer!" the FDB leader shouts. "*Man*, dem niggas don't know dat muhfucka was a prophet!"

"A prophet?" Willie repeats.

"Well, Irie Man was a prophet *and* a muhfuckin' *saint!*" the Irie Man boy counters, tearfully, rubbing his jaw. He looks like he's maybe fourteen. I think Willie hurt his feelings with that right cross.

"A prophet and a saint?" my old partner tries not to laugh.

"Hells yeah!" the boy snaps. "Irie was a man a God. Spreadin' de Word, an' shit."

"Seriously?" I ask.

"Sho 'nuff, Vee," the boy continues. "Irie been spreadin' dat shit fo' years, yo. 'Open dat ass,' dat nigga say. Fo' de 'second *cummin' a Jesus.*'"

There are nods and shouts of agreement.

"I don't think—" I start.

"Fuck *dat* nonsense," the Funky Dollah Bill leader interrupts. "FDB, now *dat* nigga, he was on dat *real* shit. Suckin' dick 'til a nigga *sees* God."

"Dat's de shit right dere!" someone shouts. People whoop affirmation.

"I'm sorry," Willie says, "what does all this have to do with being saints and prophets?"

The FDB leader huffs, exasperated with Willie's and my bewilderment. "See, dat shit, it like—like metaphor, an' shit. Like, when it come to *God*, an' shit, a nigga should be like a bitch ... an' shit."

The FDB posse shouts their approval.

"Like we *supposed* to be takin' in de Word a God—swallowin' dat shit—like a bitch suckin' dick."

"Yeah! Yeah!"

"Preach it, nigga!"

"Naw, naw." The Irie Man leader violently shakes his head. "You supposed to be totally *open* for God's Word. Like a bitch openin' dat ass fo' a nigga."

"Sooo," starts Willie, "all you fine, young brothers are supposed to—now, let me get this straight—take it ... up the ass?"

"The Word a God! Yeah!" the FDB leader shouts.

"Like ... bitches?" Willie continues.

"Hells yeah!"

"I heard dat!"

"Naw, nigga officer," the Irie Man leader counters, "we *supposed* to be suckin' de Lord's *dick*!"

"Like bitches?" Willie repeats.

"What de *fuck* dat nigga say?" a boy shouts.

Willie cocks his arm back. That boy yelps and retreats. Willie chuckles, "Punk," and then looks at both crowds. "Now, I just want to get this perfectly clear," he says, "all you strong, African brothers, all of you are ... well ... bitches?"

...

All these boys start looking around, confused.

...

Willie looks at me and smiles.

...

Give it another minute.

...

It'll sink in.

...

The Irie Man leader inhales deeply and puffs out his teenaged chest. "You *damned* right, Officer!" he cheers. "I'm a *bitch*! A *bitch* fo' de *Lord*!"

Everyone cheers. Willie shakes his head.

Suddenly, the boy slides to all fours in the middle of the street and raises his behind in the air. He thrusts his head high, and screams, "My ass is open, God! My ass is open! Fuck me up de ass, Jesus! Fuck me up de ass!!!"

The entire Irie Man choir prostrates themselves on the street and starts screaming to the heavens.

"Fuck me good, Jesus!!!"

"Give it to me, Heavenly Father! All three holes!!!"

"Oh, Lord," I gasp. "That doesn't even make sense."

"Fuck dat!" the FDB leader erupts. He throws himself on his knees and raises his hands in the air. "Come on, Jesus! I'm ready! I'm ready! Let me suck yo' dick, Jesus! I wanna *suck* it!!!"

"Uh …" I stammer.

"I wanna suck it, Jesus!!!"

"Lemme lick yo' *balls*, Lord!!!"

"Cum on my *face*, Lord Jesus!!!"

"Cum on my *ass*!!!"

Willie's cell phone rings. He quickly answers it.

"Let a nigga gobble dem nuts!!!"

Willie slams his phone shut.

"It's the coroner's. They're up to four thousand forty," he announces. "Let's go."

Chaptah Seben

"Jacking you more than Ripper
My fifth's an organ shifter
The human organism lifter"

—*Mobb Deep & Kool G. Rap, "The Realest"*

THE CITY MORGUE lies on the border of Koontown and what used to be called Niggers Run. After decades of protest claiming the name was too racially insensitive, the residents of N.R. changed the name to Giuliani. Many of us claimed that they missed our point. To which, they countered, "No. You're missing *ours*."

The morgue was originally built as a Ford SUV assembly plant during the Empowerment Zone days, but, when gas prices soared and SUV sales plummeted, Ford took their ball bearings and went home. As few jobs as there are in Koontown, the politicians took it hard—though, to be honest, most of the employees were from Giuliani, and the City Council had given Ford so many tax breaks, they were literally paying *Ford* for all those Giuliani jobs. However, the coroner, Dr. Marion C. Sims, saw an opportunity. The old morgue, he claimed, had "outgrown" its old facilities. The SUV plant was perfect. The city bought the building for a song. "Move On Up," by Curtis Mayfield.

Willie screeches the cruiser around the corner to Drew Boulevard. There's a long line of police dump trucks stretching the two blocks to the morgue plant. Willie speeds past them all, drives through the "Official" entry, flashes his badge at security, and slides into a parking space.

We get out. The conveyor belt's squealing loud and hard today. I look over. A dump truck beeps as it lifts its bucket. Body bags tumble out onto the conveyor belt. Surgical-masked uniforms straighten the bags onto the belt as they're pulled into the building. The bucket lowers, the truck pulls away, and the process starts all over again with another truck.

"The Alpha and Omega," murmurs Willie, tearing his eyes away from the squealing conveyor.

"What was that?"

"What a day," he sighs, shaking his head. "Let's go, Vee."

We enter through a steel door into the sterile lobby. A chunky, chocolaty sister sits behind a desk in an ill-fitting security guard uniform and a cheap dye job that makes her hair flame orange. She is staring at her cell phone, buds planted firmly in her ears, cackling with laughter.

Willie walks up to the desk. I follow. She keeps cackling. Willie leans against the Formica counter. We wait. She laughs and laughs. Willie finally clears his throat.

"What?!" she snaps. "Cain't you see I am *busy*?!"

Willie sighs, rolls his eyes, and flashes his badge.

"So?" the woman grunts. "I got a badge, too." She goes back to watching her phone, cackling. "Dese niggas is *crazy!*"

"Who?" I venture.

"Oh … some fools done Autotuned 'Gimme Dat' on YouTube." She starts laughing again. Willie and I obviously look confused. She looks up at us, screwing up her face. "'Gimme Dat?'" Nothing. "'Gimme dat dick, nigga,'" she sings. "'Gimme dat dick.'" Still nothing. "Pssssshhhh," she exhales, ruefully. "White folks." Her eyes bug in my direction.

I fight the urge to punch them out of their sockets. Willie places a hand on my shoulder. I do not relax. "We're here to see Dr. Sims," he announces. "Where do we sign in?"

"You got a number?" challenges the guard.

Willie produces his ticket. "Four thousand fifty," he says, flatly.

There's a ding to our left. We all look. The sign above the factory entrance door sign reads, "Now Serving ... 4048," in red lights.

The woman sighs from deep down in her belly, the burden of actual work heavy on her shoulders. "Guess you better hurry," she says, wearily. She lets loose another heavy sigh as she reaches up to the clipboard on the counter before us and spins it to face us. Her hand lands on the clipboard's sheet with a thunder clap as she points. "Sign here please."

She immediately returns to her phone and her cackling.

"Got a pen?" Willie asks.

"What, nigga?!" she roars, about to jump out of her seat.

I quietly point to Willie's breast pocket. He smiles and lifts one of his own pens. The guard relaxes. We sign in and move on.

PSSSSTTTTTTT!!!

A spray of canned perfume hits us in the face as soon as we enter. Plastic strawberries fill my nostrils. The morgue plant floor is filled with perfume dispensers. They're a little annoying, but I really don't mind too much. The stench of death would overwhelm me otherwise.

Literally tons of dead black flesh move through this morgue on a daily basis. Young men, middle-aged grandmothers, children squeak by on the conveyor belts—victims of the alphabet soup of death in Koontown—OD, HIV, GSWs—what the MEs call "K-Town Natural Causes"—to be eviscerated and examined.

The noise is unbearable. The conveyor belts criss-cross and crowd the assembly floor. They protest incessantly against the strain of all these bodies. The machine is large. It is overwhelming and loud and nauseatingly efficient.

The conveyors are on a slight incline with drainage guards along the sides so that the bodies' fluids will eventually drain into vats embedded into the floor. The body bags are seamed with Velcro. A robotic arm comes down and strips them away in one, quick motion to be reused later in the process.

The body is now fully naked, belly-down, on the belt. A panoramic camera swoops down and takes several photos for the external examination. A perfectly-calibrated, seven-foot hammer shoots up and punches the belt. The body flips on contact like a flapjack and lands on its back. The camera then returns and takes frontal exam photos.

The body then chugs a few feet down the line and stops again. A razor-sharp scalpel slices down from the ceiling and cuts a swift, precise line from the left shoulder to the bottom of the breastbone. It cuts a corresponding line from the right shoulder to meet the first at the breastbone. It modulates slightly, then cuts directly to the navel, jigs around the belly button, and continues down to the pubic bone.

The scalpel quickly disappears. Robot clamps emerge from the sides, fasten onto the skin with a click, and pull the flesh flaps away to the sides and over the victim's face.

An automated circular saw quickly appears with its maddening whine. It swoops down, and saw and bone sing a sickening aria as the ribs and sternum are cut away. By this time, several buckets have been moved up to the body on conveyor belts of their own. A gigantic robotic hand descends, picks up the chest wall, and carefully places the bones into one such bucket.

The saw returns and disappears inside the victim's throat. It quickly reappears, moves to the victim's groin, and disappears again. After it's done, it moves so the giant hand can descend on the body again. It reemerges with a handful of organs. It quickly places them in their own, separate bucket.

The saw moves in yet again. It plunges in slightly above the hairline and cuts deep into the skull. Then it whips quickly around the skull to where brain stem meets spinal cord and continues to complete the circuit above the hairline.

The giant hand comes in, grabs the skull, and there's a sickening Pop! as skull, hair, and flesh are removed from the body. Brain fluid splashes onto the belt and dribbles its way to the vats below. Then the hand sweeps into the skull and removes the brain. How something so large and robotic can do all this without doing damage is beyond me, but it does. The brain goes into a jar filled with a formalin solution.

Then everything—body, organs, brain, skull cap, and hair—is moved on down the line to separate medical examiners' stations. They have to move quickly. There's too much death in here to be lollygagging. But their jobs are made easy. There aren't too many mysteries here in Koontown. Overdose, AIDS, gunshot wounds, the occasional diabetic. They quickly record their reports into their microphones and move on to the next body.

Computers transcribe and file the reports. The robots move in to dump all the organs back, sew the body back up, zip it all into a body bag, and, if the family's there to claim it, they drop the body at their feet. If not, it is spilled into a plywood coffin, dropped into a dump truck, and hauled off to the city incinerator.

"I can't say I miss any of this," I say, as I watch the bone dust fly up on an eight-year-old girl's torso. She's in pigtails. They'll soon find their own bucket.

"Damn," Willie huffs. "Guess I'll have to come up with another surprise gift for your birthday then."

"Please do."

PSSSSTTTTTTT!!!

DR. MARION C. SIMS is the strangest, most mysterious, the ... queerest white man to ever set foot in Koontown. And that's saying a lot. J. Edgar Hoover used to have a summer home here. And this is where that old segregationist Senator, Strom Thurmond, used to visit his secret black family. But everything about Dr. Sims has been shrouded in mystery ever since he arrived in town.

Koontown finally got its first black coroner back in '89. Dr. Bledsoe-Nice was brought in by our first quasi-militant mayor, Clarence 36-24-36 X, just before his pay-to-play sex scandal brought that administration down. Dr. Bledsoe-Nice had been blessed with charisma, good looks, a Harvard education, and a bad heart. He just could not handle the strain of the Koontown morgue's 24/7 workload. He died suddenly over the corpse of a 27-year-old grandmother. Just face-planted into the woman's small intestines.

Folks screamed government conspiracy. Actually, Clarence 36-24-36 X screamed government conspiracy as federal prosecutors played the videotape of his screaming "Government conspiracy!" around the shaft of a transsexual prostitute's penis in his mouth. Nobody believed the mayor—or any of his claims—until Dr. Marion C. Sims showed up one day at City Hall, asking, "Does anybody need a coroner?"

The town did need one. Desperately. Tens of thousands of bodies had piled up at the morgue in the week since Dr. Bledsoe-Nice had passed. The Council hired Dr. Sims on the spot. No questions asked.

Those only started emerging after the Rodney King riots. Dr. Sims had claimed that Latinos had caused most of the destruction. Folks were confused. The news cameras didn't show any Latinos rioting. Nobody was even sure that Latinos actually lived in K-Town. Yet, there were all these Spanish-speaking corpses in Sims's morgue. It was then that people remembered the words of their deposed mayor and started screaming, "Government conspiracy!"

The alphabet soup that is Uncle Sam started spilling out of every African-American mouth. Dr. Sims supposedly worked for the FBI, the CIA, DoD, HHS, NIH, NASA. They even claimed the FDA.

"It's a secret government program, brothers and sisters! They call it, 'Soylent Black!'" one activist harangued. "The white man be *killin'* black *men* an' eatin' 'em! Hopin' we'll give 'em bigger penises!"

His congregation erupted in horror.

"*I* heard," one supporter yelled, "they feedin' *our* womens to *they* womens, too! Thinkin' they'll get bigger *asses*!!!"

Folks were ready to riot.

Then one, brave congregant stood up. "That's *bullshit*!" he screamed. "When men love *flat* asses! Not *fat* ones!"

They were about to tear the brother limb from limb. He saw the blood in their eyes. He quickly cleared his throat, murmured, "Naw. I heard the dick thing, too," and quietly melted back into the crowd.

The damage had already been done. People were too confused to riot. "*Flat asses? Really? Just ain't no accountin' fo' white folks.*" Everybody went home. *In Living Color* was about to come on. Dr. Sims got to keep his job and his hide. But the rumors still persisted. They persist to this day.

Personally, I think he revels in the mystery. For, while he can talk your ear off about almost anything—even government conspiracies—he remains mysteriously mum about his own past. Sometimes, I think—especially when he goes on about black helicopters, the United Nations, and the World Health Organization—he actually enjoys stoking the flames of suspicion around himself. After all, who doesn't love being the center of attention? I should know. I used to be a supermodel, after all.

PSSSSTTTTTTTT!!!

Cheap perfume smacks us in the face and loud, muffled hip-hop pounds our ears as we stand before Dr. Sims's office door. I just want to get away from the conveyor belts for a minute. Willie pounds on the door. "Detective O'Ree here, Dr. Sims!" he yells.

"Come in!"

Willie swings the door open. We quickly enter. Willie closes the door. The screeching is gone, but the music is deafening.

"What is that shit?!" Willie screams.

"Oh. Sorry." Dr. Sims turns to the stereo unit behind him and turns it off.

He turns back around with a crazed smile. "Irie Man," he informs. "A good businessman always knows his clientele."

Sims stands tall. Well over six feet. His face is cragged and slides down in a torrent of wrinkles. He has a shock of uncontrollable Einstein-white hair that would make Don King and Buckwheat jealous. His eyes are ice blue but burn with a fire that is not quite right. He looks just like all the mad scientists in every old science fiction movie ever made. To be honest, he has always creeped me out a little.

He looks me squarely in the eye and smiles. It is meant to be warm. It sends a slight shiver down my spine. He eats spaghetti and meatballs while poking around in people's intestines with that smile on his face. "It has been quite awhile," he greets. "To what do we owe the pleasure, Ms. Noire?"

"Hustle Beamon," I answer.

"The international rap mogul," he booms. "A true *pillar* of the community."

"Really?" I marvel.

"Most certainly," he declares, imperiously. "What would K-Town be without people like Hustle Beamon? If you ask me, we could use more men like him. Getting these kids off the streets. It would save this town. I might even be allowed to take a vacation every once in awhile."

I'm confused. He does know that Hustle produces gangsta rap, doesn't he? I decide to shrug it off. "Well, he has me investigating the Irie Man/Funky Dollah Bill slayings."

"Oh yes." Dr. Sims shakes his head. "FDB is on Dope Beat, after all."

"How could you *possibly* know that?" Willie snaps.

"Hip-hop is the life's blood of African-American culture," states Dr. Sims. "Of *American* culture. It is one of our lead exports to the rest of the world. Only reactionaries and troglodytes do not keep *au courant* with their own culture. And I, Detective O'Ree, am neither."

"No point in arguing that," Willie concedes.

"Not a single one, I'm afraid." Dr. Sims smiles, triumphant. He suddenly points down at his desk. There's a corpse laying on top of it. It's a large, solidly-built black man. His smooth skin screams youth—even flayed back and pulled over his face as it is. "Here. Look at this."

We comply. All of the men's organs have been removed. It's a sight that didn't use to bother me. But I've been away for over a year. And, well, this was almost me a year ago.

"The focal point of American violence," Dr. Sims pronounces grandly. "The black male body." Willie and I look at each other, confused. Before either of us can say anything, though, the doctor continues. "At first, it was the Amerindian. We were stealing his lands, he was rebelling, he had to be crushed. We paid the African little—if any—heed back then. It was the red *savage* who was the focus of our concern, our anxiety, our rage, and our violence.

"And then Toussaint L'Ouverture led a slave revolt down in Haiti. The Indian threat was diminishing. It was only a matter of time before *they* all disappeared. It was now the African's turn.

"And what to do with this?" He sweeps his latex-gloved hand across the carcass. "This, this *African. This* savage. We had taken him from *his* land. We had put him in *bondage.* We had seen what these Hottentots can do when they were angry. Those Haitians had beaten *Napoleon,* for god sake.

"When was this African on our shores going to do the same to us? It was only a matter of time. Right? When was he going to exact his revenge? It's a question we asked ourselves in 1802. It's a question we white people continue to ask ourselves to this day. Even when we were 'crazy' enough to put one of the Ethiopians in the White House."

"Actually, he's half-Kenyan," I correct.

Dr. Sims merely shakes his head. Obviously, I'm ignorant of some fact.

"So much of our energy," he continues, "so much of our blood and treasure, so much of *African-American* blood has been spilled, so much potential simply *wiped out*, all because we were loathe to discover the answer to that most menacing question.

"So many black bodies have cycled through morgues just like this one—not because of racism. Well yes, because of racism—in that 'Racism' is only 'Fear' with a more scientific-sounding name."

Dr. Sims looks down at the corpse again. "And what isn't there to fear?" he whispers, hoarsely. His fingertips start gliding—lovingly?—along the man's arm. "This gentleman here," Dr. Sims says. "Twenty-two. At the prime of his life, of his *power*. Look at the musculature."

We do. It is quite impressive. And more than a little morbid.

"The calves, the biceps femoris, the glutei. So perfect, so well-formed. So brutal. This man could easily squat—what?—two hundred, two hundred fifty pounds and run the forty-yard dash under five seconds without blinking an eye.

"Combine those powerful muscles with his well-formed deltoids and shoulders, his triceps and biceps, and you've got a punch powerful enough to deliver over four hundred kilograms of pure force. More than enough to completely shatter the human jaw with hardly even trying.

"Oh, to have been this boy," he rhapsodizes. "To have been so beautiful, so perfect, so powerful. To have been able to inflict such damage on the human body, such *pain* on the American psyche." He sighs and shudders—much like Gianni did on the night of our Paris shoot.

See what I mean? Queer.

"Come on, Doc," groans Willie. "You're giving me a hard-on here."

I'm afraid to look.

"Sorry," Dr. Sims apologizes with a slight chuckle. "I often wanted to be a boy like this. To *have* a boy like this. But no, my son had to take after me. A tall, lanky science nerd with a degree from Harvard he'll never use. If only he could've been more like his mother. Now, *she* was powerful."

"Good for her," Willie says. "I've been that boy. It ain't all you crack it up to be."

"Wait a second," I interrupt. "You said this boy was twenty-two. Both FDB and Irie Man were twenty-six."

"Why, he's neither of them," says Dr. Sims, confused.

"Well, that's who we're here for, Doc," Willie protests.

"Why didn't you say something?" the doctor asks.

"I don't know," my former partner fumes. "I guess *someone* was too busy getting horny over young black men."

"Does your wife know?" Dr. Sims snickers. He turns around, rummages beneath his stereo system, turns, and throws a manila folder at Willie. "We did those autopsies hours ago."

Willie growls in frustration and starts riffling through the papers.

"You won't understand any of it," the coroner states. "Frankly, we hardly understand it ourselves. As one of our lab techs put it, 'That's some freaky shit.'"

"What do you mean?" I ask.

"Well," Dr. Sims opens, "when the machines first sliced open the bodies to extract the internal organs, we found that there were actually no internal organs to *be* extracted."

"What?" Willie interjects.

"Nothing was there," the doctor repeats. "The carcasses were already stripped clean. Internally. We'd thought that maybe the machines had somehow lost the organs. We had to shut down operations for twelve minutes, forty-two seconds—"

He notices the look of shock on my face.

"We are *very* precise here, Ms. Noire," he states, proudly. "We have to be.

"Anyway, everything was accounted for. Except the missing organs, of course. So, we had to resume operations at half-capacity. I needed all the help I could muster to ascertain what exactly happened to our two famous victims.

"It took some time and a lot of tests, but apparently some form of highly concentrated acid was used to, basically, melt down all the internal organs to the consistency of—well, soup. We found some remaining traces of the liquid. Not very much, though. Just enough for a small sample. But in that sample, we found the liquefied remains of both men's organs as well as the unidentified substance. We're assuming it's the acid the perpetrators used. But it's nothing we've seen before. Nothing our labs can handle. I'll have to send the sample off to the boys at the National Institutes of Health—"

"NIH does autopsies?" Willie interrupts.

"There is nothing medically related happening in this world that the NIH doesn't do," answers Dr. Sims, with an odd gleam in his eye. "And, frankly, Detective, they would *love* to get their hands on a mystery such as this."

"So, wait now," Willie interrupts. "There was no evidence of manipulation at the crime scene. These two fools died while … well, you know … doing what they were doing.

"So, you're telling me, while they were—" Willie sighs deeply "—fucking, some mysterious perpetrator comes in, rams some kind of tube up Irie Man's ass, sprays this lethal acid up there, burns up all his internal organs. He doesn't scream, doesn't struggle, just takes it. Then Funky Dollah Bill doesn't see *any* of this? Doesn't jump up, say, 'Lawd hab mercy!', and get the fuck out of Dodge? He just lies there and waits his turn like a good, little bottom?"

Dr. Sims scratches thoughtfully at his chin. "Where to begin?" he asks himself. "No, we're thinking it didn't happen that way at all."

"How then?" Willie snaps. The lack of sleep and the mystery of this case are starting to get to him.

"Well," Dr. Sims exhales, "Irie Man had no signs of anal penetration— which, I'm suspecting, his fans will be happy to hear."

Willie and I glance at each other dubiously. If the doctor only knew.

"FDB's anal penetration is quite obvious, as you would expect," Dr. Sims continues. "Semen, lubricant, rodent remains. But no signs of the acid or organ solution."

I start to ask, "Did you just say—"

"Both victims," Dr. Sims interrupts, "have traces of the other's saliva and semen in their oral cavities—as it should be—but yet again, neither the acid nor organ remains."

Willie pipes up, "So then, how was this whole thing done?"

"Remember those strange, milky tears you noted in your report, Detective?" the coroner asks.

"Oh yeah," Willie grimaces. "They had no eyes in their heads. Just those weird tears on their faces."

"Well, those tears were what remained of their eyes. As though they had been melted down as well. So, what we're thinking here, and this is only preliminary *speculation*," Dr. Sims emphasizes. "We're thinking that somehow this acidic solution was pumped in and out through the victims' eye sockets."

"And they stood still for all that?" I ask.

Dr. Sims shrugs. "Unfathomable, I know. It could have only been a horrifically painful death."

"Yet, they continued pumping away on each other while their organs were being pumped out of them?" scoffs Willie.

"Who knows?" Dr. Sims admits. "Maybe they were somehow drugged. Or even hypnotized. I'm not sure we have enough of a sample to ever properly ascertain what exactly happened to those two last night."

"Oh, great," Willie groans.

"Perhaps, the boys at NIH can figure it all out," Dr. Sims offers, hopefully. Though, to be honest, there is no hope in his words, in his eyes, or anywhere in his entire office.

Chaptah Ate

"Quasi-homosexuals is runnin' this rap shit"

—Mos Def, "The Rape Over"

I CAN ALMOST see the headache forming behind Willie's eyes. No sleep and a million questions rattling around in that skull of his. The pressure on me is minimal. All I have to do is shadow my former partner and tell my boss, Hustle Beamon, what Willie tells me to tell him. Yet, there's a panging presence in my own head.

The entire weight of Koontown will soon be on Willie's shoulders, however. Funky Dollah Bill and Irie Man may have only been rappers, but, these days, rappers are celebrities. This isn't Tupac Shakur and Notorious B.I.G. People will actually want these murders to be solved. If Willie doesn't come up with a solution soon, they will red ball the case and pull every uniform and detective they can spare to solve this one. As everyone knows, too many cooks in the kitchen muddy up the crime scene. But it won't matter. Politics will demand that it doesn't. So, everybody will be filling Willie's head with useless information, crackpot theories, false leads, and malicious innuendo. The media will start screaming in his ear. The police chief, mayor, and every politician and self-appointed activist will be beating him over the head with the fact that these murders have gone unsolved.

I could see all this and hear it in his voice when he asked me to drive. I'm a civilian now. I should not be driving a police cruiser. But I readily comply. It is the least I can do.

Willie collapses into the passenger seat. He immediately throws back his head, groans, and starts massaging his eyes. "Do you know what I could really use right now?"

"The Stylistics," I answer.

"You sure do know me, woman," Willie smiles blandly to the ceiling. "Damned police cruisers. What I wouldn't give for a decent radio station right now."

I dig into my jacket pocket with my injured hand, wince, and produce my android cell phone. I pat him with it. "Here."

Willie looks. "Your phone?"

"Sure," I reply. I turn the ignition, throw the car into gear, and head toward my office. "I've got a new app. Any song you want. Just say, 'Download,' then say the title of the song and the name of the artist. It'll download the song and start playing it for you."

Willie shakes his head in wonder. "To believe how excited I was when I installed my first eight-track player in my old 1968 Ford Mustang GT 390 Fastback."

I smile. "You wanted to be Bullitt, didn't you?"

"Hell naw," Willie laughs. "His was highland green. Mine was black. I wanted to be the *black* Bullitt."

We laugh.

"Well, go ahead and try it, Willie," I prompt.

"Sure. Why not?" he shrugs. He lifts the phone to his mouth like a CB mic, and nearly shouts, "Download … 'People Make the World Go Round' by the Stylistics!"

He waits, agitated. "Stu—" The familiar, slow bass line crawls from my phone. A bright smile rests on his dark face. He leans back and lets the song creep into him. By the time Russell Thompkins, Jr., comes in with his fragile falsetto, Willie almost looks relaxed. He starts singing along.

> *"Wall Street losin' dough on every share*
> *They're blamin' it on Obamacare—"*

"Hey, Willie," I interrupt. I hate to do this, but I have to ask.

"Yes, Genevieve?" he exhales, wearily.

"You remember that stuff someone scrawled on FDB's wall?" I ask. "That

'Reel Niggaz Ain't Gay' nonsense?"

"Yeah. What about it?"

"Well, it looked like blood, I think," I answer. "That graffiti did. So, maybe it was, maybe it contains some of that acid that ate away at FDB and Irie Man's organs."

"And not the wall?"

Willie keeps his eyes closed. He obviously does not want to be bothered. I don't know why this whole mystery bothers me in the least. I'm just along for the ride. I guess old habits die hard. If they didn't, Willie wouldn't have me here in his cruiser in the first place. Sandino would be driving in my stead. I guess Willie does want to be bothered after all.

"It didn't seem to eat through their bones or skin, either," I counter. "At least Dr. Sims didn't mention its doing so."

I think I see a hint of a smile out of the corner of my eye. I turn down Tubman Walk. "I'll be sure to mention it to the kind doctor," Willie says. "I'm sure the 'boys' at NIH will be grateful."

> *"Go underground, young man*
> *Peo-ple make the—"*

"Uh, Willie," I interrupt again.

"What is it, woman?" he exhales.

"I know this is going to sound a bit crazy," I hedge, "but it's all sounding a bit crazy right now, right? I mean, two guys having their organs melted down and sucked out of their bodies while they're making love. That *is* insane, isn't it?"

Willie's lungs deflate. I can hear the wheeze. "You're about to ask me if there's anything to these vampire crack babies, aren't you, Vee?"

"Well ... uh ..."

"Sure, Genevieve. I believe that there is a horde, a school, a *pride* of vampire crack babies sucking the organs out of *all* the down-low rappers in Koontown."

"When you put i—"

"*Just* about as much as I believe some evil scientist in Mecca created white people six thousand years ago to enslave the world."

"We're not talking theology here, Willie," I plead. "It's just that none of this makes any sense."

"I'd sooner believe it's a government conspiracy," Willie says. "Hell, I'd bet that ghoul, Sims, is behind it all."

My phone suddenly rings.

"Who is it?" I ask.

Willie looks down at the display. "Hustle Beamon," he informs.

"Ignore it," I say. "All I'm sa—"

"What in the world?" Willie gasps.

"What?"

"All these white folks," he continues. "What could they possibly be doing here in K-Town?"

I tear my eyes away from the road and look. A line of white people is wrapped around the block. "I don't know. Foreclosure sale?"

"Funny, how they used to kill us for even *stepping* into their neighborhoods. Now, they're just *dying* to move into ours."

I wrap the cruiser around the corner to Father Divine Way. The line continues down the block. I follow it. A church steeple comes into view. I head toward it. So does the line. When we reach the church, Willie and I see that the whites are filing into it. Somber chorale music emanates from the open doors.

"They opened a church here?" I ask the ether.

We roll past the church. Willie whips around to read the sign. "'The Church of Racial Reconciliation?' Have you ever heard of such a thing?"

"No," I confess.

My phone rings again.

"It's Hustle again," Willie announces.

I exhale. "I guess I've been putting him off far too long," I concede. "What can I tell him, Willie?"

"Hell if I know," he shrugs. "Tell him we ain't got dick—unlike his former artist, who apparently got plenty."

SHE IS EVERY black man's dream—a Laotian-American with a big, round posterior. At least, that is how Hustle Beamon is marketing her. She goes by Likki Nice-Nice. Her hair is long, fine, and shimmering black. Her skin is almost dark enough for her to be confused for mixed. Her smile is perfect. Her eyes, "exotic." Her American, McDonald's diet has given her curves one can't even find on the roads in Asia. She is built like a sister, she's almost as dark as a sister, can even sound like a sister, but without all the "attitude" we sisters supposedly bring. After all, she is Asian, and Asian women are notoriously submissive. Right?

Her first single, "Me So Lonely," has already topped the Urban charts. She has already been on the covers of every hip-hop magazine and has graced the pages of *Ebony* and *Rolling Stone*. Some have claimed that she will soon be considered the Queen of Hip-Hop. She has presented at the Oscars and the Grammies and has been presented with both Black and Asian Image awards.

Currently, she is in a diamond-encrusted, gold string bikini, on all fours, with an apple nestled between her ample butt cheeks.

Hustle Beamon stands tall and lanky at the other end of his custom-built, private gymnasium. He smiles adoringly at her. The hip-hop executive is holding court before a gaggle of reporters. They sit on the bleachers, eyes bugging in anticipation.

Beamon is a caramel bean pole in his designer sweat suit, the Dope Beat logo of two black hands beating bongos with 9mm pistols emblazoned boldly on his back. He stands a head taller than his assistant, Avi, looking every inch the ghetto king before his subjects. He holds a notched crossbow in his right hand.

"Are you ready, Likki?" he shoots across the expanse.

We hear a muffled "Yes" from behind her behind.

"Avi," Hustle gestures.

The little white man scrambles to Hustle's side, producing a folded purple bandanna. He seems to bow before his boss. Beamon nods grandly and stoops. Avi efficiently ties the bandanna around Hustle's eyes, blinding him.

"Go ahead, then," commands Beamon.

His assistant reaches up, clamps onto the mogul's shoulders, and starts spinning him around. Faster and faster. Until Hustle looks ready to drop.

"Stop!" he orders.

Avi quickly complies. Hustle's now facing the floor-to-ceiling windows overlooking Lake Spookeldrown, away from us all. I am sitting among the reporters. There's a collective sigh of relief as the blinded Hustle raises his crossbow at the windows.

"You see," he opens, "one of the myriad problems facing the black community is our lack of business sense, of savvy, of business *knowledge*. It seems to be the same problem facing Wall Street today."

Everyone chuckles.

"However," he continues, "while the government seems more than willing to roll down Wall Street with truckloads of free money, they've completely stopped coming down MLK Boulevard with even their funky-ass cheese.

"Black folks is on they own," he states firmly. He starts slowly pointing the crossbow this way and that. The tension builds as he moves in our direction, releases when he moves away. I look over at Likki. She is trying to keep her round mound from jiggling, but she is visibly nervous.

"Sam has cried, 'Uncle,' yall. He's done all he's willing to do for the black community. It is time for black folks to do for self. Time for those of us who have prospered to reach back, *and* down, and help our own. It is time for us to spread the knowledge and wisdom we have attained over the years. For each one to teach one. And for us, black folk, to finally reach the Promised Land. To go beyond the White House straight to the Pearly Gates of Heaven."

A few reporters can't help themselves. They nod in fervent affirmation. Some whisper their agreement. One woman even starts weeping. They must work for the black press.

"That is where I and my new non-profit organization, BizZenAss, will step in," Hustle announces. He is almost ready to shoot. He steadies the butt of the crossbow in the crook of his narrow shoulder. Despite the blindfold, he lowers his head and steadies his "sight" along the barrel. His finger starts tensing around the trigger. He is facing the windows again.

"While I still firmly believe in the teachings of Jesus Christ," he proceeds, "and still claim the Lord Jesus Christ as my personal savior, it is the teachings of Zen Buddhism that have got me to where I am today."

"Nigga what?" someone murmurs. I think I recognize him. He actually works for the white media.

"Seriously," Hustle claims. "I spent a lot of my time *fighting*—fighting against racism, against oppression, fighting against the *perceived* racism and oppression of capitalism. But capitalism is neither racist nor oppressive. Capitalism is *liberation*. It is *freedom*. I only had to understand that, understand *it*.

"And it was only after I surrendered myself, my *ego*, that I fully grasped the beauty that is capitalism.

"See, the Invisible Hand of capitalism that Adam Smith explains is not simply *market* forces, it is no the Invisible Hand of *God*. It is the Hand of the *Universe*. It is the cosmic flow, a torrent of pure *energy*, force, *power* that washes over and cleanses us all. If you fight it, you will only get bruised in its wake.

"I had to come to understand it," he continues. "Understand that the Invisible Hand is bigger than me, bigger than Dope Beat Records, bigger than any *ism* that existed before it. That will even come after it. I only truly prospered after I reached this level of enlightenment. I learned that the Invisible Hand will nurture and caress and *soothe* me. That if I simply trust in It, give my entire *being* to It, that I can simply climb upon its sweaty palm, nestle comfortably within its nooks and crannies, even suckle upon the teat of its life lines, and then I, *too*, shall prosper."

He is almost ready to shoot now. We can all feel it.

"*That* is what I want to teach the brothers and sisters of Koontown," he confides. "I want to give them the ability to surrender to the universal life force of the Invisible Hand. That, if they willingly embrace It, It is *more* than willing to embrace them. To surrender is to prosper. Resistance is not only futile but infantile and even self-destructive. They need to feel the ultimate *love* of the Invisible Hand instead of constantly letting It knock them upside the head."

He spins. Fires. Twang! Thwack! "Ahhhh!!!"

Thwack!

Likki Nice-Nice is down. She isn't moving. Somebody screams. Avi tears across the gym and slides to Likki's side. No one moves. No one breathes. He thrusts his ear against her face. He shoots up, a look of pure exaltation on his face.

"She's alive! She's alive!"

Likki sits up and looks at everybody with staged clueless eyes. "What? What is everybody so worried about?"

There's a collective sigh and chuckle from the bleachers.

"The damned thing is in the wall," she tells us.

We all look. The apple is indeed impaled into the wall by the crossbow bolt. We cheer. Some whistle. Some even give Hustle Beamon a standing ovation. He stands before us proudly, bandanna removed, with eyes that sparkle almost as green as mine. He shrugs "modestly."

"I always take care of my BizZenAss," he puffs. "Any questions?"

We quickly settle down from all the excitement. Suddenly, a well-tailored, hip-laden blonde raises her hand and stands. "Carrie McCarry from *The Post*," she declares.

"Yes, Carrie," Hustle beams.

"Well, Mr. Beamon." She clears her throat. "Recently, you and other record company executives have come under considerable fire from many black pastors around the country—"

"But not their congregations," the record exec interjects.

The woman looks genuinely confused. "Why, no. I don't know," she stammers.

"You didn't bother asking, did you?" Hustle still smiles.

"No. I guess not," she admits. McCarry clears her throat again. "Anyway, many black *leaders* have called on you, in particular, to clean up the objectionable lyrics in rap music. They say it is spectacularly degrading toward women— African-American women. That rappers glorify drug use, drug trafficking, and the 'gangsta' lifestyle. They have also taken special umbrage with the supposed ubiquity of the N-word."

"Nigger," Beamon corrects.

"Pardon me?" McCarry asks.

"Nigger," he repeats. "The word is 'Nigger.' Not the 'N-word.' Unless we're talking about nematodes, or something. That's an 'N-word,' too. Are we talking about nematodes here, Carrie?"

"Uh, no. Of course not, Mr. Beamon."

"Then come on, we're all adults here," he prods. "Why do we treat that word with such childish deference? If we are ever going to get over the problems of race, we are going to have to start speaking to each other as *adults*. Not shirk and blush and titter behind our hands, 'Tee-hee, N-word.' No, it's time we call things what they truly are. 'Nigger' is 'nigger,' plain and simple. We owe it to ourselves and our children to not say otherwise. C'mon, Carrie. You try it."

"Uh ... try what, Mr. Beamon?"

"'Nigger.'" He shrugs nonchalantly. "Come on, you try it ... Nig ... ger."

The woman has turned beet red. She starts fidgeting. She looks around for support. Everyone refuses to meet her eyes. They look more than happy to not be her at the moment.

"Oh-oh, no. I just couldn't, sir," she stammers. She puts her hand on her chest, leans forward, and whispers confidingly, "You see ... I'm a ... I'm a *liberal.*"

Beamon waves his hand dismissively. "Liberal, conservative, what does any of it matter?" he chuckles. "They're all just labels. Just words. Just like nig ... ger. Go ahead. Just say it. One time. For me."

McCarry is completely flustered. She knows if she does it, she'll be denounced by everybody in this gym, have her name smeared all over the Internet, and will be fired before the sun rises tomorrow. But what can she do? One of the most powerful businessmen in the country has just commanded her to insult him to his face.

"N-n-n—" she struggles. "N-n-n—" Her face goes from red to crimson to purple. "N-n-n-negro!" She pants, exhausted.

"Getting warmer," Beamon encourages.

"N-n-nnnnnnnnnnnnAfrican! American!"

She screams. Suddenly, the woman thrusts forward and lets out a torrent of vomit. Puke splashes everywhere. People scream and dodge the spray. Carrie McCarry of *The Post* falls to her hands and knees, retching. More and more vomit spews from her mouth. She moans pitiably and collapses, unconscious, into her own waste.

"I didn't realize it was that deep," chirps Beamon, a bemused look on his face. He searches the crowd. "Anybody else?"

A portly, middle-aged man from FOKS News Radio thrusts his hand in the air. "Ooh! Ooh! Ooh! Ooh!"

"Oh no, not you, Mr. Beckbaugh," Beamon grins. "You seem a *little* too eager to volunteer."

Beckbaugh slumps back down.

"Look," Hustle says. "I know a lot of people have complaints—legitimate complaints—about rap music. I've heard them all—going on almost thirty years now. And I'll tell you now what I told people back then:

"These young men and women are messengers. They are *poets*. You might not like the message they are spreading, but it is *theirs*. You may not appreciate their poetry, but it is poetry. It *is* art.

"Many folks didn't like what Walt Whitman had to say back in the day. Yet, Walt Whitman was one of this great country's greatest poets. He was controversial in *his* time, but in *our* time, he is studied by school children and scholars alike. We appreciate his artistry. We appreciate his truth. Some day, we will be saying the same thing about these rappers, these *poets*, you constantly denigrate today."

"Yo, Hustle."

A diminutive, dark brother in shirt sleeves stands. A condescending smile spreads across Beamon's face.

"Everybody, this is Carlos Cesaire from the *Koontown Kronicle*," he announces. "What can I do for you, brother?'

"My parents are from Martinique actually," Cesaire corrects.

"Pardon the mistake, *brother*. What you know good, Carlos?"

"Well, *Hustle*," the reporter opens. "You claim that this is all poetry and artistry. But tell me: How much artistry does it take exactly to rhyme the word 'nigger' with the word … 'nigger'?"

"Sometimes they use 'trigger,' and you know that, Carlos," Hustle flares. "They're just keeping it real."

"Just like the late Funky Dollah Bill?"

"The late, *great* Funky Dollah Bill," Hustle amends. "And yes."

"As real as FDB's bio, as an example." Cesaire starts flipping through his notes. "It states that he grew up in the 'war-torn' streets of Koontown, when, in fact, he was actually raised in Shaker Hills."

Hustle shakes his head vigorously. "Never heard of it."

Cesaire smiles. "Well, Shaker Hills, as you know, is a very rich, very *white* suburb, where the houses go for anywhere from the high-six- to the low-seven-figure range. So, when FDB was rapping about 'cappin' niggaz,' was that a procedure his orthodontist father performed for black folks?"

"Bu—"

"And when he talked about 'movin' keys,'" Cesaire interrupts, "was he talking about the keys to his mother's Volvo—or his daddy's BMW?"

We all try not to laugh. It's hard. But not as hard as it is for Hustle Beamon, CEO of Dope Beat Records, the largest rap music label on the entire planet, to find an appropriate response.

"'Cause it seems to me," the reporter continues. He's got an audience now, a platform, and a full head of steam. "That all of you in the 'rap game' seem to not be 'keepin' it real,' talking about 'Re-al-i-ty'. No, it seems as though you're only peddling a very *particular* 'Re-al-i-ty'—one that not necessarily *any* of you have *actually* experienced."

Beamon wipes his brow with his purple bandanna. He fixes Cesaire with a frighteningly cold glare. It looks like he has finally found his words.

"That's it," he thunders. "Press conference over!"

Indeed, Hustle has.

"I DID NOT go to Juilliard for this shit, Beamon!"

Likki Nice-Nice storms past me in gold-and-diamond bikinied disgust. I step into her wake and into Hustle Beamon's office.

He sits with his size thirteen Nikes resting atop his mahogany desk, casually filing his nails with an emery board. He barely raises an eyebrow from the task as he yawns, "Please have a seat, Ms. Noire."

I sink into imitation leather. Several inches below where I should be. I'm a tall woman and still my chin barely reaches his desk. Cute. I look around. The walls are lined with framed gold and platinum records. There are large, blown-up photos of Hustle with every president since Reagan and the last two Popes. Every one has "My Bitch" printed on the bottom of them. Except the last. That one has "My Nigga."

Hustle examines his nails thoughtfully. "Bitch goes to Juilliard for classical violin, doesn't make the cut, I discover *her* on the set of a Stank Muvva video, make her a star, and now *she* got attitude? What she gonna do? Go back to working her momma's nail salon?"

"You could've killed her, Hustle."

"Oh, she had no problem with that," he ho-hums. He's too busy examining his nails. "What to do about these cuticles?"

I suddenly get it. "You asked her to give you a manicure, didn't you?"

Hustle puts down the emery board, turns to me, and smiles deviously. "Why, that would be culturally insensitive, Ms. Noire. And I am nothing if not a cultural ambassador. Besides, she's Laotian. Not Vietnamese."

I roll my eyes. Beamon smiles grandly, leans back, and rests his hands on top of his head. "So, where is everything on the FDB case?"

"Detective O'Ree has let me ride along with him," I inform. "We used to be partners. I think he's more comfortable having me along—especially on such a weird case."

"'Weird,' how?" he asks, casually.

"Well, you know I can't tell you too much, Hustle," I answer. "It's an open police investigation."

"But you're no longer police, Vee," he counters. "And they know who you're working for."

"I just—I just don't feel comfortable telling a civilian—"

"A *fellow* civilian."

"Right," I agree. I take a minute, gather my thoughts. "There's really not much to tell, Hustle. I'm sure you've heard by now that FDB was found with Irie Man in, well, a rather compromising position."

"I always knew Irie was gonna be the death of that boy."

"You knew?"

"Of course, Ms. Noire," Hustle chuckles. "Why do you think we always had the brother photographed with super models? Nothing kills a gay-ass rapper's career like people finding out just how gay his ass really is. That's why they all have baby mommas. Helps to throw off the scent."

I don't get it. But I'm from the suburbs.

"That reminds me," I say. "One thing that has come u—"

My ringtone goes off. Prince's "Adore." I will never stop loving that song. It's Willie. "I have to take this," I tell my employer.

"Yeah, Willie?" I answer.

"You're not going to believe this, Vee."

"We've got another one?"

"Exactly," Willie confirms.

"Is it like the others?"

"So far, pretty much. The same weird tear stains. The same writing on the wall. 'Punk Jumpt Up Punk Got Beat Down' this time."

"Did they spell it correctly?"

"Nope," Willie snickers. "Another proud graduate of Koontown High. Didn't even bother to use a comma."

"Who is it?" Beamon stage-whispers.

"You're still with Hustle?" asks Willie.

"Just about to leave, Willie," I inform. "Did you hear Hustle's question?"

"The vic was named Hercules Kennon," says Willie. "He was the lead guitarist for Ded Krackaz. Their album, *Her Peaz*, went triple platinum last year. Didn't do dick here in the KT, though."

"He actually played an *instrument*?" I gasp.

"Yeah. That's what 'lead *guitarist*' means, Vee," Willie answers.

Hot tears suddenly start steaming around the edges of my eyes. I don't know why. I guess it's like the death of an endangered species, or something. I just have to take a minute.

Hustle suddenly takes a call of his own.

"Vee?" Willie prods.

"Sorry, Willie. Yeah, I'm here," I say. "Just give me the address. I'll be there as soon as possible."

"No need," he sighs. "We're just about to wrap things up here. It's definitely going to go red ball now. I'm going to go home and catch a few zees. We can meet up again tomorrow morning. Try to rein in the ensuing chaos."

"Are you sure?"

"Yeah. I'm sure," he answers gravely. "Oh, I almost forgot. You know what other similarity this Kennon fella has with our lover boys?"

Hustle's voice is rising in my ear.

"Is this going to be another homophobic joke?"

"What? That wasn't enough?" chortles Willie. "No. Apparently, Ded Krackaz also had some kind of beef with HNIC. At least, that's what one of the uniforms told me."

Hustle's screaming now. "You keep poppin' that shit, bitch, an' you gonna find out just how *silent* a muhfuckin' silent partner can get, padnuh!"

Beamon slams his cell phone on the desk. It shatters. Pieces go flying.

"I gotta go, Willie," I hurry, and hang up. "What's the problem, Hustle?"

He waves me away and starts kneading the bridge of his nose. "Coons in a barrel," he sighs, wearily. "Like coons in a barrel."

"I think it—oh, never mind," I say. "Look, Hustle. I need to talk to HNIC."

"Can't do."

"He is one of your artists, isn't he?"

"Oh yeah. It's just that he's in Rio right now."

"What's he doing there?" I ask.

"I don't know. What could a rich, young, virile black man be doing down in Rio de Janeiro? Hmmm …"

"Oh. Right."

Hustle suddenly snaps his fingers. "Sorry, my bad," he apologizes. "He is actually back in town."

"When did that happen?"

"Hm." He scratches his chin. Suddenly snaps back. "Ow! Damned nail. Sorry. Yeah. I think he got back yesterday. Maybe last night … Yeah, definitely some time yesterday. Why do you need to talk to him so badly?"

"Rappers are dying," I state. Then, I lie, "He may be next."

Chaptah Nin

"The word 'nigger' is nothing like 'nigga'
Don't sound shit alike like 'Game' like 'Jigga'
One came before the other like aim and pull the trigga
One is slang for 'my brotha,' one is 'hang and take a picture'

—The Game, "Letter to the King"

NOTHING BEATS THE feeling of watching hollow-point bullets bounce harmlessly off your bullet-proof Prius. But those and bumper-and-bumper traffic greeted me as soon as I crossed into Koontown. It's Funeral Day, the day when all the women here gather up their grandchildren and take them down to the local funeral homes for their fittings. The kids get to choose the little suits and dresses they'll be wearing at their own funerals, pick the caskets, the floral arrangements. They even get to pick the music. They're very excited. It's *their* day, after all. One day out of every year they get to feel really important. It's also a day off from school. No one can contain their excitement.

I wish someone were able to contain the traffic, though. The trip to my office from Sherwood Forest usually takes fifteen minutes. Today, it took almost two hours. It's ten o'clock, and I'm already angry.

Even angrier now that I've stepped into my office. The phone is blaring, somebody's singing, "Let My People Go," and Grey is there, hunched over my computer, not answering my *phone.*

No more shall they in bondage toil,
Let My people go!
Let them come out with Egypt's soil,
Let My people go!

"Grey!" I shout. She does not stop staring at the computer screen. The phone is still ringing. "What in the world are you doing?"

"Collectin' shovels, gurl."

"What?!"

My cousin huffs. "Farmville ... on *Facebook*."

You need not always weep and mourn,
Let My people go!
And wear these slav'ry chains forlorn,
Let My people go!

I huff myself and answer the *ringing* phone. I snap at Grey, "Will you *please* turn off that radio."

"Ain't the radio," she declares.

I glare at her. She glances down. "Oh, please," I groan, "please don't tell me your vagina's actually *singing*."

"Hello? Hello?" I hear from the other line.

"Don't know 'bout all *dat*, Vee," shrugs Grey. "But my damn pussy won't shut the fuck up. Been tryin', tried puttin' a tampon up in dat bitch, but the damned thing just spat it out. 'Nuff to drive a nigga crazy. I mean, last night, when Night was stickin' it to me *real* good, it just kept makin' dese *gurglin'* sounds. Like it was chokin', an' shit. *Very* disturbing."

Your foes shall not before you stand,
Let My people go!

And you'll possess fair Canaan's land
Let My people go!

"Grey," I exhale, wearily, "I think this is about the most disgusting conversation I've ever had with you." I turn to the receiver. "Yes, Willie?"

"How did you—?"

"I'll be ready at my office as soon as you can get here. I'll be outside waiting."

I slam the receiver back into its cradle. Grey has returned to her … farm, I guess. Her vagina has changed its tune.

Swing low, sweet chariot,
Comin' for to carry me home...

Why does it have to sound so damned good? I've always loved contraltos.

"Please go see a doctor about that, cousin," I order as I open the door.

"You gonna pay my bill?"

"What?!"

"Ain't like you providin' a nigga wif healf care, *cousin*."

"Grrrrr."

I jerk the door open, storm through, and slam it behind me.

Comin' for to carry me hooooommmmeeeee!!!

THE TRAFFIC IS still a nightmare. Lines form block after block around

Koontown's four hundred twenty-three funeral parlors. Kids are darting happily to and fro. More Irie Man and FDB T-shirts can be seen. A bunch of little girls are wearing T-shirts with a picture of the sweetest, little black girl you have ever seen. Bright eyes, bright smile. Pigtails dangling from each side of her round, little head. "Gimme Dat" in bold, black letters.

"Hey," I point, "isn't that from that song on YouTube that security guard was listening to yesterday?"

Willie shrugs. He must've gotten some rest last night. He looks less haggard—but still harried. He now has three of the most bizarre open murder cases with his name on them. He told me the Department has refused to go red ball on them, though. Apparently, only he cares about what has happened to Funky Dollah Bill, Irie Man, and Hercules Kennon. "Hell if I know," he says finally.

"It just seems … highly inappropriate," I mumble.

Willie turns the cruiser onto Mahalia Lane. We quickly arrive at the Mottola Sound Studio compound, laced with a barbed wire fence and further protected by a manned guard tower. I can see the man's AR-15 semiautomatic rifle from here. Willie stops at the security gate and flashes his badge.

A guard peers out from his pill box, nods, pushes a button, and points. "Pull in through the gate and park immediately to your right," he instructs. "Stay in your car. Someone will be with you in a moment. Do *not* step out of your car unescorted. We are *not* responsible for what happens to you if you do."

"You know I'm police, right?" Willie says.

"You know the taxes from this compound pay your mortgage, right?" the guard responds.

Willie huffs in disgust, throws the car into gear, and does what he's told. He parks quickly and turns off the ignition. He turns to me.

"So, I talked to the hip-hop cops today—"

"The who?"

"The hip-hop cops," he repeats. "KPD has a special hip-hop unit. They follow all the rappers, producers, hangers-on, and groupies and report on any suspicious activity. If you can only imagine. We've got a huge database, going on twenty years now. And we share information with other departments around the country.

"It's a pretty cushy gig, really," he continues. "You get to go to the clubs all the time. Party, drink, do drugs. And sometimes, I hear, you get to dabble in some of the rappers' leftovers."

I screw my face up in disgust.

"Anyway," Willie sighs, wistfully, "they seem to think HNIC is our man. Apparently, these beefs run long and deep. No, that wasn't a homophobic joke. A bunch of Irie Man groupies jacked a few in HNIC's entourage a couple months back. Two fools got shot. The Internet's been ringing out for revenge for weeks now."

There's a knock on Willie's window. A pleasant-looking young white woman with black hair straightens up and smiles. "You're Detective William O'Ree?" she asks, brightly.

"Yeah, yeah," Willie says.

We get out of the car. The woman extends her hand to Willie and smiles. "Sandy Maldonado. I am HNIC's personal assistant." She points to a mammoth, charcoal brother in pitch-black sunglasses and gear looming over her. "This is Spade. I hate calling him that, but he insists." Willie and I nod. Spade doesn't move. Sandy turns to me. "Wow! Genevieve Noire in the flesh."

I smile courteously.

"I can't tell you how much I wanted to be you growing up," she continues.

"Remember that potato sack ad you did for Benetton?"

"Of course."

"That used to hang on my wall. Until I went to college, of course," she divulges. "You look like you can still fit in it."

"Well, it is a little tight," I admit, "in the shoulders."

"You look absolutely *amazing*," she gushes. "You should still be modeling."

"Thank you."

Maldonado turns to Willie. "So, Detective O'Ree, I understand you want to talk to Mr. C. Well, he's just about to go into the studio right now. You know, 'Bitch! Ho! Bitch! Ho!' is on its tenth week at Number One. But you know how it is. Can't be complacent. Gotta strike while the iron is *hot*. And it is absolutely *scorching* right now.

"But I'm sure he will be more than happy to speak to you, Detective. Mr. C. has *nothing* but respect for law enforcement. His grandfather served in Riker's, you know."

We start heading toward the studio. Suddenly … no! Yep. Oh, my. "Swing Low, Sweet Chariot" again. I swear, if Grey has followed me…

I look around. Off to the right is a large field stretching as far as the eye can see. It's filled with … yes, cotton, and a bunch of young black adults picking it and singing that old Negro spiritual.

"Who are they?" I point.

"Oh, them," chirps Maldonado. "They're singers and rappers. Singers mostly."

"They didn't make the cut," grumbles Spade.

"What cut?" I ask.

"What Spade is trying to say," the woman steps in, "is that these are recording artists from different labels whose releases did *somewhat* less than expected in the cultural marketplace."

"They shit tanked," Spade translates. "They a bunch a flops. Fools couldn't get nobody to buy they music. They end up owin' the studio an' the label *millions* a dollars an' gotta work the land 'til they work off they debts."

"How much you pay them?" Willie asks.

"The goin' rate," Spade answers. "Twenny-five cent a hour."

"Angola wages," says Willie.

"Hey, man. You think Angola the only penitentiary that got theyselves a plantation?" Spade sparks. "Hell to the muhfuckin' naw. They got plantations, manufacturin' centers, *call* centers, e'ything all throughout the prison/ *industrial* complex. All payin' twenny-five cent a hour. You throw in all dem sweatshops in India an' China an' Vietnam. Sheeeet … This shit here is the global marketplace, sun. Nigga *gotta* stay competitive."

MALDONADO LEADS US to a small dressing room. She knocks and enters. I peek in behind her. No HNIC. Just a couch, director's chair, and make-up area. A platter of broccoli, a bag of corn chips, and a large paperback book.

"He's not here," she declares, and starts to close the door.

I stop her. "What's the book?" I ask.

"Oh," she squeals. "He's been lugging that around for *days* now. I think it's, uh, *Being and Nothingness*."

"Sartre?" I ask.

"Oh, yes." Her eyes light up. They're hazel. "Mr. C. is *very* philosophical."

Hm. She closes the door and leads us down the hall. She opens a door to our left. She, Willie, Spade, and I cram into the recording booth. The engineer, a slovenly, middle-aged white man, is already there, sitting, fiddling with the endless rows of knobs and buttons.

HNIC is in the studio before large, velvet curtains. He stands tall, lean, and muscular. The headphones crown his closely-cropped hair. He flows to a beat that is not currently playing, in deep concentration, mouthing words to himself. He's wearing a tight-fitting T-shirt and designer jeans with a high thread-count and even higher price tag. He's a good-looking kid.

The engineer leans forward into a microphone. He presses a button. "Are you ready, C.?"

HNIC opens his eyes. He's startled for an instant. Surprised he has guests, I guess. He recovers, smiles, and gives the thumbs-up.

The engineer presses a button. The velvet curtains peel back to reveal a forty-person gospel choir, resplendent in purple and gold robes. A pastor with a Bible in his hand stands before them.

"And you, Reverend?" the engineer asks into his microphone.

"May the Lord bless this day," bellows the reverend.

Maldonado now beams, glows. I can feel the heat emanating from her. She leans into my ear. "You are about to witness history in the making, Ms. Noire," she breathes. "The pure artistry. The poetry. Mr. C. is like Coleridge and Pushkin, Hughes and Cullen, *combined*. The greatest wordsmith of our age."

She's sleeping with him.

I turn to Willie. We look at each other. He shrugs.

"All right," announces the technician, "'African-America,' take one."

Suddenly, a canned beat thunders and shakes our little booth. I feel as though my ears are going to bleed. Willie grabs his. I think I'm going to be sick. My ovaries are actually vibrating. Spade stands off in the corner in his shades, nonchalantly nodding his head to the beat. The gospel choir sways and claps in unison, smiling brightly. Maldonado is dancing with an orgiastic expression on her face, waving her right arm in the air.

HNIC cranes his neck to the microphone and starts:

> *"Nigga, nigga, nigga*
> *Nigga*
> *Nigga*
> *Nigga, nigga, nigga"*

The choir erupts:

> *"Niggaaaaa!!!*
> *Niggaaaaa!!!*
> *Niggaaaaa!!!"*

HNIC:

> *"Nigga, nigga, nigga*
> *Nigga*
> *Nigga*
> *Nigga, nigga, nigga"*

Oh, God. I just know I'm going to be sick now. But before I can lose my breakfast, the music stops.

"Why'd you stop, Mr. C?" his assistant asks.

"Why'd even start?" Willie whispers.

"That was pure *genius*," Maldonado continues. "Isn't that right, Spade?"

Spade nods in silent agreement—I think. I can't exactly tell. My vision's a little blurry. My head is pounding. And I truly want to be sick all over the mixing board.

"Naw, baby," HNIC disagrees, "it is definitely missing something."

"What could that *possibly* be, Mr. C?" she asks again, a little desperately. The woman looks around for affirmation. We give her none. She turns to Spade.

"Naw, nigga right," Spade affirms. "Definitely missin' *somethin'*."

HNIC snaps his fingers. "Got it," he triumphs. "I just gotta throw in a couple more 'nigga's."

The church choir claps thunderous approval.

"Amen, brother!" the preacher trumpets.

Willie groans.

"Yeah, I *heard* dat," Spade agrees.

"Genius! Pure *genius*!" Ms. Maldonado shrieks. "Let's start it up again, Darren!"

"OK," the engineer exhales. "'African-America,' take two."

I'm out of here.

I WATCH HIS mandibles working on a broccoli spear as I hear Spade crunch corn chips in my ear. He chews slowly, deliberately. All I want to do is smash my fist through his teeth and shatter his jaw. That is what a true elephant hunter, a true gbeto, would do. I can see Lucille Parsons doing exactly that right now.

We are sitting in HNIC's dressing room, and I want to kill him. I admit I have never been much of a rap fan. It never really spoke to me. I felt like it was for people other than me. In my early twenties, I did like Kid 'N' Play, Sweet Tea, and I really liked Salt 'N' Pepa. I guess it was their producer. Who could resist a man who called himself Herbie Luv Bug? As for the rest of it, though? As I said, it was for someone else.

Now, having listened to HNIC rapid-fire "Nigga" all over the studio before a church choir, I can't help wondering who exactly this music is for. What can the purpose of it possibly be? Whatever it is, it can't be good. I'm just so grateful that I don't have children. If I did, they'd be listening to this man's nonsense this very moment, and I'd be wanting to do more than just break the negro's jaw.

The rapper suddenly stops chewing his broccoli, clutches his stomach as though he has gas, and looks straight at me. He smiles. His ... his eyes ... they are large and brown, doe-like, simultaneously full of innocence and mischief. I don't ... I don't ... no, I don't want to say HNIC's gaze is hypnotic, but I suddenly find myself oddly drawn in.

Sandy Maldonado reaches over solicitously with a white bottle of Maalox. "Here you are, Mr. C.," she smiles.

He gratefully takes it and tips the bottle up. He chugs it like water and wipes his mouth with his arm. "Thank you, Sandy," he says, and starts staring at me again.

It is starting to creep me out. I grunt, "Sartre, eh?"

"Yeah," HNIC shrugs. "I decided to get into the Existentialists while in Rio."

"That's *exactly* what I would've gotten into, too," Willie inserts, dubiously, "if I'd been down there." My old partner rolls his eyes. "Existentialism."

HNIC smiles—a wry creation that lights up the right side of his dark face. I swear his eye actually twinkles. "Well, it wasn't exactly the first time I'd been there," he divulges. "Sometimes a brotha just gotta get away, clear his head, know what I mean?" He turns back to me. "I'd just finished *The Outsider* and wanted to see what Wright saw in those white boys to make him write it."

"And?" I huff.

"Just a whole lotta pages full of polysyllabic words to say you're full of shit," the rapper shrugs again. "Why bother? I'd rather read Fanon."

He says it as though he speaks French—with the nasal "N" at the end. Pretentious twit.

Willie hates niceties. He is through with them as of this very moment. "We're here about the murders, HNIC," he declares.

"Last I heard, there were two hundred seventeen in the KT last night alone," HNIC ho-hums. "Which ones are you talking about, Detective …?"

"O'Ree," Willie provides.

"Yes, Detective O'Ree," HNIC says. He looks right at me again. "Name's Kelvin Cleghorne, by the way." He turns my way with a devilish grin. "Of course, everybody knows you, Genevieve Noire."

"Not as many as used to," I say. He keeps this staring game going, I'm going to gouge out those eyes of his—right after I shatter his jaw, of course.

"Happens to much better than us," he grins. "I played some Prince for my twelve-year-old niece the other day. She begged me to turn it off. The little crack baby."

I clear my throat.

"Irie Man!" Willie shouts. "And Funky Dollah Bill. *Those* murders, Mr. Cleghorne!"

HNIC turns to his assistant. "Sandy, would you be a dear and run out to get me a couple more bottles of Maalox?"

"Oh yes. Of course, Mr. C.," she breathes. The woman darts out of the dressing room and closes the door behind herself. Maybe they're actually not sleeping together. She is way too deferential. Maybe Maldonado just really wants to sleep with her boss. Who knows?

HNIC looks from me to Willie to Spade. He suddenly upends the Maalox bottle, finishes it off, and shoots it into the waste basket. He gestures to Spade. The beefy black mountain hands him the bag of corn chips. HNIC starts downing them.

"Yeah, I heard about those," he chews.

"And Hercules Kennon," adds Willie.

The rapper nods.

"Tell us what you know about them," Willie demands.

"I know they found Irie and FDB 'attached at the hip,' I guess you can say," he smirks. Spade chuckles. "Herc, I don't know anything about what happened to him. But he was my boy. I was a big supporter. We need more black punk rock. Keep the culture fresh."

"Can you tell us why your name keeps ringing out in association with these murders?" continues Willie.

HNIC contemplates a corn chip.

. . .

He pops it into his mouth and chews merrily. "Look," he finally opens, "I have an alibi. I was in the studio day and night for the past two days working on that track you just heard."

"*That*," I yelp, "took you two days?"

HNIC shrugs. "I consider it a sardonic ode to Gertrude Stein."

"Wif a *slammin'* beat, dough," Spade interjects from behind his dark shades.

"With a slammin' beat," HNIC humbly concedes.

Willie and I must look dumbfounded.

"'A rose is a rose is a rose,'" HNIC answers. We give him nothing. "I just thought the verb and article were a bit … extraneous, I guess."

"So, what?" Willie asks. "You're some kind of hip-hop *scholar*?"

"I did go to Penn."

"The University of *Pennsylvania*?" I spout, still dumbfounded. "The Ivy League school?"

"Hey," the rapper declares. "Real niggas is *street*. Real smart niggas is *baccalaureates*."

"Hm," I voice.

"The *murders*, Mr. Cleghorne," Willie insists.

He looks at Willie. The two glare at each other for a minute. HNIC looks down at another chip, throws it back in the bag, and reaches for the broccoli.

"You ever hear of Rebelution?" he asks.

Willie and I shrug.

"Neither has anybody else," he exhales. "That was my name when I came out of college. Did a few mix tapes, released a couple of CDs on my own. Real revolutionary, Gil Scott-Heron, Last Poets-type shit. Nobody cared. Nobody bought a single one."

He sinks into his director's chair. "So, I switched it up. Became HNIC—as sort of a joke. Said the craziest shit I could think of, and you know what happened?"

Willie and I shrug again.

"I blew … the fuck … up." He laughs. "Hit after hit. International fame. I had money trucked in by the trailer-load. The shit was absolutely insane.

"But then," he sighs, "a couple years back, Irie Man comes on the scene. His shit is even crazier than mine. Talking about bitches tightening up their pussies with baseball bats. Crazy shit like that. And the brother is *hot*. He's been shot, like, ten times. I've only been shot the *once*. Everybody started saying Irie Man was the greatest rapper to ever live."

"They were fake," I divulge.

"What were?" HNIC asks.

"Irie Man's bullet wounds," I answer. "He stuck those scars on with adhesive tape. That man has never been shot—even once."

"Well, gotdamn," HNIC shakes his head. He guffaws suddenly. "Aw, what the hell? I only had Spade here shoot me in the ass for the publicity."

"Now, that don't make no kinda sense," Willie interjects.

"Detective O'Ree, you wouldn't understand this," the rapper says, "but hip-hop is *all* about legitimacy, street cred, 'keepin' it *real*.' If you gotta put fake scars all over your body or have your boy shoot you in the ass to 'keep it real,' so be it."

"And these beefs?" asks Willie. "Where brothers are willing to beat each other to a pulp and perhaps even escalate to murder? This is all about 'keepin' it *real*,' too?"

HNIC waves a broccoli spear negatively and swallows a burp. "All fake," he asserts. "Irie Man comes out and wants to make a name for himself. So, he guns after the biggest name out there at the time. Me. I don't care. He's on one of Hustle's subsidiary labels. I even worked on that first album. That song where he calls me out? 'No-Account Nigga.' Yeah, I produced it. Made a pretty penny off of it, too.

"FDB," he continues. "He's on Dope Beat right with me. I worked on *all* his albums. But he called me out, too. Hustle's publicists ran with the supposed 'beef.' We complied. To sell records, you understand. He says shit about me. I say shit about him. He says something about my momma. I talk about his DSLs." I'm confused. "His Dick-Sucking Lips," HNIC explains. "Little did I know," he chuckles.

Spade chuckles. Willie chuckles, too, despite himself.

Men.

"Irie got involved," HNIC continues, "and the three of us trade insults. Every time one of our new albums drops, we come up with new insults to continue the 'beef,' get on the cover of *Rolling Stone* eye-fucking each other, and go Gold in the first week." He sighs with a smile. "Hey, they call this shit 'The Rap Game' for a reason."

Willie's cell phone suddenly rings. He answers it. "Yeah," he says. He listens, suddenly looks at all three of us, gets up, and exits the room.

I sit here alone with HNIC and his shaded bodyguard, Spade. I wonder what Willie's talking about right now. Where that Maldonado woman is with HNIC's Maalox. The rapper suddenly proffers, "Broccoli?"

Why does he keep looking at me like that?

I screw up my face. "No, thank you."

"Suit yourself," he smiles, arrogantly. Stupid child, I'm old enough to be … well, his grandmother here in Koontown.

Willie reenters, huffing. Anxiety rims his eyes. He is obviously struggling to remain calm.

"So, do you have one of these supposedly fabricated 'beefs' with Solomon Yancey?" he asks the rapper.

"Niggassippee?" HNIC asks.

"You can*not* be serious," I groan.

"Dat was de nigga name when he was doin' his Southern thang," Spade informs.

"Yeah, but he's in television now," HNIC adds. "He writes, directs, and produces that kid show, 'Gimme Dat.' It's a big hit on *CPN*."

"So, do you have a beef with him, too?" Willie repeats.

"Not at all, Detective O'Ree," HNIC confesses. "In fact, I have a small stake in his production company, Stompin' Fetchit."

Willie huffs in disgust. "Don't think this is over with us, HNIC," he threatens. "Let's go, Vee."

Chaptah Tayn

"I think they callin' me a pickaninny"

—T-Love, "When You're Older (Ode to the Pickaninny)"

THE RAP MONEY was apparently good for Mr. Niggassippee, but it was the TV money that allowed the man to return to his birth name, Solomon Yancey, and to buy this sixty-two-room mansion on One Jig Hill. We had to take the elevator to his study, where Willie and I found the blood sign, "Dis How U Raze Yo Dawtaz?"

"I pray to God nobody's out there 'razing' their daughters," Willie quipped.

We found Yancey slumped over his iMac in his tastefully decorated den. There are the telltale signs—no violence, no signs of struggle, only death with the mucus tear trails streaking down the man's face. Willie slumps over the body with the MEs. He is angry. He is frustrated. Suddenly, homicide Detective William O. O'Ree looks old.

"Yo, Vee," Sandino says, suddenly entering the room. "You gotta come see this."

He leads me to the master bedroom. It is what one might expect—beiges, whites, with a mahogany theme. A framed photo of him with Diana Ross hanging on the wall to the master bath. I start to question Sandino, but he stops me, pointing at the large, flat-screen television playing silently on the wall.

"Can you believe the news already has his obit playing?" the detective asks. He suddenly produces the remote control and turns up the volume.

Niggassippee—a Confederate flag tied over his corn rows—jumps on the screen with, I'm assuming, his "homies." They all bounce off each other, gold teeth sparkling, champagne splashing all over soaking wet bikinied beauties. The music is loud, frenetic, with a whole lot of screaming.

"However," the newscaster's voice-over chimes in, "after a string of rather less-than-successful albums, Mr. Yancey turned his talents away from the music industry, focusing, instead, on television entertainment. After writing and directing several successful episodes of such trailblazing spy thrillers as *Spook 'N' Spanish* and *Deep-Throatin' Mama*—for which he won two Emmy Awards—Solomon Yancey got the opportunity to produce his own show, the wildly successful hit, *Gimme Dat.*"

Yancey appears on screen all cleaned up. The Confederate flag and corn rows are replaced by a perfectly bald head. The gold teeth are now capped white. He is clean-shaven in Armani. He looks perfectly respectable—even powerful. His voice is calm, reasoned, educated—all the screams drained from his larynx.

"I know that a lot of preachers and so-called African-American leaders have had problems with *Gimme Dat,*" the executive says, before a solid black backdrop.

"You know, there's a song—"

Sandino puts his finger to his lips, silencing me. His gray eyes dance gleefully.

"But I, personally, don't see the problem. Nor do these 'leaders'' congregations, by the way," Yancey continues, earnestly. "When I look at

LaSharonika Jones, I don't see anything 'controversial.' Not in the least. What I see is a *strong*, determined, *adorable* African-American girl-child who has goals, who wants to achieve, to get that *education*, who sets her sights high and flies to the moon!

"And, of course, *hilarity* ensues while she does it."

Yancey chuckles and gives the camera a playful wink.

The newscaster comes in, "It most *certainly* does. LaSharonika Jones, played by Tony Award-winning child actress, Samantha Patterson, is, *indeed*, an *international* sensation."

The picture changes.

"That's the girl…" I point.

"Her face is literally *everywhere*," the newscaster continues. "On T-shirts, children's toys. Ms. Patterson has two movies that will be out this summer. Her YouTube video has gone viral—"

I gasp.

"There are fan clubs sprouting up all over the country…"

A group of black girls have the "Gimme Dat" T-shirt. One gum-popping nine-year-old spouts, "Oh yeah, LaSharonika? Dat my BEEP! Right dere! I wanna grow up to be jus' like dat BEEP!"

"Indeed, all over the *world*…"

There's a group of giddy, Japanese pre-teens with the same T-shirt. They all cheer, "LaShalonika! Numbel Run!!!"

"*Gimme Dat* has been the Number One show on CPN for the past two seasons," the news continues, "and has already gone into syndication in over *forty-two* countries. And little LaSharonika Jones has provided the *world* with *the* most popular catchphrase since *Diff'rent Strokes*'s 'What you talkin' 'bout, Willis?'"

The picture changes again. It's from the TV show apparently, a classroom obviously filmed before a live, studio audience. Little LaSharonika stands in her school uniform, twirling her pigtails mischievously. She is being chastised by her middle-aged hippy teacher, his blonde ponytail flapping furiously. He towers over her, pointing his finger menacingly.

"I swear, LaSharonika," he nasals, "this is the absolute *last* time. You are my best student. The best student I've ever had here at Frederick Douglass."

She hams up a smile for the camera. Canned laughter titters along with her.

"But," the teacher continues, "you continue to be oh-*so* disruptive. What exactly was the point in sticking those razor blades in LaLexus's seat? That poor girl had to get over one *hundred* stitches!"

LaSharonika shrugs innocently.

"LaMercedes," the teacher continues, "she almost lost her eye over the stunt you pulled last week. And doctors still don't know if L'Acura will ever be able to have children!"

LaSharonika keeps twirling those pigtails.

"I ought to suspend you!" the teacher rants. "Have you thrown in jail! Something! What do you have to say to *that*, LaSharonika?! Hunh?! What do you have to say for yourself, young *lady*?!"

The poor girl looks up bashfully, her hand still playing in her hair. Her eyes glisten. She gives a perfectly impish smile, the same smile on all those T-shirts I saw this morning. The atmosphere stills. The camera sweeps in for a close-up.

LaSharonika speaks with a startlingly deep voice, "Gimme dat dick, nigga."

The live studio audience roars with laughter. The teacher gasps, "LaSharonika?"

My stomach leaps into my throat. I grab onto Sandino before I faint outright.

The scene cuts. The teacher's in his chair, head thrown back, his eyes rolling into the chalkboard. He pants and screams. The camera pulls back. His pants are down and ... and ... and, uh ... and that little girl has her plaid skirt hiked up around her thighs, jackrabbitting up and down on the man's exposed lap. She grunts and screams along with her ... her teacher. She suddenly slaps him in the face.

"What *you* gotta say fo' *yo*'self, Mr. White?" she growls. She smacks him again. The audience fills the speakers with guffaws. She smacks him again. "Hunh, bitch? Hunh?!"

"Y-y-you," pants Mr. White, "you get an *A*!!!"

The audience applauds wildly.

I'm blinded. Tears steam and cloud my vision. I ... I ...

I'm walking. Something has taken hold of me.

Rage?

My elephant hunting sisters?

I suddenly find myself in that *beast's* study. I think I'm next to a uniform. I think I hear a snap, the swipe of metal against leather, a distressed, "Hey!" People are suddenly looking at me. Stunned. Someone rushes forward. I have a Glock 17 semiautomatic pistol in my right hand. The trigger presses against my finger. Again and again and again. Again and again and again.

Everybody freezes. The smell of cordite is strong in the air. The gun is in my hand. It is heavy—yet much lighter. I have refused to come anywhere near one since I'd been shot. Since that bullet was lodged against my spine. It is hot. I don't like the way it feels. I drop it.

There are now fourteen fresh holes in Niggassippee's corpse.

I must have done that.

Willie looks at me. Then at the body slumped over the iMac. "Well," he says, "*that* one's gonna be hard to explain."

"AN' DAT NIGGA came at me, whinin' like, 'Yo, baby, yo. Size don't matter *none*, gurl.' An' I was like, 'Of yo' dick? Naw, nigga. Bitch got ova *dat* mole hill years ago. But a dis *rock*?! It most definitely *do* matter.'

"I mean, a *fo'* carat rock?! What kinda bullshit is *dat*? I tol' dat nigga, 'You need to go rob you some mo' Social Security checks, an' shit, an' come at a bitch co-rrect.' Ya feel me, LaCuisiné?"

The yellow tape has worked its magic yet again. The crowd outside of Niggassippee's house is truly astounding. The media are here, Irie Man and Funky Dollah Bill acolytes with their candles and chorales, little children exhausted from all the Funeral Day activities with their Gimme Dat T-shirts on and grandmothers in tow. It looks like all of Koontown is here.

Willie has taken me outside to get some air. But looking at this crowd, I still can't seem to catch my breath.

"I'm sorry, Willie," I gulp, in apology. "I don't know what I was thinking."

"Only what all of us who aren't thinking solely about money have been thinking for years," he consoles. He puts a reassuring hand on my shoulder.

"I don't know," I confess. "Maybe these fools are getting exactly what they deserve."

"Now, Genevieve," admonishes Willie, "we've been over this a million times. The Law says that only *It* has the right to put people to death. As long as I wear this shield, I will uphold that Law—personal feelings aside. And, though you no longer have a badge, I am absolutely certain that you still feel the exact, same way."

"Maybe," I shrug, none too sure. "But have you seen that show, Willie? That poor, little girl *riding* a grown man."

"Happens every show," Willie ho-hums. "People love it. What can you do?"

What would Lucille Parsons do? I ask myself.

"Go and shoot Yancey again," I answer.

"He's already dead, Vee."

"People like Solomon Yancey never die, Willie," I breathe. "They only multiply."

Willie squeezes my shoulder, grabs them both, and spins me around. He stares into my eyes with avuncular concern. His eyes pierce, dig, dig even deeper. I look away.

"We *have* to believe that what we do is right, woman," he says, adamantly. "If we don't ... if we don't, there would simply be nothing else left."

"There's always more to do, Willie," I say, desperately.

"And there always will be," he concludes. Willie suddenly relaxes, stands straight, and releases me along with a warm-hearted chuckle. "Look, why don't you go home?" he suggests. "There's nothing else you can do here. I'll have Sims cover up your little target practice in the autopsy report.

"Which reminds me, by the way. The good coroner says you were right about the blood on the walls. The samples we took were full of dissolved organs and that strange acid."

"Good," I exhale.

"He's sent more samples to his 'boys' at NIH—"

"You think he ever worked for them?" I ask.

"That blood sucker could've worked in Transylvania, for all we know," Willie says. "But the NIH has gotten nowhere so far. So, he's sent some samples to the CDC as well."

"Maybe then we can at least get a handle on what kind of acid they're using," I suggest, as hopefully as I can muster. "Maybe even who manufactures the stuff."

"Maybe," Willie grumbles. "So, go and get a good night's sleep, Vee. I'll call your office in the morning. Since you never seem to answer your cell phone."

I smile and start walking away. I don't know why I always forget to turn the stupid thing on. I guess being contacted was the least of my concerns this past year. Still, it is bad business. I need to work on that.

I begin to work my way through the crowd.

"My baby!!!" I hear a woman scream. "Dey done *killt* my babyyyy!!!"

I look. A large, middle-aged black woman in tattered house coat and ratty gray wig is on her knees before the TV cameras. Something doesn't look right. Looks way too familiar. I start making my way toward the scene.

"All right! Cut!" the reporter says, slicing his own throat with his microphone. He looks down at the distraught mother and nods. "Good job, Lameriqua."

"Thanks," she says, scratching her head. The wig dances with her every stroke.

I reach over and snatch the wig off the woman's head. She gasps. She has a well-manicured, short Anita Baker haircut. Glad to see that's back in style. But still. Even in the night, I can tell there's not a streak of gray in her hair—unlike the salt-and-pepper wig in my hand. I look closer. The lines in her face have been penciled in. This woman's not old at all. She's actually quite young.

Twenty-two, twenty-five. Young enough to be somebody's grandmother.

"Wait a second," I say, "don't I know you?"

She cringes, nervous. She tries to shy away from me. I grab her chin and move her face toward me. It dawns on me.

"Yeah, weren't you in *Raisin in the Sun* last summer? At the Robeson?" I ask. She fidgets instead of answers. "You played the sister, the Afrocentric one. Not the mother. Not the mother at all."

She still says nothing.

"You were absolutely *brilliant*," I lie.

Her face suddenly brightens. "You really think so?" she chirps, brightly. She suddenly realizes what she's done. Her face grows quickly dim.

"So, what are you doing out here in this get-up?" I ask. "Oh, wait a second. That was you outside of FDB's house the other night, too. Carrying on like that."

She sighs, deflates. I suddenly realize that her bulk isn't fat but foam rubber padding. Her eyes drop, and it takes forever for them to rise again. "You're right," she admits. "That was me, too. In fact, it's me almost every broadcast. I play the 'Mo'nin' Momma' for Channels Six, Twelve, and Twenty."

"What?" I gasp.

"They need man-on-the-street interviews," the actress informs. "For authenticity, you know. Since it's damned near impossible to find these boys' mommas, they hired me to fill the role. To show how much each murder devastates the community. So, I 'Lawd hab mercy!' and 'They done *killt* my baby!' it up for them every night."

"I knew it," I hiss. Another conspiracy theory confirmed.

"Hey, I need to do *something*. To make ends meet. Yale wasn't cheap," she rambles. "Do you know how hard it is for a black actress out there?"

"No. I don't," I say. Back in my day, I was offered at least one movie role a week. Admittedly, the same movie role, the female lead in *Monster's Ball*, but still.

I hand the woman her wig back and continue my way through the crowd again.

"Hey! A sista gotta eat! Don't she?! DON'T SHEEEEEE?!!!"

Boy, that woman can wail.

I close my eyes and shake my head. And then—no. Could it …? Oh my goodness, it *is* him. From the FDB crowd the other night.

I look back at Niggassippee's mansion. Willie is out on the veranda talking to a medical examiner.

"Willie!" I shout. "Willie!!!"

He looks up, searches the crowd. I wave my hand frantically.

"Willie!!!"

My former partner locates me and shakes his head. I viciously jab my hand in the direction I want us to go. Willie shakes his head again and leaps off the veranda, into the crowd.

Satisfied, I start running, pushing my way through the throng. "Watch it, bitch!" someone threatens. Instinctively, I swing. Thwack! The man's down holding his jaw, whimpering, before I even have a chance to realize what I've done. It's been a rough day. I keep running toward my prey.

The brother suddenly realizes that the crowd is parting before him, toward him. He sees me rushing directly at him. His eyes light up in front.

"Hey!" I shout.

He turns.

"Willie!" I yell.

"Got him!" I hear my old partner.

Willie doesn't, though. The young man sprints right past him. We both give chase.

Chaptah Eleben

"'Cause we'll put a boot in your ass
It's the American Way"

—*Toby Keith, "Angry American (Courtesy of the Red, White, and Blue)"*

(What? You sayin' Kunta Kente here *ain't* gangsta?)

THE BROTHER IS obviously not one of those health-nut, Yuppie parents you see jogging around Sherwood Forest who knows how to run with a baby stroller. Within seconds, he staggers, stumbles, and is flat on his face. His stroller shoots forward, hurtling straight toward street traffic.

"Hey!" I scream.

A good Samaritan hears me, sees the rolling stroller, and darts for it. The front wheels spring off the curb. He grabs the handle bar and halts the stroller in mid-flight. A Hummer blares by, horn honking madly.

I turn to the young man on the ground. He struggles to his feet. Willie swoops in like middle-aged lightning. He grabs the youth, yanks him beyond his feet, and slams him against a nearby wall. Air explodes out of the boy's lungs. Willie gets in his face. I join them as the Samaritan moves to return the baby stroller.

"What the hell are you doing around here?" Willie barks, sticking his badge in the boy's face.

"What?!"

"You're here tonight," I say. "And I saw you there at FDB's house the night of his murder."

"And I swear to God I saw you last night outside of Hercules Kennon's," Willie adds, vehemently.

"So?" the boy yelps. "E'y nigga come an' see a murder scene. Yall know dat."

"*Every* murder scene?" I prod. "*Every* night?"

"During *basketball* season?" Willie adds.

"Ain't no crime in dat," our suspect pleads. He is young—maybe nineteen, or so—and, with Willie jacking him by his jacket collar, really scared. Still, he is doing something wrong out here. I can feel it. I just don't know what, yet. "Why yall sweatin' *me*?"

A tall, muscular, middle-aged man with a paunch bulging in the middle of his velour sweat suit walks up with the baby stroller. He drudges up the brightest smile he can. "Here you go, Vee," he grins, heroically, and offers me the handle bar.

"Thank you," I say, coldly.

Disappointed, he slinks back into the crowd.

Willie tightens his hands around his captive's collar. "C'mon, son," he growls, "a *black* man with a *baby stroller* here in *Koontown*."

"What?" the boy yelps.

"What in the *hell*," Willie flares, "can be more suspicious than *that*?"

"What?" the boy whelps again. "A nigga cain't raise up his own *child*?"

...

We all start laughing hysterically. I wipe the tears from my eyes and look down. The baby sure is quiet for all the excitement going on around it.

"likkaniggadik"

"Did you hear that?" I ask, looking around.

Willie shrugs at me and then turns to the kid. "What game are you playing at, boy?"

Too quiet. I bend down to inspect the stroller.

"Hey!" the boy yells. "Leave LaFeceshia alone! She colicky, an' shit!"

I pull back the blanket.

A baby doll. A white one, at that. I shake my head and lift the thing.

"Ah, see!" the boy cries. "Now, look what you done did!"

The thing is heavy. Solid. Much more than fluffy, stuffed cotton. Hm. I start twisting the head around.

"You gonna kill her!" he screeches.

Willie slams the boy into the wall again. "You're only making things worse," he declares.

The head pops off cleanly. I peer inside. Just what I suspected. I turn the doll upside down.

"Noooo!!!"

A cascade of white powder spills onto the stroller bed.

"My baby! My baby!!!"

"Your 'baby,' hunh?" Willie grumbles.

"Loved her like she was my own, Officer," the youth weeps.

Willie produces a pair of bracelets. "You're coming with us."

TRAFFIC IS HELL. We seem to move one inch at a time. The siren and lights don't even help. In fact, some cars seem to move out of their way to get into ours. Koontown. What can you do?

Finally, at the corner of Hurston and Parks, a uniform stops us. He's a big, beefy, older police whose eyes are looking wearily toward retirement. He moves our way. Willie draws down his window.

"Hey, Butler," he greets, jovially. The two shake hands like old friends. "What's going on here?" he asks.

Butler adjusts his cap, a perplexed look puzzling his face. "Hell if I can figure it out, O'Ree," he confesses. "There seems to be a huge beef brewing between the followers of Irie Man and Funky Dollah Bill's followers."

"Suck dick fo' Jesus, nigga!" our perp erupts from the back seat.

We all look back at the boy. There's a mad gleam of defiant pride in his eyes. Butler shakes his head in confusion again.

"Anyway," the uniform continues, with a heavy sigh, "with all the Funeral Day activities, these fools have been bumping into each other all day. There've been scuffles here and there. Idiots screaming about being cornholed for Christ or sucking Jesus off. Who can figure it out? Killing over Eight Ball jackets. That, I get. But *this*?"

"So, they started shooting?" prompts Willie.

"It was only a matter of time, really."

"How many down?" Willie asks.

"None of *each other*, of course," huffs Butler. "But they got five straight A students and *seven* grandmothers."

"Wow," I gulp.

"All I know is, these assholes keep gunning down all the grandmothers," Butler says, "there ain't gonna be no one left to raise our children."

"You got that right," commiserates Willie. "So, how can I get out of this mess, buddy? I got a suspect here, and my foot's just *itching* to get in his ass."

"I heard *that*, brother man," Butler guffaws. "Tell you what. You just double-back here. I'll clear the way, and you can take Father Divine Way."

"Appreciate it, Butler," Willie says.

"Least I can do for a fellow officer," Butler says, "who gave me those righteous Frankie Beverly and Maze tickets."

What is it with old, black men and Frankie Beverly?

Willie does as instructed. We turn back around. Butler clears the way with his marked unit, lights, and siren. We speed down Father Divine Way in no time. There is a line down the block for that Church of Racial Reconciliation again. This time it is all Asians, though.

"What the hell?" Willie mumbles.

But there's no time for speculation. We have four open murders, a baby doll full of cocaine, and a prime suspect in cuffs in the back seat of our Crown Victoria.

WILLIE AND I sit across the table from our suspect in the cramped interrogation room. He sits staring at Willie and me and the two-way mirror behind us. Even with all the bodies falling in this case, nobody seems particularly interested in what Willie and I are doing here. There are just too many bodies falling all over town. I doubt if anyone is even watching us interrogate this boy right now.

I also doubt that our suspect is going to willingly give up any information. I can tell by his defiant posture that he's been here before. Probably too many times to count. I wouldn't be surprised if there were terabytes of information on this child in the system. It is more likely to spill its guts than Baby Doll here.

Willie hunches over a legal pad, pen poised over the yellow paper. "Let's start with your name," he says.

The boy slumps back in his chair, crosses his arms on his chest, and juts out his jaw. Willie looks up. His right hand starts shaking, ready and willing to dislocate said jaw.

"Your name," Willie seethes.

"Francis Ulysses Copper," the boy divulges. "Niggas call me, 'F.U.,' dough."

"F.U. Copper," Willie sighs. "Ha … ha … hee … hee."

Baby Doll smiles, proudly. He makes himself a bit more comfortable in his chair, ready for the long haul.

Willie rests the pen on the legal pad. He lowers his head and squeezes the tension from his eyeballs. He lifts his head again, reaches into his jacket pocket, produces a cell phone, and hands it to me. "Call Steele," he instructs.

I scroll through Willie's phone book, find the number, and hit "Call." Willie looks back at Baby Doll and casually leans forward on the table. "Have you ever heard of Commander Steele?" he asks the boy. "Commander 'Leadfoot' Steele?"

"Naw, fool!" Baby Doll spits. "Ain't *neva* heard a dat nigga!"

"Then let me have the pleasure of telling you a little story." Willie offers up such a warm smile the room actually starts heating up. "See, about ten, fifteen years ago, when Officer Steele was still a uniform, he ran into *one* too many young brothers such as yourself. Always popping off at the mouth. Trying to impress their friends. Everybody thinking they're Ice Cube, screaming, 'Fuck the police!' Do you know what I'm talking about, young man?"

Baby Doll says absolutely nothing. He is trying to remain calm and defiant, but the edges are starting to fray. It's simple confusion. He doesn't understand the point of all this, and fear is beginning to creep in. His outthrust jaw begins to tremble.

The connection is made. "We need you down the hall, Commander Steele," I say into the phone, and hang up. The boy throws a questioning look my way. I simply sit back, cross my arms, and return a satisfied grin to him.

"I think the experts call it, 'Black Oppositional Behavior,'" expounds Willie. "Brothers and sisters—such as yourself—walk around simply *aggrieved*. They feel that *every* situation, whether malignant *or* benign, is a *confrontation*. And they, of course, lash out accordingly. Fuck the police, fuck the boss. Fuck that three-ton SUV barreling down the street at them. 'I'm gonna walk out in front a *dat* bitch—as slooooowwww as muhfuckin' *possible*—'cause *dat* bitch is gonna stop fo' me. In fact, I wish a muhfucka *wouldn't* stop. I'll show *dat* bitch.'

"So, these brothers and sisters—like you, *F.U. Copper*—who suffer from Black Oppositional Behavior—let's call them, 'BOBs,' shall we? These *BOBs*, with their 'Fuck You' attitudes always end up saying, 'Fuck you,' to the absolute, wrong people—the cops, their bosses, that SUV, and they end up in jail, or without a job or even a good reference to get another one. They end up a blood smear in the middle of the road. And they always, *always* end up getting their food spat in because they've forced the waiter to return it to the kitchen one too many *gotdamned* times."

The boy is unfazed. That is what he would like us to believe. We can see his eyes dancing nervously in his head, though. He is fooling no one.

thud

It's distant, faint. But we all hear it.

thud

"What was dat?" Baby Doll quivers.

"Commander Steele," I grin.

"So, you see, Commander Steele," Willie goes on, "he's been on the street over a decade at that point. He's had too many run-ins with too many BOBs like you. He's lost count. Some say the brother had even lost his damned mind.

"And he's out there, canvassing the *'hood* for a murder investigation. A little, five-year-old girl got gunned down. A drug battle, of course. Over turf. The girl was nowhere near the scene. But you young brothers have never even taken the time to learn how to actually *aim* those damned guns you're constantly carrying. You just *shoot*. And little children die."

Willie pulls back, breathes, calms himself down.

thuD

thUD

He plunges back in. "Nobody's talking, of course, and Steele, he's had enough. Some young brother—probably your father, for all we know—finally says, 'Fuck you, 5-0.' Steele warns him. I know. I was there. He says, 'Say that one more time, and I will *literally* break my foot off in that *ass!*'

"The young brother, of course, he doesn't believe him. He thinks all police are punks, a bunch of bitches with badges—"

"Granted," Baby Doll nods.

Willie just chuckles. "Granted," he concedes. "So, the young brother, he puffs up his little peacock chest, gets right in Steele's face, and does it. He says, 'Fuck ... you ... 5 ... 0.' Steele goes *ballistic*. Knocks the boy to the ground, down on all fours, before anybody even realizes what he's done. Then, Steele does it. He actually *does* it. He *kicks* that boy so hard, you can actually hear the fabric of his jeans rip, the boy's rectum literally *tearing* to *shreds*."

Baby Doll gulps audibly.

"And the damnedest thing happened." Willie chuckles. "Steele's foot—it is actually stuck. Stuck in that boy's ass. Steele's grunting, wriggling around, trying to free his foot from out that boy's *ass*. Can you believe it? And the boy? He's crying, *screaming*. 'Get it out, Mr. Officer! Please! Get … it … OUT!!!'

"It was grotesque. Sickening. Blood was gushing *everywhere*. I thought I was going to lose my lunch right there on the street."

Willie laughs again. "But it's in there *real* good, you know. That negro must've had *the* tightest asshole in African-American *history*. Obviously, he hadn't been to prison, yet. 'Cause it just was *not* giving up Steele's foot."

thUD

tHUD

"Finally, Steele has had enough. He wants his damned foot back. So, he gives out this amazing *roar*. 'AAARRRRRRGGGGGGGHHHHHHHH!!!!' And he *yanks* with *all* his might. There's this sickening *snap*! And everything goes quiet."

tHUD

tHUD

"W-w-what happened?" the boy gasps.

"Officer Steele's leg just—it just broke off at the ankle," Willie proclaims. "He was free, but his foot stayed stuck in that poor boy's asshole. Blood spouting from both Steele *and* the boy.

"The sad thing is, they lost both that foot and that boy. That BOB was pronounced dead an hour later at Koontown Kounty, the foot *still* poking out his backside. The doctors, they tried to reattach the foot, but their efforts failed. To this day, Commander Steele walks around with a metallic prosthesis. That's why we call him, 'Leadfoot.'"

tHUD

THUD

THUD!!!

Bang!!! The interrogation room door slams open against the wall. We all jump. Commander Samuel "Leadfoot" Steele stands in the doorway. He is a big, black mountain of a man. His body consumes the entire doorframe.

"You rang?" he drones. Then he booms laughter, a laugh that shakes the molars from your jaw. He limps forward and slams the door shut behind himself.

WILLIE DOESN'T EVEN have time to grab a coffee. We left Leadfoot in the interrogation room with Baby Doll to do what he does best. Willie offered to get us some coffee. With lots of sugar and even more cream—just like I like it. But before he moves, we hear the telltale scream and Leadfoot emerges from the room, hobbling on his stump, with a big, old smile on his ebony face.

"Damn," marvels Willie, "you're getting real good with that thing, Sammy."

"Got me a new, removable ball-and-joint jobbie," Leadfoot smiles, like a three hundred-pound Cheshire cat. "You still got those Frankie Beverly and Maze tickets, right?"

See what I mean?

"Front row center," Willie gloats. "You'll be able to catch all the badly-aimed bras and panties you can handle, my brother."

"My wife will certainly appreciate that," Steele chuckles. He starts hobbling away. "I'll be wanting that foot back, of course, O'Ree," he shoots over his shoulder.

"Of course," Willie shouts after him. He turns to me. "Let's go, Genevieve."

WE RE-ENTER THE interrogation room. It reeks of feces, rectal blood, and sheer terror. I turn up my nose. Willie slams the door shut. Baby Doll's head shoots up from the table, horrified. A river of tears has flooded his face. He wails in pain.

Willie and I sit down. "So," my old partner opens, wistfully, "are you still a BOB, youngblood?"

"N-n-no," Baby Doll blubbers. "You can call me a-a-a CAN now."

"CAN?" I ask.

"One Cooperatin'-Ass Nigga."

"Good," Willie smiles, triumphantly. The homicide detective grabs his pen and prepares to start writing. "Let's start with your name, shall we?"

"Markell D'Antré Fisher," he volunteers, "but niggas call me, 'Tar Baby.'"

"You're not even that dark," I say.

He looks at me. "Darkest nigga in de fam, dough," he admits. "So dark, my ol' man was like, 'Dat nigga ain't mines,' an' got ghost. Dis nickname was all he lef' a li'l nigga."

Willie rolls his eyes in disgust.

"Anyway," Fisher continues. "I'm twenny years a age. Been dealin' since I was a sho'ty. 'Bout eleven or twelve. My uncle was lookin' at three strikes, an' got me out dere on de co'na. Got dat third one, anyfuckinway. So, the co'na a Pryor an' Parker been mines eva since. Move 'bout ten Gs a product dere a week. Her'on, crack, pills, weed. Whateva a nigga *want*, dis nigga *got*."

"That's all well and good, Mr. Fisher," says Willie, "but we're not here for the drugs. We couldn't give a shit about those. We're here about the bodies."

"Bodies?" Fisher flares. "I don't eva do no *killin's*, Officer. I'm a *drug* dealer. Not no *death* dealer."

...

We all laugh hysterically. I wipe the tears from my eyes.

"OK," Fisher guffaws. "What bodies? I'm gettin' a li'l faint here. Think I'm still *bleedin'*, an' shit."

"Smells like both," Willie confides.

"Seriously, dough," Fisher says, struggling to sit upright. "Yall got a *doctor* up in dis bitch?"

"We'll get you proper medical attention as soon as possible, Markell," I say.

"Just tell us what you know about the FDB, Irie Man, Niggassippee, and Hercules Kennon murders," Willie encourages.

"Hercules Who?"

"He was the lead guitarist for a black punk band," I say.

"A *nigga*? Playin' a real *instrument*?" Fisher gasps. "Damn. I'd a liked to a seen't *dat*."

"Well, he's dead now," Willie informs him.

"Sometimes dis game just don't make no kinda sense," Fisher mourns, looking genuinely stricken.

Willie slams his hand on the table. Fisher and I jump. Fisher screams in pain. "Stop bullshitting me, Tar Baby! Tell me what the fuck you know! Now!"

"I swear on my grandmomma's grave, Officer," the boy wails, "I don't know *shit* 'bout none a dat shit."

I believe him. Willie does not.

"Bullshit!" my old partner roars. "Why the hell were you hanging around each and every murder scene? We all know that sick, murderous *fucks* like you like returning to the scene of your own crimes. To see us idiot cops scratching our heads, wondering what the fuck you've done. You just *love* laughing at the police's own stupidity."

Fisher pleads, "But it ain't me. I ain't had nuffin' to do wif any a dat. Can I see dat doctor now?"

"No!"

The boy looks at Willie. Willie stares daggers back at him. Fisher looks to me, pleading. I shrug, helpless. I shouldn't even be here. The youth's shoulders slump piteously. He surrenders a weary sigh.

"OK, look," he opens. "I don't know much. Hardly nuffin' at all. But it's like e'ybody an' his grandmomma been talkin' 'bout de crack babies returnin'."

"Crack babies," Willie harrumphs, dropping his pen.

"I swear to *Gawd*, yo," Fisher swears to us. "Crack babies. Dey name been ringin' out fo' a few days now. Dey been gone fo' a long time, ya heard. Nobody knows where, dough. All we knows is dat dem niggas is *back*. Wif a vengeance. An' dey is *piss't*."

"And what are these 'crack babies' supposedly doing, Tar Baby?" Willie groans.

"Man, dat's de thing, right?" Fisher says. Sweat has started pouring out of his forehead. His eyes briefly roll around. He braces against the table and steadies himself. He continues, fervently, "Don't nobody really know. Some folks ack like dey vampires, an' shit. Say dey suck a nigga's blood out his neck. Say dem niggas can actually *fly*. Shit like dat. An' don't eva, eva look dem niggas in dey eyes! Dey like hypnotize you, an' shit. Make you *dey* bitches."

Willie chuckles and presses his eyeballs again.

"An' I don't know," Fisher continues. "This is prolly pure *conjecture*, an' shit. But niggas be talkin' 'bout how HNIC in charge a all a dem niggas."

"HNIC?" I gasp—despite myself.

"Well, crack babies *'sposed* to be controlled by music," Fisher elucidates. "Dey do *anythang* for a slammin' beat, yo. An', as we all know, HNIC got de hottest music goin' right now. 'Bitch! Ho! Bitch! Ho!'" he sings. "So, I figger, niggas jus' be hatin'. As we is like to do."

Willie shakes his head in the affirmative.

"After all," the boy continues, "lotta folks be sayin' dat HNIC be out dere at night actually *fightin'* de crack babies, too. Some even say he actually a crack baby his *damned* self. Who *you* gonna believe? Hard to say if *any* a dat shit be actually *true*, an shit. Or if ... or ... or ..."

Fisher's eyes turn completely white. His head reels back, then plummets. Smack! It bounces off the table. He groans, "Doctor," faintly, and passes out.

Willie and I look at him, at each other.

"Now, what the hell am I supposed to do with that, Vee?" Willie groans.

"I guess, take him to the hospital."

Willie stares at me, frowning hard and deep.

I repeat meekly, "I guess."

Chaptah Twelv

"I need a ruffneck
I need a dude with attitude
Who only needs his fingers with his food"

—MC Lyte, "Ruffneck"

I HATE TO admit it, but my cousin's vagina has a really nice voice. Night and Grey are upstairs snoring away, while her privates sing a beautiful lullaby, Sam Cooke's "A Change Is Gonna Come." In times like these—sitting alone staring at a blank computer screen, not understanding what is happening around me, confused about what to do next—I usually want chamomile tea, a warm bath, candles, and Nina Simone. But right now, the music is so beautiful, so haunting, I want to do absolutely nothing—not move, not think, not even open my eyes. I just want to enjoy this moment for as long as it lasts.

IT DOESN'T LAST long, though. By the time Grey's ... uh ... stuff moves from Sam to Al Green's "Beware," Night and Grey are awake. They are screaming, and they are loud.

I suddenly realize that the bandage on my hand is ragged and dirty. In all the excitement and confusion, I've completely forgotten to change it.

I go downstairs past my makeshift gym and enter my bathroom. It's a typical basement bathroom. Peeling, stained white linoleum, white walls, simple commode and sink. I keep a few medical supplies under the sink. I retrieve them and open my first aid kit. Everything I need is there.

I carefully unwrap the bandage. The wound on my palm has scabbed over, but that scab is tender and doesn't look quite right. Brownish red with tinges of yellow and maybe even green. I hope it's not infected.

I can't take that chance. These hands used to be worth millions. I take the mercurochrome out of the kit and unscrew the top. I then needle a nail underneath the scab and—*hhhssssss*—rip it off. It hurts, but I expected nothing less. Fresh blood trickles over the pink skin of my palm.

I turn on the tap, wait for the water to get hot, then run my hand into the flow. Oh, yeah. This hurts, too. I retract my hand, grab a hand towel, and begin to dry my hand. My palm is tender, and I dance the cloth around the wound. Satisfied, I pour the mercurochrome over the re-opened wound. What was that song Nina sang about Mississippi? Yes. *That* word.

I quickly wrap my hand in a fresh bandage and leave the tacky, little bathroom. After all the money I had spent remodeling the upstairs for Grey ($57,201.37, but who's counting?), I didn't want to spend one more dime on this place. But what if somebody came down here and saw this bathroom? Would they go away thinking that *this* is the way Genevieve Noire actually *lives*? I'm going to have to get somebody in here. As soon as possible.

I climb the stairs. Night is pacing furiously in his street clothes, frantically puffing on a Kool. I cough. "No smoking," I gag.

Night glares at me, fury dancing in his eyes. "You ever fuck a talkin' *pussy,*

Vee?"

"There is still no smoking in my office, Night," I repeat. "You know that."

He throws the cigarette on the floor and stomps it out. He keeps stomping and stomping—harder and harder—until I think he is about to fracture the bones in his foot.

"It just keeps laughin' at me!" he screeches. "An' *laughin'*!!!"

He furiously spins on his heel and charges out of the building.

Disgusted, I pick up the ground-out cigarette and throw it in the wastebasket. I'll have to empty the trash soon before it starts smelling like an ashtray in here.

THE MYTH OF the Crack Baby was given birth on July 30, 1989, by a Conservative muckraker at the *Post*, Jerry Hammer. He claimed, at the time, that a physician friend of his told him that something strange was going on in the neonatal wards of this country's urban hospitals. The pundit claims to have wheeled over to the nearest ghetto hospital to investigate. Supposedly, this is where Hammer found "a bio-underclass, a generation of physically damaged cocaine babies whose biological inferiority is stamped at birth." He'd reported that exposure to crack in the womb was about to produce "a generation of severely damaged children" and that "the dead babies may be the lucky ones."

The doctor whose study the journalist abused, Ira Chasnoff, cried foul. He said, "It's interesting, it sells newspapers, and it perpetuates the us-vs.-them idea."

It definitely did sell newspapers. It also sold TV news advertising spots, and news cameras crowded neonatal wards across the country, filming every skinny black baby they could find.

It caused a panic. Pure hysteria. I personally did twelve "Save the Crack Baby" charity events in the '90s. Everybody wanted to punish these abusive, drug-addled mothers. Harsher drug sentences were passed into law. Women were rounded up and thrown into jail by the droves. And, when a Conservative think tank intellectual declared, "This is not stuff that Head Start can fix .... Whether it is five percent or fifteen percent of the black community, it is there," we ended up punishing the children as well. Education funds to the inner-city were cut around the country.

"That was their real target," my could-have-been ex, Ashanti Moor, once told me. "They'll do and say anything to prove that black folks are inherently inferior and don't deserve shit. And they know they've got to *lie* in order to do it."

I didn't want to believe Ashanti. I knew the media air brushes and Photoshops, but outright *lie* ...? I couldn't stomach it. I had done all those benefits, after all. Ultimately, though, I found out Ashanti was telling the truth. I found out that researchers found minimal damage to the "crack baby's" brain development or her behavior and that prenatal exposure to cocaine was less harmful than exposure to alcohol and/or tobacco in the womb ever were. But by then, it was too late—too late for the women convicted of exposing their fetuses to crack, too late for Head Start, too late for Ashanti and me. By the time I had finally come around, he had already been dead for over a year.

And it is definitely too late to dispel the Myth of the Crack Baby. Now we have two myths—the crack baby and the vampire—married to one another and wreaking havoc on the Koontown streets.

None of it makes sense. The fact that we now have a string of four celebrity murders. The freakishly horrific way in which they have died. The fact that no one has seen anything and absolutely nobody is talking. Well, all right, that's pretty much "Business as Usual" in Koontown, but still ...

The only thing that makes sense is that people are scared—and rightfully so. I don't want my organs liquefied inside my own body and sucked out through my eye sockets, either. So, we're all terrified of something. Something mysterious and strange and absolutely lethal. And if it's not vampire crack babies—and, it most definitely is not—it must be HNIC.

The young man I met, Kelvin Cleghorne, does not seem the type. He is articulate, intelligent, and, with those eyes of his, a bit charismatic. I really can't see him as a homicidal maniac. But one thing all those years in the KPD has taught me, one never knows. People are strange. Homicide, even stranger. We all have this little beast within us capable of the ghastliest deeds. It is a miracle that beast is not released more often. A true blessing that the lion's share of humanity has managed to keep it buried within.

I turn on my computer, wait for the thing to boot up. Stupid Windows Vista. I go and make myself that chamomile tea. I faintly hear my cousin Grey sobbing upstairs. The woman never does *anything* faintly. She must really be hurting.

...

No. I refuse to go deal with this now. I have murders to solve.

I return to my computer and start my search on HNIC né Kelvin Cleghorne. I scroll past pages upon pages of mostly favorable reviews and articles. The celebrity gossip. HNIC seen with this woman and that woman and this woman and that woman—her? My goodness, Mr. Cleghorne sure does get around. This is the same man who wrote "Bitch! Ho! Bitch! Ho!," right?

Women.

Ah, here we go.

"Local Rapper Wanted for Questioning." "HNIC Arrested in Federal Drug Trafficking Case." "Rapper's Gun Tested in Triple Homicide." "HNIC Arrested Outside Paris Nightclub—Two Dead." "Rapper in Jail for Aggravated Assault." "Rapper Jailed for Shoot-Out with Police." "Rapper Jailed for Unpaid Parking Fines."

I can't believe this is all the same man I just met yesterday. No, wait. A small part of me can. I've been around crime, death, and murder too much to not believe the worst in people.

According to all these news reports, Cleghorne is definitely one of the worst. A lot of dead and injured bodies seem to be cluttered around his feet. How this boy isn't rotting away in some super-maximum penitentiary out in the middle of nowhere is beyond me. He most certainly has money, but even the U.S. Mint can't print enough cash to stop all this dirt from sticking. Still, all these charges seem to have been dropped. It doesn't even appear as though Kelvin Cleghorne has ever even been shackled with probation. Something is just not right here.

I pick up my cell phone, scroll through my phone book, and make a call.

"Hey, Jon Vee!"

"Hello, Hustle," I greet. "Where are you right now?"

"The K-Town Fashion Fest."

"The what?" I ask.

"You haven't—well, I guess you have been outta the game for awhile," Hustle Beamon chuckles. I can hear music and cheering in the background. "Anyway, the K-Town Fashion Fest is where the world's top fashion designers fly in all the most influential journalists, industry insiders, rappers, producers, video hos, and drug dealers to show off their new spring line."

"Drug dealers?" I groan.

"Hey, I once paid White-Nose Parker over there on Clayton Powell to sport my gear for six weeks," Hustle informs. "Sold half a mil in merchandise in Koontown *alone*."

"Unbelievable."

"Not really. Think about it, Vee. It's all about 'The Street,'" Hustle continues. "Before Jordan started sportin' their kicks, Nike was only *one* syllable."

I drink the last, cold dregs of my tea. "Look, Hustle," I finally say, "can we meet up somewhere? I need to talk to you."

"All right," he agrees. "I'm not too far from Toomer Way. I can meet you over at your restaurant in, say, twenty?"

"My restaurant?" I ask.

"Yeah," he chirps. "La Bête Noire. You own it, don't you?"

"No," I groan.

"They at least named it after you, right?"

"Um, Hustle," I exhale. "Just meet me there in twenty minutes, OK? And please, Google the definition of that term before you do."

WHY WHITE PEOPLE are moving into Koontown is no mystery. The commute to work is much shorter, and the housing is a lot cheaper—so much cheaper, in fact, that the new residents can build and staff charter schools with the money they have left over. Three are going up just around the corner from where I park my bullet-proof Prius.

Why they chose Toomer Way to settle is a bit confusing, though. And the rapidity with which they have made-over this neighborhood is absolutely mind-boggling. Century-old septic tanks have been replaced with a state-of-the-art sewage system. Lead is no longer a problem for their drinking water. The old nuclear waste site has been scrubbed clean and turned into an absolutely stunning toddler park. Children now glow from pure happiness instead of uranium-235.

Toomer Way itself is completely unrecognizable from what it was even last year. Cracked pavement has been replaced by some kind of rubbery hybrid. It's very easy on the joints. The joggers must love it. Trees have been planted. What was once a dilapidated lane of abandoned store fronts, liquor stores, check-cashing places, pawn shops, a chicken shack, and street-corner pharmacies has been replaced by a real pharmacy, an organic food market, several clothing boutiques, a few bars, and some very cute restaurants (La Bête Noire being one of them). Only the chicken shack remains, but it's about to be torn down for a new police station/firehouse/public library complex. There are even rumors that the city will be remodeling and reopening St. Martin de Porres Hospital after thirty years of dormancy.

Toomer Way is the most celebrated, shining example of what its new residents and Mayor Cummings are calling "revitalization." One cannot help being impressed.

I stroll past the Gurdjieff-Ouspensky Learning Center and enter La Bête Noire. Edith Piaf plays subtly in the background. Toulouse-Lautrec prints line the wall. It all reminds me of a gaudy replica of my time in Paris with Gianni. I immediately want to leave.

Expensive suits—white and black—and the smart, savvy, tailored women who accompany them fill the restaurant. The atmosphere is subdued, full of people who want to be noticed dining here but don't want to appear to be wanting.

Hustle sees me and casually points my way with a conceited, gangsta smirk on his face. He is wearing a diamond-studded Yankees cap, several ostentatious rings on his skeletal hands, and an expensive track suit. It is hard to believe this man is the owner of a billion-dollar, multinational enterprise with truly global reach. I guess this is the standard uniform of the modern-day hip-hop mogul.

I quickly join the record executive and sit down.

He smiles humbly. "I'm really sorry about that 'Bête Noire' thing, Jon Vee," he apologizes. "I really didn't know."

"Honest mistake," I accept.

He reaches over to a chilled wine bucket. I suddenly notice that there's a wine glass sitting before me. He produces a bottle. A 2003 Marcassin Estate chardonnay. I refuse to be impressed. He can easily afford a $250 bottle of wine. He probably just ordered it for its price tag.

"You should try this," Hustle encourages.

"I really shouldn't."

"Are you afraid the boss will find out?" he chuckles. He pours the wine into my glass. It sparkles in the light. "I'm sure he'll be OK with it."

I try never to sniff. I really don't know much about wine. I sniff despite myself. "It smells kind of … I don't know … nutty?"

"That would be hazelnut," Hustle divulges. "The more sophisticated palette will also detect brioche, white fruits, liquefied rock, and *just* a hint of gun flint."

"Gun flint," I smirk.

"Call it, 'Gangsta Juice,'" Beamon laughs. "But seriously, Genevieve, I swear to you this is *the* best chardonnay California has to offer."

I finally take a sip, let the wine linger on my tongue, the aroma fill my mouth. I reluctantly swallow. "Is that …?"

"Yes," Hustle beams, "orange blossom. The 2003 is absofuckinlutely *devastating* in its subtlety. Not too sweet, just the right amount of acidity, and *never* too oaky. They have reached utter BizZenAss. The perfect fucking balance, baby."

I take another sip. I hate to admit it, but the man is right.

A finely-trimmed, sandy blonde waiter comes and deposits a healthy bowl of mussels before Beamon, the black shells struggling not to overflow the lip. "I hope you don't mind," Hustle says. "I'm a bit of a regular here. I can't resist the mussels. Please. Help yourself."

"I better not."

"Oh, come on, Vee," he prods. "You've gotta help a brother out here. The best part of mussels is getting to the bottom so you can sop up the sauce. They got this buttery cream sauce with saffron. Blow your damned mind, yo."

Now I have to admit that I'm a bit confused. The man I see before me is not the Hustle Beamon I have casually known these past twenty years. This is not the gangsta street poet hip-hop advocate full of double negatives and attitude. If it were not for that ridiculous get-up of his and the diamond-encrusted ball cap, I would almost swear that this man is actually … *cultured*?

"What?" Hustle asks. He seems to be searching my face for meaning. "Yeah," he smiles, "you must be hungry. I'll tell you what. They've got an absolutely *amazing* poached salmon with a Golden Osetra caviar garnish. You try that shit, you will *never* have to have sex again."

"OK. Hold up," I flare. "Where in the world did you learn all this stuff, Beamon? Koontown High? 'Slangin' rock' on the corner of Delaney and Butler?!"

Hustle smiles at me, bemused. "Where did you get that, Genevieve?"

I shrug. "I've read your bio, *Jonas* Beamon."

He leans over his mussels and lowers his voice. "Let me tell you something about hip-hop," he opens. "See, just like any other consumer product, hip-hop has an *image*. A façade it puts before the world. You know. You were a super model. It's nothing but branding. Designers used you to promote their brand. You used them to brand yourself.

"We do the exact, same thing in the music business," he continues. "When people see the Dope Beat label, they have a fairly good idea what they're going to get. We give it to them. When they actually wanna cop a rap album, they expect that sort of ... *predictability*.

"We have an image. An image they expect. An image they crave. And, to a certain extent, an image they hope rubs off on them. To a certain extent.

"See, a fool like me. I'd rather be in anything else—jeans, T-shirt, Savile Row, hell, even a lab coat. Anything would be better than this—" He sweeps a hand over his outfit. "But the Hustle Beamon is no longer the man before you. Hell, I'm not a man at all. I'm a corporate brand. I am an *image*.

"So," he breathes, "the industry—me, everybody in it—we give these fans that image. Some of us actually *live* that image. But a lot of us, frankly, are nothing but a bunch of *poseurs* who know how to give the people not what they *want* necessarily—but what they have grown to *expect*."

"And which one are you, Hustle?" I ask.

"I think I've already answered that one." Beamon looks away from me and searches the table. He finds his fork, grabs a shell, and digs a mussel out of its ancestral home. Good, for a second there I was afraid that Hustle Beamon is actually European and would've dug in with his hands. I'm not sure I know who this man is anymore, but at least I know he's a fork-wielding American.

"Bitch! I said, 'Straw!'" a man yells. I turn. A few tables over, a black man light enough to be a Noir points his big, meaty finger at his waitress. He is solidly-built, clean-shaven, bald-headed, well-dressed, and furious. I can see his hazel eyes burning from here. "Who the *fuck*," he roars, "drinks wine wifout a *muhfuckin'* straw?! Dat shit is *unsanitary* ... an' ... an' shit."

"Our people," I mutter, shaking my head.

"You don't know who that is?" Hustle whispers. I shake my head. "Hunter Wentworth. Eighth Ward. City Council."

I shake my head again. "You mean he represents Toomer Way here?"

"Yep," my employer confirms. "He's already declared. He's running against Sweetdick next year."

"For mayor?" I gasp.

"Right," Hustle chuckles. "Sweetdick's running scared, too. All these white folks backing homeboy over there. With their white folks' money. They say Sweetdick's off the wagon again, just holed up in his office all day on that dust."

"Did Clarence 36-24-36 X teach us nothing?"

"Who knows?" Hustle shrugs. "But you know Sweetdick. He ain't going down without a fight. He's already put the word out that Wentworth is actually *white*."

I look back over at the Councilman. He's waving his hands in the air, roaring, "Bitch! Ho! Bitch! Ho!" The people at his table laugh encouragingly, waving their hands along with him.

"Not acting like that, he isn't," I say.

Hustle points a mussel shell at me with a self-satisfied smile. "Exactly."

"So, Hustle, speaking of *poseurs*," I open, "nice pronunciation, by the way. You sound almost as though you may actually speak French."

Hustle shrugs nonchalantly, concentrating on his mussels.

"Anyway," I continue, "speaking of *poseurs* in hip-hop, which one is Mr.

Cleghorne?"

He looks up. "HNIC?" Hustle suddenly starts studying my face again. There's that smirk again. "That was bullshit, wasn't it? When you said his life might be in danger?"

It's my turn to concentrate on his mussels. I grab an empty half shell and an occupied full one. I scoop the rubbery mollusk out of its shell and start chewing.

"He's a suspect, isn't he?" he probes. I continue chewing. "Need I remind you, Ms. Noire, that you actually work for *me* now?"

I swallow. "It's not as though I need the money, Hustle."

"That's good to hear," he admits. "I was actually worried when you finally accepted my offer."

"To be honest, I missed the action."

"Face it, Jon Vee, you're too young to retire. We both are," Hustle says. "And since you *are* working and working *for me*, I do expect you to answer my questions. That's what I pay you for."

"Then I quit," I declare, stonily. "Now, answer *my* question, Jonas."

Hustle leans back in his chair, rests his hands on top of his baseball cap, and laughs. "You are one, *amazing* woman, Genevieve Noire." He leans forward again. "No. Mr. Cleghorne is most definitely no *poseur*. We didn't have to teach him one damned *thing* about being a 'gangsta.' It was like he was *born* to the shit."

"So, all that stuff I've been reading about him—the murders, the drugs, the parking fines—he actually did all that stuff?"

"And a whole hell of a lot more."

"How can you do it, Beamon?" I ask. "How can you take such despicable human beings, allow them to make such reprehensible music, and make them rich, make them powerful and influential? How?"

"BizZenAss."

"I don't buy it."

Suddenly, Hustle looks off to the side. His eyes are miles away. I wait. He eventually turns back to me.

"You remember the '80s, Vee?" he asks. "Remember how *white* they were? How isolated, how *embattled* we black folks felt? Like we were being buried *beneath* Reagan's 'City on a Hill'?"

Frankly, I don't. My Daddy simply *adored* Reagan. I nod, anyway.

"Then along comes rap," he continues. "'The Message.' Damn, woman. Talk about the *ultimate* 'Fuck You' to Uncle Ronnie. Remember Kurtis Blow?"

"Before these brothers came along, what did we have? Bill Cosby? Sidney Poitier? Real feel-good negroes, you know. Michael? Prince?"

"Hey!"

"Don't get me wrong. I love 'em all, too. Where would I be without them?" he admits. "But they weren't exactly the most *masculine* examples of black manhood, were they?"

I concede nothing.

"Then LL comes along. And he's like, 'Fuck all yall. I'm blastin' my muhfuckin' radio in all yall bitches' ears, and I *dare* you to reach for the volume.' And Run-DMC were like, 'Naw, white boys, *we're* the Kings of Rock.' And they said it, they were actually *proud* to be black. No process. No high heels. No faggoty-ass prancing on stage.

"I mean, here I was, just a confused, mixed kid from Bethesda—"

"I thought you were from Koontown," I interrupt.

Hustle smiles, a mischievous gleam in his eye. "A confused, mixed kid from Bethesda," he repeats, "searching for an identity. A well-worn copy of *Black*

Poets in my back pocket. Wandering around, aimless. And these brothers come along. They're young, they've got *gorilla* balls, and they're *black*. So black, white folks are up in arms. They're screaming that it's not real music, that it's *dangerous* music. That it's music they wanted to ban. Put stickers on it telling little white kids to stay away or burn in hell.

"Hell, those Old School rappers were so black, our *own* parents wanted the music destroyed. So black even black *radio* refused to play it.

"I gotta tell ya, Vee," Beamon sighs, "I was soooo high on the stuff back then. In those early days. I just loved it all. The Fat *and* the Skinny Boys." He leans back in his chair. "I'm like Nice & Smooth, Genevieve. I'm a hip-hop junkie. And that's why I have the label. I'm always chasin' that first high."

He sips on his chardonnay.

"And HNIC," I ask, "he does that for you?"

"He used to," the man admits. "With that first album. Now, it's just BizZenAss. I will ride that flow until it slows to a trickle."

"I need to talk to him, Hustle," I urge. "ASAP."

"I'll tell you what," he says. "I don't know where the boy is right now. He is constantly in the wind. And getting a hold of him during the day is like trying to raise the dead. But I know that tonight he's going to be at the Übernoggin joint. Doing some A&R work for me."

"Übernoggin?" I ask. "I have no clue what that is."

"It's not a *that*," he corrects. "Übernoggin's a woman. She is *all* woman."

"Where can I find her?"

"You can't," he replies. "She only surfaces once, maybe twice a year to host these parties of hers. They're invitation-only. Completely on the down-low. Negroes privileged enough get an email about an hour or two before the party kicks off. And, I gotta tell ya, everybody who gets that email drops whatever the hell he's doing and rushes straight to the spot."

"But Cleghorne will be there tonight?"

"Oh yeah," Hustle confirms. "It's his job to be there."

"So, how will I find this party?" I ask. "Are you going?"

Hustle throws his hand to his chest in a "Who? Me?" gesture. "Oh, God no," he laughs. "I've left Übernoggin's joints alone *ages* ago. But I *do* get the invite. Once I get the email, I'll text you and tell you where the party's at."

Suddenly, Hustle reaches into his tracksuit pants pocket. He produces his iPhone and studies it for a second. He stands, a scarecrow in silk. "Sorry, I've got to take this one, Vee." He starts walking away.

"An' I tol' dat bitch," we overhear Councilman Wentworth regaling. "You *best* be gettin' back on dat damned *track*. Nigga gotsta git *paid*, na'mean?"

His table laughs.

Hustle chuckles, derisively. "Yale."

He rolls his eyes, shaking his head, and answers his phone. "Yeah. What is it?" I hear him snap as he exits the restaurant.

Wentworth's waitress places a small, earthenware bowl before the Councilman. His face curdles. He picks up his spoon and starts poking at his soup.

"Genevieve?"

I turn and smile. "Lucille? What are you doing here?"

Lucille Parsons does not look happy. She towers over me in rage. "It's bad enough that you're already working for that limp-wrested race traitor," she snaps, vehemently. "Now, you're going out to lunch with him?"

I have never seen my mentor, my gbeto, the woman who pulled me from the abyss, looking so furious. She looks ready to decapitate somebody with her teeth. I don't know what to say. She peers at me—eyes burning—as though she expects me to actually say something, though.

"Oh, Hustle," I wave off, "he's not that bad, Lucille."

"Bullshit," she spits. "With all that genocidal music he peddles to his people. And *those* people."

. . .

"Did you know that *sixty* percent of all rap sales are to *white* people?" she seethes. "Do you think that *garbage* doesn't affect the way they think about us?"

"I'm sure—"

"Sometimes," she interrupts, careful to control her wrath, "sometimes, you have just *got* to call a spade a spade, Genevieve. And Hustle Beamon is one spade I'd like to bury six feet under."

I still don't know what to say. In all honesty, I'm afraid to even open my mouth. However, before I can conjure up a single word, Lucille Parsons spins on her expensive heel and storms out of La Bête Noire. I just hope, with what she was just saying and the way the woman can handle a bo staff, she doesn't run into Hustle out there.

"Yo, bitch!" Wentworth screams. The entire restaurant goes completely silent. "What de *fuck* is up wif all dese muhfuckin' *onions* in my soup?"

"B-b-but, Councilman We-We-Wentworth," the waitress stammers, tears in her eyes, "y-you ordered F-F-French *onion* soup."

"What?!" he snaps. "You gittin' *smart*, bitch? Wif *me*?! You *best* know who you talkin' to! I'm the *muhfuckin'* pimp up in de Eif Ward!"

I leave my seat.

"I-I-I am s-so-sorry, Councilman," the waitress weeps.

I make my way to the Councilman's table.

"Fuck 'Sorry,' ho!" growls the politician. He jumps out of his seat. He reaches back and flips his suit's tails.

I quicken my pace.

He reaches for the small of his back.

"I got 'Sorry' fo' yo' ass," he growls.

He pulls something from his back.

I leap. I swing.

Thwack!

A pistol flies out of his hand and skitters across the floor. The room gasps. Wentworth yelps, grabbing his left cheek. He looks up with tears in his hazel eyes. "Genevieve Noire?" he squeals.

My right fist crashes into his cheek again. He spins. I uppercut a left under his chin. Wentworth is a tall man, about my height. A large man. More than twice my weight. He crashes into the wall. The entire room rattles on impact. My right, my left, my right, my right again crash into his face until he slides to the floor.

My cell phone rings.

"Hold on a second," I say to the downed politician. I dig my phone out of my jacket pocket and read the Caller ID. I quickly answer. "What is it, Willie?"

"We've got another one, Vee."

I groan. "All right, come get me," I say. "I'm at La Bête Noire. Over on Toomer."

"Checking up on your employees?" Willie asks, earnestly.

"I do not own this restaurant, Detective O'Ree," I fume. "In fact—"

"Uhhhh," Wentworth moans. I land a kick to his solar plexus. He immediately doubles over.

"I'm going to assume," I continue into the phone, "that I probably won't be welcomed back here any time soon."

Chaptah Firteen

WILLIE AND I return to the organ/blood scrawl on the hallway wall one more time, still scratching our heads.

"Don't Eva Let De Lion

Tell De Giraffe'z Storee"

"What the hell?" Willie exhales.

"I think it's an African proverb," I inform him.

"Great. Next time I see a gotdamned Wolof griot, I'll question *him* about these fucking murders."

The old homicide detective storms off to the victim's bedroom, where the body lay. I readjust my latex gloves and move onto the victim's study, confused as to how they can spell "giraffe" correctly, yet misspell "story."

Absolutely nothing about LaSchwanika Compton-Stuyvesant's death is making much sense right now. She's been murdered just like the rappers—her organs liquefied and vacuumed out of her eye sockets—except that she's not a rapper.

Dr. Compton-Stuyvesant is a professor of literature and a writer. A very successful writer. Last year, she was the literary world's latest sensation. Her novel, *Smoke Dem Niggaz*, captured "the gritty reality of America's inner city streets—the pain, the despair, and, ultimately, the *hope* that burns within all of us." That's what most of the critics said, anyway. It spent most of the year on the *Times'* Best-Seller List, *USA Today*'s, and even *Ebony*'s. The movie is in post-production right now. The TV pilot has already been shot. There is even talk of a perfume and video game.

Compton-Stuyvesant has won tons of literary awards. Most I've never heard of. But I know that *Smoke Dem Niggaz* has won the National Book Award and the Pulitzer Prize. The Brits even made an exception and made Compton-Stuyvesant the first American winner of the Man Booker Prize for her debut novel. They said that the novel spoke to "all of us—whether British, a member of the Commonwealth, or American—whether we be white or black or anything else in between."

In a way I don't want to admit to myself, I understand why the others were killed. Obviously, I would've contemplated killing Niggassippee myself if I had actually known of his existence. I wouldn't be surprised if Lucille Parsons and my fellow elephant hunters had plots cooking up his demise. But this woman? LaSchwanika Compton-Stuyvesant? She was a literary jewel. A black diamond shining on the world. Why did she have to die?

I hope to find the answer in her study. But I can find nothing so far. Masks from Kenya and Ghana line the walls along with pictures of the author with some really famous people—Quincy Jones, Keith Ellison, Dr. Ben Carson,

Dr. Bill Cosby, Dr. Dre, Oprah, Tyler Perry, Lucille Parsons. There's a large bookcase filled to overflowing on the rear wall. A large flat-screen television occupies the front wall. Sandino's already been here and turned it on. It mumbles in the background as I continue my search. In the middle of the room is a large, cherry wood desk with a laptop resting in its center. A tech will be coming in to search the hard drive for clues any minute. For now, though, I am only concerned with what's in the desk itself.

I open the top drawer. There are pens, pencils, a few erasers, rubber bands, paper clips, loose change. Nothing out of the ordinary. I dig deeper. Bills, bills, and more bills. Wait a second.

I pull out a little pamphlet. "De Rulez a Ebonikz." I start flipping. Nothing but blank pages. A compact disc falls out of the folds and crashes onto the desk. I ignore it, keep flipping through the pages. Ah, here we go. Finally, some text:

"Dey ain't no rulez, nigga.
You got served!!!"

I chuckle despite myself. I look down at the fallen CD. Hm. It reads, "Nigga Narrativez." Now, what could *that* possibly be?

"It's on!" Sandino announces, breathless, from the doorway. He enters the room, produces a remote, and turns up the volume on the television.

An elderly, silver-bobbed white woman is on the screen. She is all in black with chunky red glasses. She speaks in hushed, erudite tones weighed down by gravitas. The screen below her reads, "Samantha Rose. *Book World.*"

"The literary world has been starved for a new African-American voice for far too long," Rose whispers, huskily. "LaSchwanika Compton-Stuyvesant was that voice. Bright, articulate—"

"Of course," I grumble.

"—tragically comical. A truly *authentic* voice. She spoke the *agony* of the street. She was the street. She was its pain, its despair, and, ultimately, Professor LaSchwanika Compton-Stuyvesant was the *hope* that burns within all of us. And now," Samantha Rose weeps, "that hope is *dead*."

"Wow," Sandino gulps.

Zamani Mandinka, the author with a few Pulitzers of her own with *Cry Me a Ribber* and *Uncle Tom's Cadillac*, appears with her beehive of salt-and-pepper dreadlocks. Her eyes are raw and watery. She speaks with a British accent—though we all know she's from Mississippi.

"I have been looking to pass the mantle of 'the Queen of Black Literature' for decades," Ms. Mandinka declares. "I felt that I had finally found a worthy heir in LaSchwanika. The heroine—that crack commercial sex worker—LaFarfignewton Jones—she was so compelling, so ... so awe-inspiring. Her pain, so real. Her despair, so ... *palpable*. And that woman's *hope*—" Ms. Mandinka bites her knuckle to stanch the tears "—her *hope* spoke to *all* of us—even my students here at Cambridge."

The porn actress, Ann Nzinga, star of the *Analubian Queen* series, wails on the screen. "I cain't b'lieve dey done *killt* my *bitch*, yo!" she screeches.

Sandino turns to me, confused. "Do you think ...?"

I shrug.

"Dat gurl could spit her some *mad* wisdom!" Nzinga continues. "An' yall niggas know I know sumt'n 'bout *spittin'*!"

That *Raisin in the Sun* actress is back in her Momma wig and housecoat. She's on the ground, pounding it with her fists. She looks up at the camera, brown face drenched in tears. "My baaaaaaabyyyyy! Aw, Lawd Jesus hab mercy!!! My baby gooonnnnnneeeeee!!!"

"Genevieve!" I hear Willie shout from the bedroom. "Could you come here, please?"

"Be right there, Willie!" I shout back. I look down at the CD. "Nigga Narrativez." I doubt it has anything to do with the case. I'm just curious. I pick up the disc and pocket it. "Coming!"

Willie meets me outside of Compton-Stuyvesant's bedroom. He looks frazzled, annoyed, angry, too many things at the same time to list here. "Did you find anything, Genevieve?" he asks.

"No," I lie. "These are the cleanest murder scenes I have ever seen. They're almost museum pieces."

"Tell me about it," he grunts. "Well, Sweetdick just called."

"The mayor?" I ask.

"These ... *negroes* have just killed a black woman with a degree," he says, wearily. "A PhD, no less. You know they're on the Endangered Species list, right?"

"I did hear something about that."

"Might as well have just offed a *fucking* bald eagle." He starts rubbing his eyes again. "Anyway," Willie sighs, "rappers are one thing. This is a whole fuckin' other. *Now*, City Hall is interested. I've got to roll down there immediately. You coming?"

"Sure, Willie. Sure."

He smiles and starts heading for the door. "Sandino!" he shouts. "You're coming with us!"

"Sure, boss!"

Before I go, I turn to look at LaSchwanika Compton-Stuyvesant, professor of literature and literary sensation, one last time before Dr. Sims gets his hands on her at the City Morgue and cuts her to pieces.

She looks so rested, so peaceful, laying there on her bed. Her reddish-brown plaits spread around her head like a halo. Her milky, caramel skin seems to glow in this light. She almost looks like a Noire angel—though her skin is a touch too tawny. I heard she even had sparkling green eyes like mine. I can't tell now, of course. They have been liquefied and sucked out of her head.

No, none of this makes the least bit of sense.

No sense at all.

THE COLD, STEELY gaze of Lucille Parsons greets us as we enter Mayor Hordace "Sweetdick" Cummings's office. The television screen dully transmits her regal image in a cream-colored pantsuit. Microphones crowd her face. Her words are distinguished—but lifeless. She just does not seem her fiery self.

"LaSchwanika Compton-Stuyvesant was a sister-in-arms," she drones. She was? I don't remember her at any of our elephant hunter meetings. "She died trying to uplift her people. *Black* people. We will be feeling her loss for centuries to come."

The television clicks off. Mayor Cummings lowers the remote control atop a mountain range of powder cocaine on his desk. He looks like Al Pacino at the end of *Scarface*. Wired, exhausted, at the end of his rope. He rests his head back against his leather chair and moans audibly.

"Have a seat," he croaks.

Willie, Sandino, and I comply, looking at each other nervously. At the mayor's cocaine mountain. At the door. Federal troops can come storm his door at any moment. It wouldn't be the first time.

Everybody in Koontown—the entire world, in fact—knows about Mayor Cummings's history of drug and legal trouble. It started way back in his Freedom Riders days.

He was an activist working for the Student Non-Violent Coordinating Committee, trying to integrate the white high school in Ofay, Georgia. His efforts were getting him and his cause nowhere. Anybody he tried recruiting would soon end up being rounded up by the racist sheriff's department. Having had enough, Cummings desperately called for a large, nonviolent rally outside of Ofay High.

Miraculously, nearly every black person in a twenty-mile radius of the school showed up before its doors to protest. Predictably, every sheriff's department in a three-state radius showed up to beat every protestor within an inch of their lives. Inexplicably, the man who called for the rally, a young Hordace Cummings, was nowhere to be found.

At first, everybody thought that the white police had gotten to him and dumped his body in an undisclosed location. They feared they would never find the man. But they did. At SNCC headquarters. The white police hadn't gotten him at all. The white powder had. He was found, "sick," covered in crusted-over vomit, a needle in his arms, and a nearly fatal dose of heroin in his veins.

After centuries of racial animosity, violence, and bloodshed, the black and white citizens of Ofay, Georgia, banded together to run Hordace Cummings out of town. Seeing that they actually *could* get along and work together, Ofay was soon integrated. In fact, the town's current mayor is, indeed, African-American. He and his Cambodian-American lesbian sheriff have the town running smoothly—and prospering.

Cummings spun this profound humiliation into victory and ran with it all the way to the Koontown mayoralty. His victories here and in Georgia only further encouraged his drug use. His abuse became legendary. He would even appear at press conferences high as a kite. It was only a matter of time before the federal government took notice.

When they did, it wasn't hard to catch him. They simply strolled into his office one day with heavy armor and light machine guns. He was so high he offered the uniformed DEA agent a hit off the homemade banana spliff he was smoking. They gave him twenty years, but he only served seven. Getting out just in time for Clarence 34-26-34 X to hand off the keys to the Mayor's office on *his* way to the federal penitentiary.

The folks in Koontown love Mayor "Sweetdick." Their problems are *his* problems. Literally. He has a problem with drugs, more than enough problems with the Law, and so many baby mommas he can't even remember their names—only referring to them by number. He's so drug-addled, though, he even gets those wrong.

Personally, I can't stand the man. But what can I do? I'm from the suburbs. I just get far too nervous around him. I always feel like I'm about to be either impregnated or charged as an accessory.

Cummings moans again, his head reclined against his leather chair. Willie, Sandino, and I look at each other once again. This is all too weird. Even for the mayor. And there's a strange sound coming from somewhere I just cannot identify.

"Like I ain't got it rough enough, O'Ree," Cummings roars. "With that white boy, Wentworth, breathing down my neck. Those crackers with torches and the noose in their hands, circling around a brother. Did you know there was a demonstration outside my office today?"

"What are white folks protesting about?" Willie asks. "Better housing?"

"Not white folks," Cummings growls. He lowers his head and finally looks at us. "It was that damned peacenik, Reverend Goodblood. *He's* claiming that all these dead rappers are victims of a government conspiracy."

"Are they?" I accidentally blurt out.

He smiles at me. Hungrily. I suddenly feel naked. "And how are you, Ms. Noire?" he leers. "I haven't seen *you* in ages. Ooooohhhhhhh."

Willie leans across me to block Cummings' view and plants an elbow into the cocaine. He quickly withdraws and brushes the powder off his sleeve. "Was it, at least, peaceful?"

"With all those Irie Man and Funky Dollah Bill disciples? And those 'Gimme Dat' kids?" the mayor asks. "Surprisingly, yes. Only three grandmothers dead and seventeen straight A students hospitalized."

Sandino shakes his head approvingly. I groan. So does Mayor Cummings.

"I mean, here I am," the mayor continues, "about to roll out this new 'Tough on Crime' legislation, ready to beat that white boy back to Harvard—"

"Yale," I correct.

"—Yale," he amends. "I've even Photoshopped him in bed with a bunch of white bitches. And how the hell am I supposed to do all this—how am I supposed to be tough on *crime*—when we've got dead *writers* littering the streets? Did you know they were already talking Nobel Prize? After only *one* novel? Not since Pasternak—"

"Only one," Willie interrupts. "Only *one* dead writer."

"So *far*," Cummings objects. "What the *hell* are you doing out there, Willie? You too busy makin' googly eyes at Vee here to do your fucking *job*?!"

"Motherfu—"

Willie jumps out of his chair. Sandino jumps out of his. He grabs Willie before my old partner can do anything we will all regret.

"I oughtta bust your ass right now!" Willie yells.

"What?" Cummings guffaws. "For drugs?"

"Fuck the drugs! I said, 'your *ass*,' n—"

WHAM!!!

We all turn. The door has been slammed open. A harried-looking secretary hyperventilates in the doorway. "The Governor's on the phone, sir!" she gasps. "Line one!"

"What the—?" Mayor Cummings looks around frantically. His hands dive into the mound of powder. It starts snowing in the office. I sneeze. He finally retrieves the receiver, blows some coke off of it, and puts it to his ear. "Hello?"

"Hm-mm." He slumps his head back into his chair. "Hm-mm. Hm-mm." He's nodding. "What?!"

He jumps out of his chair.

THUD!!!

"Ow!" comes a squeak.

The mayor stands, rigidly, behind his desk. His penis stands, erect, peering out over the cocaine mountain. Some rustling. Suddenly, a young, half-dressed sister scuttles out from beneath the mayor's desk like a cockroach and quickly crawls out of Cummings's office.

"You've got to be fucking *kidding* me!" the mayor screams, desperately.

Another frantic secretary joins her colleague in the doorway. She pants. "The FBI is on Line two, sir! The CIA on Line three!"

"Fuck!"

The mayor's hand searches frantically in the Colombian snow. "Yeah! Of course!" he screams into the phone. He slams the receiver back into its cradle. He finds the remote control, stabs at it madly.

The TV flashes on. A young, distraught white woman is on the screen. Her eyes and nose are red from crying. She has an uncontrollable mane of curly, reddish-brown hair and sad, green eyes. She holds on desperately to a ragged tissue. Below her reads, "Rachel Torch—Author's Sister."

"What?" Sandino mumbles.

"Our family," Ms. Torch sobs, "we're a very *accepting* family. We don't just *accept* other cultures. We *embrace* them. Some of *my* best friends are Amish—"

"You *can't* be serious!" Cummings erupts.

"The Society of Friends, Line four!" announces a new secretary.

"So, we have grown up with a *profound* respect for African-Americans and their culture," Ms. Torch continues. "But Sarah—"

"Sarah," Cummings blubbers.

"—she always took it—well—she took it too far. She didn't just *identify* with the black struggle. We all did. But she ... uh ... she—we just always suspected that Sarah actually wanted to *be* black.

"It was more than just listening to rap music and dressing like the rappers and adopting some of the slang. We all did that—"

"Tipper Gore on Line five!" yet another secretary declares.

"Damn," huffs Cummings.

"No, with Sarah, it was so much more. She didn't just want to *act* black or *be* black. She actually thought she *was* black. All the kids in high school called her a ... a ... 'wigger.'"

"The Attorney General on Line six!"

How many secretaries does this man have?

"And then, she went and changed her name to *LaSchwanika*?" Ms. Torch scoffs. "We thought she had gone too far then. But then she came out with that *book*. That, that *Smoke Dem N-Wordz*."

"Why didn't you come forward then?" an off-screen reporter asks.

"Oh, we wanted to," Ms. Torch claims. "But the publisher threatened to sue."

"Koonington Press on Line seven!"

"And then she started winning all those prizes and awards," Ms. Torch continues. "We were afraid to say anything."

"The Nobel Committee, Line eight!"

"So, Ms. Torch, why did you feel the need to come forward now?"

"Well, it's—it's just not *right*," she states, fervently, swiping fresh tears from her emerald eyes. "I mean, she's dead now. And everybody's claiming she is the greatest *black* writer of her generation—"

"Zadie Smith, Line nine!"

"—but she's not black. Not in the *least*. Sarah Rebecca Torch is a beautiful, white woman—"

"Oh ... God ..." Cummings trembles, now crying himself.

"The President of the United States, Line ten!"

"Not only that," Ms. Torch continues, fervently. "Sarah was a beautiful, *Jewish* woman."

"Mossad, Line eleven!"

"The Mossad!" Cummings wails. He's standing behind his desk, catatonic, his pants around his ankles. His junk? ... Well, now I understand why he has so many baby mommas. "I'm a dead man," he croaks.

Willie, Sandino, all ten secretaries, and I stand frozen. The mayor has become an automaton. He stiffly raises the remote and turns off the television. All is silent. Nobody knows what to do. We are all too confused. Suddenly, the air outside vibrates as though it is slicing itself to ribbons. Helicopters?

"That's probably the National Guard right now," Cummings declares, woodenly. He collapses back into his leather chair. His penis pokes him in the solar plexus. A small sigh escapes his lips. "What the *fuck* have you done to me, O'Ree?"

"Me?" Willie flares. "Get off the crack, Sweetdick!"

"Crack?! Ha. That is *soooooo* ghetto." The man laughs. Long. Hard. Maniacally. He quickly stops, snapping the laughter like a twig. He suddenly stares, glares, at Willie. An insane fire in his eyes. "You're fucking me, O'Ree!" he roars. "Fucking me! Right in the ass! With a *dick* full of razor blades!!!"

"Like I need this shit right now," grumbles Willie, rubbing his eyes.

"You know what, *Detective* William Orpheus O'Ree of the Koontown Police Department—Homicide Division, you are right," Cummings smiles, menacingly. "You don't. You *don't* need this shit at all."

Willie leans forward and buries his hands elbow-deep into the Mayor's stash. Cummings lurches forward as well. They are face-to-face, close enough to tear off the other's nose with his teeth. "Go ahead, motherfucker," Willie seethes. "Do it!"

"All right then, bitch, have it your way," Cummings smiles. "YOU … ARE … OFF … THE … CASE!!!"

Chaptah Foteen

"I'm just trying to say the way school needs teachers
The way Kathie Lee needs Regis
That's the way yall need Jesus"

—Kanye West, "Jesus Walks"

"LIKKANIGGADIK"

"Did you hear that?" I ask, looking up into the night. Large airplanes drone overhead.

"C-130s," Sandino proclaims, gazing heavenward as well. "Heavy military transport planes."

Descending black circles engulf the indigo sky.

"Airborne," Willie sighs, a reverential glow on his face. He smiles briefly then quickly turns serious again, looking at Sandino and me. "Koontown's gonna burn tonight. No greater crime on this Earth than killing a white woman."

"I just can't believe that Torch woman had everybody snowed," Sandino says. "I mean, *Lucille Parsons*. She's the pro-blackest woman in the world."

"Well, Lucille hasn't been quite herself lately," I mumble.

"How so?" Willie asks, intensely.

I didn't realize I had said anything. I'm taken aback. Briefly. Then I start thinking—about the beating she gave me the other day, her violent reaction to seeing me at lunch with Hustle Beamon this afternoon …

I shrug. "I don't know," I confess. "She's just not."

Suddenly, my cell phone chirps. I pull my phone from my jacket and look.

"What is it, Genevieve?" Willie asks.

"A text," I answer. "From Hustle. Telling me where HNIC's going to be tonight. It's over on Jack Johnson Boulevard."

"What is?" Sandino asks.

"Uh, some woman named Übernoggin's having a party in a warehouse over there."

"Übernoggin?!" Willie guffaws. Sandino howls hysterically, too.

"What's so funny?" I ask.

"*HNIC*? He's gonna be at *Übernoggin's* tonight?" Willie asks, incredulously.

"Yeah. Why?" I ask, a little flustered.

Sandino laughs even harder.

"Why, don't that beat the bitch?" Willie chuckles.

"So, you know about Übernoggin's party?"

"Vee," says Sandino, patronizingly. "There is not a single man in Koontown who *doesn't* know about Übernoggin's 'jams.'"

"I guess I'm not a 'single man' then."

"No. You are not," Sandino concurs. "You will never be invited nor will your presence be particularly welcomed."

"We're gonna need back-up," Willie urgently declares. "Jon Vee, can I drop you back at your car? You can drive yourself there?"

"I'll call Leadfoot and Watts right now," says Sandino, whipping out his cell phone.

"What's the big deal?" I ask. "It's just a party."

"If it's an Übernoggin party," Willie says, "I want every man I *trust* there to have my back."

"Yeah," snickers Sandino, "before some man you *don't* trust has it."

"But, Willie—"

"Look, Vee," Willie barks, "we need to stop these murders before K-town turns to ash before our eyes. All roads seem to be leading to HNIC. If he's at Übernoggin's, then we gotta go to Übernoggin's. Whether we like it, or not."

"Don't act like you don't like it, Willie," Sandino jabs. He starts dialing numbers.

"But, Willie," I repeat. "Mayor Cummings just threw you off the case."

The two homicide detectives laugh heartily again.

"Oh, come on now, Vee," Sandino says. "Willie's a maverick here. Everybody knows that."

"And everybody knows," Willie adds, "including Sweetdick back there, that I do my best work when I'm actually *off* the case."

I shrug, confused.

"Now, let's go solve this motherfucker!" Willie triumphs, heading for the police cruiser. "After I do something first."

"FUCK YOU, NIGGA!!!"

A young teenager in an FDB shirt sprints past as I put my Prius in Park. A baby-faced soldier charges after him with bayonet and rifle muzzle leading the way.

"Come back here, you little prick!"

I step out of the car and hit the car alarm button on my key ring.

"likkaniggadik"

OK, am I going crazy? Did anybody else hear that?

"AAARRRRRRGGGGHHHHHH!!!!"

I look. The teen has turned a corner. The soldier is nowhere in sight. Koontown. What can you do?

Father Divine Way is simply teeming with people. Restless, anxious people—afraid of what tonight may bring. There are gunshots off in the distance. An explosion. Everybody cringes. Some gasp. Others scream. Everybody looks for the fireball. Somewhere off by Porch Monkey Projects. Nowhere near the gentrifying Toomer Way.

I find Willie and Sandino. They are flanked by Commander Samuel "Leadfoot" Steele and the equally beefy Lieutenant Maurice Watts. I haven't seen the latter nor his graying mutton chops since the Standish case that got me shot. He is one of the few police I can still trust. He won't be putting a slug in my back.

"Vee," he purrs, warmly. "It's been a koon's age, hasn't it?"

He spreads his arms wide. I walk affectionately into the embrace.

"It *has* been awhile, Maurice," I concur, smiling. "How's the rib business treating you?"

"Still got that barrel over on Famous Amos," he says, releasing me. "Two more years. I retire and open up a spot for real." He beams proudly and then gives me an appraising eye. "You need to come down, gurl. Put some meat on dem bones."

"She's about to get all the meat she can handle down at Übernoggin's," Sandino laughs.

The others guffaw grandly.

Men.

"What are we doing here, Willie?" I ask.

"Going in," he states, and starts making his way through the bustling crowd toward the Church of Racial Reconciliation.

I MUST CONFESS. I am not much of a believer in God—much less an actual church-goer. We Noires believe that we have been blessed with our outstanding beauty—but not blessed *quite* enough. Therefore, we don't owe the Big Guy anything. I don't necessarily believe all that, but it is hard going against the way one is raised. Besides, all those zeroes in my bank account from modeling seem to confirm my family's faith.

The Church of Racial Reconciliation is itself a mystery. The first time Willie and I rolled past the place a couple days ago, it seemed like nothing but white people were coming in here. Last night, the crowd was entirely Asian. Tonight, however, the church is packed to the gills with black folk. Sweaty, exhorting black folk enthralled by the message the preacher is screaming at them. A message, by the way, I can't imagine any white or Asian person actually appreciating. In fact, I can only imagine their being enraged by what their pastor is now saying.

"We are at WAR!!! people," he exhorts. "WAR!!!"

He wipes his slick forehead with a handkerchief and takes a sip of water.

From the back of the church here, it's a little hard to tell exactly what the man is. From the message, I can only assume black. His hair is black and close-cropped. The kind of cut that refuses to reveal whether the hair is fine or kinky. His skin is tawny—or rather, "high yella" (pardon the phrase). But at the moment, he is red-faced with rage. The blood nearly bursting from his face.

"It is a four hundred-YEAR war that we are LOSING!!! brothers and sisters!" he continues. "African slavery was the ONLY immigration policy these white folks could EVER agree on. They was like, 'Africa, give me ALL the niggas you can spare! Shit! It ain't like WE wanna work!"

"Amen!"

"I heard *dat*!"

"Then! Once we BUILT this country! Once we made it the GREAT nation it is TODAY! them SAME white folks was sayin', 'Ah, yeah, *Africa*? Could you, um, take them niggas back? We through with 'em now.' And Africa was like, 'Ah, hell naw, cracka! They YO' problem now!!!"

The rafters rattle with laughter. Even Willie chuckles.

OK, I admit it. that was a *little* funny.

"And don't think we WASN'T a problem for all these white folks!" the pastor screeches. "They couldn't have all these niggas runnin' around FREE! Now could they?!"

"You got *dat* right!"

"Preach! Reverend! Preach!"

"So AMERICA treated us BLACK folk like every OTHER problem America has ever faced! They went to WAR!!!

"They Jim CROWED us! They LYNCHED us! RAPED our mothers and daughters! Even some of our MEN!"

"BOOO!!!!"

"Them white folks broke up our FAMILIES! Pumped HEROIN in our veins! Shoved CRACK down our throats!"

"Speak! Brother! Speak!!!"

"Police with body armor! Police with automatic weapons! Police with tanks! And helicopters! Is this FALLUJAH, people?! Is it NORMANDY?! The shores of TRIPOLI?!!! Naw! It's Koontown! What is it, my peoples?!!!"

"KOONTOWN!!!"

"Koontown, USA!!!" he screams. "And right now! As I SPEAK! In Koontown, USA! The police! The National Guard! The FBI and CIA! They are marching down our very STREETS! Knocking down our DOORS! Shooting our GRANDMOTHERS and STRAIGHT A STUDENTS! Singin' 'God Bless America' the ENTIRE time!!!

"Pardon my French here, my peoples—but that is BULLSHIT!!! THEY may be singing, 'God BLESS America!' But yall know, I am SCREAMING, SCREAMING!!! "GOD *DAMN* AMERICA!!!"

The church quakes in cheers, "Amen!"s, hoots, hollers, African war cries. The reverend, drenched in sweat and fatigue, slinks out of the room, wiping his face furiously with his handkerchief.

Willie taps my arm. "Let's go, Vee," he says. I follow.

A rapper with a large, gold cross swinging across his chest jumps up on the altar, a microphone in his hand. Gospel music booms from the band off to the right.

"Fuck tha police
Comin straight from the underground
Young nigga got it bad cuz I'm brown!"

WILLIE AND I find the pastor in a small office behind the altar. He is seated, his feet resting on a little, cheap wooden desk, toweling off beneath a portrait of Black Jesus. Willie knocks and enters, flashing his badge. I don't know why we're here. What this man can possibly have to do with our case. But I trust Willie O'Ree with my life. I enter behind him.

"Detective William O'Ree," my old partner introduces himself. "Koontown Police Department. Homicide Division."

The reverend slowly places his feet on the floor and straightens his rickety, old chair. Recognition flashes in his eyes as they settle on me. He smiles.

Willie points my way. "And this is—"

"Genevieve 'Jon Vee' Noire," he beams. "My goodness, how I have always wanted to meet you."

I can only imagine. I smile in awkward appreciation.

"So," Willie says, "Reverend ...?"

"Booker," he answers. "Crispus Booker."

"Yes, Reverend Booker—"

"Please," the man urges. "Call me 'Cris.'"

"OK, *Cris*," sighs Willie. "That was quite a ... *powerful* sermon you delivered out there."

"Oh," the pastor blushes, "you heard that?"

"Yes. I did," Willie says. "Tell me something. You call yourself, 'The Church of *Racial* Reconciliation.' Is that sermon out there something white folks can reconcile themselves with?"

"Well, that wasn't for *them*, Detective," Reverend Booker pleasantly answers.

"You *do* have white parishioners, don't you?" I ask.

"Oh. *Hundreds*," he answers. "In fact, the Church of Racial Reconciliation is the most *diverse* congregation in America."

"Really?" I marvel.

"But, to be honest," the preacher continues, "our services are *perhaps* the most segregated."

I'm confused. It must show on my face. Reverend Booker smiles patiently at both of us.

"What we at the Church have come to realize," he explains, "is that we Americans don't want to actually *reconcile* our racial notions about each other with each other. No, we rather want those racial notions to be *reaffirmed*."

No. I'm still confused.

"We give people that *reaffirmation*," he continues with an angelic smile, "so they can actually feel *reconciled* with what they already believe—racist or not."

My stymied look turns to scrutiny. I now see that the reverend's close-cropped black hair is indeed course—but straight. His skin is milky with just a *hint* of brown. His features are fine. I originally thought Reverend Crispus Booker was black. Now, I am not so sure. He can be anything. Black? Mixed?

"In other words," the man of the cloth continues, "we give the people what they want."

Puerto Rican? Cuban? Dominican?

"How so ... Cris?" asks Willie.

"Take, for instance, tonight," Cris says, leaning forward in his chair. "Tonight we had a black audience. A *poor*, black audience. They feel under attack. And tonight, with the National Guard moving in, rightfully so. So, I tell them what they want, what they *need* to hear. They go home feeling better—*reaffirmed* in their belief that they are, indeed, an endangered species. That whitey's out to get them.

"If this had been a more ... *bourgeois* black crowd, I would've told them that they have worked hard all their lives. That they are reaping the benefits of said hard work. But they can't let down their guards no matter who's in the White House. Racism is still alive and kicking. And that they have to continue their good works—reaching back to help their poorer brothers and sisters still stuck in the grips of poverty and mental slavery."

Willie nods approvingly.

"African and Caribbean parishioners," Reverend Cris continues. "I tell them that they may be black. But not like *those* blacks. They are working hard, going places. They don't owe anything to anybody. They are *better* than that."

Maybe he's a Haitian "mulatto." Brazilian?

I look up at the Jesus portrait. I can no longer tell what He is, either.

"I'll tell my Arab and North African members that they need to extend the olive branch to their Muslim cousins. For that is the only way to stop the oppression our people face today."

Our people? I guess he could be Libyan. Egyptian? Definitely not Moroccan. Lebanese?

"Latinos. 'Keep your heads down. *La migra* is on your ass. But trouble don't last *siempre, tu sabes*?' Keep hope alive."

No. *Definitely* Cuban.

Jesus now has blonde hair and blue eyes. I need a nap.

"I fill Asians full of that 'model minority' stuff. South Asians, too. Tell them more Americans should follow their example of hard work and dedication to the family and that affirmative action is really *killing* them."

I guess he could be Punjabi. Polynesian?

"And white people," the good reverend sighs, heavily. "I say, 'Look, we've done all we can for *those* people. It's time *they* lift *themselves* up by their *own* boot straps. Just like *our* grandparents did when they emigrated here. Nobody gave *them* a hand-out—which is the furthest from the truth, but it's what they like to hear. *Those* immigrants worked *hard* to get what they got. It's time for those *other* people to do the same, stop asking Uncle Sam to solve all their problems, and stop *bitching*."

All right. I got it. He's Italian.

. . .

Maybe Greek. Hell, Crispus Booker could be *Swedish*, for all I know.

"It seems like you got everybody covered," nods Willie.

"You should hear my Native American sermon," the pastor beams, proudly. "You know, the funny thing is," Cris continues, "if there actually *had* been Caucasians in the audience tonight, they wouldn't have heard *any* of that stuff you did. No, they would've gone away thinking I was railing against affirmative action."

"How is that even possible?" I wonder.

"When it comes to race," the reverend smiles, "people hear only what they *want* to hear."

"Impossible," I object.

"What exactly did *you* hear tonight, Ms. Noire?"

"Exactly what you said."

"And what was that?"

The pastor's smile is so smug, I want to knock it off of him. But I can't. I'm too confused, frankly. I look up. Jesus is black once more. He's smiling omnisciently. A shiver runs through me.

"So, how can I help you, Detective? Ms. Noire?" Reverend Booker asks.

"You already have," admits Willie. "I was just curious about this place."

"Glad to be of service."

Willie starts leading me to the door. He suddenly stops. "You go ahead, Vee. I'll catch up."

"OK."

I head out the door. I turn. I hate to eavesdrop, but …

Willie is suddenly on his knees, his hands folded in prayer. Reverend Booker stands over him, his hand resting atop Willie's short fro.

"What is it, my son?" the pastor breathes, gravely.

"I-I-I don't know, Reverend," Willie confesses. "It's just—just that—look, I grew up in Koontown, right. I'm quite proud of that fact, you know. I'm proud of my *people*. I became a cop to protect them. To show my gratitude. My love. I wanted to give back, to give thanks. For all the things they have given *me*."

"And don't think we don't appreciate that, Detective," Reverend Booker soothes.

"I don't know if they do, though, Reverend," Willie swallows. "Not anymore."

"How so?"

"I don't know. It's—well, things have *changed*. I don't know when. Don't know how. Maybe it was all that Black Flight in the Seventies and Eighties. It's like all those folks took all their money out of the community. And, maybe, they took its *soul*, too.

"It's like … like *they* left and … and Koontown didn't know how to *act* anymore. See, there has always been poverty. Always been crime. But there was always pride, too. And *respect*. It's like folks don't have any *respect* anymore. Respect for each other. Respect for *themselves*.

"Like all the *black* folks left the 'hood. All the *African-Americans*. And all that's left is a bunch of triflin', thievin' …"

"No, no," coos the reverend, patting Willie's head. "I understand. You don't have to say it.

"Look, Detective O'Ree, maybe folks around here don't say it enough, but we *do* appreciate what you're doing for us. We don't show it, but we really do look up to you. You're our hero, Detective. And, in our own strange way, we *do* respect you."

"Thank you, Reverend."

"No problem," he smiles, avuncularly. "But let's face it, Detective O'Ree. Our people are, indeed, troubled. They are under a lot of stress, a lot of strain. And, frankly, under all that pressure, at times, it can get to them. And, admittedly, at times, our people *can* act quite … well, you know … *niggerish*."

Chaptah Fifteen
(Even a broken clock's right twice a day)

"Bitches ain't shit
But hos and tricks
Lick on these nuts and suck the dick"

—*Dr. Dre, Snoop Dogg, Dat Nigga Daz, Kurupt, Jewel, "Bitches Ain't Shit"*

THE WAREHOUSE DISTRICT on Jack Johnson Boulevard seems deserted. Broken street lights, broken windows, near-total blackness, and scurrying rats. I pull up to the address Hustle Beamon has given me for the Übernoggin party. The windows are intact, but they are all blacked-out. I would assume this place was abandoned, too, if it weren't for the throbbing disco music vibrating my Prius. Sylvester and Two Tons of Fun. "You make me feel mi-ighty real!"

I get out of the car and turn on the car alarm.

"likkaniggadik"

There it is again! I look around. Willie pulls his Crown Victoria in the space behind mine. The men don't look too eager to get out of the car, but they eventually do. I have never seen them look so apprehensive. These are men who have stormed doors with known killers on the other side. Yet, right now, the sight of a mouse would probably have them hiking up their skirts. Sandino swallows hard on air.

"Are you all ready?" I ask, a little irritated.

"Sure," Sandino gulps, again.

I move toward the warehouse. Alone. I turn. I glare. They are so tense. I glare harder.

"Oh, all right," Willie surrenders. He moves up to join me. "You stay back, Vee."

"What?"

"Believe me," he adds. "They are *not* gonna want you here."

Sandino, Leadfoot, and Watts push up in front of me. I comply, for now, and trail the men. We take baby steps to the warehouse.

A large, iron door greets us. Above it hangs a sign, "Spitterz Iz Kwitterz!" Willie knocks. Watts, barely six feet himself, tugs at my sleeve. "Get down, woman," he hisses. I crouch down, confused, so I no longer overshadow him. From between the others' shoulders, I see a gun slit open in the door. Words are exchanged. Seconds go by. The heavy iron door finally creaks open. The men hustle themselves and me inside. The music blares. I can see nothing, though.

"So, I *tol'* de Congressman!" I hear from behind. Two elegantly-dressed men in their thirties and Joseph Abboud stand off to the corner with glowing drinks in their hands. One continues, "I said, '*Fuck* dem tax-payin' *bitches*! We *pimps* up in dis *muhfucka*!"

"So, did they fire you?!" the other asks.

"*Hell* naw, *nigga*!" the first one beams. "You lookin' at the new VP a Operations at Goldmann-Sachs's Asia Portfolio!"

The second one is absolutely radiant. He reaches out, grabs the VP by the scruff of his neck, and plants a grand kiss on the former's lips. The VP grabs back, and the two men start pawing at each other, tearing at each other's expensive suits.

I finally rise from my crouch.

"What de *fuck she* doin' here?!" I hear.

I turn. A coal-black mound of man hovers over Willie and the others. Leadfoot and Watts are giants, but they look small in comparison to this behemoth. Willie looks like a malnourished gnat.

"Yall niggas know! Ain't no *bitches* allowed up in *here*!" the mountain roars.

Instinct has me moving up to join my former partner. Fear should have me running as far away as possible. But old habits are hard to break. Willie flashes his badge.

"I don't give a *fuck*, nigga!" the man bellows. "Rules is *rules*! An' dem *muhfuckas* say, 'No! Bitches!'"

The mountain moves. Willie moves.

Thwack!

My partner's right fist lands square in the middle of the big man's jaw. The big man laughs condescendingly.

"Give it a second," Willie instructs.

Suddenly, the big man groans. His eyes roll back in his head. His hands reach out, grab air. His legs buckle, and he is down. I marvel at Willie. He smiles, clutching his right hand. "Now, where the hell is HNIC?"

We look around. Strobe and disco lights streak madly. Otherwise, the place is incredibly dark, incredibly massive. The rapper could be anywhere. There are men lined against the wall—talking to each other, drinking, just staring out of dark sunglasses. There is a small bar area way off to the right. All I see are shadows over there.

There is a railing about five feet in front of us and then nothing but air beyond it. It sounds as though below that air must lie the dance floor. I move to the railing. Alone. Again. I turn back, nod for the "men" to join me. Sandino and the others wave me off. With a shrug, I move onward.

I reach the railing and look down.

OhmiGod!

I turn back, gasping. I rub my eyes, not believing them. I hear chuckling. I turn back and … and … and I look again.

No. It is not a mirage. Not a nightmare.

It is one oily, writhing mass of moaning, screaming, ecstatic black flesh. Every hue and shade of blackness. Hard bodies all. Not a single female in all that mess. Hugging, kissing, licking, sucking, and pumping. All men. Ejaculate flies everywhere. On butts, on backs, on neatly-trimmed beards. I can hear the slurps from here. Drowning out that old Dynasty song booming the sound system. "I don't want to be a freak … but I can't help myself …" It's like none of these men have ever heard of safe sex. Damn you, Cookie Johnson.

I want to turn away. But … but … I can't. HNIC is probably down there, and we need to talk to him. Can't it wait until tomorrow?

…

No. I … I have to look.

I don't see him, though. I do start seeing people I recognize, though. There's my banker. The owner of that revolutionary book store over there on Madhubuti. That fool Sergeant Perkins in a sling I must've given him outside of Funky Dollah Bill's the other night. My hairdresser on Baldwin and Hughes. Well, that's not really a surprise. But still…

I finally give up. I turn away. My eyes hurt. I rejoin the men. They seem unusually bunched together. They're snickering.

"Spitterz Iz Kwitterz!" Sandino guffaws.

"What in the world's going on here?" I ask, rubbing my eyes. "It's like every man in Koontown is here tonight."

"Come on, Vee," smirks Willie, "everybody knows that ninety-five percent of the African-American male population is on the Down-Low."

I knew it. "What does that make you, Willie?" I ask.

"A Five Percenter," he smiles.

"You're a Muslim, O'Ree?" I huff.

"A salaam alaikum," he chirps, raising a power fist.

I look at Leadfoot and Watts. They both shrug. Leadfoot offers, "Me and Maurice are Fruit of Islam on the weekends."

I am beyond belief. "You, Maurice?" I flare. "With a *rib* stand?"

"Hey," he interjects, "God made pork, and pork don't hurt."

I finally turn to Sandino. He looks at me with those gray eyes of his. "What, Vee? I'm Nicaraguan, *chica*."

I rub my eyes again and exhale slowly. "Now," I breathe, "how in the world are we supposed to find HNIC in all that … that … that *that*?"

"He's not down there," I hear. I turn. HNIC's bodyguard, Spade, stands before me.

I nearly faint with relief.

"Where is he then?" I ask.

"Follow me," Spade orders, turns, and starts walking away.

We follow. He skirts us along the wall, passing men yet to join the fray downstairs. Spade leads us down a dark stairwell. We have to step around a couple of loving couples before we reach the ground floor. I try not to look at what's happening on the dance floor, but I can't help myself. I spent a lot of years in the fashion industry, yet I have never seen anything like this.

We finally reach a long line of young men in the latest hip-hop fashions.

Hustle would be happy—I think. His line is fully represented here. Spade finally reaches a door and knocks. A gun slit opens. Darting eyes appear. Whispered words I can't hear over the Jay-Z ("Get, that, dirt off your shoulder") playing are exchanged. The door finally opens.

Spade turns. "Vee," he points.

I step forward. So does Willie. Spade puts a meaty hand on the detective's chest. Willie looks down. I can see the thoughts flashing through my old partner's mind. They are quite violent.

"Sorry, sir," Spade apologizes, respectfully. His tone seems to mollify Willie. The detective visibly relaxes. "This is Übernoggin's lair. I can't let you in."

Willie looks back at Sandino, Leadfoot, and Watts. Their eyes say it all. They contemplate the bum's rush, decide it's not worth it, and finally concede.

"All right," Willie finally says. "We'll be right out here if you need us, Genevieve."

"Just, for the love of God, make it quick, woman!" Sandino yells over the music.

SPADE LEADS ME inside. The door slams quickly behind us. A heavy bolt slides into place. The room is dark but for a single spotlight. In the glare bobs a large black woman's buttocks covered in glitter. I can't quite see, but her head seems to be bobbing as well. Two male legs are spread to either side of the buttocks. I can see the logos on the bottom of the man's sneakers. I faintly hear him groan. Suddenly, the man's hand reaches up and moves to the woman's head. Her hand flicks up and swats it away before it can settle on her auburn weave, which I can now see cascades out in a five-foot radius.

"What in the world is going on here?" I huff.

Spade smiles, devilishly. "Übernoggin," he answers. "Come on, Ms. Noire."

He leads me around the edge of the room. My eyes adjust to the darkness. Suddenly, I see that the walls are lined with men in business suits—some white, some Asian, but mostly black and Latino. They stare intently on the scene with pens, paper, and Blackberrys poised. They stare at the couple on the floor as though their lives depend on the two. I'm afraid to see if any are masturbating. I wouldn't doubt it, though.

Spade takes me to an empty chair, gestures for me to sit. I do. He disappears into the darkness.

"Hello, Ms. Noire."

"Kelvin," I return.

HNIC is seated next to me in khakis, Polo shirt, and dark sunglasses. He has a bag of licorice on his lap. "How you doing tonight?" he asks.

"I have never seen a single pornographic movie," I declare. "After tonight, I doubt I ever will."

"Don't think of it as pornography," he suggests. "Think of it as the future."

I turn to look at him. "What?"

"That's Übernoggin over there," he points. "You ever see a fortune teller? How they read tea leaves? Bones? Tarot cards?"

"Of course."

"Well, Übernoggin reads semen."

I feel my jaw go slack. My mouth gape.

"Seriously," continues the rapper, earnestly. "I don't know how she does it, but she's been servicing every up and, well, coming rapper and producer for

the last two decades now. And, I guess, by the taste, the texture of their spooge,
she can tell you the trajectory of their careers."

I'm still speechless.

"It's incredible, really," HNIC confesses. "But the woman's never wrong.
You noticed all the men along the wall?"

"Yes."

"Record execs," he informs. "Every single one of them. Übernoggin only
has these jams of hers twice a year. Every aspiring rapper from around the
world lines up. She sucks them off. Tells us where their careers are headed.
Then, the labels bid, depending on their needs. And Übernoggin gets a healthy
finder's fee."

"Sounds like a scam," I finally manage to say.

"You'd think," HNIC admits. "But the woman's *never* wrong. That's how
Dope Beat ended up with Niggassippee."

"Did she predict his death?"

"You know, come to think of it," he scratches his hairless chin. "She *may*
have. I don't know. I wasn't there. But that sounds about right. Licorice?
Asparagus?"

I wave him off. He crams three licorice twists in his mouth.

"What did Frau Übernoggin predict for you?" I ask.

The young man grins. "Never needed her," he boasts. He finally swallows,
then produces a bottle of Maalox and takes a sip. "You should read her books—
"

"She's written a book?"

"She's the most successful negro in the biz," he says. "*Video Ho* and *Video
Ho Tellz Mo'* spent over a year each on every Best Sellers' List you can think
of."

"Unbelievable."

"Not really," he shrugs. "She outed *a lot* of celebs in both of them, but they're really both heart-warming tales about a single mother trying to raise her son the best way she knows how."

"Serially fellating rappers and producers?" I ask, incredulously.

"Sure, that kid's gonna be fucked up knowin' Moms here done sucked every brother's dick this side of the Nile," he admits. "But at least he'll be able to afford the therapy. Think of all those poor kids out there who can't."

I don't want to. The man being serviced by our hostess is reaching climax. He moans, groans. He thrashes around wildly, trying desperately not to grab hold of the woman giving him so much pleasure.

"The money shot," HNIC smirks. He leans forward in his seat. "Pun intended."

"AAAARRRRRGGGGGHHHHHHHH!!!"

Übernoggin immediately jumps to her feet. She is in nothing but a G-string and glitter. The fat ripples all down her backside.

"I said not de face, nigga!" she screeches. She lifts a meaty leg and stomps her foot down on the aspiring rapper's privates. He immediately doubles over in agony, screaming. "Trick bitch!!! Where my towel at, *muhfucka?!*"

"likkaniggadik"

"Did you hear that?" I ask.

"You did?" HNIC asks, in return.

"likkaniggadik"

"Oh, shit," HNIC yelps. He suddenly looks worried. He grabs my arm. "Let's go."

"Wha—"

He stands, pulls me up with him, and starts dragging me briskly toward the exit. "Spade!"

"How many times I tell yall fools?!" Übernoggin continues to storm. "Neva! In de! Face!!! Now, what you lookin' at, nigga?!"

I turn. A sinewy, tall black man, two pounds away from being malnourished, stands before Übernoggin, staring at her through dark sunglasses. A scowl plastered on his dark face. He suddenly whips off his glasses. A shock goes through the woman. She stands rigidly still, erect. She seems paralyzed, hypnotized, staring into the man's eyes.

What the—?!

Two tendrils whip out of the man's eyes and smash into Übernoggin's own eyes. The woman goes limp, held up only by the tendrils impaling her skull. I hear the flush of liquids. Something sounds like it's sizzling.

I run.

So does everybody else. Chairs scrape and tumble. Men scream and stumble. Fall. Chaos. A mad rush to the door.

Spade grabs me. He grabs HNIC. The big bodyguard punches, smacks, kicks people out of the way. We reach the door. Spade rips the bolt from the door. He throws the door open. We plunge into an even greater chaos.

"AAAAHHHHHHHHHH!!!!!"

A naked brother runs straight at HNIC, Spade, and me, sheer terror in his eyes. A black shadow swoops.

"likkaniggadik"

The man's swept into the air, screaming. Spade reaches out. Too late. The man and shadow disappear up into the disco lights.

"Pull up to the bumper baby,
In your long, black limousine"

"Damn," Spade hisses.

Men scream all around us. Flesh smacks against flesh in flaccid horror as each man scrambles for his own life. Men push us from behind as they charge out of Übernoggin's lair. My eyes dart frantically. I can't find Willie and the others.

"Willie?!" I scream. "Sandino?!!!"

"Vee!!!" I hear—I think.

I see nothing, though.

HNIC snatches my arm. "Let's get outta here!!!"

"I can take care of myself!" I protest.

"Not against *dese* muhfuckas, you cain't!" Spade screams. A strange tension constricts around his dark sunglasses. It makes me believe him.

"OK," I surrender.

HNIC pulls me forward.

"likkaniggadik"

"AARRRGGHHHH!!!"

Spade clubs and punches a path through the naked throng to the staircase. Men are clawing at each other, slipping and slapping at one greased body after another. Spade grabs shoulders and flings brothers away like discarded trash. We climb doggedly over bodies. Screams mark our every step.

Spade suddenly stops. We are almost at the top. He straightens and tenses. An emaciated man stands at the top of the stairs. Limp, naked bodies lay strewn at his feet. The wraith suddenly whips off his sunglasses. His eyes … they glow *yellow*?

"Don't look!" HNIC barks. He buries my head in his chest.

"Bring it, *muhfucka*!" I hear Spade cry.

"likkaniggadik"

Whoosh!

Thud!!!

Two heavy bodies tumble past us, knocking us down on top of several naked men. Hands everywhere. Hands scratching, clawing, punching, pawing. Screams all around. The rank stench of musk and terror suffocating. I cough. I plead. Hands yank me to my feet. HNIC looks at me—concern tearing at his eyes. He has lost his sunglasses.

"You a'ight?!"

I nod. "I think."

He pulls me up the stairs. We claw our way to the top. "Spade?!" I look back. HNIC's bodyguard has the wraith by the throat. The thing hisses, thrashes, its eye tentacles thrashing madly in the air. Spade suddenly flashes a Desert Eagle revolver, slams the gun into the thing's mouth.

BOOM!!!

Blood, brains, skull, teeth. A crimson mushroom cloud balloons out of the back of the thing's head. It goes limp. Spade throws it down. He looks up at us. "Go! Go! Go!!!"

I run. HNIC runs. We club and kick everyone in our path.

BOOM! BOOM! BOOM! Rat-a-tat! Tat!

Gunshots tattoo the warehouse. That must be Willie and the boys, but I can't see them.

"likkaniggadik"

BOOM! BOOM!

I continue to run, wishing, for the first time in a year, that I actually had a gun.

WE FINALLY REACH my bulletproof Prius. Bodies are everywhere. Running madly. Swooping through the air. Strewn all along the cracked pavement—lifeless, bloodless.

One of those things is hovering over a body right now. Its eye tentacles buried deep inside the sockets of its victim. The tentacles pulsate with life. Slurp, slurp.

"Come on, Vee!" HNIC screams.

A throng of crazed nudity surrounds my car. They yank frantically at the door handles, pound on the glass, scream to the heavens for mercy and deliverance. HNIC hops up and slides across the car's hood. He reaches the driver's side door and starts pounding on the men who are pounding it. I rush up behind him as he finally clears the way.

My keys jingle in my hand. Calm down, Vee. Calm *down!*

I finally hit the Unlock button. The locks click open. "Thank God!" a nude brother dives toward the door, pushing me out of the way. I elbow him in the back. He collapses. I open the door, slam him in the head. He groans. I push, push, PUSH! him out of the way and get in. HNIC slams the door shut behind me.

"What?!" I scream.

He holds up a finger. A hand lands on his shoulder. He spins, strikes. He jumps back on the hood and leaps to the other side. Men are pounding the windows all around me. I breathe, slow it down, clear my eyes, my thoughts. I push in the ignition. The car starts.

Men scream as HNIC peels them from my car. They fall away slowly. Men are suddenly yanked from the back as well. HNIC finally rips open the door and dives inside. He slams the door shut. A back door opens and shuts. I look. Spade heaves breathlessly in the backseat.

"Gits ta gittin', woman!!!" he pants.

I punch the accelerator. Brothers jump on and bounce off the Prius's bulletproof armor. I gain speed. They fall away and begin melting away into the night. The speedometer springs to forty-five, fifty, sixty.

THUD!!!

The roof reverberates. A body ricochets off it and lands in the road in front of us. I smash the accelerator into the floor. The engine purrs. The headlights catch a wraith in its glare. It springs to its feet, turns, and flashes a scowl. Its eyes are mad, yellow. I bare down on it.

THUD!!!

The thing bounces off the front fender, against the windshield, into the air. I look in the rearview mirror. It struggles to its feet. A black SUV barrels over it, barely noticing the body it has crushed. The truck's headlights glow menacingly in my mirror.

"Who's that?" I ask.

HNIC turns. "Waldron and Roach?" he asks Spade.

"Shit," I hear the bodyguard. "You carrying?"

"Just the .22."

"Give it here."

I see HNIC move frantically out of the corner of my eye. "Who are they?" I ask.

"The hip-hop cops," Spade informs. "Try an' lose dem bitches!"

I'm a cop. Was a cop. Will always be a cop. But I owe these men tonight. I whip a right onto Dessalines. My tires squeal. I struggle not to hit the sidewalk. Fail. The car jumps the curb.

Lamp post!

"Ahhh!!!"

I fight the wheel. Strain the cords in my neck. Engine, tires protest. I jump off the curb. Exhale. Right myself onto the street. Punch the accelerator.

I look in the rearview mirror. The SUV struggles with the turn. The headlights slide in my mirror. Slide. Keep sliding. Out of sight.

"What the—?" I gasp.

Suddenly, another pair of headlights appear. They make the turn easily.

"Are there more hip-hop cops after you?" I ask.

"No," HNIC answers. "Only Waldron and Roach."

"Then, who—?"

"Oh shit!" Spade yells. "Go! Go! Go!"

I strain, trying to push the accelerator through the floor.

"Here, K!"

Suddenly, HNIC has the .22 back in his hands. "What's this gonna do, Spade?" he asks, exasperated. "*Annoy* them?"

"You gotta git us outta here, gurl!!!" Spade roars.

They roll their windows down. Air rushes in. I concentrate on the road. HNIC and Spade lean out of their windows and start firing. The Desert Eagle roars. The .22 titters. I hazard a look in the rearview. Bullets spark off the SUV. Its windshield shatters. Gun flashes come from the pursuing vehicle.

Ping! Ping! PingPingPingPing!

I have got to get us out of here.

"Ha! Ha!" Spade cheers. "We *bulletproof*, niggas!!!"

Got it!

I race down Dessalines. Past Rainey, Wilson, Wideman. A red light flashes before me. I ignore it. I screech a right turn. HNIC and Spade scream, teetering out of their windows, still firing.

"Sorry!" I apologize.

I tear the Prius down John Wayne Boulevard. We're out of Koontown now. On the edge of Giuliani. The SUV still follows. Starts gaining. I push. Fifty-five, sixty, seventy, seventy-five!

Sirens scream. Just as I expected. I look in the rearview mirror. One, two, three, four, *five* police cruisers give chase. I hear helicopter blades over the bullets bouncing off my car. A spotlight washes over us from above.

The SUV doesn't care. It continues to gain on us. Their gun flashes split between us and the pursuing police cruisers. The police return fire. The night fills with bullets. This is not going the way I expected.

Think, Vee! Think!

Right!

I whip the car right—back toward Koontown. "Get back inside! Now!" I yell.

"What?!" HNIC screams, ducking his head back into the car.

"We're going back into Koontown!"

"Oh, shit!"

The rapper dives back into his seat. "Spade! Get back inside! C'mon!" he urges, desperately, as his window mechanically climbs toward closing.

Spade settles back into his seat. "What the—?"

"Welcome to Koontown!"

I drive beneath the billboard. We're greeted with a barrage of automatic gunfire. I flinch but keep driving. Sparks fly everywhere. Bullets bounce willy-nilly. There's an explosion.

I gasp. Slam the brakes. The Prius spins to a halt.

We struggle to catch our breaths. I open my eyes. The SUV is in flames. The result of a rocket-propelled grenade's direct hit. The police cruisers are parked safely two blocks away. The GPD never, ever ventures into Koontown. We're safe. Finally.

A sigh of relief. HNIC looks impressed. Spade laughs.

"Damn, you good, gurl!" the bodyguard hoots.

I smile.

"likkaniggadik"

THWACK!

The car's hit. It flies. Turns.

CRASH!!!!

The hood slams into a brick wall and slides to the ground.

My head. I'm … groggy. Can't …

I groan. I'm foggy. I'm trapped, pinned. The car's on its side. Only the shattered driver's side window separates me from the sidewalk. HNIC groans, struggling to pull himself off of me.

"likkaniggadik"

Loud, metallic tear. Air. Something has ripped the passenger door off its hinges.

"Oh, shit!" HNIC gasps.

A sinewy, black arm thrusts into the car. Its hand grabs the belt loop on HNIC's khakis and yanks. The rapper screams. He goes flying into the night. I hear a distant thump.

I scramble madly. There's no place to go.

"likkaniggadik"

I look … up. There's one of those … those things. I hear a groan somewhere. The beast … it whips off its sunglasses. Its … its eyes … they're … yellow? They glow … glow like … fire …

I … I … I …

"Ugggghhhhhh…"

Chaptah Siksteen

"Fuck the world, fuck my moms and my girl
My life is played out like a Jheri curl
I'm ready to die"

—Notorious B.I.G., "Ready to Die"

THE WIND SCREAMS in my ears. Pounds, penetrates, splits my eardrums with every sigh. I can barely think. The noise shatters my skull. To even think about opening eyes causes agony. Breath is a struggle. It should be an impossibility. I am dead. I saw the eyes. I saw their glow. I know what happens afterwards. The tentacles, the acid. The burn, the sucking. Body turned to dead husk in the literal blink of an eye.

But the wind. The pain. I am not dead. I can't be. There is no pain in death. Is there?

I open my eyes. Death is a bright, sunshiny day in a verdant meadow. The green is Technicolor. Nothing found in real life.

Death is a dream. With brilliant colors and violent wind.

The gale continues to pound. My head is filled with static. I can't think—only see. And the wind is nothing. The green grass rests peacefully at my feet. The flowers are still. A baobab tree stands sentinel atop a hill before me. Its massive trunk sprouts stoutly from the earth. Not a single leaf ruffles from its sturdy limbs.

I look through the sun's burning rays. They are strong enough to blind. Yet, I can see. Though there is nothing to see. Not a single human in sight. Only grass and flowers and that giant of a tree.

It calls to me.

Genevieve Noire.

That is my name. It knows me. The dead have no names. But the baobab knows mine. It is calling me. I don't seem to have a choice.

My legs move without me. They glide easily against the gale. The hill is nothing. I move quickly, weightless. I am before the tree before I realize I want to be before it.

> *"... like a ship without a sail,*
> *Like a boat without a rudder..."*

A woman's rich contralto reaches my ears through the wind. I look. No one in sight. The baobab's trunk is as round as a house. I walk the base, letting the song guide me.

> *"...like a kite without a tail ..."*

Finally, I find her. A big, bulky black woman sits on a stump. She's dressed like one of those slaves in *Gone with the Wind*. Her dress is threadbare and tattered. Her apron is stained with fresh blood. Her handkerchief wrapped tightly around her nappy head.

> *"...like the Spring without the Fall,*
> *There's only one thing worse in this universe..."*

A small campfire burns at her bare feet. She's lurched over it, poking at a skillet with a wooden spoon.

"Aunt Jemima?" I croak.

She looks up, beaming a smile that blinds. "I'se in town, honey!" She lifts a china plate stacked high with flapjacks. "Pancakes?" she proffers.

I can't protest. My legs move forward, stop at her feet. My knees bend, my hands reach out. I am seated before her with the plate and a fork in my hands.

Aunt Jemima smiles grandly. Her teeth are perfect and as white as ivory. She holds up a plastic bottle. "Maple syrup?" she asks.

"Real maple syrup?" I ask.

"Wif sodium benzoate, sodium hexametaphosphate, caramel color, an' high fructose co'n syrup, a co'se," she beams.

"Of course," I mumble. I eat greedily. The pancakes are gritty—buckwheat. The syrup is tinny. But I can't stop. My fork stabs, impales, lifts, shovels in and out of my mouth over and over again. A blur.

"Whoa! Slow down, gal!"

I can't. I want to. I swear I do. But my body won't let me. My hands whip more pancake into my mouth before I can even swallow. I start to cry from the sheer terror of it.

Please … stop …

Aunt Jemima whips a meaty hand into the air. The pancakes, plate, and fork disappear. The food vanishes from my mouth. The dead don't eat. Right?

"I need to get home," I finally manage to say, voice cracking, mouth desert dry.

"But you *is* home, chile," Aunt Jemima insists. Her voice is so warm, so gentle and comforting, so motherly, I just want to curl up in her arms, rest my head on her ample bosom, and weep.

"No," I counter. "This is *not* my home. You are *not* my mother."

"Co'se not, chile." She smiles rivers of warmth into my soul. "I'se yo' auntie, gal."

"Trust me, nobody in my family's looked like you since 1821," I scoff. "We have the portraits *and* the photographs to prove it."

The smile disappears in quivers. Aunt Jemima tries to maintain her dignity, but she can't. Her mouth quakes. It starts blubbering. Tears trickle, then stream. The woman lets out an ear-shattering wail. Leaves from the baobab rattle and fall to the ground. We are showered in green.

I swallow the lump in my throat. I scoot to her and bury my head in the folds of her ratty apron. The blood comes off on my face. "I'm so sorry," I plead. "I don't know what made me say that. Please forgive me, auntie. *Please!*"

She pats my head. Then starts stroking my hair, playing with it, massaging it through her gnarled fingers. "Yo' hair is so *fine*, gal!" she marvels. "How you do dat?"

"Miscegenation," I whimper.

"Hmm," she voices. "Now I don't feel so bad."

I have no clue what she means by that. I suddenly look up at her, tears in my green eyes. "Am I dead?"

"Could be," she dodges.

"But, here … I don't belong here."

"All my chillums is welcome home, chile."

"No, no, no!" I scream. "It's not my time! I know it! It's not!" I start hyperventilating. "I have got to get home! I–I –I have *got* to stop those … those *things*!!!"

She reaches down, puts her sandpaper finger to my chin, and lifts my head to hers. She gapes at me.

"And dem *eyes*," she breathes.

"Yeahyeahyeah," I snap. "Just tell me how I get back to Koontown. I need to get back."

She studies my face. My skin starts itching under the scrutiny. I feel like a piece of meat. I can only imagine what's going through this woman's mind.

"Well, chile," she smiles brightly, "anytime I'se wanna go home, I jus' do de Hambone."

"Seriously?"

She smiles and opens her mouth even wider to release her contralto. "'Hambone, Hambone, where you been?'"

I chuckle and sing along. "'Round the corner, and back agin'—'"

"*Niggers* do the Hambone!"

Aunt Jemima and I gasp and turn. My Daddy stands in the bright sunlight. He is tall, statuesque, and bulging with rage. His light skin glows crimson like a second sun. I swallow hard. I'm in trouble.

He moves faster than lightning. His hand snatches my collar.

"*Noires* do not!!!" he yells.

Daddy yanks. I fall to the ground. He growls, furious, like a beast. A demon. His eyes glare red. I scream. He pulls me away from my auntie.

"My baby!!!" she wails. "Lawd hab mercy!!!"

I kick. I claw at his hands. No good. He's too strong. Dust billows around my dragging body.

"Stop that *right now!*" my father roars. "You're coming with me, Genevieve!"

"But, Daddy!" I screech. "Daddy! You're *dead*!!!"

Chaptah Sebenteen

"My neck, my back
Lick my pussy and my crack"

—*Khia, "My Neck, My Back"*

DESPITE WHAT A lot of people say and believe, Koontown has a long, proud history. A long, proud American history.

Like the rest of this country, Koontown is built on Indian land. Nobody knows which tribe—though every woman here with "good" hair claims to have a Cherokee princess hanging in her family tree.

When Europeans started encroaching on their lands, the native tribe banded behind one Chief John Killacracka, who, unfortunately, lived up to his name. In their first midnight raid, Chief John killed exactly *one* Caucasian before dying in a hail of arquebus fire. After that, the colonists took their revenge, slaughtering every man, woman, and child with buckshot and smallpox, and claimed the land for themselves.

Eventually, all this territory fell into the hands of one family, the Cromwells. They ruled ruthlessly for centuries. Thousands of slaves died under their yoke. They whipped. They starved. They fathered generations of tragic mulattoes. And they grew rich beyond measure.

A slave revolt ended their reign in 1875. The Cromwells neglected to tell their illiterate slaves that a civil war had been fought, the Emancipation Proclamation become law, and that they had actually been freed a decade earlier. When these slaves found out, they were more than a bit perturbed. They exorcised that perturbation on Jessup Cromwell's skull with a hatchet. The rest of the family's skulls fared no better. The slaves had been *very* perturbed.

The emancipated laughed with glee, awash in their former master's blood. They cackled and heckled the man as he crawled blindly toward hell's gates. Brains and blood exposed to the heavens, the young Cromwell choked out his final words:

"Always knew there were too many damned *coons* around here."

The slaves didn't know if the man had been referring to them or the thriving raccoon population on his pine tree plantation. It didn't matter, though. They loved it. The new town erected on Cromwell lands had a new name.

"Coontown."

It's a name that stuck until the 1920s. It was the time of the Renaissance. The New Negro. Marcus Garvey. Colored folks were achieving, striving. They had a newfound pride in themselves, their history. They demanded dignity. Rights. They protested vigorously for the right to have 'negro' spelled with a capital N. People died in the streets. They were lynched. But eventually, they won. "Negroes" could hold their heads high, knowing when white folks wrote, "No Negroes Allowed," they had to do it in uppercase. In honor of this Civil Rights victory, "Coontown" became "Negrovillea." Flowers strewn the streets in mad celebration.

Negrovillea had its ups and downs, its booms and busts. But through its entire history, it had its own businesses, its own leaders, and its own culture.

The barbershop quartet, the blues, ragtime, jazz, rock 'n' roll. They all had their births here. People flocked from around the world to partake in Negrovillea's culture. To revel in it. Celebrate its "jungle savagery." To study and copy it, and eventually to adopt it as their own.

But that all changed with the Civil Rights era. "Integration" was the word of the day. Black Flight went Concord. Black people with money could not leave fast enough, flocking to Sherwood Forest and the surrounding suburbs. Restaurants, clubs, doctors' and dentists' offices, law firms. They were all shuttered up, abandoned—to eventually be replaced with pawn shops, check-cashing places, and liquor upon liquor store. What had been a thriving metropolis became urban decay.

Boys no longer grew up to be doctors, lawyers, and Pullman porters. They soon aspired to become pimps, playas, and NBA stars. The girls no longer wanted to grow to become nurses and teachers. They grew to become pregnant.

"It was that damned Moynihan Report," the activist Ashanti Moor once railed at me.

"What?"

"Daniel Patrick Moynihan," Ashanti spat. "He comes out with that report in the '60s telling the world how triflin' black folks are. The drugs, the violence, the out-of-wedlock births. Like white folks weren't doing the same things. But he goes on to say it was all *black* folks. That it was a black thing, and white folks needed to understand. But they couldn't possibly understand. They weren't *black*. They weren't *niggers*."

I didn't understand. I barely understood anything the man ever talked about. I'm from the suburbs. But I was smitten with Ashanti Moor. My incomprehension never stopped me from listening to whatever the man had to say—in *rapt* attention.

"See, Vee," he continued. "Society is nothing but an agglomeration of social agreements. We all stop on red because we *agree* that red means stop. We agree not to put our elbows on the table because that is not proper etiquette. All up and down every society—in matters large and small—we all agree on how to conduct ourselves. Society couldn't function any other way."

That made sense enough. I must've shook my head because he went on.

"So then, this Moynihan Report comes out, right? And he's like, 'Look how these niggers act.' Fuckin' like jungle bunnies, gettin' high *all* the damned time, killin' each other. White folks wring their hands for a minute. Johnson starts all these programs. Nixon implements some, cuts others. And you siddity negroes were like, 'Yeah, look at these niggers. Peace! I'm out!'"

"My father was police here," I protested.

Ashanti smiled, wryly. I wanted to be offended, but that smile … those eyes … they just drew me deeper into his tirade.

"And the Left Behind," he continued. "The negroes who couldn't afford a Sherwood Forest *mortgage*, they look at all the abandoned businesses, the loss of jobs. They look at all those white folks wringing their hands, all those federal programs, how their *own people* jetted on they black asses, and they look at that *report*. And they're like, 'You right, Massa Dan, suh, we *is* niggas. We best start actin' acco'dingly.'"

"All because of this report?" I asked, skeptically.

"Before that report," Ashanti fumed, "black out-of-wedlock births were at around twelve percent. *Twelve percent*, Vee. Now, they're at seventy. Gangs used to be like Jets and Sharks shit. Brothers dancing, snapping their fingers, hitting each other upside the head with chains and two-by-fours. Now, they got AK-47s. And then, when the government started shipping *crack* into the 'hood, that was all she wrote."

He leaned over the table and grabbed my hand. A wave of electricity surged through me. We were at the famous Chinese check-cashing restaurant, Mr. Ching-Ching's. I was afraid I was blushing before all those people, but they were too busy digging into their teriyaki chitterlings to notice my embarrassment.

"That's why I'm on this campaign, baby," Ashanti confessed, vehemently. His eyes seared my flesh. So much knowledge, so much passion. At that moment, I could see myself spending the rest of my life beside Mr. Ashanti Moor. "Our people, we've been 'niggas' for too long, Genevieve. We've been shootin' up, shootin' sperm, and shootin' each other, all in the name of being real 'niggas.' And people *believe* that bullshit, too. They believe that's all we are. But, Vee, we are so much *more*, baby."

"So," I swallowed, "we're coons?"

"Hey, now." He stiffened in his chair, releasing his hold on my hand. He pointed angrily. "My *daddy* was a coon. *His* daddy was a coon. His daddy and his daddy and *his* daddy. We been coons ever since the Pilgrims chained us to Plymouth Rock.

"You forget. It was *coons* who built this country. *Coons* fought in the Revolution and every war since. It was *coons* who killed that racist rapist Jessup Cromwell. *Coons* fought and *died* for their freedom.

"It was *negroes* who fought for integration," Ashanti continued. "*Blacks* who embraced that shit. And *African-Americans* who lavish in it now. And they *all* want to forget that it was the *coon* who got them there. And, whether they like it or not, it is the *coon* who will ultimately set us free.

"But not just *any* coon," Ashanti thundered. "Naw, Jon Vee. It's a new breed of *coon*. A *super* coon. Educated, strong, a *militant* coon with an AK in one hand and a thesaurus in the other. The *übercoon*! With a *Kay*! Sissy!"

It was a powerful speech. Ashanti Moor was a powerful man. He had me believing. The entire town believing. He made Mayor Clarence 36-24-36 X believe. He even got the mayor to change "Negrovillea" back to "Koontown"— with a *Kay*! Sissy!

There was no telling what Ashanti Moor could have accomplished. He could've possibly been the nation's first black president. He most definitely could have been my husband.

But none of us ever got a chance to find out. One tragic Sunday, when he was giving a fair-housing speech at Mt. Zion AME Church, a man jumped up from the middle of the crowd, shouted, "Get yo' dick outta my ass!" and gunned Ashanti Moor down at the pulpit. He had been pursuing me forever. I had been reluctant, that Paris night with Gianni constantly barring my way to something greater. But I had finally given in. Finally admitted to myself that I loved Ashanti. I kissed him just before he went to speak in front of that church, and they gunned him down. Right there. That day. In cold blood.

It was a singular loss to the city, the country, the world. And, of course, to me. Ashanti was a singular man. I had never seen a man with such knowledge and passion and charisma. I had never seen such determination, drive, and raw power. I had never seen a man whose eyes burned with all of that. Eyes that could hold you in their sway, that could burn their fire into you and make that fire yours. Eyes that could burn with such passion and focus, joy and love.

I had never seen eyes like that before I had met Ashanti Moor. I thought I would never see them again after we buried the man. But I have. I did. Last night. And those eyes belonged to Kelvin Cleghorne.

HNIC.

I FLOAT SOMEWHERE between consciousness and sleep. In, out. In, out. I am in a place I cannot recognize. It is Africa. It is not Africa. America. But far from the United States. My memories are foggy. My head, a cloud. I should be in pain. But, for some reason, I am numb to it all.

There are things I can remember. The down-low party. The penises and sperm. Übernoggin. Her death. Testicles. I remember bullets and John Wayne. There was an explosion, I think. There were tentacles … and those eyes. But there is a solid, black void. A space, a time I simply cannot remember.

I twist and turn. I am in sleep. And there are images—hazy, fuzzy images—that dance along that ebony cloud. Blood, cuts, scratches, gashes. I am shattered and splintered. I should be dead. I should be eating buckwheat pancakes beneath a baobab tree.

But there is Kelvin. There is Spade. Grey, crying in the distance. Wailing. A mournful song emanating from her crotch. There is a bed—her bed. And mirrors. And I see …

I see Kelvin. Looming over me. I am nude, shattered. There is blood. There are cuts. And scratches. And gashes. And Kelvin and his eyes and his mouth. And that mouth is voracious. It is over me, on me, all over me. There is no place it has not touched, a crevice it has not explored.

And I tingle. All over. It is fog. A pleasure fog. I groan and moan and celebrate in its tantalizing nature. It is not real. It is only a dream. It is not real. It is not sexual. Yet, it heals. There was blood. And cuts and scratches and gashes. But they are no more. They were a dream. I am whole. Even the gash on my hand from the saw grass is healthy and pink.

BOOM!

An explosion. I wake, gasping. I'm in Grey's bed. Alone. I look up. I stare back at myself in the ceiling mirror. I am fully clothed and confused. I have no clue what happened to me last night. No idea how I got here. And I can't even begin to imagine why everything smells like grape Kool-Aid and alcohol.

I get up and take a shower.

THERE IS A jumble of thoughts muddling my head that even a good, hot shower can't seem to clear up. It all has to do with Kelvin Cleghorne. I simply cannot reconcile what I saw last night with what I've been hearing and reading about the gangsta rapper.

The young man I saw last night was strong, determined. He was heroic. He saved my life—of that I am positive. The Kelvin Cleghorne in my dreams ...

Well, anyway, how can those two men jibe with the drug-trafficking, murdering, traffic-violating HNIC I've been hearing about? How can this be the same man who recorded "Bitch! Ho! Bitch! Ho!" and "African-America (Nigga, Nigga, Nigga)"? How can he be the same person behind all these murdered rappers? Can he be simultaneously controlling these blood-sucking creatures and be at war with them? If he were the former, wouldn't he have let me die last night? Wouldn't he have thrown me in with Übernoggin to have my life sucked out of me? Wouldn't he have, most of all, saved his own skin and not have been concerned in the least with mine?

But he didn't. Instead, he grabbed me in Übernoggin lair. He and Spade fought to save not only their own lives, but mine as well. And while I can't be certain, I think they brought me back to my office last night. They had fought while I drove. That made sense. That was self-preservation. But they didn't need to bring me back here. They could have left me in my car—my poor, shattered, bullet-proof baby—to die. But I'm sure they did not. I am almost certain that they did not.

Could that dream have been real? Kelvin's eyes? His tongue?

I look down at my hand. The gash *is* gone. It *is* healed.

I swallow hard. I shut off the shower, the smell of grape Kool-Aid totally gone. I towel myself, go down to the basement for some fresh clothing, and quickly dress. None of this makes sense, and it needs to. Quick. Those things are terrorizing the city. The National Guard is occupying it. People are dying as I dress.

I need to find Willie. I need to solve this thing. I need for the world to make sense again.

OF COURSE, IT only gets more confusing as I climb the stairs to my office.

There is Grey. At my desk. Typing? She couldn't actually be working, could she?

"What's going on here?" I ask, my voice gravelly.

"Oh, Lawd!" Grey wails. She shoots up from her chair, circles the desk, and bounces her mighty girth my way. I cringe. She hugs me. I can hardly breathe.

"You OK, gurl! You OK!" she screeches in my ear. I pull away. She grabs me by the shoulders, examines me, spins me around, examines me some more. "Oh, Lawd! I di'n't think you was gonna make it, gurl! But here you is!"

"How did I get here?" I ask, turning back to face her.

"I done nursed you all *night*! Cold compresses! Aspirin, an' shit! An' here you is!"

I look my cousin in her eyes. They are bloodshot and puffy. Their bags weigh down her entire face. For the first time in my life, I actually believe my cousin is telling the truth. My cousin ...

I guess we *are* family, after all.

I smile. "How did I get here?"

"Dat nigga, HNIC, brung you here," she smiles, coyly. "Dat nigga *fine*. I di'n't know you knew his ass."

"I don't."

"Coulda fooled me, Vee," Grey counters. "De way he was fussin' ova you, an' shit. Den he had me an' dat nigga, Spade, leave you two alone upstairs fo', like, a *hour*. Speakin' a Spade. How can I git *dat* nigga's dick in *me*?"

"Give me a rest," her vagina grumbles.

"You shut up!" Grey shouts at her torso. "It been like a *day* since I had me some!"

"Where's Night?" I ask.

Grey shrugs. "Fuck dat nigga. Up an' disappear cuz my coochie laugh at his stank ass."

"Fuck the fool if he can't take a joke," her vagina adds.

I can't believe I'm starting to think this is normal. I point at my computer. "So, what were you doing over there? Building your farm?"

"Naw, gurl," Grey chuckles. "Been writin' a novel. Three, actually."

"You?" I ask. "Writing a novel?"

"Three," Grey corrects me.

"*I've* been writing them," her stuff corrects her. "This bitch hasn't written a thing in her life."

I look at Grey. I know my anger shows. She looks down, sheepishly. "What about all those college papers you had to write?" I bark.

"You know …" Grey starts hemming and hawing. "You know how it is, Genevieve. Make a nigga cum, he bound to do anything fo' a sista. So, I suck a few dicks, get me a couple papers wrote."

I groan.

"I got straight As, gurl!" Grey screams. "What's de problem?!"

Yes. We are family, I have to remind myself.

"So now you—and your vagina—have started writing novels. How did all this come about?"

"Dat disk you dropped off," Grey chirps. "'Nigga Narrativez.' Makes it all easy. You jus' type in a few things here an' dere. Damned thing damn near writes itself."

"I punch it up a little," adds her honey pot, proudly.

"When Night's punk ass di'n't show up," Grey continues, "I was bo'ed as *hell*. An' my gurl here suggested we try de disk. An' we *good*, Vee. Wrote three books real quick, sent 'em off to Koonington Press, an' dey gonna publish dem shits *today*. Dey say we a mix 'tween Toni Morrison, Iceberg Slim, *and* Zane," Grey marvels. "Who Toni Morrison, cuz?"

"She's a novelist," I inform, a little queasy. "The first African-American to win the Nobel Prize for Literature."

"Oooh!" Grey coos. "You think I can git me one a *dem*?"

"Sure. Why not?" I shrug. "Look, I need to get out of here. Find Willie."

"He in Koontown Kounty Hospital," my cousin informs.

"What?!"

Grey reaches over to the desk and flashes a bunch of pink slips of paper at me. "I took messages!" she beams. "Willie's at KKH. HNIC called a couple times, too, seein' if you's a'ight."

"You ... you took messages?"

My eyes feel warm. I might just be about to cry. Grey smiles warmly.

"We family, gurl," she soothes. "Family take care a dey own."

I swipe at my eyes. "I've got to go," I say, heading to the door.

"You be careful, Genevieve," warns Grey. "Dem National Guard niggas is off de *hook*, you hear? Helicoptas came in last night an' shelled de Porch Monkey. Started gunnin' niggas down in de streets like dey was Palestinians, an' shit."

"The Porch Monkey?" I squeak.

"Gone, gurl," Grey repeats. "Hundreds a grandmuvvas dead. Twelve Straight A students *an'* a gotdamned puppy. Niggas killed a *puppy*. Some folks talkin' 'bout torchin' Toomer Way tonight in retaliation."

I've really got to go. I grab the door handle and swing the door open.

"Ooomph!"

My stomach ... Hit. I double over in pain, clutching my belly. Tears spring to my eyes. I look up. A body swings in the doorway. Not *a* body. *Night's* body. His pale, albino flesh glistens in the sunlight. He is completely naked, dangling from a rope. His sockets gleam black where his eyes should be.

There's a piece of paper pinned to his chest.

"Do U C Whut Eye C?"

Grey screams bloody murder.

Chaptah Ateen

"Recently police trained black cop
To stand on the corner, and take gunshot
This type of warfare isn't new or a shock
It's black-on-black crime again nonstop."

—*KRS-One, "Black Cop"*

GUILT FILLS MY eyes. It's all I can see.

I felt guilty leaving Grey behind with her boyfriend Night's corpse. I didn't have a choice, though. I have to stop this thing. I should've stopped it days ago. There are just too many missing pieces to the puzzle. The pieces I have don't fit, yet. They don't even seem to be a part of the same puzzle.

Night's naked body hung from my office's doorway. I had to leave him up there. I didn't want to corrupt the murder scene. I took Grey up to her bedroom. She was beside herself. Screaming and crying and tearing at her weave. Her acrylic nails digging deep into her caramel flesh as she scratched furiously at her arms, drawing blood. Her vagina and I did our best to console her. To no avail. I guess she really loved that man. Who was I to stop her from mourning however she saw fit?

I called in Night's murder directly to the KPD's homicide division. I tried pulling my Celebrity and FOP Cards, but they were having none of them.

People are dying all over the city. They said they'd do their best, but they'd get to my office as soon as possible.

I couldn't wait. I couldn't leave Grey alone. Not the way she was. She wailed for me not to worry, that she'd call a couple of her "gurls". They could come over to be with her. But I know my cousin. Her world is Man. She has no "gurls"—no matter how you spell it. No one would be coming to console her. With Night gone, I am all my cousin has.

My cousin …

I waited a half-hour. Each second crawling along my skin like a colony of ravenous fire ants. I finallyed reach out to the elephant hunters, the gbeto, my sisters. I called Lucille Parsons. I called Yvonne, Cynthia, Augustina, Vanessa, Sonya … No one answered. I texted. Nothing. I hoped they were out there fighting this thing. But, if that were the case, why didn't they call me? We are sister-warriors. We drank each other's blood, swore the same oaths, committed to the same cause. If they are fighting, I should be by their sides. It made absolutely no sense. But what, in the last few days, has?

Desperate, I finally called Naima. She answered, chirping happily, until she realized it was me. It was probably my imagination, but there was an edge—a nervous edge—to her voice when I announced myself. When I told her what I needed—that I needed her to babysit my cousin while the police came to investigate—she hemmed and hawed. She was supposed to be on a flight. To Stockholm. To be with her Swedish wife, Annika. She was supposed to be leaving any minute now.

She was lying. The National Guard and Mossad have closed Eugene Bullard National Airport to civilian traffic. They're using it to run their military operations—sending in fresh supplies and troops and refueling and rearming between bombing runs. I told her this, told her it was on the news. I could hear my gbeto wilt over the phone.

Naima got there right before the police. She looked antsy. She apologized, said she was nervous to come out, what with all the shootings and bombings and did I hear what happened to the Porch Monkey? You can still see the smoke.

She looked so frayed. I felt guilty for imposing, but what choice did I have? Still, I almost told her she could go back and wait for her flight to Sweden.

But a few homicide police arrived on the scene. I didn't know them, didn't recognize them. I didn't trust them. Not after the Standish case. The bullet in my spine started aching in these detectives' presence.

I was disappointed. I hoped that Sandino would've been called here. I wanted to know what happened to him, Willie, Leadfoot, and Watts last night. But he was nowhere in sight. I asked the detectives if they knew where he was. They said they didn't know, acted as though they didn't even know the man. I knew they were lying, but I didn't have time for their mess, Naima's apprehension, or even my cousin's mourning.

I simply went downstairs, grabbed my bo staff and an old katana I had laying around. I haven't really practiced with the sword lately. It felt awkward in my hands. Guns are too much for me right now. The staff simply isn't enough. The katana is the closest I can come to comfort facing what I have to face. I took it, the staff, Grey's keys, and headed for my cousin's Hummer.

I feel guilty driving this huge beast. Not because it's Grey's. Technically, it's mine. My name's on the title. It was my cash ($47,513—no, I am not counting) that bought the stupid thing. It's just … the gas mileage. These beasts cannot be good for the environment. How I miss my little bullet-proof Prius.

THE DAY HAS a cordite haze hanging over it. So much gunfire. The bombs and rockets. The streets are nearly deserted. There's shattered glass and debris all along the roads. I crawl the Hummer along. Snipers take potshots from the rooftops. I knew allowing Grey to buy a camouflage-green Hummer had been a mistake. These fools think I'm military.

But, so does the military. I roll easily through several checkpoints. The Apache helicopters roaming the skies let me pass without a shot.

I am still cautious, careful, my eyes darting for any sudden movement. But hardly any exists. The little that does is uniformed. Police and soldiers. They patrol the streets—rifles aimed, bayonets pointed. They are young. They are nervous. Hundreds have died. Thousands are in the hospital. Some troops have been Medivaced to Germany. Yet, there is tension, the realization that everybody's been let off light so far. There is definitely more to come. There can never be enough blood. It simply has to tire itself out. There's a strange energy in the air, telling us all that the bloodletting is just getting started.

All of this because that woman, LaSchwanika Compton-Stuyvesant—no, Sarah Torch—died last night.

"likkaniggadik"

I peer up through the windshield. A helicopter gunship hovers menacingly overhead. I tense. I dream of Stinger missiles, mujahidin, Afghanistan. What can a bo staff and katana do against something like that?

I swallow hard and drive on. It is all I can do.

I COME ACROSS a makeshift checkpoint. Barbed wire's lined across the street. Fires burn in two oil drums. A squad of pimple-faced kids in combat fatigues stand guard. I can see their anxiety from here.

I slow the vehicle to a stop. A freckle-faced boy points his rifle at me and rushes toward my window. Another soldier follows in his wake. I slowly reach to the passenger's seat and retrieve my license and detective's badge. The first soldier taps my window with his rifle muzzle.

"Roll this fucker down!" he orders. "Now!!!"

I comply. The window creeps downward. The boy's terrified. I can smell it on him. He has probably spent the day being shot at—shooting. I don't want to give him any excuse to loose another round.

"ID!" he demands.

"Hey, dude!" his companion erupts. I refuse to look. No sudden movements, Genevieve. "That's Jon Vee Noire."

"Who?!" Freckles barks.

"The super model!"

"What the *fuck* is a super model doing out here with all this shootin' goin' on?!"

"I have to get to the hospital," I answer, evenly.

"What?! You broke a nail?" Freckles laughs. "You have to get the *fuck* outta this vehicle! That's what you *got* to do!"

"Aw, come on, Brandon," the other whines. "The woman shoots *ads*, not soldiers. Besides, she's a cop, too."

"Retired," I correct.

"Bullshit!" Brandon yells. "Who the hell's gonna believe a supermodel cop?! Out! Now!"

"All right," I agree, trying to hide the contempt in my voice. "I'm getting out."

I move as slowly as is humanly possible. The energy is building. I have to fight it. Fight the anger, the fear. Less than a year ago, I was riddled with bullets. I spent months in painful convalescence. I walked with a cane. I learned to live with a bullet in my spine. My shooters were known. They were never prosecuted. They, too, wore uniforms. Blue—not green. Bold—not camouflaged. But the guns were the same. And they were pointed at me. Just like the one Brandon has mere inches from my skull. I don't like it. Every part of me wants to take that gun away from this freckle-faced boy, turn it on him, shove it in *his* face, ask *him* how it feels.

Breathe …

I do. Slowly. It counters the staccato beat of my heart.

I step down from the truck. Glass crunches underfoot. I slowly raise my hands and face Brandon and his fellow soldiers. My green eyes meet his blues. I try to quench the fire behind mine. But his twitch. He recognizes the contempt. He grins and steadies his rifle against his shoulder.

"Goddamnit, Brandon!" his friend shouts. "What the fuck are you doin' this for?"

"Why the fuck am I here?!" Brandon screams, never taking his eyes off of me. "Hunh, Shane?! Why?! I'll tell you! 'Cause these *assholes* can't control themselves. 'Cause, no matter what we give 'em, they destroy it! 'Cause every time we *fuckin'* turn around, they gotta fuck it up! Burnin'! Lootin'! Killin'! You'd think this was fuckin' Fallujah!"

"Well, Vee doesn't have shit to do with it!" Shane argues. "Hell, she's famous! Like she needs to be lootin'!"

Brandon's index finger inches toward the trigger. "For all we know, Shane, this bitch is high on crack gettin' her boyfriend to pull the shit out of her ass."

"That was Whitney!" Shane screams.

"Look, Brandon," I finally say, as calmly as possible. "My arms are getting tired in the air like this. And, though it may not sound like it now, I'm getting incredibly angry here. Angrier by the minute, actually. By ... the ... second.

"I'm not just angry at you with your gun here," I continue. "I'm angry at this entire situation. I am angry that the National Guard is here—in *my* city— shooting everything and *everyone* in sight. I am angry that the Porch Monkey Projects are now rubble. I never lived there. But there are people—*my* people— who did. And a lot of them are dead now. Many more are without homes. So, yes, I am angry. Angry at the people who did it.

"But see, Brandon," I sigh, "the people who did that. They aren't here right now. They are hundreds of feet in the air. They're shielded from my anger. If they were here, standing before me, pointing a *gun* in my *face*, I would let them know exactly how *angry* I am.

"But, instead, there's you ... Brandon. Pointing that gun in my face. You ... Brandon ... now, you are the *focal point* of *all* my anger. My *rage*. And ... Brandon, I know you've seen the movies. I know you've heard the lyrics, seen the news reports. So, ... Brandon, I know, deep down in your heart, you know *exactly* what I mean when I say, Hell hath *no* fury like an *angry*, black woman.

"And ... Brandon, don't let this good hair, light skin, and green eyes fool you, boy. I ... am ... a ... *black ... woman*."

Brandon's finger suddenly twitches away from his AR-15's trigger. He blinks the sweat from his eyes.

"A militarily-*trained* black woman," I add.

Brandon slowly lowers his rifle. He releases a nervous laugh. "I'm so sorry about the misunderstanding, Ms. Noire."

"Uh-huh."

"Say," he smiles, affably. "Could I have your autograph?"

I AM FURIOUS now. All I see is red. But it quickly turns milky and curdles and becomes nausea twisting my gut. Dusk has descended on Koontown. I struggle to find a parking space at Koontown Kounty Hospital, fail miserably, and wind up parking the Hummer blocks away.

Lines snake from all directions into the hospital. Wounded men, women, and children, bleeding, struggling to stand. They inch along. Step by painful step. They moan, they cry, they lean against each other for support. Many are dying. Some have already died. Others will die before they reach the hospital's doors. The survivors will simply step over them. When this is all over, someone will be by to collect the bodies.

"likkaniggadik"

Helicopters churn overhead, keeping a watchful eye on the ghastly procession.

I walk by quickly. Determined. Too many people know me. They scream my name in recognition, hope, agony. I squeeze my eyes and quicken my pace. I look up at the Apache helicopters, praying they don't decide to shoot. There's an explosion off in the distance.

The emergency room is pure chaos when I enter. Nurses, interns, doctors rush to and fro, harried, looking as though they have never known sleep. The wounded and dying press frantically against each other, jostling for help. They claw at anyone who looks like medical staff. The staff begs for patience.

The blood is thick. The desperation, asphyxiating. I look for someone, anyone to tell me where I can find Willie's room. In my search, I see a little black girl. She sits calmly in her "Gimme Dat" T-shirt and bloodied bandages as the world screams around her. Blood mats her nappy pigtails. She has obviously suffered. But she plays happily with her black dolls—Trap Barbie, Track Barbie, and Bottom Bitch Barbie—as the world screams around her.

"Where my money at, bitch?" Bottom Bitch barks at Track. The former doll smacks the latter, who yelps and falls to the little girl's lap.

The sight of her is so precious, so depressing. I want to cry. I stand frozen. Several people bump into me. I barely move. The poor girl notices me. She looks up—with eyes as green as mine—smiles, and waves.

The tears are hot in my eyes. They scald.

This all ends tonight.

I kNOW WHAT I expect to see when I reach Willie's hospital room, and my steps are leaden because of it. My old partner will be lying there—as I once lay in the vision Lucille Parsons provided me—unconscious, tubes jutting profusely from his wounded flesh, monitors beeping a morbid symphony. The man teetering preciously between life and death. These will be his last moments. I will be his final witness.

When I finally get someone to tell me where William Orpheus O'Ree rests, it takes me even longer to find the room than if I would've simply searched blindly. My step is a crawl. The elevator seems to stop at every floor. I examine every room number I pass as though searching for a clue—I examine, reexamine, double back like I'd missed something, then go back to examining a number I'd already scrutinized.

Finally, I reach it, Room 11858. I inhale, exhale, close my eyes, open them. I take one, final push and open the door.

It is not what I expected.

Willie is lying there, reclined, bandages covering his arms, legs, and head. But only one tube. An IV needled in the crook of his right arm. He's not on the precipice. Not in the least. He has the remote in his hand, watching TV (a Western, by the looks of it), cursing under his breath.

I stand in the doorway—dumbfounded, but grateful. Willie turns. "Oh, hey, Vee," he greets casually. "Have you seen this?" he asks, pointing at the television.

I enter the room, take the chair next to Willie's bed, sit, and look up at the screen. Stagecoaches fill the screen, kicking up dust. A mad scramble to be off-screen.

"What is this?" I ask my former partner. "Some old John Wayne movie?"

"No," he answers. "*KNN*."

"The news?"

"Yep," he exhales. "News of the riots has gone global. White folks from all around the country have packed up their belongings and are headed this way. They know real estate's about to get *real* cheap."

I am speechless.

"There'll be a land grab in the old K-Town tonight," Willie sighs, heavily.

He raises the remote and snaps off the television. He looks at me gravely. There's a line of stitches below his left eye. It looks like he's suffered burns on his chin.

"Did you know I had an older brother?" Willie suddenly asks. "About ten years older than me?"

"No, Willie. I didn't."

"He was in the Army—101st Airborne—in Vietnam. He even fought in the Battle of Hamburger Hill. Maybe you saw the movie?"

I shrug.

"One of Don Cheadle's first. You should check it out," he advises. "Anyway, my brother, Oscar, did two tours in Vietnam. They took their toll on him. I was a kid back then, but Oscar, he never seemed the same after that.

"He was distant—sometimes terrifying. My brother could get real quiet—get this stare. And every time he got it, he would clear the room. I mean, there could be this party going on, everybody really gettin' down, blue light burning in the basement, the whole nine. Then, Oscar would get this stare, and everybody was so terrified, they'd just go home. And this is Koontown we're talking about here, Vee. *Real* thugs and gangsters and other fucked-up veterans. And they'd be like—'Gotta go!'

"Well, whatever was haunting my poor brother finally caught up with him. First, it was alcohol. Then heroin. Crack finally got him in '92."

"I'm sorry, Willie."

He shrugs. "I got to talking about him to my momma—she was the only person Oscar would talk to really after he got back from the war. Never married, never had kids. A real drifter. A real *scary* drifter. Anyway, I asked Momma what Oscar saw over there. What drove him to all that madness. And she insisted that it wasn't the war, at all. That he was normal after his two tours. She said it was 'that hospital.' At that military base he was stationed at after his tours were up. Fort Detrick. Ever hear of it?"

"No," I admit.

"They used to do experiments there," Willie informs me. "Chemical and biological weapons. Anthrax, and the like. Nixon signed some treaty with the Soviets and claimed to shut down the research on *offensive* biological weapons. They continued research on *defensive* weapons, though. And what's the difference, really? Hunh, Genevieve? Any defensive weapon can become offensive, right? And what *kind* of weapons aren't both, really? So, I started wondering. What exactly do they *do* over there at Fort Detrick?"

"Why's that, Willie?" I ask.

"You see, Genevieve, Oscar, he never really talked to me. I was his younger brother, a little shit, as far as he was concerned. But sometimes, when he was drunk, he would *mutter*. Say the weirdest shit you could think of. About experiments, operations, drawing blood, injecting drugs. On soldiers, on little kids, I don't know. It was all too weird, and the man was drunk—or high—or both. I thought my brother was crazy, to tell the truth. I just thought Vietnam snapped him."

"But it didn't."

Willie gives me a long, hard look. He quickly looks away, out at the night. "See, when my mother told me that ..." he continues "...about the hospital. Well, it was all just too weird. By the time he died, I was already a cop. A grown-ass man. I was just tired of seeing my brother constantly in trouble. Tired of seeing the shit he put our momma through. Frankly, I was glad he died. To see Momma's suffering finally end. I thought her talk of secret government experiments was just her way of coping. Of her not coming to terms with her oldest boy dying a crazy-ass junky. But now ... after last night ... you gotta wonder ..."

Willie trails off. I can see the memories playing across his face. I'm glad I can't see what they are. They are obviously causing the old man pain. He swipes quickly at his eyes. He inhales, labored, exhales deeply.

"Sandino died last night," he finally croaks.

"No," I whisper.

"Leadfoot and Watts, too," he continues. "Those *bastards* got 'em all."
He suddenly turns to me. His glare burns my flesh. "What we saw last night,
Genevieve. That wasn't some myth. That shit was real."

"I ... I know, Willie," I stammer.

"And those weren't crack babies—or vampires—or crack baby vampires,"
he amends. "It's like ... well, what if the government *didn't* close down Fort
Detrick? What if they were doing more than just screwing around with anthrax?
What if they were doing some *real* hardcore experiments? Some real science-
fiction shit, or something? What *if* what we fought last night was something
they created?"

"I don't know, Willie," I hedge. "That seems kind of far-fetched, don't you
think?"

"So does brothers with tentacles shooting out of their *gotdamned* eyes, Vee,"
Willie growls. He thrusts his bandaged arms at me. "You see these? These are
burns, Genevieve. From those fucking *tentacles*. I didn't imagine these burns.
And I most *definitely* did not imagine the fucking *pain* they produced."

"I know."

Willie leans back in his reclined bed. He rubs his eyes and gets a hold of
his breathing. "So, I got to thinking," he continues, looking back at me, "and I
borrowed one of the nurses' cell phones. You know you can access the Internet
on those things?"

"That's how you downloaded that Stylistics' song the other day, Willie," I
answer.

"Amazing," he breathes. "I remember the days of party lines and listening
in on other folks' conversations and when you knew it was important when
somebody was calling you long distance."

He chuckles. I join him.

"So, I started surfing the Net on this nurse's phone," the old detective continues. "Looking up whatever I could on Fort Detrick. Not much there, really. Just wild speculation, innuendo, conspiracy theories, specious documents, like, what was that? Roswell? Area 51? Anyway, I did come up with something interesting, though."

"Which was ...?"

"Our friend, Dr. Marion C. Sims," Willie opens. "He *did* work at NIH for a time before becoming K-Town's coroner. But, before *that*, he was a physician ... at Fort Detrick."

I jump up. My chair skitters across the floor and crashes. I head for the door.

"Wait!" Willie yelps. I turn. He struggles to sit up, groaning all the while. "I'm ... I'm coming with you, Genevieve."

"No, Willie," I object, harshly. "I got this," I say, and sprint out the door.

Chaptah Ninteen

"I hate you for no reason except you're black
I'm gonna kill you by poisoning your crack
You came from Africa, I wish you'd go back
You're a fucking nigger because you're fucking black"

—*Vaginal Jesus, "I Hate Niggers"*

(Sure, they're a White Power group,
but, for some strange reason, the lyrics seemed to fit)

DUMP TRUCKS LINE up for miles down Charles Drew Drive—heading straight for the morgue. The bodies are piling up. I press the accelerator to the floor. The Hummer speeds past the morgue's entrance faster than the bullets sailing through this night. I don't want to register my name and be buzzed in. I want to take Sims by surprise.

I screech to a halt on Henrietta Lacks Lane. I jump out of the Hummer. I strap on my leather harness and attach the katana and bo staff to my back. I cling to shadows as I approach the morgue's chain link fence.

The back of the building is humming with activity. Men in white biohazard suits glow in the moonlight. They dart in and out of the morgue warehouse burdened with large coolers.

I quickly hop the fence, careful to make as little sound as possible. I land smoothly and crouch low. There's not much natural cover here. A flat-top parking lot. But the lot is full of vans. I inch my way to the closest one and hopscotch my way among the shadows until I am near the exit.

THUD!

"Sa bi!" I hear a man curse through his surgical mask.

A cooler has fallen. Its contents have spread along the concrete. I look. Fresh meat in plastic bags. No … not meat … no …

Hearts? Maybe. Livers …?

My stomach turns. I look at the men as they scramble to clean up the mess. Other men file past, loading their coolers into the back of the nearest van. They are short, wiry. I look closer. Asian? Maybe. They continue snapping at each other in a language I don't understand. Part of me wants to brandish my sword and let it sing through their tongues. But I'm here for Sims. And, if he doesn't tell me what I want to hear, my katana will most definitely find its voice tonight.

The men continue to argue. Others have stopped to listen and laugh. I dart to the building, plaster my back against its brick, and use their distraction to slip inside the morgue.

The conveyor belts whine and hiss in protest. The noise in here is deafening. The machines can barely keep up with all the bodies being dumped their way. There's a high-pitch whine echoing throughout the building as belts, scoopers, scalpels, and stitching needles work faster than they ever have before.

Below the cacophony, I hear the thump of a bass, the scratch of turntable needles. Funky Dollah Bill music. I head toward it and Sims' office. I duck, crouch, and crawl. Nobody seems to notice. I reach the door as quickly as possible. I reach up for the doorknob, grab it, and turn.

Open dat ass

Bitch, you know dis dick pleases
Open dat ass
A second cummin' like Jesus

I crawl into Sims' office and slowly close the door. The good doctor doesn't notice me. He is dancing behind his occupied examining table with a bowl of marinara spaghetti. He chews, sings, and dances to the music while a cadaver lay exposed on the table.

I spring to my feet. Sims yelps, his hair turning even whiter, and drops the bowl of pasta into the body's exposed chest cavity.

"Ms. Noire!"

"So, you're trafficking in human organs now?" I ask.

Sims' pale face brightens for a moment. Then deflates. Whatever fight he may have had suddenly seems gone. "It's the only way to meet budget," he confesses. "Besides, who wants all these young, healthy organs going to waste? There are people *dying* out there, Ms. Noire."

"Do the families get a cut?" I ask. He answers with a frown. "Do they even *know*?"

...

"I'm not here for that, anyway," I growl, frustrated, angry.

Sims seems relieved. A nervous smile creases his cragged face. Then, the old man scrutinizes me, my combative stance, the weapons strapped to my back. "What *are* you here for, Ms. Noire?" he finally asks, swallowing hard.

"These crack babies," I answer. "Vampires, whatever they are."

"What makes you think I know anything about that?" he swallows.

"Your demeanor," I answer, blandly. "And Fort Detrick."

He suddenly stiffens. Then relaxes with a strangled laugh. His right hand starts creeping. He doesn't think I notice. Thinks he's being smooth. "I don't know anything about that," he states, plainly, regaining a bit of his composure.

A drawer starts sliding. He hears it. I hear it. We both know we both heard it.

"I assume you're going for a gun, Dr. Sims," I exhale, wearily. "I also assume you know that I will beat you mercilessly before you reach it."

Sims slumps and sighs. He removes his hand from the drawer. He suddenly reaches for the cadaver and pushes. It slumps to the floor with a sickening splat. His saucy pasta spills from the thing's chest. I look away, disgusted. Sims wearily sits on the edge of the table.

"How did you find out?" he finally asks.

"I didn't," I admit. "Willie did. Apparently, his brother was stationed there."

I move behind him and open the drawer. A Mark VII Desert Eagle .44 Magnum. A very serious gun for a man expecting very serious trouble. I tuck the hand cannon's 10.6-inch barrel into the small of my back and move back toward the door. I settle beside it, ready to ambush anyone who might come through it. Sims' eyes never leave me the entire time.

Defeated, he finally sighs. "Yes, I remember," Sims admits, "Private First Class Oscar B. O'Ree. I was hoping the detective would never discover his and my connection."

"What did you do to him there?" I ask. "What did you do to all those poor people?"

"Ms. Noire, you're fairly young," he flatters. "Do you remember the Cold War at all?"

"Yes. I do."

"It all seems silly now," the doctor states, "But we really *did* think the Soviets a threat. Here, they couldn't even feed their own citizens, but they could blow up the world twenty times over.

"So could we, mind you, but what would happen afterwards? What exactly would *total* world annihilation mean? We knew. It meant exactly what it said. There had to be a way to avoid such catastrophe."

He clears his throat and looks pensively off into the distance. "And that way was beefing up our first-strike capabilities," Sims expounds. "Destroy them before they had a chance to destroy us. And, by the Seventies, we were *fairly* convinced that we could wipe out the lion's share of the Soviets' nuclear capabilities before they could retaliate. But that would not only include limited nuclear strikes, but also invasion.

"And *everybody* knows invading Russia is pure folly," the old man continues. "Those bastards beat Napoleon *and* Hitler. They know how to fight. Even if we wiped out *half* their population with a nuclear attack, we would've *still* had to face one hundred *million* angry, desperate Russians.

"There would also be the inevitable problems of supply lines, moving in materiel. *Feeding* all those troops we would need for an effective invasion. Most of the available food would be too dangerous to touch due to radiation. Whatever good food there would've been, would've been horded or destroyed by the Russians. And what would the troops do for water? These were all very serious problems, Ms. Noire, *monumental* problems."

"OK," I say, confused.

"What you're facing out there," Sims waves, "is the solution."

"What?" I snap.

"I had a colleague," the coroner continues, "a biophysicist, Lynch. Willie Lynch. He pondered that question for years. And he finally came up with an absolutely *brilliant* conclusion."

"Which was …?"

"Willie said, 'What if we bred soldiers who were not only resistant to nuclear material but who could actually use that material? Digest it?' See, we could actually have soldiers *feed* on the nuclear waste that was *poisoning* the rest of the population."

My stomach flutters in disgust. "And you somehow ... did this?"

"Sure," Sims answers. "Crick and Watson were credited with discovering DNA in '53, but the Nazis were conducting genetic experiments in the Thirties. The Brits stole their secrets during the War and gave them to us. By the time we announced the mapping of the human genome in the Nineties, the knowledge was nearly forty years old.

"Willie Lynch and I were experimenting, trying to create these 'super soldiers' at Fort Detrick during Vietnam. We didn't perfect the science, however, until the mid-Eighties at the National Institutes of Health."

"What did you do?" I gulp. My head's swimming. I'm now leaning against the wall for support.

"Created an auxiliary digestive system," Sims informs, proudly? "See, the tentacles, their stomach acids that can dissolve anything, break it down, extract the necessary nutrients, and excrete all superfluous matter—*including* nuclear materials."

"So, how did all these 'super soldiers' of yours get loose?" I ask, breathlessly. "How did they come to terrorize Koontown?"

"They were born here."

"What?!" I scream.

"It was an *experiment*, Ms. Noire," Sims groans. He almost looks ... sorry? "We forced prenatal care on welfare mothers, pregnant women in prison, whomever. We gave them injections, told them it was a new polio vaccine. It would protect their babies in utero."

I groan.

"We didn't think it would actually *work*," he confesses. The doctor suddenly looks down at his feet.

"And you did all this … when? The mid-late Eighties?"

He nods.

"The crack baby story," I gasp.

"A cover," nods Sims. "We did some testing, realized that our experiment actually *did* work. We had to cover up our tracks. Make sure that some nosy intern didn't realize that these newborns actually had *two* digestive systems."

"You and Willie Lynch?" I ask. He nods gravely. "You're *barbarians*."

"What?" he erupts. "Do you think that—our experiments—that they were something *new*?"

"No," I agree. "Everybody's heard about the Tuskegee Experiment."

"Do you think *that* was new?"

Sims' cold blue eyes radiate with righteous indignation. He stares at me. Furious. What's he about to do? My hand creeps toward my back. Sims noticeably relaxes.

"Look, Ms. Noire," exhales the good doctor, "we've been experimenting on black people since this country's inception. Have you ever heard of fistula?"

"Some kind of vaginal disease in Africa," I respond.

"It's literally a hole," the coroner states. "It develops between either the vagina and the bladder or the vagina and rectum. Usually from a complicated birth—but sometimes through sexual abuse, as well. Without proper medical attention, women suffer from severe ulcerations and infections to the vaginal tract. Also paralysis from nerve damage, and a very distinct, very *strong* odor. Yes, it's mostly in Africa now. But thousands of women in *this* country used to suffer from the disorder. That is until my namesake, C. Marion Sims—"

"I know what 'namesake' means," I snap.

"More than just a pretty face, I see."

I nod, curtly.

"Well, Sims, he cured it," he continues. "He had two slave women. I can't remember their names. It's not important. But basically, he continuously operated on his 'girls,' suturing their vaginas, ripping out the stitches, over and over again, until he perfected his technique and the cure. All without the aid of anesthesia."

"What?!"

"Oh, the doctor had it," Sims shrugs. "He just refused to use it on them. It was common 'knowledge' in the nineteenth century that the African did not experience pain," Sims informs me. "And this is the Father of American Gynecology. There are statues, medical departments, you name it, dedicated to the man."

My stomach knots. There's a rage building. I want to kill this man. *And* his namesake.

"But it's not as though Sims is alone in this, either," continues the coroner. "Sure, there was the Tuskegee Experiment, but, even before that, medical students needed cadavers to perfect their skills. Where do you think they got them? Damned near every skeleton you see hanging in your high school biology class or doctor's office is some poor, black schmuck who couldn't protect himself against the grave robber.

"Drug tests?" he adds. Sims is trying to overwhelm me, disorient me with my own rage. It won't work. It ... won't ... work. "Ritalin?" he asks. "We tested that drug on poor, black kids before we deemed it safe enough to be administered to white children. And *that* practice continues to this day. With other drugs."

"What are you—?"

"We find some ignorant welfare mother, tell her that her little boy or girl has some behavioral disorder, and start administering drug trials on the poor tyke. The mother's happy because she now has a 'disabled' child and gets a little extra in her welfare check. The government is more than happy to 'help.' And drug companies are ecstatic that they can continue their free drug trials and can't wait to see the profits they'll reap down the road for them."

"Why are you telling me all this?" I steam. I wipe the tears from my eyes.

"You think Willie Lynch is somehow different. You think that *I'm* different," he bellows. "You think we're *fucking* animals, don't you, Ms. Noire?"

I shrug. My tears betray enough.

"Well, we're not," he snaps. "We are *doctors*. Men and women of *science*. We are no different than the other proud men and women who preceded us. Who will proceed us. It is a *tradition*, Ms. Noire. A fine, *proud* tradition of curing society's ills."

"Built on the backs of unwitting black people," I seethe.

"Yes," he concedes, with a dismissive wave. "But those 'unwitting black people' are the backbone—if you will—of American medicine. And American medicine has cured untold *millions*."

"And that's what your 'super soldiers' are doing right now, Dr. Sims?" I ask. "*Curing* people? Is that what you and your *son* are doing?"

"My ... son?"

Sims looks genuinely perplexed.

"Hustle," I say. "Hustle Beamon. He's your son, isn't he?"

"What ... what ... what are you talking about?" he blubbers, "flummoxed."

He's lying.

"Hustle told me himself that he was a confused 'mixed' kid from Bethesda," I inform. "You worked in Bethesda, didn't you, Dr. Sims? That's where NIH is headquartered, right?"

He remains silent.

"The other day," I continue, "while you were marveling over that poor, dead black boy, talking about how *muscular*, how *powerful* he must've been, you'd said that you wished your *son* had been more like that. More like his *mother*. And not like you—a long, lanky, *twerpy* scientist. And I started wondering, Did this man marry a black woman?"

"Yes, I did," he confesses, tearily. "Dorothea. She died ten years ago."

"You also said that your boy had a science degree from Harvard that he wasn't using," I roll on. "Then, soon after, I was at a press conference with Hustle. And he used the word ... 'nema—nematodes.' I had to look that one up. Roundworms, right?"

Sims nods.

"Only a science geek would know something like that," I say. "Or a *scientist*. Definitely not some two-bit hip-hop mogul.

"Then later," I exhale, "Hustle and I were having lunch, and that councilman, Wentworth, loses his mind. Hustle scoffed at him, something about his going to Yale. And I figure the only people who'd hold Yale alumni with such utter contempt would be *Harvard* alumni."

"And for good reason," Sims interjects.

"If you say so," I counter. "And the other thing that's been bugging me is ... what in the *world* is an old white guy like you doing listening to *rap* music all the time?"

"I am disappointed in you, Ms. Noire," Sims says, haughtily. "You, of all people, pigeonholing somebody by *race*."

I don't take the bait. "Still," I say, "it's not just any rap music. You only listen to Dope Beat artists. *Hustle's* label. Now, I could understand if we were talking about old Kid 'N' Play—or Salt 'N' Pepa—they were great. But *Dope Beat*? All that bitches and hos nonsense. It was just too suspicious to ignore."

"I don't know," Dr. Sims says. "It all sounds a little thin to me."

"Thin, yes," I grant. "But there *is* meat on them bones." I peel myself from the wall and move toward the doctor. "Hustle Beamon *is* your son. And for some reason, you told him about these super soldier crack babies of yours, told him how to control them. And now he's got them running all around Koontown, killing white women and bringing the wrath of Uncle Sam and the Mossad down on our heads."

Sims looks tired, defeated. The bags under his eyes sag, dispirited. His blue eyes are dull and watery. "I concede nothing," he finally announces.

"I don't care what you concede," I object. "You're coming with me. You're getting your *son* to stop this nonsense. Now."

I move to grab the old man.

"likkaniggadik"

CRASH!!!

His office door slams open and shatters against the opposite wall. I jump back. A wraith leaps into the room and grabs Sims by the throat. My hand snaps back for Sims's gun.

BOOM! BOOM! BOOM!

Click. Click. Click!Click!Click!Click!

They're still coming. Hissing! Clawing! Screams! Tentacles snap the air. I throw the gun.

I reach. Katana in hand. I swing and swing. Slash and slash. Blood sprays everywhere. They're still coming! Still … coming!

I slash more. Swing more. I kick. Desperately. I scream. Grunt. Cry.

I … I …

Chaptah Twenny

"Our nation is protected by some pro-Black niggas"

—*X-Clan, "Fire & Earth (100% Natural)"*

I RUN. I don't know how. How it's even possible. Eyes. Fangs. Tentacles. Hisses. "likkaniggadik." Screams. Katana. Blood. Acid. Spray. Space. I run. Conveyor belts squealing empty. Bodies, bodies, more bodies. Naked. Eviscerated. Buckets of blood. Organs. Technicians. Night. Biohazard suits. Sprawled. Twisted in agony. Huff-huff-huff. Running. Gasping. Legs. Arms. Lungs. Screaming in protest. Throat raw. "likkaniggadik" I jump. Fence rattles. Claws. Grabbing. Scratching. Tentacles. Spitting. Hummer. Keys. Rattle. Bangs. Screams. Hiss. "likkaniggadik." Tentacles slamming on windshield. Glass cracking. Tires squealing. Breathe. Breathe. Breathe. Ignition. Turn wheel. Punch gas. "likkaniggadik." Hisses. Ohgodohgodohgod. Bodies fall. Crunch under tires. Cracked windshield. Fire. Everywhere. Explosions. Road blocks. Punch gas. Men scream. Women scream. Uniforms firing. Wood shatters. Bullets spray. Punctured steel. Ohgodohgodohgod. Fire. The night red with it. More speed, Genevieve! One large blur. One loud brake squeal. Tires whining in protest. Out the Hummer. "likkaniggadik." Run. Door. Open. Dodge. Slam close. Click. Lock! Lock! Lock! Catch breath. Breathe. Breathe. Fall to floor.

"What happen to you, gurl?"

GREY'S LARGE BROWN eyes emerge from the haze. They are moist and leaking tears, and they're merely inches from my face. Her breath, fresh and minty. I try to shake the cobwebs from my head.

"How long have I been out?" I croak.

"Dunno," Grey answers, wiping the tears from her caramel cheeks. "Couple a seconds. What happen to you, gurl?"

I struggle to my feet. "I don't know," I wince.

I look down. I'm covered in blood and gore. There are holes in my clothes from the crack babies' tentacle acid. I must look a mess. If only Gianni could see me now.

"I'm gettin' worried, gurl," Grey trembles, sincerely. "You 'bout to get yo' ass killt."

I look around frantically. I need help. I need to make some calls. An explosion rumbles nearby.

"Is Naima still here?" I ask.

"Yeah," Grey harrumphs. "Tried to get dat bitch to leave. Tol' her I was fine. We got writin' to do."

"Another novel?" I ask, distracted.

"Got three on the *Essence* Best Seller list," Grey triumphs. "But a bitch be ready fo' some mo' *literary* j'ints, an' shit. Workin' on *Night Fallz* right now. Fo' my nigga."

Grey starts blubbering.

"Where is she?" I ask, looking around. "Naima?"

"Oh, dat bitch upstairs," Grey whimpers. "Dey runnin' a *De Reel Dyme Piecez a de KT* on *CPN*."

"Naima!" I yell.

"Yeah?" I hear.

"Could you come down here please?!" I bark back. I turn to Grey. "Could you go downstairs and get me a fresh set of clothes?"

She turns up her nose. "You ain't gonna take no shower first?"

"Don't have time."

"Hmph." She turns and waddles downstairs.

Naima emerges, chuckling to herself. "That LaFreqya sure is a trip." She suddenly looks up at me and gasps. "What happened to you, Genevieve?"

"Too much to explain right now," I say, hurriedly. "Look, we've got to get the gbeto together. We've got to stop this mess right now."

Naima stiffens, fidgets nervously.

"What is it?" I ask.

Suddenly, she can't look me in the eye. I lunge toward her, grab her by the shoulders.

"What is it?" I repeat.

Computer, desk, ceiling, floor. She looks at everything except me. I shake her. Shake her as hard as is humanly possible.

"Talk to me, Naima," I demand harshly.

Tears start welling in her eyes.

"What?!"

The woman steadies herself. Her eyes cool. She runs a hand through her auburn curls. There's an aura of shame to her, but her undying Moni dignity shines through. She clears her throat. "The gbeto," she opens. "We're not coming."

"What?"

"We won't be helping you, Genevieve," she states.

"Why not?" I squeak, desperately.

"It's Lucille," Naima answers. "She says that this is not our fight."

"But this is *my* fight," I argue. "And we're supposed to be *sisters*, aren't we? We took a *blood* oath, Naima. We swore to be there for each other, to *protect* each other."

"Everybody knows that, Genevieve," she answers, coolly. Something has shifted within her. An iciness. A glacier covering the place where shame had just been. I know now this woman is not there for me, never will be, probably never was. "What *you* have yet to realize, Genevieve *Noire*, is that we gbeto are here for a much *higher* purpose."

"Higher than saving our people from the National Guard?" I yell. "From these genetic *freaks* running amok? Sucking the organs out of the very people we have sworn to *protect*?!"

Naima smiles. She sends a chill through my spine. "Lucille thinks that a lot of good will come out of this … *incident*—"

" '*Incident*?'"

"—and we all agree," the proud elephant hunter continues. "We gbeto will be there to sift through the ashes. We will rebuild a better Negrovillea. A place where we can raise good, decent, *respectable African-American* children. With *real* names. Where we can thrive and prosper and take our rightful place in *civilized* society."

I let Naima go. There are so many things I want to do right now. Smash that smug smile of hers into her esophagus. Stomp her until my foot feels spleen. Splinter every bone in her body.

Instead, I back away. Farther. Farther. I don't want to be anywhere near the woman. I will hurt her. She will hurt me. She, too, is a warrior, after all. A warrior who refuses to do battle. I can barely hide my contempt.

"You're right," I breathe. "Your battle is most definitely *not* mine. I doubt if it ever were."

Naima smiles imperiously. "Good," she chirps. "Now can I go back upstairs and watch *De Reel Dyme Piecez*? I love me some LaFreqya."

I nod dumbly. Naima looks triumphant. She turns and bounces back upstairs. I slump down to the floor and put my head in my hands.

"HELLO? VEE?"

"Yes. I need you. Right away."

"I'll be right there."

"Good. And bring the big guns."

"I WISH I was in Dixie—Hooray! Hooray!" sounds the car horn outside. I get up from my computer searching, head to the window, and look out. A stretch Hummer is double-parked beside Grey's H4. Two figures rush out of the vehicle and head straight for my door. I move to open it and do so before they can knock. Kelvin sweeps inside with a woman at his side. He has a .45 in one hand and a bottle of Maalox in the other.

I still don't know if I can trust HNIC. I don't know what choice I have. Willie's laid up in the hospital. Sandino was the last police I could trust—and he's dead. Lucille Parsons and the elephant hunters have sold me down the river. Hustle is somehow behind this chaos. And what use is Grey?

Kelvin Cleghorne is all I have left in all this insanity. Perhaps it is crazy to trust the man. But he did save me last night. He may have even healed me. What would you do in my situation?

The man reeks of sweat and dirt. He looks harried, drained. He has most definitely been busy. Doing what? is the question.

"Vee," he pants, "this is Clarise Hammond. You might know her as C-Word."

"I don't," I say, and offer my hand.

Clarise ignores my sleight, beams, and eagerly shakes my hand. "Genevieve Noire," she revels. "I can't tell you how many times I damned near burned my scalp off, trying to get my hair like yours."

I look down at the short woman. She has a baseball cap pulled backwards over a short natural. She wears a baggy football jersey and loose jeans. She is an even brown with strong Caribbean features. She is comely—if a bit masculine. Any taller, she could possibly be a model.

"I'm sorry," I apologize, sincerely. This is not the first time I've heard that complaint.

"Don't be," Clarise smiles, warmly. "My hair was only one of *many* issues I had to come to terms with."

"She's a *lesbian*," Kelvin stage-whispers. Clarise hits him in the shoulder. "Damn, woman. You walk around with a strap-on and basically *fuck* Yo!Nutz on stage. Ain't like it's a secret."

"It's called an *act*, Kelvin," she spits. But there's no venom to it. In fact, this feels a bit like of a routine itself.

"Where's Spade?" I ask.

"We're double-parked," Kelvin answers.

"I'd think the police have better things to worry about tonight," I say.

"You'd think, wouldn't you?" he adds.

"Hell, fool," Clarise says, "the hip-hop cops are all dead."

"True," he agrees. "Spade's outside, Vee. In the Hummer. Actually, most of the team's out there. We've got a couple more stops to make, then we're good to go. What did you have in mind?"

"Team?" I ask.

"We're crack baby hunters," Clarise answers, proudly.

"Rappers *and* crack baby hunters?" I ask, incredulous.

"Almost as ridiculous as a super model cop, eh?" Kelvin smiles, sardonically.

"So, how do a bunch of rappers become crack baby hunters?" I ask.

"Remember a couple months ago?" he asks. "There was a spree of spoken word artist killings."

"No, I didn't notice," I confess.

"The perfect test run," Clarise adds. "Killing an anonymous population no one would notice was missing."

"I just had a hunch," Kelvin says. "I just thought the crack babies were back."

"How?" I question.

He shrugs. "I was just right, is all. So I assembled this team and hunted a bunch of them down. I thought that'd be the end of them. Obviously I was wrong."

"But if you kill all the crack babies, who's going to buy your music?" I ask.

"White kids," Clarise and Kelvin answer, in unison.

I shake my head in understanding.

"Besides," Clarise adds, "we're not all rappers."

"Does Hustle Beamon know about your extracurricular activities?" I ask.

"No," Kelvin answers, visibly confused. "I don't think so. Why?"

"I was just at the morgue," I start. "Had a talk with Dr. Sims, the coroner."

"Why?" Clarise asks.

"Well, apparently, he was involved in inventing these 'crack babies'—"

"Inventing," Kelvin interrupts. Suddenly, his eyes become clouded over with confusion. He takes a swig of his Maalox.

"Um. Yeah. A few decades ago, he and a Dr. Lynch—"

"Willie Lynch?" Clarise interrupts.

"Yeah. You've heard of him?" I ask.

"Rumors, mostly," she responds. "Been swirling around since I was a kid. He's all over the Internet."

"I don't think it's the same guy, Clarise," Kelvin mumbles.

"Anyway," I continue, "they were working for the government. Trying to solve the problem of how to invade the Soviet Union. Decided they needed to create a group of 'super soldiers.'"

"You're joking, right?" Kelvin groans. He shuffles back toward my desk and crumples against it.

"No," I say. "It took them a couple of decades, but they finally succeeded in the mid-Eighties."

"The government *invented* crack babies?" the man asks, stunned.

Clarise, no less shocked, moves over to his side. She plops down next to him.

"Crack babies are a myth, Kelvin," I say. "A myth trumped up by the Conservatives so they could attack Head Start funding."

"Nobody likes a smart nigger," Clarise grumbles.

We all nod in agreement.

I add, "Sims and Lynch *used* that myth to cover up what they'd done."

"But ... but ... it can't be," he croaks. "I ... I ..."

Clarise pats him on the shoulder. She looks up at me. "Did Sims tell you how to stop them then? We have our own methods, but what did he say?"

"He didn't get a chance to *say* anything," I inform them. "A bunch of those super soldiers bust in on us. They killed him—I'm pretty sure. I don't know. I was lucky to escape with my life.

"All I found out was that he and Lynch invented them and that, somehow, his son knows how to control them."

"His son?" Kelvin yelps.

"Hustle Beamon."

"What?" he gasps.

"That's it!" Clarise erupts. "I'm rippin' up my muhfuckin' contract soon as this shit is over!"

"Hustle Beamon is Marion Sims' son," I respond.

"He's *mixed?*" Kelvin breathes.

"I don't see how that's important," I continue. "But yes. And he's the head shot caller behind all the slain rappers. And I guess that writer, too. I don't know why. Have no clue what he's thinking. But we've got to stop him now. He's obviously gone insane, and all of Koontown has caught his madness."

"All right." It looks as though I've overloaded Kelvin's circuits. He seems dazed, confused. He takes another swig of Maalox and stands. Tall. He straightens his clothes. The confusion slowly melts away as he grooms himself.

He looks at me. Those big, brown eyes are steely, determined once more. He looks strong and proud again. The reincarnation of Ashanti Moor. "Let's do this."

"HNIC in de *house!*" Clarise trumpets.

The three of us move to the door. A throat clears behind us. We turn. My cousin Grey stands in the doorway, her tremendous girth crowding the frame. She looks furious, a stainless steel, polymer-framed Ruger P97 .45 ACP auto pistol pointing skyward. Nice.

"I'm goin' wich ya," my cousin announces.

I move toward her. "I don't think so, Grey," I say.

"Gurl, two nights straight you come back more dead 'an alive," she says. "What de hell I supposed to do if you get dead?"

"I'll be all right, Grey," I reassure, touched. "I'm trained for this fight. You're not."

"Gotdamnit, Vee. Dis bitch right here from de Porch Monkey, ya heard?" Grey proudly proclaims. "Just let me take out my earrings, an' we good to go, gurl."

"Family takes care of its own," I counter. "I won't be able to do that if you come along, Grey. Just lock up behind me, take the twelve-gauge from downstairs, and don't open the door for anyone."

Grey nods, tears in her eyes. Damn family. What can you do? I reach for my cousin and hug her tightly. She bear-hugs me in return.

"And finish that novel about Night, cuz," I croak.

"We will," her vagina reassures.

Grey and I separate and chuckle.

"Take care of yourself, Genevieve."

"I will, Grey," I smile, fondly. "Hey, uh, can I borrow that Ruger?"

ONLY A PSYCHOPATH looks forward to killing. I still have nightmares over the first life I'd taken. LaDiDante Farrell. Fourteen years of age. Why a dumb kid would ever point a weapon at a police is beyond me. I guess the child wanted to die. It doesn't matter now. Only the nightmares do.

I plan to have even more of them over the crack baby I expired tonight. And over even more after this night is over. I dread the promise of it all. But less than I do my own death. Less than if I were to abandon Koontown altogether. The thought has crossed my mind. But what are nightmares when compared to human life?

So, along with Grey's .45, I have grabbed a spare katana and bo staff from downstairs. I've strapped a snub-nosed Taurus .22 to my right ankle. I also snagged a pair of workman's goggles. I may not be a psychopath, but I am, by no means, crazy either.

I put the sword and staff in the back of the stretch Hummer. It sags with weaponry. AK-47s, AR-15s, Uzis, .45s, .22s, 9mms. Even a battle axe. You would think these musicians were actually a gang. No wonder they're so scared of the hip-hop cops. I suddenly start wondering if all those reports about HNIC and his killing and drug trafficking are true. Wonder if it really matters right now. The enemy of my enemy ...

I shut the hatch and move to the front passenger door, eyes darting in the darkness. It seems to take forever, but I finally climb into the front seat. Kelvin is seated next to me. Spade's in the driver's seat.

"Welcome back to the party," the big man grins behind dark shades. I suddenly feel old, my first thought being *Should he be driving with those things on? It's night time.*

Kelvin turns around in his seat as Spade starts the Hummer. We move. "Everybody knows Jon Vee."

A chorus of assent. I turn to look. C-Word sits directly behind me. By her side is an attractive, cream-colored sister in expensive make-up and weave. She's all peaches and cream in different shades of pink. Far from the warrior we need tonight. More like a beauty queen. Ironic, I know.

"This is Yolanda," Kelvin introduces. The woman nods.

"Yo!Nutz," I guess.

"In the flesh," Yolanda smiles.

Behind the two women are two men. A wiry brother in a black Winnie the Pooh T-shirt with an afro Mohawk that reaches the ceiling. And a completely bald, buff white man in the same shirt.

"A skinhead?" I marvel.

"A former SHARP, actually," the white man announces, proudly.

I look at Kelvin, questioning.

"Skinhead Against Racial Prejudice," Kelvin answers.

"I used to be World Church of the Creator—before the split," the white man says, from the back. "Then, my mom went and married a black man. Hard to hate the black race when half your family's half-black."

"You could half-hate us," the Mohawk brother laughs. "Or is that a quarter-hate? We black folk ain't too good at maf, ya know."

The others laugh.

"Quarter-hate the man who helped me perfect my wrister?" the SHARP scoffs.

I look at Kelvin again.

"Wrist shot," he elaborates. "Hockey, Vee."

"Sorry," I shrug.

"Anyway, that's Brudda Spearchucka," Kelvin says, "and that's Blue-Eyed Devil. The lead singer and the lead guitarist—"

"Axeman," Blue corrects.

"Axeman," Kelvin amends. "They're from the Pooh Nannies."

"The what?" I ask.

"Pooh Nannies," Brudda repeats. "Afrocentric death metal. 'I Fucked a Kennedy.' You ever hear it?"

"Sorry," I apologize.

"Hell," Clarise chuckles. "Vee probably hasn't bought any new music since Luther turned corny."

"I like Jill Scott," I protest, a little offended. Probably because C-Word is mostly right. Mostly.

"Celebrate dat Queendom, sista gurl," Clarise doffs her cap.

"Shit," Spade fumes, peering at his side view mirror.

"What is it?" Kelvin asks.

RAT-TAT-A-RAT-TAT-A-TAT!!!

Ping! Ping! Ping!

Bullets bounce off the Hummer. More rounds chew up the asphalt around us. Spade suddenly punches the accelerator. The stretch Hummer gains speed.

"Apache!" Spade yells, over the incoming rounds. Metal sings staccato all around us. I instinctively reach for my holstered Ruger.

"Blue!" Kelvin yells. His eyes dart furtively. But there's nothing he can do. Nothing any of us can do against an Apache helicopter.

"Got it!" Blue-Eyed Devil responds. He moves quickly, darting beneath his seat. The skinhead quickly emerges with an armed rocket-propelled grenade. Before I can blink the sweat from my eyes, the man has his window down and is leaning out of the speeding Hummer. Brudda Spearchucka holds onto the belt loops of his jeans.

"Steady, Spade!" Brudda commands.

"Got it!"

"Ahhhh!!!!" I hear Blue scream.

WHOOOOSSSSHHHHHH!!!

BOOM!!!

"Eat that, motherfucker!!!" Blue roars. He plops back down in his seat. "Are we there, yet?" he whines, in a little kid's voice.

I roll down my window and take a look. The shadow of a wounded Apache recedes into the night. Smoke trailing defeatedly.

"I gotta go Number Two, Daddy," Blue continues.

"Me, too!"

"Me, too!"

"Don't make me turn this car around," Spade jokes. "Don't think I won't."

The hurtling stretch Hummer reverberates with laughter.

THE LINE OUTSIDE of Sojourner Truth Elementary School wraps around the block. All children with young women. Federal troops escort the line with rifles and bayonets.

"What's going on?" I ask.

"Sweetdick called a State of Emergency," Kelvin answers. "They're making all the kids report to their PPO."

"He wants them to sign up for health care?" I squeak.

"No," the rapper answers. "Pre-Parole Officer."

"*Pre*-Parole?"

"It was supposed to be a Scared Straight program," he elaborates. "But you can't *scare* these kids. Their lives are already a fucking nightmare." He exhales deeply. "So, now they're treating the program as vocational training."

"So, Sojourner has one of these PPOs," I groan.

"Yeah. One," he says. "We're here to see her."

"Who's that?" Clarise asks.

"The new member of our team," Kelvin proclaims. "She's a singer/songwriter."

The others groan. Spade parks.

"Let's go," Kelvin says, gesturing for me to get out of the car.

"likkaniggadik"

"Did you hear that?" I ask, looking around.

"Everybody out," Kelvin orders. "They're around here somewhere."

I continue looking. Maybe it was my imagination. I don't see any of the crack babies. Just soldiers, children, and their guardians.

The air is tense. The night glows orange from distant fires. We can hear gunshots and explosions. Koontown is burning. But here there is nothing but angry looks and itchy trigger fingers. There must be at least a hundred children out here. Some kindergarteners.

I'm frozen. The rest move on toward the school. I can't remove my gaze. All those children. All those grandmothers.

"Are you coming, Vee?" Kelvin asks, up ahead.

I swallow my disbelief and follow them. We trace the child trail into the building. It's lit up, fully active. A handful of school nurses move along the line with trays filled with tiny cups of water and pills. They stop occasionally to dose a child and move along once the child is medicated. Ritalin. I think of

Koontown's former coroner and wonder if this night will ever end.

The line ends at a door. Kelvin knocks and enters before there's time for a response. The rest of us file into the room. It's crowded in here. The office is more of a broom closet, really. Maybe a waiting room. There's another door on the opposite side of the room.

A brown-skinned woman sits wearily at a tattered, wooden desk, pen poised over paper. There's a woman on the other side of the desk. She might be thirty. A six-year-old girl sits on her lap, yawning in her "Gimme Dat" T-shirt.

"But my grandbaby didn't do nuffin'," the thirty-year-old whines in protest.

"Not yet," the other woman yawns. There's a large cardboard box at her feet. She reaches into it and retrieves a tiny ankle monitor. "Just have LaBarricudika wear this until the State of Emergency's over. Come back after that, and we can talk."

She hands the ankle bracelet to the grandmother, who huffs as she clasps it onto the little girl. LaBarricudika's dark face immediately brightens. She lifts her scrawny leg and marvels at her new, electronic jewelry. "Cool," she sings, and jumps off her grandmother's lap.

She flings the office door open and darts out. She yells, "Eat a dick, LaTalapia! Tol' you I be gettin' one, too! Bitch!"

"LaBarricudika!" Grandma screams. "Get yo' ass back here fo' I cash you out like my welfare check!"

The woman growls and storms out of the office.

Before anyone else can enter, Kelvin closes the door. "Everybody, this is Martina Canales," he announces. "She's on my new album—and a new member of the team."

"Aw, hell naw!" Yolanda protests.

"What is it, Nutz?" Kelvin sighs, wearily.

Yolanda looks Martina up and down, a sour look on her face. "What are you?" she huffs. "Dominican?"

"Puerto Rican," Martina answers, firmly. There's an edge to her dark, brown eyes. Like she's just been offended.

"Hmph," Yolanda continues. "I saw that Rosie Perez documentary. Yall Puerto Ricans are *Taino*."

"Oh, one of *those*," Clarise spits.

"What is this all about, Kelvin?" Martina asks.

"Yeah," he says, "what is this all about, Yolanda?"

"Your bitch here—"

"Bitch?!"

"—is *Taino*," Yolanda repeats. "It's bad enough you've got Jon Vee here."
"Hey!"

"Hell," Kelvin counters, "Blue is *white*."

"But he ain't *white* white," Yo!Nutz declares.

"Um ... thank you?"

"Damned near a nigga, really," Clarise contributes.

"I wouldn't say—"

"Wait a second," Martina interrupts. "You're saying I shouldn't be a part of your *precious* team because I'm of *Puerto Rican* descent? Because I'm *Taino*—and not *black*?"

"*Basically*," Yolanda snaps, hands on hips with a tiny neck roll.

Martina's brown face darkens with blood. Anger flaring brightly. She struggles for control. "I'll have you know, my grandma—"

"Oooh," Yolanda scoffs. "Your *grandmother*."

Martina's hands fly up in surrender. "You know what," she flares," you can go to hell. I'm outta here."

She stands up, turns—

"*Dyamn*," Brudda squeals.

—to reveal the biggest, roundest, most bulbous behind I have ever seen.

"Naw, nigga," Spade declares, "she black."

Martina turns and looks down at her own backside. Face going crimson.

"I stand corrected," Yolanda apologizes. "Welcome to the team, gurl."

"Yo, baby," Brudda Spearchucka coos, "come an' holla at a brotha—"

WEEEOOOHHHHH!!! WEEEOOOHHHHH!!! WEEEOOOHHHHH!!!

A siren.

"Shit!" Martina curses. She crashes into the door behind her desk. It slams open. She sprints into the other room.

We all dart after her. Papers flutter. The woman flies into a well-suited torso hanging halfway out of a window. She punches furiously into the right kidney. A man yelps repeatedly in pain. He flails frantically.

She uppercuts her right fist into the man's crotch. Suddenly, his body crumples. Martina reaches out of the window. She returns with a handful of sandy blonde hair. The head attached to it belongs to a middle-aged white man in a lot of pain. Martina reaches back and smashes her right fist into his face. Over and over again. The man starts whimpering. She throws his head to the floor. She reels back and lands her foot several times into his gut.

Impressive.

"Please, Martina, please," the man cries.

"What did I tell you would happen if I ever caught you around here again?" Martina barks.

"You said you'd kill me," the man whines. "But everybody says that."

"Martina?" Kelvin asks, apprehensively.

"This is Paul Whiteman," she pants. "Whiteman's Historiographical Investment Properties." She lands another kick to his stomach. He groans. "Tell them what you do, Whiteman."

The man struggles to a seated position. He is bloody. He straightens his jacket, combs a trembling hand through his golden locks. He composes himself as quickly as possible, though the blood continues to drip from his nose, and looks up at us with a warm set of cobalt blue eyes.

"We at W.H.I.P.," he begins, "combine education and national security. A strong educational system is the first weapon in the nation's fight against crime. So, through strenuous scientific research, we—"

"They build prisons!" Martina erupts.

"Well ... yes," Whiteman stammers.

"Tell them what you were doing here, *Paul*," the PPO demands.

Whiteman looks up at all of us nervously. Fear plain on his face. His Adam's apple bobs repeatedly in his throat. He looks about to cry. He finally looks at Martina and shakes his head. No.

"W.H.I.P. and companies just like it look at fourth- and fifth-grade failure rates. He was here, trying to steal school records."

"Why?" I ask.

"Today's failing fourth- and fifth-graders are tomorrow's convicts," Martina informs. "They look at failure rates to determine how many prisons they're going to build and sell to the state."

"Oh, fuck naw," Clarise groans.

"Murk dat nigga," Yolanda growls.

"Fuck it. I'll do it," Spade volunteers. The big man lurches toward Whiteman.

The man scrambles frantically along the floor away from Spade. "Wait!

Wait!" he screeches, throwing up his hands for protection. "Y-y-y-y-you can't kill *me!*"

"But I made a promise," Martina grins, devilishly.

"B-b-but," Whiteman stammers. "It's not like I'm the only one. It's an industry, Ms. Canales. Killing *me* won't solve anything. My competition will be right behind me. Right through that window! There *will* be others!"

BOOM!!!

All that was in Whiteman's head blows out of the back of it. The man crumples to the floor. The wall painted a chunky red behind him.

The pistol smokes ominously in Blue-Eyed Devil's right hand.

"Not if we kill enough of you motherfuckers."

Chaptah Twenny—Wun

"The super duper nigga that'll buck
We had to tear this motherfucka up
So what the fuck?"

—Ice Cube, "Tear This Motherfucka Up"

"SONOFABITCHCOCKSUCKINWHITEWHORE!!!"

Even among all the chaos, Welfare Queen has not stopped birthing her babies.

"It's a girl!" the uniform police officer announces, swaddling the babe in a pink blanket.

"Shit!" Welfare Queen curses.

He disappears to the back of the building. Another uniform arrives to catch the placenta before it falls to the slick floor.

It was a harrowing trip to King of Sheba's Hair Care and Beauty Salon. The authorities are on the look-out for Kelvin's stretch Hummer after Blue disabled that helicopter. There were roadblocks all over the city. They planned to shoot us dead first and question our corpses later. I'd never shot at a uniform before—police or military. The very idea goes against a lifetime of training. Frankly, it made me a bit nauseous. But horror trumps apprehension every time. The first bullet that singed my hair made me more than ready to fire back. We shot our way through roadblocks on Vesey and Prosser, Newton and Cleaver. Kelvin, stuck in the middle seat, frantically texted on his phone the entire time. He didn't stop until we reached King of Sheba's.

"Cumguzzlinhos!!!"

The placenta oozes into the police's latexed hands.

Pimpnakang waddles out from the back. He has a red-white-and-blue headband around his glistening Jheri curl, a cut-off sweatshirt with a Rising Sun and Japanese characters, way-too-short shorts, striped knee-high socks, diamond-studded Gazelle glasses, and original Air Jordans. I swear I hear Joelski Love's "Do the Pee Wee Herman" playing in the background.

"What took yall so long?" he asks, beaming a gold-tooth smile.

"They're on us like white on rice, Pimpnakang," Kelvin answers.

"Glad yall's asses didn't get burnt," the fat man chuckles. "Come on, yall."

We follow the Old School Bruvva to his basement.

"Fuckwaddicklessniggas!!!"

CEILING LIGHTS COME on. We are greeted by faux-wood paneling, shag carpeting, and vintage basketball posters. Dr. J, Kareem Abdul Jabar, Bernard King, Magic Johnson, a baby-faced Michael Jordan, and Kurt Rambis.

"Hol' up," Kang orders. "Wait a minute."

The pimp disappears into a side room. There are greedy smiles on my new teammates' faces. Martina and I look at each other, confused. I simply shrug.

Pimpnakang quickly reappears, wheeling in a squeaky cart covered in a white sheet. The others move forward to join him. Martina and I trail behind. The big man grips the sheet. "Waddadadang," he beams. He throws the sheet off the tray. It's full of bullets of every caliber and empty clips. "Funky fresh out de box!!!"

The others cheer.

"Now, dat's what I'm talkin' 'bout," Spade trumpets.

They start grabbing at bullets and clips. Curious, I pick up a round and study it. "Ostentatious." Hm. I grab another. "Perspicacious." I pick up another. Another. Polysyllabic words are etched into every round.

"What is this?" I ask the room.

"De only way to kill dese damned crack babies," Kang answers.

"What?"

"You can shoot them," Kelvin elaborates. "But crack babies have incredible healing powers. They regenerate rapidly, making most bullets fairly useless."

"Crack babies don't die," Brudda grins.

"They multiply," comes the chorus.

"Head shots work," Kelvin continues. "So do shots directly to the heart. But who's that good?" I am. "The only truly effective weapons are books."

"Books?" I blurt out.

"The Classics, mostly," Clarise adds. "Anything with big words in it. The Victorians. The Russians are especially effective. Burns right through them. The Renaissance is the best, however. I once threw *Their Eyes Were Watching God* at one of them. The nigger *literally* exploded."

"Zora Neale Hurston?" I gasp.

"Yeah, Vee," Kelvin reaffirms. "But you ever try to fight loaded down with copies of *War and Peace*?"

"Or *Being and Nothingness*," I add.

Kelvin smiles, the gleam back in his eyes. "The isms are all good, too. Existentialism, objectivism, nihilism, Communism. They seem to thrive off of capitalism, though. Adam Smith's a no-go. But you could probably take out an army of them with *Das Kapital*, and shit. But the weight still holds. They'd tear you apart before you could gather the strength to throw the first volume."

"Gravity's a muhfucka," Spade adds.

"Ooh, dat reminds me," Pimpnakang says. He bends down with a groan and groans even louder when he comes up with a box of little red books. "Got a shipment a Mao today."

"You are the *man*, Kang," Blue booms.

They start loading themselves down with copies of the Little Red Book. Blue hands me a few. I pocket them. I don't believe a word they're saying, but it's better to be safe, right?

"The next best thing," Kelvin continues, holding up a 9mm round, "is these. Bullets with SAT words on them. I don't know why, but big words burn their flesh, shatters their eardrums, do all kinds of weird shit to these fiends."

"It's their Kryptonite," Yolanda adds. "Take as many as you can carry, gurl."

"All right," I comply. I empty my .45 clip and load it with "Peripatetic," "Omnipotent," and several words I won't even try to spell. I do the same with the .22 strapped to my ankle. I load and pocket even more clips. I may not believe in their theories, but I've been a huge believer in speeding bullets for years.

"Two more things," Pimpnakang announces. He claps his meaty hands. The stereo suddenly blares. "The freaks come out at night," Whodini sings. "Shit," Pimpnakang curses. He claps again. The stereo shuts off. "Yo!" he yells. "You can come out now!"

The door Kang previously entered opens.

"likkaniggadik"

A blindfolded wraith leaps out at us. We gasp and aim. Suddenly, the thing snaps back and crashes to the carpet. I blink, see a leash. It writhes on the floor, clawing at the choker collar around its neck. But the leash is being held firmly by a brown-skinned Asian woman.

I look down at the suffering beast. It whimpers like a wounded animal.

"Believe a nigga now, Vee?" Kang asks me, smiling gold teeth. "Dese crack babies is *crazy*, ain't dey?"

I nod dumbly. Words are hard to form. "Why?" I finally croak. "Why do you have it—*him*—tied up like this?"

"Not like we want it loose," Yolanda quips.

"When HNIC texted us Hustle was behind all this," Kang starts, "I knew we needed some help in findin' de nigga. He probably already in de wind. Who knows? But dese fools can track like *nobody's* bizness. So, me an' Lin got us one."

"How?" I ask.

"Funyans, Cool Ranch Doritos, you know dese niggas can only digest junk food."

"And the Crack Baby Cocktail," the Asian woman, Lin, adds triumphantly. She looks familiar. I can't place her in her black sports bra and yoga pants. But I swear …

"What?" I ask.

"Tangueray gin and purple Kool Aid," Kelvin smiles, taking a swig from his Maalox bottle.

"Really?" I say, looking at the rapper.

"They can't resist," he says, looking away. "So, what are you doing here,

Likki?" he asks the Asian woman.

That's it. Likki Nice-Nice, the R&B singer from Juilliard. The one with that hit ... "Me So Lonely." It was hard to recognize her without the gold swimsuit and the apple perched between her butt cheeks.

"It's Lin," she demands, heatedly. "And I want Hustle my damned self. I am *classically-trained*, for god sakes. I want in. Here." She tosses a diamond-encrusted Pirates baseball cap. "It's Hustle's. Give it to the crack baby. He can track that bastard down for us."

"All right," Kelvin agrees.

"Naw, not again," Yolanda objects. She glares at Lin. "Can you fight?"

"Of course I can," the singer says, defiantly. "I'm Asian."

"Right," Yolanda scoffs. "All Asians know karate. Just like all niggas eat chicken and watermelon."

"Well, I *do* enjoy the occasional pig foot," Brudda Spearchucka mumbles.

Lin hands the crack baby's leash to Pimpnakang and approaches Yo!Nutz. The two women glare at each other. This doesn't look good.

Suddenly, someone clears his throat. We all turn. It's Brudda. His eyes dart to Lin's back side.

"Aw, naw," Yolanda groans. "Not again."

Lin's gluteus is just as big and as round and as bulbous as Martina's. Much bigger than mine or Yolanda's or Clarise's.

"What are we doing wrong here?" Yolanda whines.

"I don't know," Brudda admits. "But yall sistas sho' is fallin' *behind* in the *ass* race."

"Oh, come along then," Yolanda surrenders, welcoming Lin to the team.

WE STRAP THE crack baby to the hood of the Hummer and give it—
him—Hustle's cap. Blue-Eyed Devil sits on the roof with an Uzi trained on our
captive. The night is eerily quiet. All we hear is fire crackling. Everywhere.
An orange halo illuminates the dark sky. But there are no more gunshots in
the distance. No explosions. No helicopters or Stealth bombers in the air.
Something is very, very wrong here. Brudda, Lin, Yolanda, and Clarise pile
into the vehicle. Kevin gets in. I get in behind him. Spade squeezes behind
the steering wheel and starts the engine. The stretch Hummer quickly creeps
along.

The night is truly quiet. It was not an illusion. Not a momentary blip on
the radar. Nothing but rats move. There are no delinquents in the streets. No
National Guard, no police. No rifles nor bayonets.

"What in the world is going on?" I mutter to myself.

The mystery is soon answered as the crack baby slowly leads us toward
Toomer Way. A crowd has gathered on the edges of Koontown's white enclave.
Angry and restless. Spotlights flood the night white. Helicopter gunships hover
ominously overhead. Soldiers and police are everywhere. So is every remaining
resident of Koontown. If they are not in the hospital or the morgue, they are
here. Right now. And they do *not* look happy.

Spade edges the truck to the edge of the crowd and cuts the engine. The
crack baby hops frantically on the hood, pointing manically at the crowd. He
strains at the leash. We can hear Blue struggle to restrain the poor thing.

"What are we doing?" we hear Blue scream.

Spade looks at Kelvin. Kelvin looks to me.

"Can we ask it—*him*—where he wants to take us?" I ask.

"Naw," Kelvin confesses. "Crack babies speak a form of Ebonics no one can
understand."

"Hm." Alternatives run quickly through my mind. None seem to suffice. "I guess we'll have to walk then."

"Through *that?*" Yolanda blurts out.

"Yeah, *Yolanda,*" Kelvin snaps. "Through *that.* Now, let's go."

We file out of the Hummer and move to the back hatch. "Come on, Blue," Spade summons. He opens the hatch and reaches into the back. He pulls out a bandolier full of bulleted clips and puts it on. He then straps an AK-47 and AR-15 to his massive back, grabs an Uzi and works the gun's slide. He looks at us through his sunglasses. "What you fools waitin' fo'?"

We quickly go to work. I find my harness, put it on. I slide my katana and bo staff onto my back. By the time I'm done, everybody's loaded and ready to go. Pistols and automatic weapons everywhere I look. Blue has a devilish gleam in his eyes, twirling a mammoth battle axe from hand to hand. He also has an AK-47 strapped to his back.

"You ready, Axeman?" Brudda smiles.

"Fuck 'em like a Kennedy," Blue chuckles.

"In like Arnie," Brudda responds, "and out like Jack."

"Take my twelve inches," Blue continues, "and fuck 'em in de back."

The two Pooh Nannies share a complicated hand shake and perverse laughter.

"Booyah!!!"

SQUEEZING THROUGH AN angry mob is a lot easier with a growling, slavering crack baby leading the way. He strains savagely against his lead, howling, jostling, jumping, stomping, sprinting ahead. He knocks some people over. He bowls into others. It's all Blue can do to control him. When the crack baby's victims turn to protest, they look at the blindfolded, wild wraith and quickly move aside. For the braver among the offended, seeing a group of heavily-armed rappers and an ex-super model squashes any remaining qualms.

I swear we're going to get arrested. People just can't walk openly in public with automatic weapons—even in Koontown. But nobody really seems to take much notice. Or do everything in their power not to notice. We are obviously trouble. And there's enough of that going around right now. More than enough to choose from. Why choose trouble with that crazy HNIC and all his parking violations? There's a riot about to happen. You could either walk away with an autographed bullet in your behind or a brand new, flat-screen television. An easy choice in most people's book.

The riot is so close I can almost touch it. You can definitely feel it, taste it in the air. As we move through the crowd, I can see the tension. It bunches up in limbs and shoulders, in everybody's eyes. They all look ahead. I can hear a voice, but I can't make out the words.

Oddly enough, just the sound of that voice soothes me. I suddenly have a feeling of calm wash over me. Peace, solidarity, fraternity. I don't want to hurt my fellow human beings. Race no longer matters. It is but a fiction. A social construct. All that matters is the human race. And we must work together. Work for a better future. For each other, for our children.

I look up ahead. On the platform with a bullhorn in hand, Reverend Crispus Booker from the Church of Racial Reconciliation addresses his people. I am still trepidatious about confronting these super soldier crack babies, but about the pending riot, I have no worries. Reverend Booker will bring peace. I can feel it wash over the crowd as we approach the platform.

"The Reverend's right," I hear a middle-aged white man say. "These *people* have been taking advantage of our good will for *far* too long."

What?

"And now they actually want to burn down our *homes*?" the man continues. "I call Bullshit on that! I didn't join the NRA for nothing! Let's go, Chad!"

"Right behind you, Biff," Chad growls, angrily. "Come on, Muffy! What's taking you so long?!"

"I just hope they don't *rape* me," Muffy whimpers.

The three white people start pushing their way back through the crowd toward Toomer Way. They recruit other white people and a tiny procession starts flowing—a milky stream in a sea of bubbling oil.

The crack baby continues to lead us toward Reverend Booker's stage. I still can't hear his words, but I can hear the urgency in his voice. Perhaps, on that stage, he can see something I cannot. Maybe he can feel what I do down here on the ground—that something's still not quite right with this mob.

"Yo, dat nigga *right*," I hear a black man shout. "Dese crackas been rapin' an' killin' us niggas fo' too damned long! Time to start *head* huntin', niggas!"

"I *heard* dat," his friend agrees. "Le's go, LaMuffetia!"

"God, Tyrell," the woman whimpers. "I jus' hope dey don't *rape* me."

Oh, no. I push ahead, past Kelvin, the others, and the crack baby. I work my way desperately through the crowd. I push, elbow, punch. I scream for people to get out of my way. Some curse, others recognize me. Most ask for autographs. More still snap pictures on their camera phones. I will be in *The Koontown Enkwirer* next week. "Super Model Loses Mind—Says Crackers Done Stole It."

I finally make my way to the foot of Booker's stage. Breathless.

"Genevieve?!"

I look around.

"Willie?"

I make my way to my old partner. He is standing next to the Mayor and looks absolutely haggard. There's a gray pallor to his skin. He leans on a cane. His eyes are bloodshot. And bandages peer out around the edges of the trench coat he is wearing.

"It's not working," I pant.

"What?" he asks.

"Whatever the pastor's saying," I respond.

"What are you talking about?" Mayor Cummings flares. "Reverend Booker's message of peace and reconciliation is exactly what the city needs right now. Look, even the National Guard has started putting daisies in their *own* rifles."

"It's like he said before, Willie," I counter. "People are hearing what they want to hear. There's going to be a riot."

Suddenly, there's a chorus of boos.

"Shut de fuck up, white boy!!!" someone crows.

The crowd cheers.

"Sell-out!!!"

"Uncle Tom!!!"

"Sounds like it, Sweetdick," Willie grumbles.

"B-b-but," the reverend stammers, through his bullhorn.

"'But,' my ass!!!"

A malicious laughter surrounds the stage.

"Did I already kick you off the case, O'Ree?" the Mayor fumes.

"Of course," Willie groans.

"Then, what the *fuck* are you waitin' for?!"

"I say we get dis nigga!!!"

More cheers.

Willie exhales, heatedly. "Vee, may I borrow your phone?"

I hand it to him. He starts pushing buttons.

"What the hell?" Cummings barks. "You can't call in the cavalry, O'Ree. They're already here!"

"Uh-huh," Willie drones, concentrating on my phone's screen.

"Not to mention," Cummings continues, vehemently, "there are over *five thousand* Conestoga wagons on the border full of *white* settlers. I'll never get re-elected if *they* move in!"

Willie looks up and smiles. "All right, Vee," he says, "let's go help the good reverend out."

Willie hobbles to the stage's stairs. I help him up the aluminum steps. He is breathless by the time we reach the platform. Reverend Booker looks just as drained. The color has fled his light face. The rest of his body is equally sapped. He sags. His remaining energy is gathered in his raw throat, but that, too, seems to be extinguishing quickly.

"I say we *lynch* dis chinky bitch!!!"

"But violence has never solved anything," Booker weeps, defeated.

"Tell dat shit to de Nazis!!!"

"An' de Indians!!!"

"Fuck dat! Tell dat to de *muhfuckin'* po-lice!!!"

Mad applause.

"I say we burn dis whole *muhfucka* DOWN!!!"

More applause.

"W-what?" Booker stutters, into the bullhorn. "Burn down your *own* neighborhood?!"

"Own neighborhood?!" a brother in the crowd guffaws. "Don't a single muhfucka own a *single* piece a *muhfuckin'* property up in dis bitch! We renters! All we be doin' is burnin' mo' a de *white man's* shit!!!"

"Yo! Tyrone! Where you goin', nigga?!!!"

"Uh … um … I … uh … I think I lef' de stove on…"

"Home owner," Willie whispers to me. He taps the preacher on the shoulder and points to the bullhorn. "Could I have that for a second, Reverend?"

Booker readily complies. Willie takes the bullhorn. He pushes my android phone's screen, puts it against the bullhorn, and lifts them both high into the night sky.

"It's electric!" the bullhorn erupts.

Suddenly, the familiar Eighties synthesizers blare their electronic beat.

"Oooh! Dat's my *jam*!!!" a sister screeches.

The crowd cheers.

"You can't see it," Marcia Griffiths sings.

"It's electric!" her chorus cheers.

Just like magic, the crowd shifts and parts. I can hardly believe my eyes. I rub and reopen them. The mob has suddenly formed into line after line, stretching as far as the eye can see.

"You gotta know it," Griffiths croons.

"It's electric!" her chorus again. "Boogie woogie! Woogie!"

I feel as though I'm at one, massive black wedding reception. The crowd moves in a perfect grapevine four steps to the right. Their feet meet. One giant handclap. Gay laughter. They move to the left. It's as though they can't resist.

"Amazing," I marvel.

"I can't believe it," Reverend Booker mumbles.

The crowd slides backwards, steps right, then left, click their heels, and clap again as the music plays.

"The record for Longest Electric Slide is four hours, twenty-seven minutes, and fifty-two seconds," Willie informs us. "I don't think this'll last that long. We need something else. Something better."

"It's electric! Boogie woogie! Woogie!"

Clap.

"I might have a solution," we hear.

All three of us turn, desperately. A tall, well-built middle-aged black man stands at the edge of the stage. He has close-cropped hair and a perfectly-trimmed beard. I suddenly wonder if I saw him at Übernoggin's jam. He certainly looks familiar. None of that matters now. Not if he actually does have a solution.

He wears a black-and-red striped T-shirt with "B.A.D.-Ass." stenciled in green across his massive chest. Suddenly, other brothers climb onto the stage behind him. They are grim, serious, and incredibly well-groomed. They certainly exude confidence and a strange sense of reassurance in their own B.A.D.-Ass T-shirts.

"Oh la oh la ay," Marcia Griffiths sings, as the music fades.

The crowd groans. Willie pulls down the phone and bullhorn. He starts jabbing frantically at my android. Nothing. "What the hell?" he curses, as boos rise from the crowd.

The lead B.A.D.-Ass. brother steps forward and takes the bullhorn from Willie's hand. My former partner takes little notice, punching at my phone like it's personal. The B.A.D.-Ass. clears his throat and speaks into the bullhorn.

"Brothers and sisters!" he roars, authoritatively. "My name is Martin Luther Malik al-Shabbazz Washington-Carver, and I am with the B.A.D.-Ass. organization. Black Area Dads Association. We are a not-for-profit group of proud, African-American men with good jobs, better incomes, and even stronger families. We believe that the most *revolutionary* act any young brother can commit is to raise his children. After all, any man can *father* a child—but it takes a special kind of *man* to be a *Dad*!"

Emphatic applause.

"Yall niggas married to white women?" a disgruntled grandmother yells.

"Well, uh …" Washington-Carver stammers. "Some of us … sure. And some Latinas and Asians, too."

"Uh-huh!!!"

Boos.

"But mostly *sistas*!" Washington-Carver screams.

More applause—less emphatic, though.

"Now, let me ask you a question!" the man recovers. "What is it that *every* young black man wants to know?!"

"How to make dat paper so's a nigga ain't gotta work?!"

Grunts of assent.

"How to get dese bitches *pregnant* an' on welfare so's a nigga ain't gotta work?!"

Grunts, clapping.

"How to get dese *white* bitches pregnant an' on welfare so's a nigga ain't gotta work?!"

Hoots, hollers, ferocious hand-clapping and foot-stomping. Whistles.

Washington-Carver rolls his eyes and holds out his hand to calm the crowd. "No, no, no!" he screams. "What every young black man really wants to know is who his real father is!!!"

"Uh-huh!!!"

"I heard *dat*!!!"

"Preach, nigga!!! Preach!!!"

"Fuck *dat* nigga!!!"

"I sure know I do," the B.A.D.-Ass. leader confesses, tearily. "And, if you do, too, we of B.A.D.-Ass. have gathered a database of *thousands* of black men's DNA. We have *dozens* of brothers right here, right now, willing to *claim* their children.

"And, if you really want to know who your *real* daddy is! If you want to be reunited with your *real* family! If all you grandmothers out there just want a damned *break*—"

"Damned right!!!"

"—we have set up tables over there to your right," he points. "Just line up, swab your mouth with these cotton swabs—for your own DNA—and we'll give you your paternity tests right here and now!!!"

For the second time tonight, I watch all of Koontown line up in perfect order. A strange sense of hope radiates the crowd. It glows a beautiful blue against the orange-fire halo brightening the Koontown night sky. There's laughter, joking, a few cheerful tears.

Washington-Carver turns to us, a proud look beaming on his face. He gives us a self-assured wink. Suddenly, I realize where I've seen this man before. I look to Willie.

"B.A.D.-Ass.," I open, "they're police, aren't they?"

Willie nods. "Yeah, Vee," he admits. "It's a round-up. A lot of cold cases are gonna get solved tonight."

"I knew it was too good to be true," I grumble.

"Yo, Vee!" someone shouts.

Kelvin and his crew stand at the foot of the stage. The crack baby is on all fours, scrambling around mindlessly.

"HNIC?" Willie asks me, tension surging to his shoulders.

"It's not him, Willie," I say. "Hustle Beamon's behind all this. Kelvin and his group are helping me." I turn to Kelvin. "What took you so long?"

"You know," he shrugs. "The Electric Slide. You coming?"

"One second." I turn to Willie. "We're going to stop Hustle right now. Put an end to all the madness. Do you want to come along, Willie?"

"I ..." The old man suddenly stops. There is a war going on in his face. Conflicting emotions do battle. I can tell he wants to come with us, to fight until his very last breath. I can tell he also realizes that this fight may very well take his very last breath. I can tell William Orpheus O'Ree is actually scared.

"It's OK, Willie," I soothe, putting my hand on his shoulder. He winces. "You're grievously injured."

"Yeah," he chuckles, awkwardly, "grievously."

"OK," I nod.

"OK," he nods, in return.

I jump off the stage and join the others. We race headlong toward Hustle Beamon's hideout.

Chaptah Twenny–Tu

IT TAKES FOREVER to walk through Toomer Way. Whatever they heard Reverend Booker say, it inspired the white residents of Koontown to arm themselves—rapidly and heavily. Streets are barricaded. Windows are boarded up. It seems that every darkened pane has a pair of gun muzzles and blue eyes peering out of it.

Blue fashions a white flag out of his underwear. The group of us walks steadily down the middle of the street. We make no sudden moves. We make sure our weapons are pointed skyward. We know that even a fidget on our part will bring down a storm of bullets. We stay tense and ready for the metal deluge. But the whites don't make a move, either. They are content to watch and aim. They don't want any trouble from us.

Unfortunately, their children want our autographs. After the first boy screams, "HNIC!" and dashes out of a darkened building toward us, chaos ensues. We are suddenly inundated. The children cheer and chirp, shoot pictures and beg for signatures. Kelvin, never one to disappoint his fans, apparently, poses for pictures and signs pieces of paper, photographs, napkins, whatever.

C-Word and Yo!Nutz are less accommodating. The kids want their autographs, as well, but their last album only went Gold. The two women feel that their fans—these children—let them down. They make the rug rats work for every pen stroke.

Then, someone realizes that the bronzed Asian woman in sports bra and yoga pants is none other than the hot, new R&B sensation, Likki Nice-Nice. Suddenly, a middle-aged wave of Caucasian manhood crashes upon us. Their hormones seem to lead the way. They preen and boast before the singer. They laugh too loudly, pose, and strut. Beg for autographs, pictures, her phone number, URL, whatever she can spare. Suddenly, the wives rush out of their darkened houses, rifles in hand, to retrieve their husbands.

Before we know it, we are leading a parade out of Toomer Way. However, when we reach the border, Jack Johnson Boulevard, the parade abruptly stops. They beg us to stay, have dinner, a drink, to spend the night. Please email us. Call us. Feel free to come back. Any time. Really. We would love to have you.

But they refuse to cross that boulevard and leave the safety and sanctuary of Toomer Way. You can see the fear on their faces. The sweat and moistening eyes. The frantically bobbing Adam's apples.

It is night time, after all. They let us go—reluctantly. But there is absolutely no way any of them will leave Toomer Way.

WE ARE BACK on Jack Johnson Boulevard. The warehouse district. My stomach clenches. I almost lost my life here last night.

The crack baby goes crazy. He hoots and hollers, jumps high in the air, starts somersaulting along the cracked pavement. Blue curses, trying to control the thing. Though nothing but skin and bones, the crack baby is a super soldier and stronger than any of us. He lopes forward, lifting the two hundred fifty-pound Pooh Nanny in the air. Blue screams as the thing drags him forward. He struggles mightily to hold on but eventually lets go, landing flat on his face. His battle axe skitters across the street. He scrambles to his feet and gives chase.

"Blue!" Kelvin shouts. "Let it go!"

Blue stops and turns. "Why?" he asks.

"I know where the place is," Kelvin admits.

"But it'll warn the others," Yolanda objects.

"Doesn't matter," their leader concedes. He pulls out a pair of goggles and straps them across his eyes. The others follow his lead, putting on shades or goggles. "This'll be fucked-up whether it tells its buddies, or not," he says. "Let's go, yall."

I grab Kelvin by his arm. The others move ahead.

"Where are we?" I ask.

"Hustle's mix tape warehouse," he answers.

"I thought mix tapes were illegal."

"They are," the rapper admits. "And we'll prosecute your token store here and there for selling them. But they're great marketing tools. Can't sell without 'em."

"Is this hard for you?" I ask, searching his goggled eyes.

"What?" he asks. "Making mix tapes?"

"No," I say. "Going after these crack babies."

...

"You're one of them, aren't you, Kelvin?"

"What makes you say that, Vee?" he asks, straining to chuckle.

"Pimpnakang said they heal quickly," I start. "And—I don't know how you did it—but you actually *healed* me last night. And I woke up this morning smelling like grape Kool-Aid—"

"*Purple* Kool-Aid," he corrects, with an awkward smile.

"And alcohol," I finish. "Probably Tangueray, right? The Crack Baby Cocktail." The young man shifts uncomfortably. "Then there's the Maalox. He said all they can digest is junk food—at least their primary stomachs, I'm thinking. And you, Kelvin, you eat junk food *and* health food. But every time you do, you down gallons of Maalox."

"Hm."

"Then there are your eyes," I continue.

"What about them?"

"They're so … I don't know … magnetic. Almost hypnotic, really," I say. "I don't know … when I look at you, I feel like you're trying to put me under a spell, or something—just like those crack babies do."

Kelvin chuckles warmly. "Are you sure *that's* what it is?"

I put my hands on my hips.

"You're right," he finally admits, lowering his eyes. "Half-right, anyway. My mother was a crackhead. My dad is a corporate attorney for Knott, Seaux, Black & Blue. I'm half-crack baby, Genevieve."

Kelvin swallows hard. He looks up at me, tears steaming his eyes. I try not to look directly at him. I feel so bad.

"Obviously, I don't have those tentacles and devour human organs," he continues. "But my saliva *does* have amazing healing properties. I heal pretty quickly, too. I'm also addicted to junk food, but I can eat regular food. It's just hard to digest. That's why all the Maalox."

"And you're obviously educated," I add.

"Penn, remember?" He sighs, heavily. "Frankly, Genevieve, it's nothing I'm proud of, but God doesn't burden you with anything you can't handle, right?"

"I'm so sorry, Kelvin," I whisper. "Are you sure you can do this?"

"I have to, Genevieve," he growls, adamantly. "These crack babies have to be stopped. Before they destroy all we've worked for here in Koontown. And, if I don't stop them—if *we* don't stop them—who the *fuck* will?"

I don't know what it is. His passion, his pain. The fierce determination in those very sad eyes. Suddenly, I think of Ashanti Moor, the Koontown Krusader. All that I felt for that man. How I haven't felt the same again. Until this very minute. With this very man. This ... this gangsta rapper.

I don't even know how my hand finds his chin, how it lifts it. No clue how my lips find his. But they do. And they press. They search and drink in all that is Kelvin Cleghorne, Head Nigga in Charge.

Kelvin separates us and smiles.

I suddenly blush. "M-m-m-my god," I stammer. "I don't know why I just did that. I'm sorry. I'm old enough to be your grandmother."

"Damn, Genevieve," he swallows. "I'm twenty-five years of age."

"A very young great-aunt then," I grin—like a little schoolgirl.

WE COWER IN the shadows. The warehouse is fully lit. Full of activity. Fully-naked wraiths move busily to and fro. They are burning compact discs, packing them in their jewel cases, loading them into cardboard boxes. You can see their rib cages all the way out here. They look absolutely famished.

And here we are, a potential feast, crouching mere feet away outside, ready to sacrifice ourselves for the good of Koontown.

"Why are they naked?" I whisper.

"Hustle doesn't want them pinching the discs and throwing them up on the Internet before their release dates," Kelvin says. "These things are *highly* coordinated."

"We goin' in, or what?" Yolanda hisses, clutching a Heckler & Koch P2000 SK pistol.

Martina nods her assent.

"Is Hustle even there?" Lin asks, eagerly.

"Doesn't really matter," Kelvin answers. "There are a lot of crack babies in there. Take them all out, and Hustle'll be reduced to just fucking up the music industry."

"And television," Spade adds.

"And books and movies," Blue contributes.

"You get the idea, fools," their leader snaps. "Clarise, Yolanda. Yall don't have any outside projects or endorsements, do you?"

"Naw, we only have our Dope Beat contract," Clarise fumes.

"What did I tell you about diversification?" Kelvin admonishes. "You should at least have a reality show. Something."

"We know, we know," Clarise exhales, wearily.

"You, Lin?" Kelvin asks.

"I don't care," she says. "I want to go back to the Philharmonic, anyway."

"OK, then," Kelvin says. "Clarise and Yolanda, you go to the back. If Hustle's here and tries to escape, you grab him. If we fail, he'll never know you were here. You can keep recording."

"You sure?" Yolanda asks. "What about you, K?"

Kelvin shrugs. "Just go."

"To believe I went to Wellesley for this shit," Clarise smirks. "If Momma could see me now."

She and Yo!Nutz dash into the night and disappear around the side of the building, crouching low the entire time.

"So, how we goin in?" Brudda Spearchucka asks.

Kelvin looks to me. "Vee?"

"No need to be subtle. Let's just go straight in—fast and hard," I say. "Fuck 'em like a Kennedy, right?"

"ONE! TWO! THREE!"

Spade and Blue-Eyed Devil's massive feet slam against the heavy metal doors. They fly inward and crash against the wall. The two large men swing their AK-47s to their hips and fire into the massive warehouse.

Ping! Ping! Ping!

Sparks fly. Flesh opens. Throats scream. Bodies fall.

We flood in behind them. Lin, Brudda, and I sprint right. Kelvin and Martina move left. We all fire. I aim for a forehead. The Ruger booms in my hands. I hear a scream. A faint sizzle. The head disappears from sight.

I look for another target. Bodies are flying everywhere. Bullets smack into all resistance. Smoke starts rising. From our guns. From the crack babies' bodies. Wounds sizzle and smoke. Cordite and burnt flesh fill my nostrils. I simply fire at whatever moves.

"Fuck!!!"

I look. A crack baby sits atop Brudda Spearchucka. They wrestle for the punk's gun. Another naked wraith jumps on the duo, its elongated penis smacking Brudda in the face.

"Oh, God!!!" he wails, and starts gagging.

I dash. Raise my pistol. Squeeze. Bullet finds brains. Blood sprays. The remaining crack baby looks up, hissing.

WHOOOOOSSSSSHHHHHH!!!

A tentacle smashes into my goggles. I groan. Stumble. Drop the gun. Acid sizzles. I drop to my knee. A shadow moves past me. A woman screams. I look. Lin flies. Her foot lands in the side of the baby's head. They go flying. She rolls on the floor, comes up firing. The baby's head flies off—chunks at a time.

"Vee!" Lin screams.

I turn.

The talon catches the side of my head.

"Ugh."

Stars. I twirl. I point my gun—no gun. I click air. The thing cackles, swoops in. Catches my jaw with a right hook. I twirl, gain momentum, lift my leg. My roundhouse catches its head. Snaps its neck back. I stop, reach behind, brandish my katana. Strike. The crack baby shakes its head. I remove the blade from the thing's shoulders. Blood sprays to the ceiling. The body collapses at my feet.

The right side of my goggles is cracked and partially melted from the stomach acid. I can't see. Useless. I rip the glasses off my head. Throw them to the floor.

"likkaniggadik"

I crouch, spin, rip the .22 from my ankle holster, and come up firing.

THUD!!!

"Oooomph!"

The flying crack baby lands on me. Its momentum drives us to the floor. It looks into my eyes. I swing the .22's muzzle to its temple. Squeeze the trigger. More blood and brains go flying. I struggle beneath the beast's weight.

I finally get to my feet and start firing at anything that moves. Crack babies fly through the air. More gunfire. More screams. Blue? I don't see him. Is he down? I keep firing, aiming as best I can.

Click! Click! Click!

I duck behind a table. My hands search frantically for a replacement clip. I eject the used one. Jam the fresh clip into my gun.

What …?

A powerful heat suddenly washes over me. A strong light blinds. I am suddenly … pulled to my feet. I slowly turn to the light. Against my will. I have no will. My body moves without me. I see nothing but the light. I hear nothing. But I feel the light, revel in its heat. I move away from the table, find an aisle, and start walking toward the brilliant illumination.

It seems as though the battle has ceased all around me. Guns have been silenced. They clatter to the floor. I throw down my Taurus and sword. I involuntarily reach back for my bo staff and let it drop to the concrete.

Suddenly, a figure emerges from the light. Glorious blond hair, a fluorescently white robe. It billows and flows in a wind of its own making. Arms stretch out toward us, beseeching.

"White Jesus?!" I hear someone gasp.

Despite myself, I fall to my knees. I don't understand. I don't even believe. None of us Noires do. We never did. Yet, here I am, kneeling before a god I don't even think exists. Yet, here he is, glorious in the light—white and beautiful. All-powerful. All-knowing. I am suddenly ashamed of my own disbelief.

But who can resist White Jesus?

"That is right," God bellows. "I am here. White Jesus. Here to save you silly negroes from yourselves. Just like in all the movies."

"Bruce Willis!!!" someone wails.

"Vee! Vee!" I hear through the mystery. Someone's tugging at my clothes.

I look up, confused. All I see is the Light.

"Only White Jesus can save you people," White Jesus continues, so beautifully I want to cry. "Put down your guns. Believe in peace. Believe in me! Give unto Me what is Mine!"

"Yes, White Jesus!" I scream. "Save me! SAVE ME!!!"

"That's not White Jesus," a woman whispers.

"What ...?"

Thwack!

"Ow."

My head. A new light burns out the old. I grab my head and shake. Suddenly, I see Lin standing over me.

"What?" I repeat.

"That's not White Jesus," the woman repeats, heatedly. "It's Avi. Hustle's assistant."

"How do you know?" I gulp.

"I'm Buddhist," Lin declares. She starts pulling me to my feet. "Come on. I think I saw Hustle. Let's go!"

I struggle to stand. I look. Lin's right. The light has lost its luster. Without all the shine, I can plainly see that who I thought was the Messiah is nothing but Hustle Beamon's lackey in white robes. I let Lin pull me along.

"It's not White Jesus!" I yell, over my shoulder. "It's Avi!"

"No, silly negress," Avi booms. "I am the one, true Savior. White Jesus! I swear to Me!!!"

"Motherfucker!" I hear Blue yell. "Get the Jew!!!"

I hear scuffling, screaming. I don't turn. Lin has us running down a hallway. Suddenly, Hustle appears, running across a perpendicular hall. We turn right and follow. His diamond ball cap flies off his head as he ducks into a doorway. We sprint after him. The door slams in our faces.

"Come on," Lin pants, stopping at the door.

I nod, breathlessly. "One … two … three!" I count.

We kick simultaneously. The door groans on impact. We kick again. The door jamb splinters. We kick again. The door flies open. We rush inside. Hustle Beamon turns to face us, an ominous smile on his gaunt face. Like he expects us. Like he actually wants us here.

"What …?" I exhale.

THWACK!!!

"uggghhhhh…"

Chaptah Twenny—Free

I DON'T THINK I've been out long. Don't think I've traveled too far. I can still hear the battle raging in the distance. I groan. My arms are stretched out, held on either end by crack babies. I raise my head and turn it to the right. Lin is in the same position. I look straight ahead. Hustle Beamon gloats at us, leaning against a desk, filing his fingernails.

"Always knew you were more than just a pretty face, Vee," the rap mogul smirks, maliciously. "I'll take care of you in a minute."

He places the emery board on his desk and stands. He nonchalantly moves toward Lin. He carefully lifts her head. She looks at him with nothing but disdain.

"And you," he spits. "After all I've done for you. Lifted you out of the slums of Juilliard. Made you an R&B star. Made you famous! And I *never* asked—*never asked* for *anything* in return. No manicure, no pedicure, no Happy Ending! And this is how you repay me!"

"You shot an arrow at my *ass*, Hustle!" Lin yells.

"That was only BizZenAss, woman. Nothing personal," he refutes.

"However, this bullshit *is*."

He claps his skeletal hands. A shaded female crack baby enters the room. Hustle moves aside. The super soldier stands before Lin and her two captors. The singer struggles ferociously.

"What the hell are you doing, Hustle?!" she demands.

"You know, Likki, Pac and Biggie sold way more in death than they ever did in life," Hustle declares, icily. "The same with Hendrix, Morrison, Janis Joplin, Otis Redding. You're about to join some *very* prestigious company, girl."

"No! Hustle! No!!!"

"Funny thing about fame," he continues. "People don't realize that it's actually not worth it until *after* they've actually attained it."

"But I went to Juilliard!!!"

The mogul snaps his fingers. Lin screams her throat raw. My stomach twists in knots. The female crack baby whips off her glasses. Lin thrashes her head from side to side. The crack baby grabs the singer's chin and holds it in place. Lin cries. Tears stream down her face from clamped eyelids. The wraith places her fingers on the left lid and pries it open.

"No," Lin whimpers. "Please ..."

It's too late. The R&B sensation goes slack as her eye meets the super soldier's. She sighs briefly. Their eyes lock. The tentacles fire into Lin's orbs, smashing them. There's a sickening squish. The two females are linked. The tentacles pulsate with fluid. I can hear the acid burn through Lin's poor body. Slurp! Slurp! Slurp! The crack baby vacuums my comrade's innards clean out of her body.

I empty my own stomach, vomiting all over the floor.

Hustle laughs heartily. "It *is* hard getting used to," he cheerily admits. "But you won't have to worry about all *that*, Jon Vee."

He strides my way.

"So, do me the honor," he opens, "how did you figure my little scheme out?"

"Once I realized that Sims was your father, it was easy," I declare.

He gives me an odd look—like he may actually be impressed. "Continue," he urges.

"See," I say, "I thought it was weird how everything just kept pointing so conveniently to Kelvin. *Too* conveniently. It just wreaked of a set-up."

"Because you're attracted to the boy?" he asks, calmly.

"No!" I object. Too vehemently. Hustle offers up a condescending grin. "Not at all," I reaffirm. "It's just that everybody was connected—*obviously* connected to Kelvin—"

"HNIC, you mean," he interrupts, gloating.

"I don't use that word," I lie, haughtily. "Kelvin had a very public beef with both Irie Man and Funky Dollah Bill. And that other one, too, I think…"

"*Niggassippee.*"

"Yes, him," I concur. "But he's also produced some of their records. For all I know, they were all friends. You yourself said a lot of this drama in hip-hop is just that. Drama—to sell records.

"So, knowing that, it made it harder to believe that Kelvin would actually kill those other men. I mean, Mr. 'Sippee was even completely out of the rap game. He was producing that utterly *atrocious* kids' show, *Gimme Dat*. Reason enough to want his death, but why actually kill him? I couldn't figure that out. And I couldn't figure out why you so vehemently wanted me to believe that Kelvin was so dangerous. It almost seemed like you were selling him down the river. It didn't make much sense, at first."

"At first," Beamon echoes, his thoughts seeming to be elsewhere.

"There was Hercules Kennon who wasn't even a rapper, but an actual musician. And that woman, Compton-Stuyvesant. I mean, Torch," I correct myself. "Why would some two-bit gangsta rapper kill an award-winning novelist? Black or white. It just didn't make any kind of sense."

"Does if the nigger's actually *crazy*," Hustle proffers.

"Oh, someone's crazy, all right," I agree. "But not a total whack job. And there had to be an underlying logic to all this death. It took me a little while to piece it all together. There were just too many things that didn't seem to fit. Until I did some research and discovered that these people *were* actually connected. Connected to *you*. But you know that already, Hustle."

Beamon leans his lanky frame against his desk. He picks up his emery board and returns to inspecting his nails.

"Dope Beat Records, subsidiary labels," I start. "You're a silent partner in Mr. 'Sippee's production company, and you hold a controlling interest in Koonington Press, Ms. Torch's book publisher."

"And your cousin Grey's," he adds, ominously.

I ignore the threat. Hustle Beamon is not leaving this warehouse alive.

"What I can't understand is, first, how you can control these … these super soldiers," I admit.

"The music," he states, plainly. "You know how negroes are with their music. Keep those booties shaking, and you got 'em. Like the song says, 'Enslave their asses, and their minds will follow.'"

"Hm, that makes sense," I admit. "The other thing is, why would you want to kill all these people, Hustle? They're your business partners, your associates. You make money with them. Quite a lot of money, actually. I haven't read your book, yet, but this does *not* seem like good BizZenAss, Beamon."

"Well, these fools are definitely worth more to me dead than they are alive," he says. "FDB and Irie Man sales are through the roof. Especially with those cults of theirs popping up out of nowhere."

"So, that's the reason?" I spit, disgusted.

"No, Genevieve," Hustle objects. "The reason is Revolution."

"Hunh?"

"Look," the rap mogul opens, looking me straight in the eye. "I may come from a privileged background and may be of mixed-race parentage, but I was treated as *black* growing up. I was a first generation Integration Baby. People were quite hostile to my existence. They said our family didn't belong in their neighborhood. I shouldn't have been in their schools. That I better not have gone anywhere near their daughters.

"See, I might've been light-skinned, had a white family background, spoke proper English, and had money in the bank, but, just like the residents of Koontown here, those white folks treated me like a *nigger*. You could see it in their eyes. Hear it coming out of their mouths."

I nod, believing.

"The *main* thing that saved me was my family—especially my mother. *She* was the one who constantly told me I actually wasn't what those crackers were calling me. *She* stood strong against their racism. And *she* would smack me upside the head if I ever *once* acted like they said I should."

"She was the perfect role model."

"Yes," he smiles, fondly. "But there were others. We had proud, strong brothers and sisters back then—like Diahann Carroll, Sidney Poitier, Bill Cosby, Richard Roundtree, Cicely Tyson, Lena Horne. We had athletes like Arthur Ashe and Kareem Abdul Jabbar. We had educators and Civil Rights leaders and activists and even musicians who constantly reminded us that we black folks, indeed, were *not ... niggers.*"

He looks away briefly. He's getting heated. On the verge of losing control. He must be trying to calm himself down. His chest heaves in and out—in search of that BizZenAss?

"But then something happened," Hustle Beamon continues. "*The Chronic* sold *millions*. And the culture changed. Suddenly, hip-hop took over. And only one certain *kind* of hip-hop. Oh sure, it was militant for a minute, and there had been 'happy rap,' and even *female* MCs. But then, the labels had their model. It was going to be 'All Niggaz, All de Damned Time!'

"We have had nothing but niggaz for almost twenty years now, Genevieve," Hustle cries, desperately. "Everywhere you look, all you see *is* niggaz. Niggaz in the music. Niggaz in the movies. Niggaz in politics. Even niggaz in our fucking *books*, Vee. Now, how the hell are we supposed to raise up our sons and, especially, our daughters, when wherever they look, all they can see themselves as is as a bunch of *niggaz?*"

"But Hustle," I open, confused. "You've contributed to all this. You've profited from it. In fact, you are the *largest* purveyor of all this nonsense you say sickens you."

"I know, Vee," the record exec huffs. Something takes hold. He suddenly smiles grandly. Energetically. He sweeps toward me. "It was a power move, can't you see? I started my own label. Grew that bitch to a multinational, billion-dollar enterprise. Got the money, got the clout, got ... the ... *money*. Now, every single company that produces that *nigga* bullshit is under *my* control. Not the white boys'. *Mine*."

"Congratulations?"

"Thank you." He stands back. His chest puffs up. "'Cause now, it's time for the Revolution! It is time to *clean house!*"

"What are you talking about, Hustle?"

"Please call me, Jonas."

I nod.

"Don't you see, Vee? Most of those 'gangsta' rappers are dead and gone now, thanks to me," he triumphs. "My army and I have killed them. There are a handful left, but it's only a matter of time. Ms. Torch was only an opening salvo. I've bought Koonington Press, and soon I will go after every negro who's bought a copy of Nigga Narrativez. They have *all* got to go!"

"Grey?" I gasp.

"Now, that depends on you," Beamon states.

"How so?"

"You can join me, Vee," Hustle encourages. "I've been chasing you for almost twenty years now because that's all I've ever wanted—for you to join me. You can head up your own publishing house—produce books and magazines and websites we can be proud of again. Or you can have your own label. You can produce *real* R&B with *real* singers with *real* voices being accompanied by *real* musicians on *real* instruments. Hell, we can even take over Niggasippee's production company. Produce movies, television. Dramas and comedies where black folks aren't always killing each other."

I admit, it does sound good. But it doesn't sound quite right. There is something missing. Before I can open my mouth, though, Hustle Beamon continues flapping his.

"We can *actually* have a 'No Nigger' policy," he continues, eyes blazing madly. "I don't care how you spell it. We will never have to hear another African-American utter that *despicable* word in the public sphere ever again.

"We can usher in a whole new Renaissance, Genevieve. We can build a new Afrikania. No more Koontown, no *Negrovillea*. No more coons. No coons, no porch monkeys, jigaboos, spades, spear chuckers. None of it! Just proud, strong, and *beautiful* African-Americans!"

"Afrikania?" I mutter.

"Yes," Hustle beams. "It will be *amazing*, Genevieve! Can't you see it?!"

"I think I can," I admit.

"What do you say, Ms. Noire?" Hustle asks, enthusiastically. "Will you join the Revolution?"

"Indubitably, Jonas," I chirp.

The two crack babies holding my arms suddenly cringe. The female who killed Lin flinches.

"Abscission," I voice.

Their grips loosen.

"What?" Hustle snaps. "That doesn't even make sense."

I struggle to remember as many SAT words as possible.

"Frowzy!" I shout. "Frigidarium!"

All three crack babies fall to their knees, screaming, clawing at their ears.

"Seditious!" I yell. "Nostrum!"

"likkaniggadik!" they screech.

"Shut up!" Hustle screams.

I lead with my left and crash my first into the man's jaw. He sprawls across his desk. The crack babies move toward me.

"Insentient!" I yell.

They fall back to the floor, writhing. I reach into my jacket and produce one of Mao's Little Red Books. "Heptarchy!" I dive at the female and shove the book against the thing's forehead. "Vendible!" Flesh burns. Smoke rises from her head. She writhes furiously, trying to claw at me. I dodge as much as possible as the book burns into her flesh and bone. "Polyhedron! Polyarchy!"

The creature stops struggling, dead. I rise.

"Ooomph!"

Hustle's blow lands square in the middle of my back. Such a scrawny man. But he definitely packs a punch. I go reeling.

CRASH!

"Uhhh…"

I smack into the wall. My hands are too slow. My nose smashes against the wood paneling. Stars. I shake my head, trying to clear it.

SMACK! SMACK!

Fists.

"Pugilism," I groan. The crack babies scream.

"What the hell are you doing?"

"Sedulous," I whimper.

"Iikkaniggadik!!!"

Hustle looks to his beasts, confused. There! I rush the mogul. I tackle him to the ground. As soon as his back smacks the floor, I release. I spin in the air, land on my back, come up in a crouch. Each hand rips out a Little Red Book. I throw them at the crack babies. Reflexively, they catch them and start screeching. The sound is utterly inhuman. It tears at my ear drums.

"Bestial!" I shout, triumphantly.

Their screeching grows louder. Their flesh burns and melts around the miniature tomes. They writhe in pain, unable to let go. Their tentacles whip the air. They tumble to the floor, smoke rising from their struggling forms.

Hustle storms toward me. He raises his foot to kick. I grab his foot and twist. He spins to the ground. I scramble. Land an elbow into his prone kidney. He howls. I scramble farther up. I work my arm under his chin, clamp my hands together, and start choking.

"Why—why—" he struggles "—why not j-j-join the R-Rev-Revolution, Genevieve?"

"Because …" I grit, trying to choke the consciousness out of the man. " … I am petty … and bourgeois …"

Hustle chuckles his last breathes. His head slumps over, unconscious. I struggle to my feet, heaving air into my lungs.

"I am a *Noire*," I declare, proudly.

THWACK!!!

The world goes white.

I fall …

"···ON MY OLD Kentucky hoomAAARRRRRGGGHHH!!!"

I land hard. But soft. The ground is lumpy beneath me. And clothed? I shake my head, completely confused.

"What is this all-fired balderdash about now?!" I hear the ground erupt.

I shake my head again. I was just standing over Hustle Beamon. Something hit my head—I think. Then everything went white. I felt as though I were falling, hurtling. Then I landed here.

Here?

I open my eyes. Darkness above. A huge light to my left. A … spotlight?

"It's a negress!" I hear a woman shriek.

There's grumbling. A smattering of … applause? I don't understand. I feel hands on my back.

"Why, gal!" the ground roars again.

I feel it push. I roll over, hit hard wood, and land on my belly. I try once again to clear the fog from my head. Suddenly, two large, white eyes peer down at me. Curious, terrifying. More eyes follow. They shine brightly in dark masks. Burnt masks. Burnt-*cork* masks?

Black face?!

I shriek and scoot across the floor. Suddenly, the air around me erupts in laughter.

"Why, you'd think she's gone and seen her a Ku Kluxer!" someone bellows from behind the masks. The laughter swells.

I see a stick, a broken banjo neck. I snatch it off the floor and point it at the men. There are four of them. In black face and old-timey barber uniforms— striped shirts and arm bands. Their faces are covered in ghastly blackness. There are huge, white smiles painted on them from ear to ear.

"Where am I?" I shriek.

More laughter.

"From the looks of it …" sounds a familiar voice.

Suddenly, the four minstrels separate. The missing puzzle piece breeches the gap. Lucille Parsons. I just knew it. I've known Hustle Beamon for a long time. All he's ever cared about was money. All of the sudden, he's talking about Revolution. And actually killing people in its name. I knew there had to be a master behind his puppet.

And now she's standing above me, tall, majestic. She looks around with nothing but disdain for the four men in black face.

"…I'd say we're right in the middle of a nineteenth-century minstrel show," Lucille declares. She scrutinizes the men's costumes. She leans in closer to look around their eyes. "You're negro, right?"

"Shhhh," one of them hushes.

"Who are you?" she asks. "The American Four?"

"Dem niggas?!" their leader scoffs. "Naw, gal, we de Hamtown Students."

"Right, then." Lucille looks back at me. "We're looking at about 1875 here, Genevieve."

"Eighteen sebendee-six," the leader corrects.

I look up at her. "You took me time-traveling again, Lucille?"

"Yes, I did, Genevieve," she admits, proudly. "I wanted to talk some reason into you. After all, I'm thinking 1876 is probably a pretty shitty time to be stuck in, don't you? Even for a negress with such *fine* features as yourself."

"She can always start her a gaudy house," one of the quartet volunteers. "By the horn spoon, I'd be her very first customer … off de *reel*."

Lucille looks down at me on the stage's floor, satisfied.

"You planning to leave me here?" I ask.

"If you don't wise up and join the Revolution," she answers.

"Join you and Hustle? And form a new Afrikania?"

"Dey's goin' to *Liberia*, yall!!!" one minstrel announces to the crowd.

The audience behind them cheer emphatically.

"Huzzah! Huzzah! Huzzah!"

"Don't book return passage!" someone yells.

"How did you do it, Lucille?" I ask. "How did you convince Hustle to have all those people killed? To join forces with you and your so-called Revolution?"

"The 'Power of the P'—as the young folk say."

"Persuasion?" I guess.

"*Pussy*," she gloats.

"Really? He's, like, thirty years your junior."

"What can I say? The boy has a great-grandmomma fetish."

I fight back a shiver. "Well, you *are* one helluva woman, Lucille Parsons," I admit.

"That I am," she smiles. "So, are you going to join us, Genevieve? Go back to the present day and rebuild Afrikania with your gbeto? Or am I going to have to leave you here … with *these*?"

I shrug. "No. I'll go."

"What? No fight?" my mentor asks, genuinely astonished. "I expected more from you, Ms. Noire. I expected … *a fight*."

"I'm tired of fighting, Lucille," I exhale. "It seems like I've been fighting my entire life. And I don't even know for what anymore."

"For the Revolution," Lucille volunteers. "It is high time we exterminate the vermin and let our humanity *thrive*. I am *ecstatic* knowing you will be by my side … daughter."

Her eyes gleam madly. There seems to be blood in her smile. I fight back a squirm. I try to produce tears. A smile. I must look happy, ecstatic. It must look like all the fight has gone out of me. It *must*. "Here," I smile, wearily, "help me up … mother."

I raise my left hand to my mentor. She gladly leans over and takes it with a victorious smile. I lunge forward with a grunt. I shoot my right hand straight toward the woman's belly. The broken banjo neck in it plunges straight into Lucille Parsons's gut.

"No," the old woman gasps, absolute horror and betrayal bug her eyes out. Blood dribbles out of her stunned mouth.

She collapses right on top of me. We crash to the stage. I lie here. Paralyzed. Lucille gasps atop me. I feel her blood seep out and wash over me. I start to cry.

"Why …?" she rasps. "Why … Genevieve …?"

"I don't know, Lucille," I whisper/weep in her ear. "Who are we to judge? To say who's a real … *nigger* … and who's not?"

She titters—almost girlishly. Blood dribbles down her mouth. She struggles to speak.

"What is it, Lucille?" I ask, gingerly.

"I ... I ... I have seen the nigger, Genevieve," Lucille croaks. "And she is ... she is ... *us*."

She lets out one, last sigh, and her head slumps against my shoulder. I feel nothing. Hear nothing. Not a single breath. My mentor, my hero, the woman who pulled me from the fog, lifted me out of my hospital bed, and gave me life and gave that life purpose, Lucille Parsons, Civil Rights activist and advocate for her people, is dead. On the sepia stage of an 1876 minstrel show.

"Huzzah! Huzzah! Huzzah!"

The crowd cheers wildly. The rafters reverberate with their love of the show we've just given them. My tears know no end.

"Come on, fellas!"

The four minstrels move and lift Lucille off of me. I lie here. Frozen. Covered in my hero's blood. I did this. I killed her...

BEFORE I KNOW it, the men lift me up, too. The crowd is beside itself. Roses and carnations are thrown onto the stage. They land at my feet. I am dazed, stunned, beyond belief.

"Encore!" they cheer. "Encore!"

"What should I do?" I whisper. "I need to get back home."

"Well, chile," I hear a woman say.

I turn. "Aunt Jemima?"

"I'se in town, gal!"

She smiles brightly, waddling up to me on the stage. The crowd goes ballistic. Apparently, Aunt Jemima was a fan favorite—even back in 1876. She pulls me to her bosom and gives me a suffocating bear hug.

"Any time I'se wanna go home," she continues, "I jus' do de Hambone."

I pull away. "That's it?" I ask. "Just do the Hambone?"

The minstrels shake their heads emphatically.

"With *style!*" Aunt Jemima amends, shaking her "jazz hands" at her sides.

"Uh … OK," I say, hesitantly. I turn to the minstrel leader. "Pardon me for asking, but you all are black, right?" The man nods. "How can you do it? The black face thing? I mean, isn't it just a *bit* degrading?"

"Gotta make dat paper, *bitch*," he snaps at me.

I shake my head. The more things change …

"Don't you worry none, chile," Aunt Jemima advises. "You jus' do yo' Hambone an' gits on *home*."

I nod. I clear my throat. Stiffen. The crowd lurches forward in anticipation. I see nothing but pale faces, handlebar moustachios, and parasols. I'm embarrassed, humiliated. Part of a minstrel show—and I don't even know my part. Noires don't do the Hambone. We have spent centuries learning how not to do it.

I straighten my clothes. Clear my throat again. I try to remember. Back. Visiting Grey and Uncle Connelly and Aunt Umfoofahloofahklik!klak!klik! back at the Porch Monkey Projects before my aunt hightailed it back to Africa. Remember the old-timey men who used to sit out in the front of the high rises. Doing their old-timey dances. Singing their old-timey songs.

My voice is barely a whisper.

"Hambone, Hambone, where you been?" I croak, meagerly.

The crowd boos.

"Put some *feelin'* in it, gal," Aunt Jemima encourages.

"Hambone, Hambone, where you been?" I sing, a little louder.

"Put yo' *whole* foot in it!" she yells, and starts slapping her thighs and chest.

Oh yeah. Right.

I slap my right hand against my thigh, the back of my leg, and my sternum. I do the same with my left. It's herky and it's jerky. Not much rhythm to it.

"You can do it, gal! You can do it!"

"Hambone, Hambone, where you been?" I repeat.

"Round the world an' I'm goin' again," sings the barbershop quartet in four-part harmony.

I chuckle uncomfortably.

Then, something happens. A warmth, a power suddenly radiates through me. My voice gains strength.

"Hambone! Hambone! Have you heard?!" my voice rings out.

"Papa's gonna buy me a mockin' bird!"

I laugh. The warmth is whole now. My voice is clear and strong. My hands gain a rhythm all their own. Whatever it is has taken hold. I am *its* now. And it is bigger than me. Bigger than the Noires. It is past. It is present. It is future!

"Hambone! Hambone! Trying to eat!"

It's America. Africa. It goes beyond Africa and America. It follows the old routes. To Brazil, Central America, the Caribbean. All throughout the Middle East. To India. To China. All the way up through Europe. Even ancient Rome. It is bigger than all of them. It encompasses the entire world. All of human history. It is written. Has never needed to be written. It is a part of me. Always has been. Always will be. I cannot shake it if I try. It will always be there for me. Accept me. Love me.

"Ketchup on his elbows! Pickles on his feet!"

"It doesn't matter what others think of you," my father once told me. "It's what you think of yourself."

My clapping becomes furious. I stomp hard enough to shatter fillings.

"No matter what you do in this world, no matter what other folks think …"

"Look at him holler!" I sing. "Look at him moan!"

"… you just got to maintain that dignity, child …"

"That hambone just can't hambone!!!" I shriek.

My hands are a blur. My slaps echo throughout the spellbound crowd.

"As long as you can hold your head high," Daddy said. "Don't shit-else matter, Vee!"

"Hambone!" We all sing. "Hambone!!!"

I end with a flourish, slapping and dancing, and throwing my hands in the air. The crowd erupts frantically. I can hardly catch my breath. My ears ring with applause. Flowers hurtle toward me. Cheers. Whistles. Shouts.

I close my eyes in triumph.

The world, once again, flashes entirely white.

Eppylog

"Ladies first, there's no time to rehearse
I'm divine and my mind expands throughout the universe"

—Queen Latifah and Monie Love, "Ladies First"

I SIT HERE in my office, staring blankly at my computer screen. Not knowing what to do with myself. I am tired. Battered, bruised, beaten. The bullet lodged in my spine aches. I can't believe it didn't kill or paralyze me with all it's been through. The last few days have been madness incarnate. Hell, itself. I want to cry, but my eyes are too exhausted. They refuse to even make the effort. I'm not sure I will ever recover. So many people never will.

My kiss has, once again, proven fatal. A decade ago, I kissed Ashanti Moor, and he was immediately gunned down in church. Last night, I planted one on Kelvin Cleghorne's unsuspecting lips, and Koontown has lost another good brother.

I refuse to believe those earlier news reports about the man. About his supposed drug dealing, homicides, and traffic violations. They were plants, fakes. Kelvin Cleghorne *was* a good man. That is all there is to it.

Fortunately, for his memory, all of Koontown feels exactly as I do. The kids have burned all their Irie Man, FDB, and "Gimme Dat" T-shirts. They now sport HNIC polos. Their candles now burn for that great man. Unfortunately, they will never know how he saved the entire town. How he gave his life for his fans, for his people.

Nobody's talking. Yo!Nutz and C-Word are each walking around with a bloody T-shirt, claiming that they were his one, true love. I won't even pretend that I was—but I could have been. Oh, how I could have been.

These women are lying. About their love with him, about their "suspected" pregnancies, and about the true nature of Kelvin's death. Nobody would believe a bunch of super soldier crack babies killed the legendary rapper. However, *everybody* believes that his death was a government conspiracy—possibly carried out by the National Guard.

That's what the two female MCs are saying. I don't blame them. A lie needs to be told. Just not about the love. But those rumors are skyrocketing their own CD sales. The same is happening to HNIC's records. And Avi, Dope Beat Records' new CEO, promises to release Kelvin's entire vault—including his earlier work as Rebelution.

Similar promises are being made in regards to Likki Nice-Nice's unreleased material. And the Pooh Nannies. Neither Blue-Eyed Devil nor Brudda Spearchucka survived last night's encounter with the crack babies.

But neither did the crack babies themselves. Only their corpses remain. Spade has promised to continue the hunt. So has Martina Canales. But both of them seem to think the threat over.

If only Dr. Marion Sims were still alive to pay for what he and Willie Lynch has done to this town. But Koontown's coroner is dead. The authorities found him eviscerated in his own office. The scene was so gruesome, grown men— trained professionals who deal with death on a daily basis—lost their lunches on the spot.

A similar fate did not claim the coroner's son's life, though. Hustle Beamon, apparently, took matters into his own hands—placing a .45 in one of them and a 9mm in the other. They still don't know exactly how he did it, but the hip-hop mogul apparently succeeded in firing both guns simultaneously. His skull shattered beyond all recognition. I actually don't think he did it, though. My money's on Spade and Martina. But I'll never snitch.

I also won't talk about what happened to Lucille Parsons. She's been missing, of course. And obviously, her body hasn't been found. I think my former gbeto suspect that I had something to do with it. But they'll never confront me about it. To do so would only force them to admit to being accomplices in Lucille and Hustle's plot. I don't know if they were or weren't, but I highly doubt they want to be put in a position to say yea or nay.

I don't know what will happen to the elephant hunters from this point on. I believed in the sisterhood, believed we were about something. Something positive. But now I don't know. That school was great, but Lucille's plot obviously was not. I wish I could return to my sisters, but they weren't there for me when I needed them most. I don't know if they ever had been. I doubt if I will ever find out.

I can't believe I'm saying this, but Koontown is definitely better off with Hustle Beamon and Lucille Parsons dead. I know it's a bit ironic that the person who decided at least one of their deaths can and actually did condemn them for deciding who should live and who should die, but it'll literally take decades for my city to recover from the devastation they brought upon it.

The B.A.D.-Ass./police round-up worked spectacularly. Thousands of people volunteered their DNA in the hopes of discovering the identities of their real fathers. Instead, they found themselves accused of crimes everybody thought long-forgotten. Hundreds of cold cases were closed last night. Thousands were taken off the streets.

Millions of dollars worth of property were saved. Koontown did burn. Whole swathes of it. But most remained unharmed. Including Toomer Way— of course. So, the devastation wasn't as widespread as many had feared—and others had hoped. Most of the Conestoga wagons turned right back around to go back to wherever they came from, taking the National Guard with them. Koontown has not been changed enough for their tastes. The risks of living in the KT far outweigh the benefits of the depressed real estate market.

Others were undaunted, however, and several, intrepid white settlers have decided to homestead within city limits. Toomer Way is expanding rapidly as I sit here. I wonder how Mayor Cummings feels about all this. He's got to think he'll never be re-elected with this influx of newer, paler residents. I heard on the radio this morning that he's launching a new Tough on Crime initiative later this week.

I wonder how Willie feels. I've tried calling my old partner several times this morning. He refuses to answer his home, office, and cell phones. I even called Koontown Kounty to make sure he isn't back in the hospital, but the nurses told me he'd been discharged last night.

I know that old fool. He's still smarting form missing the battle with the crack babies. He probably thinks himself a coward. That he let me down, himself down, and all of Koontown. But he has nothing to be ashamed of. He was grievously injured, after all. And, with all that man has given to this city over the years, he most definitely deserved *one* night off.

I said all this in the messages I left for him. I hope the old coot listens. Hope he comes out on the other end of the funk he must be feeling today. He is too good to let his supposed "failure" haunt him.

Looking at this debacle, my cousin Grey seems to be the only one the better for it. Sure, she lost her long-term lover, Night, but that albino brother wasn't really much of a loss. By the looks of it, he only weighed Grey—and her vagina—down.

Now, that dynamic duo is flying high. And all over the country. *Night Fallz* has already joined her other three novels on Best Sellers lists around the world. Critics have dusted off what they'd just been saying about LaSchwanika Compton-Stuyvesant née Rebecca Torch, claiming that Grey Noire truly captures "the gritty reality of America's inner city streets—the pain, the despair, and, ultimately, the *hope* that burns within all of us."

The new CEO of Koonington Press has rewarded my cousin with a six-figure advance for her new novel, which should be coming out any day now, and a thirty-city book tour. Grey called me earlier this morning from somebody's private jet, on top off the world.

It's all so hard to believe. I know, what hasn't been these last few days? But my Grey, my cousin, an internationally best-selling author? I don't think I have ever seen the woman crack a book. She has never expressed an interest in reading or writing. According to her own privates, Grey never studied or written a single paper while in college. Yet, here she is, a literary sensation. Time has called her the best African-American writer of her generation. She may just get that Nobel Prize, after all.

And, to believe, all of my cousin's newfound success is because of that silly, little computer program I found on that white girl's desk ...

Nigga Narrativez ...

...

Hmmmm ....

BILL CAMPBELL

is the author of *Sunshine Patriots*, *My Booty Novel*, and *Pop Culture: Politics, Puns, and "Poohbutt" from a Liberal Stay-at-Home Dad* and the co-editor (along with Edward Austin Hall) of *Mothership: Tales from Afrofuturism and Beyond*. He lives in the Washington, DC, area and terrorizes the countryside with visions of blackface and watermelon.

www.rosariumpublishing.com

Mothership:
Tales from Afrofuturism and Beyond

Edited by Bill Campbell and Edward Austin Hall

Mothership:
Tales from Afrofuturism and Beyond

Edited by
Bill Campbell and Edward Austin
Hall

Cover by
John Jennings

978-0-9891411-4-7

What Is Afrofuturism?

Let These 40 Amazing Authors Show You ...

Linda D. Addison * **Rabih Alameddine** * Lisa Allen-Agostini *
Lauren Beukes * Joseph Bruchac * **Tobias Buckell** * Indrapramit Das *
Junot Díaz * Minister Faust * **Jaymee Goh** * Kawika Guillermo *
Carlos Hernandez * Ernest Hogan * **Thaddeus Howze** * Darius James *
N.K. Jemisin * Tenea D. Johnson * **Victor LaValle** *
Rochita Loenen-Ruiz * **Carmen Maria Machado** * Anil Menon *
Silvia Moreno-Garcia * Farnoosh Moshiri * **Daniel José Older** *
Chinelo Onwualu * **Andaiye Reeves** * Eden Robinson *
Kiini Ibura Salaam * Sofia Samatar * **Charles R. Saunders** *
Nisi Shawl * **Vandana Singh** * S.P. Somtow * **C. Renee Stephens** *
Greg Tate * **Tade Thompson** * Katherena Vermette * **George S. Walker** *
Ran Walker * **Ibi Zoboi**

www.rosariumpublishing.com